Stories and Lies

The True Account of Tåsan Sulac

N.K.Hart

Tangible press

Printed in the United States of America
First Paperback Edition, 2019

ISBN: 1-7334579-1-7
ISBN-13: 978-1-7334579-1-0

Library of Congress Control Number: 2019905295

Dedicated to Edward Wojciechowski whose excitement and praise boosted my spirit and with the gifted citrine quartz in hand, I made my way forward.

Thank you kind friend, you are loved. –NK

Not only is the universe stranger than we imagine - it is stranger than we can imagine.

Sir Arthur Stanley Eddington (1882 – 1944)

Part One

The Twisted Ascent

I was sure that the dream materialized around me as I had a vivid recollection of falling to sleep. Nevertheless, there I was, standing in the bright warmth of the mid-noon sun, gazing out over a misty, unfocused scape. As I lazily ran my eyes over the surroundings, I became acutely aware of an overwhelming sense of optimism that seemed to penetrate my being right down to the bone.

As I focused on the feeling permeating my being, I asked myself from where did this come from? What caused me to feel so happy and light?

I stepped through the scape barely aware of my feet as I wondered, again, at my sudden enthusiasm that sprang from nowhere. I stopped. I concentrated. Was it family? Was it friends? Could it be that my life, to this point, was so perfect, so untroubled that I lived as in a dream, floating along, no cares and no worries?

No answer was forthcoming.

When Tåsan awoke, the hour was just before the dawn. He reached for his e-dev and retrieved four messages, selected the second in the list, pressed a series of iconographs and held the device up to his ear.

"Yes, just this minute." He listened. "I'm very serious about this." The dream of optimism began to fade. "I'm thinking it's more an act of discipline." Enthusiasm barely remembered. "Trust me. I'm confident."

One

The Nascency of Naiad Five

It begins as it began on Naiad Five, the third planet from the sun at the center of the Niles Galaxy. Tåsan Sulac's home planet.

Naiad Five has come to support a sizable population who built their civilization in sustainable balance with the environment and in harmony with five other planets, Eros, Erantu, Astor and Lux, and Sador, all of which share the habitable zone surrounding their sun.

Today the chief commerce among the planets is the production of tungsten and niobium, necessary alloys for the manufacturing of various metals used throughout the Niles Galaxy and outward, to include the Hedorrion Galaxy as well. The uses of these metals vary from planet to planet. On Naiad Five, the various alloys are used in the building of shuttle hoppers and space jets which are always in demand. On Erantu, metal alloys are a huge part of the inter-planet trading system and are consumed by many local companies in the production of large inter-stellar craft and their supporting accoutrements. On Cimtun 8, a niobium distillate is prized for its strength and used for mining drills and eco-structures. These businesses are typical of the type of trades that generate large profits that have driven inter-planet economies for several generations.

Less than three centuries ago Naiad Five, and specifically the small, provincial town of Merula, was chosen as the seat of power for the then newly formed Intersolar and Space Alliance (ISA), consisting of a handful of leading citizens from as many local planets whose main intent was the unionization and peaceful co-existence of business interests throughout the prosperous and civilized settlements about the territories.

9

Merula has spread outward from its humble beginnings, across the gently undulating plateau to occupy three hundred and twenty two square milia. It is situated between the high Phyllite Cliffs that loom in the east and the raucous wild lands that lay in the west. Merula residents enjoy mild weather in the summer quads with the most spectacular sunsets most every early evening. Winter quads can bring periodic storms that light the sky with flashes of gold and drive the rains and fill the gullies to capacity. On clear winter evenings, the view of Datos, Naiad Five's moon, its pocked face in a purple haze, and the stationary asteroid belt that encircles the sun, cast their long shadows across the land.

Since ISA's humble beginnings, many and many more representatives from planets, moons, and far-flung outposts have joined them, making it a large and very powerful entity.

The complex occupied by the Intersolar and Space Alliance, nicknamed ISA City, is large, almost as large as Merula itself. ISA City is home to representatives and dignitaries as well as their families. There are judges, law experts, and support personnel who work amid the myriad of meeting chambers, courtrooms, and offices distributed over ISA City grounds that is situated amid homes and schools and connected with by-ways, movers, trans-tubes, and shifters.

ISA's cooperative beginnings eventually evolved to include law making, judiciary oversight, law enforcement, dispute reconciliation, and conflict resolution.

The ISA board members established the Inter-Galaxy Command (IGC) as the group responsible for carrying out directives as set forth by them. The role of the IGC, initially that of arbitrator and ambassadorship, resolutely changed to include investigations and enforcement of ISA directives with the capability of performing military-like actions if necessary. With the seemingly infinite resources of the Intersolar and Space Alliance, the IGC grew powerful and held sway over the known limits of habitable space as recognized today.

The Inter-Galaxy Command chose as its base of operations, a remote site situated some seventeen linear milia from Merula and named it, Firmus Opulentia. Reliable Might.

Along with its expanding power and responsibilities, the IGC garnered a respectable reputation and upheld its long-standing traditions with style and pomp. Many found this blend of authority and statesmanship appealing and the allure of a career within such an organization drew applicants from across all the known galaxies, including all the various habitable territories in the Allodial Expanse that lay between.

And so it was three generations ago when Arronson J. Sulac, joined the IGC as a Class II Technical Cadet and worked his way through several rankings to become Brigadier General and who proved to be instrumental in the development of the disciplinary regulations that still survive today. His son, Tariand, joined the IGC and fought with distinction in the War Between the Galaxies in 31725.82.

Following strong family tradition, Tariand's son, Amans Sulac, entered the IGC as an officer and distinguished himself as a persuasive mediator and an outstanding military figure after accumulating several impressive achievements, including the brokered peace agreement between the Crosians, inhabitants of Titus, Crosus' largest moon in the Hederrion Galaxy, and the people of Sador, a planet in the Niles Galaxy. The Sadorians were exploring space, looking for metals and minerals in which to exploit and the Crosians, upon discovering the large trolling ships and their locations, first took umbrage, then declared open hostilities. They not only threatened war, they prepared for it.

The IGC sent Captain Amans Sulac out to investigate the allegation and to do what he saw fit in order to settle the dispute. After an inordinate and tense amount of time, Amans' power of persuasion and sense of balance finally won out and the now memorable Crosus Sador Pact still stands.

After his graduation from university, Amans married his sweetheart, Rebetta. Shortly after accepting his first commission that promoted him to Major, their eldest son, Arron, was born, followed by a second son, Tåsan, and three years later, their daughter, Stellanova.

When all three children were old enough to attend basic school, Rebetta resumed her career as a master chemist with the Institute of Inter-Space Geologic Research.

Life for the Sulacs went smoothly enough, punctuated now and again by the brief absences that Amans' call to duty required of him or when Rebetta's research would need her to travel to a new archeological or mining site to perform advanced analysis of unusual conditions.

Growing up, Tåsan was close to his brother Arron. They shared many boyhood adventures like racing jetbikes and climbing to the top of giant dodon trees, but it was his sister, Stellanova, that opened his mind to imagination and details. When she was a young child, she had once shown him a tiny pebble that she had plucked from a garden path and provided the wildest story of how that pebble had travelled great distances and met such extraordinary creatures along the way just to live in their garden. Stellanova was fascinating in her wild imaginations. While Tåsan was close to Arron, sharing brotherly interests and responsibilities, it was Stellanova he held nearest and dearest to his heart. And being the second child of three, Tåsan felt he lived in the better of two worlds.

When still a young boy, Tåsan was fascinated with the stories his father would tell of his life in the IGC. He would sit rapt as he heard tales of adventure and excitement, of flying through space to prevent war and to save the day. The stuff of real legends. Tåsan and Arron both admired their father and loved to hear tales of IGC encounters throughout the galaxies. Amans tried to frame his stories in such a way as to compel both of his sons to consider careers with the IGC.

In his teens, Tåsan kept his grades up easily enough but in his spare time, would push his physical limits by engaging in pulse rocket racing across the Cirrian Flats that ran a rough eight milia along the base of the Phyllite Cliffs to the east. The danger was in the rules. Pulse rockets had to stay within a fifth of a nolan from Naiad's surface, which was crowded with outcropped rock formations and low crevices. Riders had to speed through the course as fast as possible. Simple.

Once, after Tåsan had completed a rather tricky upgrade to his racer's fuel system, he organized a race to test it. He contacted two of his friends who then contacted a few of their friends. Before the day was done, several racers were eager to participate and a fairly large crowd of spectators had responded as well. The race was organized for the following weeks end and had turned into quite the get-together.

Arron and Stellanova went along, too. The air was electric with excitement. As the racers started to take their places, talk among the onlookers became animated.

"Modvig has painted his pulse rocket a bright sulfur yellow. Oh! There he is now!" The yellow rocket slowly drifted past and eased in next to the others already positioned at a starting line.

Another comment heard among the groups, "There must be at least eight riders here today. Should be a good race."

Stellanova, standing with Arron and two of his friends, had been watching the crowd with interest. Her excitement had been growing steadily as the pulse rockets began to organize into a starting position.

"Oh look! There's Tåsan's flame red pulse rocket. He's jockeyed it into position."

Tåsan stood astraddle his racer, helmet off, talking with the friend to his left. They were smiling and laughing with each other. Tåsan scanned the small crowd and when he saw Arron and Stellanova, gave a big smile and waved to them.

Stellanova waved back and called out, "Good fortune, be safe!" but couldn't be sure Tåsan had heard her over the excited chatter of the others gathered about.

Shortly, the eight pulse rockets were lined up. Their riders twitching to begin, hands on throttles, engines humming and ready.

Off to the right, a tall kid in a bright blue jump-jacket, raised his hand to the sky and after a brief moment fired a popper pistol signaling the race to start. Stellanova had held her breath in anticipation.

The roar of the pulse rockets as they leapt off the line was deafening and the exhaust flare of so many racers lit up the area in a flash of red and gold.

The rockets sped off down the course, closely hugging the terrain and weaving around the tall and twisted sandstone rock formations that dotted the landscape.

Tåsan loved the feeling of joy as his insides lightened with the speed. He would sharpen his focus and his determination as the course flew past in a blur. With his resolution screwed on tight, he usually won his races. His friends called him crazy but he knew it was a matter of skill and yes, there was a bit of nerve involved, but he laughed them off in friendship.

Tåsan's focus was on the race, his eyes were glued to the terrain ahead. He gave a small thought to his ground-hugging altitude and an awareness of how well his fuel system modification was performing, otherwise it was all about the speed.

He could make out two rocket riders just behind and to his right. Tåsan smiled with the thought that he had outpaced five other riders but his confidence never wavered. He pulled his rocket's throttle again, gaining more distance from his companions.

Just ahead, a close grouping of sandstone pinnacles blocked the riders from their straight path. The two riders trying to catch Tåsan had started their turns to course around the pinnacles but Tåsan had another plan.

Watching the race, that was by this time some three milia down the flats, Stellanova became concerned when she realized that Tåsan was not turning his rocket to steer around the pinnacles. She lowered her digi-lenses and gazed unbelievably into the distance.

"What is he doing? Doesn't he see the rocks?"

Arron had also been closely watching the race and as the seconds clicked on, he said, "Oh, I think I know what he's up to. He's found a way through the maze. If he makes it, he could win the race."

Stellanova was shocked. "What do you mean 'if he makes it'?" and lifted her digi-lenses to her eyes to bring the scene into closer focus.

Tåsan loved racing. He knew that to win, once in awhile you had to take chances. Once in awhile, opportunities would pop up and decisions and plans would have to be performed quickly with little thought except for the feeling of confidence that the plan would work. This was one of those times.

Tåsan, with speed near full throttle, headed straight for the rock pinnacles. When he was within margin, he leaned his racer down on its side to squeeze between and under two formations and punched the rocket's thrusters to push ahead. His last thought, as he threaded the rocket through the narrow opening was a vague desire that he didn't swipe one of the engines off on the way through.

Stellanova was no stranger to Tåsan's riding style. She had watched one of his races before and had even cheered him on but was never so afraid as when Tåsan leaned his racer so far over. She had been holding her breath and as Tåsan shot through the pillars of sandstone, she sighed in relief just as the crowds of friends sent up a cheer and clamored in amazement at Tåsan's performance.

Tåsan gave a whoop of pleasure as the pulse rocket shot out into the daylight and he pulled far ahead of the other racers. The day was his.

~

During his first month at university, one of Tåsan's professors sparked his interest in astrophysics by demonstrating to the class how one would go about using innate planetary energies to propel a craft, even as large as an inter-stellar transit ship, in concert with boron supplied warp drives to gain speed while maintaining a tactical advantage.

Tåsan was in. He excelled in astrophysics and started dabbling in advanced astronautical engineering. As his studies moved forward, Tåsan frequently found that he was deep in the retrofit of his pulse rocket jetbike. Every time he learned of a new method of propulsion or stability, Tåsan immediately re-engineered the doctrine to fit his racer and made the modifications. Eventually his classes and hobbies led Tåsan into a serious interest in spaceship mechanical systems and from there it was an easy step into a relatively new field of study, Cognitive Problem Solving As Used in Artificial Intelligence. He couldn't wait to build an intuitive drive interface for his racer.

Tåsan's parents were so pleased with his newfound excitement for the technical and esoteric aspects of space and travel. Amans felt that Tåsan's future lay with the IGC. Rebetta just loved Tåsan's excitement for his studies no matter where it led him. His brother Arron was well on his way to becoming a professor of Advanced Spacial Mathematics and Stellanova showed promise as a Biomechanical Engineer as applied to terra-forming planets and to the establishment of off-world settlements. Rebetta couldn't have

15

been happier.

As their university years neared the end, Stellanova and Tåsan spoke a lot to each other about their hopes and dreams for their futures.

One afternoon, Stellanova joined Tåsan as he worked on his racer. He was determined to integrate the custom modifications he had devised earlier, into the racer's exhaust system in an attempt to divert the proto-fume exhaust vapors past the drive motor thereby boosting the RPM's. It was proving to be more complicated than Tåsan anticipated and he was up to his elbows in engine grease.

Stellanova set two cold frosties down on the workbench. "I brought you a nice chilly drink, ready to take a break?"

"Yea, as soon as I tighten this bolt," said Tåsan, concentrating on a nut that wasn't cooperating. "Aaugh, almost..."

"Tåsan you only have two more quads until you graduate. Are you getting excited?" asked Stellanova.

"Well, yes," replied Tåsan, "and no," reaching for a malwrench just out of his grasp. "Stella, would you?" wriggling his fingers to indicate that they were two inches too short.

Stellanova moved the malwrench closer. "What do you mean, 'No'?"

"Oh it seems I've just gotten into the rhythm of education and now I'll have to actually show something of myself."

"Aren't you going to follow father's footsteps and join the IGC? It's what you've been saying for at least three solars."

Tåsan had wrenched the wheel cog of his racer to the specified torque and sat back on his heels to inspect his handiwork. "I think the new titanium bearings should stand up to the increased temperatures very nicely."

Tåsan moved his greasy hand toward Stellanova's face to tease her. She laughed as she feigned indignation and slapped his hand away even as she took a step back. "So? IGC?" she said.

"The entrance exams aren't until the end of the solar year, I'll probably take them but until then," Tåsan wiped his hands and had busied himself with his tools, moving them from the bench to the drawers when he stopped and looked at Stellanova. "Until then, I'll see what else comes up. I don't think I'm in a hurry."

Stellanova said, "Good. I'm glad that you said that," and pulled a rolled up sheaf of papers from her back pocket. She excitedly unrolled the papers and laid them on the workbench, smoothing them down before she turned her bright eyes to Tåsan.

"My Bio-Eng professor told the class about a relatively new dig site on Eros. I would love to go check it out. I want to put my education to a practical matter. I'm planning to complete a survey and design a terra-environment for my upcoming Off World Structures class. Extra credit...a sort of 'pre-credit' that I intend to hand in right in the door, on the first day of class."

Tåsan had taken the top few pages of Stellanova's stack of papers and had breezed through one or two, furrowing his brow with concentration. "Seems like a worthy goal, Stella. Do you think father would approve of you jetting off to Eros?"

"Actually I've already spoken with father about it. Mother thinks it would be a wonderful opportunity." Stellanova stopped talking long enough for Tåsan to look up from the papers. "There's only one catch," she said.

Tåsan smiled, he knew about father's "catches" having been snared by them before. "As long as you're back by dinner?" he laughed.

"Not exactly," Stellanova replied. "As long as you take me."

Tåsan had put the papers down and was leaning on the workbench. When Stellanova voiced father's "catch" he straightened up and said, "What? As long as I take you?"

"Look," Stellanova said, riffling the papers and producing a star-chart, "Eros will be closest in orbit during the solstice months, just after your graduation and during the break between my quads. We could borrow father's Hopper. It would take two days out plus two days back. We could spend a week or two exploring the Eros dig site and when I've gathered enough information and scans, we come home. It would be like camping, except better." Stellanova looked at Tåsan, trying to read the look on his face. Was that acceptance or rejection? She couldn't tell but trusted that she had sold him on the idea. "Did I make it sound so appealing that you can't resist?"

Tåsan was building a mental picture of it all, his mind racing; timelines, obligations, schedules all flew to fit together for his consideration. At length he spoke, "Well..." and paused to watch Stellanova's expression of heightened expectation slowly start to change to one of seriousness, "Okay! I'm in!"

Stellanova exploded into a happy dance, jumped up and down and smiled brightly. "Thank you, thank you, thank you! This is going to be great!" And took Tåsan's hands in hers and attempted to swing him around.

Her exuberance made Tåsan smile and he danced a little jig to please her and in a wink of the eye, Stellanova scooped up her papers and was hurrying from the shop, calling out as she went, "Wait 'till I tell mother! There's so much to do, I'm so excited about this!"

Tåsan stood for a quiet moment thinking as he absentmindedly picked up a tool and looked at it, without much recognition, and thought, *"I had probably better speak with father, do a system's check on the Hopper, and think about the eventualities of Eros."*

~

The solstice months came soon enough. As he expected, Tåsan graduated at the top of his class. The weeks of preparation for his final exams were brutal. There were long hours of study and review, anxiety and sleepless nights, and times when exhaustion forced all cognitive thoughts from Tåsan's overtaxed mind, causing him more than a bit of frustration.

Exams seemed to flow and to his satisfaction, Tåsan submitted his seventy-five-page thesis on "The Abhorrent Behaviorism of AI Malware on the Androidal Circuitries of Deductive Reasoning" on time.

Tåsan breathed a sigh of relief as he stepped out of his last exam auditorium and into the warm afternoon air. The study-square between the buildings was full of students, many with heads down, noses in books cramming for their tests and those who had recently completed their exams and who were excitedly talking with friends in small groups.

Tåsan stood for a moment in the sunshine, enjoying the warmth on his face and arms, feeling joyous but almost empty, like there was something missing.

"Tåsan! Hey Tåsan, over here," called a voice.

Tåsan shielded his eyes with his hand and looked around. He

had heard his name being called but had not, with any certainty, determined its point of origin. Subsequently, he saw his friend, Romis, standing with two other friends, waving at him from the center of the study-square. It was a quick few steps and Tåsan joined them.

Romis greeted Tåsan with a big smile, "How're your exams going?"

"Real well. I've just finished my last one," answered Tåsan. "How about you?"

"Yes, done! Finished up about fifteen minutes ago and have been enjoying my new freedom ever since!"

The small group laughed and all agreed, in excited tones, that it was good to be done with the exam stress that had been the bane of their last two quads.

Romis said, "Some of us are planning a small celebration this weekend. We're going to meet at Vector Eight around mid-morn and have one last pulse rocket race down the Cirrian Flats and out across the Rocky Reach. We're marking the end of university and our new beginnings. We may not have another opportunity to be together like this again. What do you think? A little race, some food, the best of company. Are you in?" Romis looked at Tåsan with excited anticipation, anxiously waiting his reply.

Tåsan smiled and said, "Yes..."

The small group gave an excited cheer and Romis clapped Tåsan on the back.

Raising his voice to be heard above the chatter, Tåsan said, "I've got to warn you, I've modified my racer!"

Romis said, "That's alright! Winner buys drinks!"

The group stood together for another minute or two before the young friends started to drift off to other engagements. Tåsan was no exception. He had promised to call his mother the moment he was out of his last exam and still had a bit of preparation work to do before his trip to Eros with Stellanova. They were to leave when the moon, Datos, was in its third quarter, which was coming up next mid-week. Tåsan felt that his To-Do list was getting longer with each passing day. He would have to take a good look at it and see if there were any items he could delegate to Stella, not that she had much free time, either.

19

Stellanova's excitement about her trip to Eros was over the top. She had packed and repacked three times already and had spent countless hours researching Eros to gain advanced knowledge of its weather and topography in an effort to maximize on the best time to be there and the most optimum place to set up a working base camp.

Tåsan had to smile at the thought of Stella's exuberance and at how serious she was about the purpose of this trip. She had asked him four times if the Hopper could carry the load of all the equipment and would there be room to bring back geological samples. The last time she asked, Tåsan put a hand on her shoulder and smiled at her as he patiently explained that, "Yes. The Hopper will easily carry everything it's expected to. Please don't worry about this, Stella, cross it off your list as 'Done'."

She had smiled back at Tåsan and relaxed her posture. "Okay, thanks!" was what she had said before dashing off to the next thing.

Tåsan loved his little sister and knew that for all her worry, the trip would be fine and her design of a fully integrated terra-formed community would be innovative, advanced, and above all, appealing. Tåsan had no doubt about it.

• • •

The trip out to Eros went flawlessly. During the down times, Tåsan and Stellanova read books, listened to music, studied Eros terrain charts, or played word games, made more exciting by agreeing that whoever lost would have to do the grunt-work of cleaning up the Hopper's cramped living space.

After studying the land charts and conducting a long-range survey, Stellanova selected a base campsite less than one milia from the dig. She wanted to be close enough so that transport to and from the site was fairly easy but far enough away not to interfere with measurements and calculations.

They had been on site for twelve days when Stellanova announced that she had gathered all the data she could, had checked it against the most current Eros information found in her text books, and had studied it from every angle she could think of. It was complete. There was nothing left to do but to pack up and go home.

20

Stellanova was very animated at dinner that night as she and Tåsan sat together munching a hot mixture of proteins and vegetable starch and sipping frosties.

"I bet it feels good to be done," said Tåsan.

"Yes," Stellanova replied, "I don't know what else I could do. I have all my data, that I've reviewed three times, and I've checked and rechecked my pictorial scans, and organized the sub-surface structure surveys. I'm pretty sure I have all I need."

They ate in silence for a moment as Stellanova thought more about her expedition.

Tåsan helped Stella with her site measurements and offered suggestions when she asked his opinion about how he would organize the files or when she needed technical help with a piece of equipment. Otherwise, it was her show and he was impressed with her organizational skills and her methodologies. The way she approached this project, aside from the initial stress of trying to prepare for every conceivable contingency, was thoughtful and solid. Her data collection was systematic and thorough. Maybe too thorough. Maybe all the way to redundant. But Tåsan agreed that it was better to have too much data than not enough because there was just this one trip and Stella had better have everything she needed by the time they left.

"Stella," said Tåsan.

"Hmmm?" breathed Stellanova.

"Tell me about your design. From all this data, you're going to do a three-part build of a new city?"

• • •

The Hopper was packed; everything had been accounted for and securely stowed for the flight home.

Stellanova sat in the co-pilot's seat leaning forward as she reviewed the pre-flight checklist.

Tåsan had completed the inspection of the craft from the outside, slowly walking around the Hopper, taking time to look carefully at intakes and exhaust thrusters. It would do no favors to the craft if dirt or dust, or worse yet, some sort of microbial or bicrobial "creature" were blocking the engine mechanics. It also gave Tåsan the opportunity to refocus his mind to the technical aspects of the trip. He had, at times, let go of the daily routines of living with so much technology that he actually had enjoyed himself. It was nice being carefree. But the trip had come to an end and it was time to return home.

After securing the bulkhead door and taking a fast tour of the Hopper's interior, Tåsan took his command chair and began the pilot's preflight requirements list.

After a minute Stellanova said, "Everything good outside?"

"Yup. No obstructions. We should lift up without a hitch. How's the co-pilot's list coming?"

Tåsan knew that Stella was an experienced co-pilot and had several hundred hours, nearly a full quad, of flying time to her credit. How could she not have? Growing up with two older brothers definitely had an influence on her. And she took to the sky like an Avabird.

"Almost done. Just checking the nav-program now, to make sure it loaded completely," answered Stellanova as she leaned forward to twiddle a dial, fine-tuning the aft-scan monitor.

Tåsan looked at the panels in front of him and said, "We'll be ready in five. Last chance, Stella," glancing at his sister. "Are you sure you've got everything you need? Eros won't be back for another duquad."

Stellanova looked up from the blinking altimeter display and smiled, "More than ready. I've got all my data and my data backups. Good to go. Besides, I've really been craving mother's homemade parsit and serra grain stew." She gave a sideways glance at Tåsan, before excitedly adding, "Let's call ahead. Maybe she'll have pity on us poor travelers and put one together for our homecoming!"

...

Liftoff was flawless and the Hopper performed like a champ. It took a few minutes to steady the craft through the rough atmosphere of Eros and another handful to position her onto the course home.

When all was settled, Tåsan flipped the craft into auto-pilot and sat back in his chair, releasing the tension from his shoulders and looking out through the shields at the stars that hung in the black inky blue sky, like brilliant cut diamonds.

Stellanova completed her tasks and swiveled her chair to face

Tåsan. "I've engaged the long-range motion sensors in case there's any stray asteroids out here and the rad-sensors are on, too. Can't be too careful."

"Make sure the audio is up to at least .2 so we can hear it if we're not especially paying attention to the controls."

Stellanova checked and adjusted the dial then turned her eyes to the perpetual night sky of space that lay before them. After a moment she said, "I'm going to have a hot tea, want a cup?"

As she got up, Tåsan replied, "Yea, sounds good, thanks."

Stellanova made her way to the Hopper's galley, that is to say, the chiller and the warming plate tucked into a small cabinet along the fuselage, about mid-ship. She retrieved two cups and a box of tea buds and was about to measure out the portions of water when the long-range motion sensors sang out a warning sound. She stashed the cups back in the drawer and quickly moved forward to regain her seat.

Tåsan had switched the sensors to the viewing screen and was concentrating on the monitor, searching for signs of moving objects.

"Is it asteroids?" asked Stellanova.

"I don't think so," answered Tåsan. "They're moving too fast."

Two distinct blips danced across the screen. One closely following the other. After a moment of watching them, Tåsan said, "Let's map and track them. Maybe we can guess what they are by their speed."

Stellanova switched on the recording device to capture the relevant information generated by the sensors. She also lowered the volume of the sensor's warning alarm since it was obvious that she and her brother were fully aware that something was active in their proximity.

Tåsan spoke, "According to my calculations, those two objects are traveling at about 17.2 rads per hour, much faster than asteroids."

Tåsan and Stellanova watched the blips in silence for a few moments, then the leading blip made a fast jerky change of course. The following blip overshot but quickly recovered and raced to close the distance. After the scenario had played out once more, Tåsan said, "Stella, fasten your belt," as he disengaged the

23

autopilot and took the engines out of pulse. "I'm going to follow 'em. I'm curious to see what's the big hurry."

Tåsan set the course and pulled the throttle lever as he turned the port side thrusters. The Hopper banked into a steep and quickly accelerating turn and seemed to leap forward as they gave chase.

"Are you sure that's a smart idea?" asked Stellanova, trying to keep the anxiety out of her voice but feeling the fear start to tighten her throat.

"Maybe not but I'm going to get close enough to see what's going on. It may be nothing more than a couple of friends playing games. Don't worry. It'll be okay. Just want to check it out, that's all."

The next dozen minutes passed in silence, except for the low hum of the rhythmic pings of the motion sensor as it reported the whereabouts of the two racing objects.

Tåsan had heard from his father that the IGC had recently issued a warning that privateers had been operating in this sector of space. It was reported that they had more or less sprung up out of nowhere and were wanted on Sador for robbery of a government shipment of boracite, a very dangerous compound used in the mining industry, and for the aggravated assault of a shipping handler in connection with another robbery two days later.

Tåsan's intuition told him that the two blips on his motion sensors probably had something to do with just that. Privateers.

There wasn't a chance he was going to mention any of this to Stellanova before they started the trip to Eros. He didn't want her to get upset. And he was surely not going to say anything now. He looked over at her and saw the worry gently creasing her brow. She looked like she was controlling her fear and was keeping it together well enough but Tåsan didn't know for how long.

"We'll just tail them for a while. I won't get too close and it looks like they're too busy to bother with us. Probably won't even see us."

Stellanova looked over at Tåsan and he smiled at her and said, "Just a little adventure before we go home."

She smiled in return but cinched her safety belt tighter...just to be sure.

It took twenty-two minutes to catch the two blips. Tåsan held the Hopper at a discrete distance behind and stayed close to their boran emissions trails hoping to distort any image of the Hopper that may be picked up.

"Stella, can we get a telephoto shot of them from here?" asked Tåsan.

Stellanova busied herself with bringing the sensor cameras online and adjusting the aperture speeds to account for the distance. When she was satisfied she said, "Cameras are ready. The autofocus should account for any changes you make in speed and direction. Are we close enough to make them out?"

Tåsan peered at the images, now magnified five times on the screen. "I can almost make out the registry ID on the rear panel. Hold on." He nudged the Hopper closer. "Almost." Closer still. "Got it!" and pushed the camera's scan button. Five successive shots were taken before the Hopper's rad-sensor sounded.

With fear in her voice, Stellanova asked, "What's that?" Her eyes frantically searched the flight panels for anything out of the ordinary.

"I think we've been made. The rad-sensor reports that we've been scrutinized by a low level rad-beam coming from the trailing ship," answered Tåsan, adding, "Time to get out of here." He immediately braked the port side thrusters even as he pushed the starboard thruster to full, effectively spinning the Hopper in a 180° half-circle before he revved all the thrusters full ahead and accelerated like the hot wind across the Rocky Flats to speed back the way they had come.

"The trailing ship is in pursuit!" cried Stellanova. "They're gaining on us!"

Tåsan took a split second to scan the doppler rad screen and gently pushed the Hopper's velocity forward. He had already neared the top of the Hopper's range and was concerned about an engine overload. It wouldn't do to blow an engine with possible trouble on his tail. In hindsight, maybe it wasn't such a good idea to get involved but his curiosity had been overridden by his indignation with the thought of a "little guy" getting taken by a "bad guy". Now, he wasn't so much worried about himself, he felt that he could handle what may come, but he shouldn't have been so reckless with Stella onboard.

"They're still gaining, Tåsan," Stellanova said, almost in a whisper.

"I still have some evasive moves up my sleeve. We're not down, yet," said Tåsan as he concentrated on the control panels and his thruster positions.

The ship had nudged closer still in its determination to chase the Hopper. Stellanova had run the registry numbers and read the results. "It's a Class-N ship, normally holds six crew members. Standard equipment includes protowave bombardment. Oh, and get this: reported stolen over nine days ago."

Just then, the ship loosed a protowave that shot forward and grazed the rear port panel of the Hopper. Alarms sounded and lights blinked all over the cabin.

Stellanova screamed, "We've been hit, they're firing at us!"

Tåsan uttered a profanity and jammed the thrusters forward causing the Hopper to shudder as it lurched to make its new speed setting. Within seconds, the Hopper had put a huge distance between it and the pursuing ship.

"Where are they now, Stella?" Tåsan asked, not daring to take his eyes from the thruster data screen as it reported temperatures slowly climbing through the warning zone closer to the danger zone.

"Long range motion sensors are saying that they've changed direction. They're no longer following us."

Tåsan said, "Check it again. Let's make sure they haven't changed their minds."

Stella concentrated on her panels and icons and Tåsan heard the small snaps of switches being flipped and the clinks of dials as they indicated changes. He also became aware of Stella's heightened dread and ventured a quick glance at her face. The look across her face was dead serious and her jaw was clamped tight. Finally she spoke.

"Long range says they're eighteen vectors away. Now nineteen. They're headed further away."

Tåsan eased off of thrusters until the data screen told of temperatures returning to normal, but he held the Hopper steady, wanting to increase the distance between them and the ship as steadily as possible.

When he was sure about the Hopper's performance, Tåsan said, "Let's expect we gave the first ship the time they needed to out-distance the Class-N."

"What makes you think they weren't together?" Stella looked at Tåsan.

Finally he answered, "It looked like a chase, not a game."

Stellanova thought about the implications of Tåsan's statement. She was not coming up with anything good.

Tåsan seeing the consternation in Stellanova's eyes asked, "Were you frightened?" and gave a little laugh to tease her.

"No!" she said in her defense, although she knew that wasn't completely true.

• • •

The remainder of the two-day trip home was smooth and uneventful. Stellanova stayed vigilant watching for any craft that might be following them or any that might stray too closely. Neither of which happened.

Tåsan kept the Hopper's speed up after calculating fuel consumption against time to ensure they arrived with a little boron to spare. They would arrive six hours earlier than expected.

"Should we call ahead to tell them?" asked Stellanova.

"Yea. Ask mother about the parsit stew. And Stella, don't mention anything about the wild spacecraft chase I took us on. Don't want to worry her over nothing. Besides, I want to speak with father about it first. I want to hear his opinion on the matter," said Tåsan.

Stellanova smiled. "Okay. No worries."

• • •

The parsit stew tasted so delicious and was even better than that! Their mother, Rebetta Sulac, had turned the evening meal into a kind of celebration. She prepared the stew as requested, but had dropped in special root vegetables and a pena grain that brought up the spice heat to a very tasty level.

Stellanova helped set the table, using the fancy dishware and the crystal goblets as indicated by her mother.

"Thank you, dear," Rebetta said as she gave Stellanova a smile and a little hug. "I'm so proud of you! You went on a fact-finding mission and returned without a terrabug bite or a Brush Clover rash to show!"

"Ha! That was the easy part," said Stellanova. "The hard part was making sure I had everything I needed before we left."

"It's always that way but as long as you're prepared and thorough, you'll be, most likely, able to make up the difference of anything you find missing," remarked Rebetta.

"Oh, that reminds me," said Stellanova as she turned and started for her room, "Just a second," and disappeared down the hallway. Momentarily she was back and held out her hand to her mother. She held a small package, carefully wrapped in linen and tied with the long green vine stems of a bindweed plant. It was adorned with a large Chata bloom that Stellanova had press-dried to preserve.

"For you, mother, to thank you for letting me go to Eros."

At just that moment, Tåsan, along with his older brother Arron came in from the back balcony where they had started a conversation about the difficulties of picking a career and about post-university choices, in general.

Tåsan had heard Stella mention Eros and joking said, "There wasn't too much on Eros to be thankful for! It was desolate, too many rocks," and he gave a short laugh as punctuation.

Stellanova joined in, "What? My company wasn't good enough for you?"

Arron added, "Told you Stella, Tåsan's a bore, should have taken me instead!"

Stellanova turned to her mother, "Go ahead, open it up."

There were a few moments of quiet as Rebetta undid the ties and unfolded the linen wrapping. Stellanova was starting to bounce a little in anticipation and she thought her smile couldn't get any bigger.

Finally, with the last flap of linen pulled back, the gift was revealed. Nestled in the linen were eight rocks of varying size and weight.

"What?" exclaimed Arron, "A bunch of rocks?"

Rebetta saw immediately what they were. Her knowledge in advanced geologic chemistry had brought her into contact with rocks like these all over the galaxy. But it was her passion for painting that recognized their value. She noted each one in turn. Sanguine, chrome, cadmium yellow, vary rare, cobalt, her favorite, manganese violet, along with a small, smooth stone of iron and a big jagged piece of zinc.

"This 'bunch of rocks', Arron, will supply me with enough pigment for at least two more paintings." And turning to Stellanova, "Thank you, Stella, this was very thoughtful of you," and hugged her again.

• • •

After the meal, Amans brought out a bottle of Tradorian Berrywine and poured a small dram for everyone.

"To celebrate Stella's great achievement and to guide fortune to her project." Amans raised his glass and the family joined him.

"Hear, hear," said Arron before taking a sip.

Stellanova smiled and thanked everyone for their kind thoughts and then blushed a little when Tåsan said, "Tell them about the skittle bug, Stella!"

Stellanova told a brief but embarrassing story of how, when out at the site one day, she had reached into her travel pack to get a note card and a skittle bug popped out, apparently very angry at being disturbed. It had stood its ground, clicking and chirping at her, even as she waved a stick at it in an attempt to frighten it away. Finally it turned, gave a jerk of its back leg and trundled off.

"I felt foolish standing there with only a stick," said Stellanova. "Honestly, I thought that little bug was going to charge at me!"

When the conversation had all but run out, the family started to drift away. Arron was helping Rebetta clear the table and Stellanova, after a series of tired yawns, excused herself and went to her room.

Tåsan asked Amans if he could speak with him privately.

"Sure, son, let's go to my study," replied Amans and led the way. Inside the room, Amans motioned for Tåsan to take a seat in one of the overstuffed chairs by the window and gently closed the door before joining him there.

Amans poured another drop of Tradorian wine for them both then asked, "Is everything alright?"

Tåsan was quick to say that, yes, everything was good, that

29

there was nothing to worry about then took the next ten minutes to tell his father about the run-in with the Class-N ship on the way back from Eros.

Amans listened carefully and had only interrupted Tåsan's narrative twice to ask clarifying questions.

When Tåsan had finished the report, he said, "Just as we were landing, I sent a brief comm to the IGC field line but thought it best to tell you myself."

Amans considered all he had heard then spoke, leveling his tone, "I know that I don't really have to tell you this but I am compelled to say that it was more than foolhardy to chase down a ship full of privateers. I thought that I would have taught you to be more responsible than that. You could have been in real danger." Amans looked at Tåsan, who nodded in thoughtful agreement.

"However, your report, along with the ship's coordinates, have probably assured their capture and arrest by the IGC, so I have to add: good work son. At least that was correct."

"Thank you, father," said Tåsan. "I'd like you to know that I didn't start out to chase privateers. I had no way to know that until later."

"Then why did you give chase?" asked Amans.

"I simply had a feeling that something was wrong. I merely wanted a closer look. To see if I could help."

Amans furrowed his brow, clearly troubled by Tåsan's remark. "Acting on feelings alone is a fool's errand and will always end with dire consequences. This situation could have ended very differently." Amans waited for Tåsan to respond.

Tåsan knew his father was concerned about the incident and thought it wise not to push him further by continuing to argue the merits of his own decisions. It would be wiser to gently let the discussion end.

"You are right, father. My decision to follow the Class-N without supplemental intel could have ended in another way."

Amans said, "It might have ended badly. You should thank your fortune that it did not."

"I do thank fortune, father," said Tåsan, "that the IGC will end the privateer's crime spree."

"Yes," said Amans, leveling a look at Tåsan before adding,

30

"The IGC will intervene and take care of the situation. As they are trained and practiced to do."

The two sat in silence for a minute lost in their own thoughts.

Amans leaned forward in his chair which broke Tåsan's loose consideration of the conversation with his father. The look on Amans' face had softened from the disciplinarian frown that moments before barely hid his anger, to that of understanding and Tåsan smiled in return.

"One more small drop of wine, son?" Amans asked as he reached for the ornate silver bottle.

Two
Badges of Honor

The trip to Eros was a nice diversion and for Tåsan, a much needed reprieve from the rigors of preparing for and taking his final exams. On Eros, he felt he could breathe easier and take chosen moments to appreciate his surroundings. Often Tåsan found himself looking up at the night sky with no particular thought occupying his mind's attention. But while the trip was pleasant, it was wholly over.

The time for the Inter-Galaxy Command placement exams, scheduled for the first week of fall, was fast approaching and Tåsan quickly realized that he needed to pick up his pace.

Submission deadline for his personal biography, his presentation letter, and his transcripts was next week. All the information had been gathered together but Tåsan took his time carefully packaging it so that the narrative flowed. He wanted to convey to the admissions board that he was a man of excellence; he was capable, and multi-dimensional. Tåsan had word-smithed his bio at least three times before he was satisfied and then had asked his mother to look it over.

After reading it through, Rebetta and Tåsan sat in the kitchen over tea.

"What was your overall impression?" asked Tåsan.

Rebetta held the pages in her hands, slowly leafing one, then the next until finally she spoke. "I think this submission package is very well done. It speaks to a young man who has worked very hard, succeeded in his educational endeavor, and is excited about entering the IGC."

Tåsan thought to ask another question, "You don't think it's a little overdone, do you?" and quickly asked another, "Does it come off as boastful or, worse, desperate?"

Rebetta gave a small laugh, amused at Tåsan's concern. "No, I don't think it sounded over egotistical. There's the right amount of confidence without making it sound as if you're bragging or exaggerating the facts. I think it's fine. I think it's ready to send."

Rebetta's comments made Tåsan feel so much better. He then relaxed and let go of some of the anxiety that had been slowly building for days. He had been very concerned with the way he might be perceived by members of the admissions board, many of whom were familiar with the Sulac family name. Being the fourth generation to join the IGC, Tåsan was all too aware of what that meant. He did not want to treat it as an entitlement nor did he want to create the impression that he didn't care, that the IGC wasn't important to him. It was a very fine line to walk.

Tåsan thought that as a last step before submitting his application, he would ask his father's opinion.

• • •

A few weeks later, Tåsan received notification from the IGC: he had been accepted into the academy. In two weeks, Tåsan was to report to Phaton Center Hall on the main IGC complex for placement testing exams. He was so happy and excited that he was sure his face muscles would be sore from all the smiling he did. He immediately sent an e-note to his father, Amans, informing him of his acceptance and thanking him for his support. Tåsan then called his mother with the good news.

Stellanova had come home from her day and overheard Tåsan speaking with Arron about deadlines and placement tests and instantly knew the news.

When Tåsan had ended the call with Arron, Stella hugged him and said, "Good job! Are you happy?"

"Thanks Stella, yes, I am happy," smiled Tåsan.

"Then this calls for a celebration. How about a nice, cold Triton ale down at the Crossroads? Maybe Jess or Romis are there and you could tell them the good news."

"Okay, but no ale for you! It's a school night."

Tåsan sent a family e-note telling them that dinner was on him. He would buy some Sadorian home dishes and see them around eight that evening.

...

Could the time have gone any quicker? Tåsan hadn't thought so. All of a sudden, the placement exams were only six days away and Tåsan found himself the busiest he had been in weeks. He filled the intervening time with studies of IGC protocol and procedures, organizing his personal belongings, performing maintenance on his pulse rocket, meeting with friends, and trying to plan for the upcoming exams.

The placement exams were very important and no one knew this better than Tåsan. His exam scores, coupled with the admissions package would determine the rank at which he would begin his academy training. Tåsan knew that it was near impossible for anyone to score at a Captain's level or above but starting at a Commander's level wasn't unheard of. It was very difficult but not impossible, and Tåsan felt that aiming at the level of Commander was a worthy goal to reach for.

Still, a small particle of doubt lodged itself deep in Tåsan's conscious, below the plans, behind the studies, and under the dust of the last few years. When it surfaced, Tåsan couldn't quite put his finger on what caused him to worry. Was it doubt about his abilities? His intentions? Or was it a fragment of something much bigger but that lay deeper still...was it doubt about joining the IGC?

As the days ticked down, Tåsan put away any doubts he had and submerged himself in preparations. Soon enough, he found himself on his pulse rocket, riding out to the IGC complex, Firmus Opulentia, located north of Merula. It was his designated time to take the placement exams and he was ready. Tåsan was very confident that he knew what he should know and anyway, it was too late to shore up on additional knowledge at this point because the game was on. He would know in a very few hours where he stood.

After parking his rocket, Tåsan strode the wide walkways flanked by manicured landscapes and stood for a moment at the bottom of the stairs leading up and into the front of Phaton Center Hall. He breathed in, held the air briefly in his lungs, and as he slowly released it, thought, *"This is it,"* and took a decisive step forward and up.

...

At the end of exam number five, the final one required, Tåsan put his stylus down and stretched out his back. His shoulders were a bit stiff but other than that, he had made it through the six and one half hours of testing.

Finally Tåsan could take a moment to look around the auditorium.

The room was very long and quite wide with windows all along one wall that offered a view into the garden beyond that was crisscrossed with paths and dotted with benches. There were leaded sky windows in the high ceilings that appeared to magnify the outward view. Tåsan thought it would be wonderful to sit in this room on a dark moonless night and just gaze out into the vast star filled sky. As he sat looking up, an Avabird landed on the sky window just above him and squawked its loud call to no one or nothing in particular before flying away. It brought Tåsan's thoughts back.

As Tåsan sat quietly, he noticed two things. The auditorium's wall hangings seemed to be a pictorial of the IGC's history with many of the pictures showing the glory of this famous battle and that renowned Admiral, posing in fine splendor looking almost regal.

The other thing Tåsan noticed were the applicants still present in the auditorium, almost all were of varied citizenship. He recognized a small group of Sadorians with their wild shocks of red curls and their stocky builds. Sitting two tables to Tåsan's right was an applicant that appeared to be from Cimtun 8. He sat hunched over his exam tablet with his head bowed in concentration, but from his long thin limbs that showed the faint color of lapis lazuli, Tåsan guessed his eyes were probably the subtle color of green moss with large black pupils that all those born on Cimtun 8 possess.

Tåsan was struck by the varied representation from so many of the other planets and outer worlds. He was sure he couldn't name them all and as he sat quietly looking around at all the different faces, Tåsan started to feel his excitement rise at the prospect of working with and getting to know so many different cadets.

For the first time since university, Tåsan started to feel as if he could truly belong in the IGC. He thought he could make a go of it, be part of it, and succeed.

~

Tåsan was working on Stellanova's Drifter808, adjusting the mini-thruster and cleaning the citron injectors. She had asked him to look at it after it had threatened to stall as she was attempting to cross a busy intersection on her way through Merula's shopping district.

The chime of his e-dev signaled an incoming message.

Tåsan wiped his hands and picked up the device to look at the screen before deciding to answer or let it go to the message queue. It was a recorded text message from a Major C. T. Barlet. Tåsan opened the screen and read the text. The message informed Tåsan that he had passed his placement exams, scoring in the top five percent with total points in the high nine hundreds. He was to report for officer training in one quad, on the first day of the new solar year. The message ended with, ((*Congratulations Lieutenant Tåsan Sulac. Welcome to the Inter-Galaxy Command.*))

Tåsan read the text through a second time before composing a text of his own, addressed to his family, excitedly sharing the good news and thanking them, again, for their steadfast confidence in him.

As he touched the transmit button, his excitement rising, he could only think to jump on his pulse rocket and race across the outback. He called Romis, who agreed to meet him in one half hour. Tåsan then grabbed his helmet and was off.

• • •

The remainder of the quad was a blur for Tåsan but he managed to complete everything he needed to do before his scheduled move to the IGC training complex.

After the initial stir of excitement that Tåsan's news brought, the family settled back into a sort of routine where work, studies, and life in general carried on. Soon enough, Tåsan's departure time arrived.

Preparations for the move proved harder than Tåsan had anticipated.

Regulations allowed for three travel cases and one modest mode of ground transportation per cadet. The boxes could be stuffed to capacity but no alcohol or pharma was allowed.

The ground transport part would be easy, Tåsan would take his pulse rocket, but that also meant that he would need a couple of tools. He, at first, filled a small toolbox with the essentials but as time went on, he added several more tools until he couldn't clamp the toolbox's lid closed. He then decided that it was more likely that he would be able to borrow basic tools when needed, so repacked his toolbox with specialized tools that would be harder to find later.

Filling the first two travel cases went surprisingly quick. Tåsan packed several wardrobe changes, boots, shoes, his riding gear, the toolbox, and his personal bath items. However, the third case proved to be a puzzle.

"Should I take...?"

...

Eventually, Tåsan packed the third case with his e-devices, a selection of manuals, his camping gear, and all the material he had on AI systems including a small robotic Cyclops he had built as a demonstration of how robotic logic could progress. He wasn't sure he would have any time for fun or personal studies but thought it wouldn't hurt to take these items along, just in case.

The three cases stood by the front entrance ready for the short haul to the IGC training complex a few milia outside of Merula.

Tåsan was sitting on the front staircase saying goodbye to Stellanova. He was dressed for the short pulse rocket ride out to the complex; his helmet propped up on the stack of cases.

Stellanova linked arms with Tåsan and said, "Don't worry about the travel cases, the delivery transport will be here in an hour. They said they would have them to you by mid-afternoon."

"By then I'll know where my quarters are and will transmit the info to them. I'll copy you, too, so you'll know also."

They sat for a brief moment before Tåsan said, "The first quad is going to be crazy. New faces, new places. I just hope that my studies don't get in the way."

Stellanova gave a short laugh and smiled. "I'm surprised that you need any classes at all. You've been telling me for years that you already know everything." And gave his arm a gentle punch for emphasis.

37

"I know! Right?" smiled Tåsan.

Arron called out to Tåsan as he came down the stairs, "Coming through." Causing Tåsan and Stellanova to get up from their places. "Looks like you're about ready to leave. Glad I caught you before you left so I could say goodbye."

"Yes," said Rebetta as she joined the siblings, "The day has arrived and a bit quickly at that. Are you excited, Tåsan?"

"I think I am, mother. It's nice to have a clear direction in which to move," he said.

The family stood in a small group with each of them hugging Tåsan and smiling as they voiced their valedictions for his success and requests that he send update comm's to keep them apprised of his accomplishments.

Rebetta relaxed her embrace and held Tåsan at arms length and smiled. "Let me know if you need anything."

"I'm already missing your parsit stew! That can't be good," smiled Tåsan.

"I promise we'll have it for your first dinner home," said Rebetta.

Arron added, "Now there's a worthy goal!"

Tåsan took up his helmet and opened the front door and stepped out. Part way to his parked rocket, he turned and raised his hand as he called out, "Everyone take care!"

A few moments later, Tåsan was on his way.

~

Incoming officers in training were given two hours to locate their quarters, clear all personal effects from the grounds and hallways, store their transports, and obtain their Quad One assignments before reporting for general assembly in the Cirrian Auditorium.

Tåsan was fortunate in that his three travel cases had shown up early. He tipped several tenges and had the cases stowed in his quarters. After parking his rocket and waiting through the queue for his training class schedule, Tåsan found that he had fifteen minutes before he needed to make his way to the auditorium. He decided to familiarize himself with the training grounds.

The first thing Tåsan noticed was the distinct separation of the academy training buildings from the main IGC complex. Overall, the training complex consisted of several ornate and imposing buildings that were clustered around a large open space and separated by landscaped gardens of tall trees and wild-looking shrubs. The signage on the buildings hinted at the studies being taught within: Advanced Mathematical Theorem, Energy and Propulsion Sciences, Engineering, and a host of other subjects.

Shortly, Tåsan found his way to the Cirrian vestibule and thought to take a leisurely stroll around the displays before heading in to find a seat. Dominating the center of the space and subtly lit as to draw attention, stood a large sculpture of the IGC acronym and logogram rendered in semi-precious stones with added holographic imagery. The movement of the display was mesmerizing.

To the left was a large portrait of A. J. Padue, the founder of the IGC, posed serenely and confidently in front of a backdrop of planets and stars, presumably an artist's perception of the scope and breadth of IGC's domain.

On the right of the vestibule was a large triptych that almost covered the entire wall. It was an intricate depiction of what must have been every significant battle or acquisition the IGC had ever been involved in. Tåsan stood trying to make sense of what he was looking at and, while small vignettes presented themselves, the significance of the mural as a whole escaped him.

Scattered here and there were displays crowded with awards, medals of heroism, and other compensations that attested to the magnitude of the IGC's sphere of influence.

Tåsan decided to look at the displays another time and made his way into the auditorium. After a few brief hesitations, he found a seat about halfway down the aisle, between other incoming officers, whom he acknowledged with a nod and a brief greeting.

The noise in the auditorium was slowly climbing to a clamorous level and the air was filled with excitement. Just when it didn't seem that it could get much louder, the house lights started to dim and the audience came to quiet attention as a tall figure of a man strode across the stage to the podium.

He stood erect and quiet, surveying the faces before him. When he was sure that all eyes were on him, he spoke.

"Good afternoon ladies and gentlemen and welcome to Firmus Opulentia, headquarters of the Inter-Galaxy Command. I am Major

39

C. T. Barlet and I am in charge of this Officer Training Academy.

"By virtue of your hard work and brilliant admissions scores, you all have been admitted into a very prestigious organization, respected throughout the known galaxies and their beyonds, as the governance responsible for the general security, safety, health, and welfare of all member citizens and their business concerns.

"As such, the IGC fully predicts that each and every one of you will rise to their expectation that at the end of your training, you, too, will be an intrinsic part of the establishment.

"The next series of quads will not be easy. You will be pushed to go farther than you thought yourself able. You will reach further into your minds as your education takes hold. You will push your physical selves to arrive at and maintain peak performance. For it is common knowledge that mental acuity and physical wellness are paramount to efficiency.

"And all this while enjoying yourselves."

Major Barlet paused and smiled as the brief sound of hushed laughter rippled across the auditorium.

At length, Barlet continued, "At the end of your training, you will have gained improvements in yourself and built an appreciation for the wide and varied universe we share with a diversity of individuals. You will be leaders and adjudicators. The IGC expects nothing less.

"Thank you."

A polite smattering of applause followed Major Barlet as he turned and left the stage just as another man appeared and made his way to the podium.

"A quick word, if you will. I'm Major Sedwik, in charge of Internal Trainee Affairs. Your training schedules will officially begin tomorrow morning. Consult your assignments and the class locations map so you are not late to start times. The remainder of today may be spent organizing your quarters, familiarizing yourself with your new environment, and reviewing academy regulations. After that, officers in training, your time is your own."

Sedwik took a step back and turned to leave.

The chatter in the auditorium immediately started up and everyone rose to their feet and prepared to leave.

The man who had been sitting to Tåsan's right, turned and

smiled. "Hello. I'm Castell Brann," and held his hand in greeting. Castell was the same height as Tåsan, with thick, unruly black hair, green eyes and a long, slender nose.

Tåsan briefly took his hand and smiled in return. "Tåsan Sulac. Glad to make your acquaintance," and added, "From your accent, I'm guessing you're from Astor."

"Yes, Astor is my home planet. I'm from a community called Avados, close to the northern belt."

The auditorium was slowly emptying out and Tåsan found that he and Castell were edging along the aisle about as fast as could be expected.

Castell asked, "And you? Where is your home?"

"About seventeen milia from here, my family lives in Merula. I've grown up here."

By this time, the two recruits were edging out of the auditorium and into the bright vestibule where small groups of trainees stood, excitedly introducing themselves and exchanging comments on classes and schedules.

Tåsan asked Castell, "Where are you quartered?" and quickly added, "I'm in Res A, Q-D."

Castell smiled, "A coincidence! I'm also in Res A, Q-H. What a turn!"

Smiling, Tåsan said, "Great! I've already stowed my gear, how about you? Need any help?"

"No," replied Castell, "I arrived early so managed to stack my belongings before getting my Quad One schedule. If I work at it a little at a time, I could probably have my quarters organized by the end of the week."

"Well, in that case, let's explore the grounds, maybe catch an ale, and compare schedules before calling it a day."

"Happily," agreed Castell.

• • •

As it turned out, Tåsan's classes did not overlap with Castell Brann's. However, they frequently ran into each other in the residence hallways and between classes. Tåsan liked Castell and during the next several weeks, the two became friends.

Tåsan's Quad One classes, in print, looked to be fairly simple but were far from it.

41

Coming from an IGC family, Tåsan thought he knew just about all he needed to know about the Inter-Galaxy Command. His IGC Standards class had quickly proven him to be fairly lacking in basic IGC knowledge and it was embarrassing to say the least. The history of the IGC was long and colorful and populated with interesting characters. The IGC's relationship to the Intersolar and Space Alliance, the ISA, read like a father son relationship until the son, in this case, the IGC, became a formidable entity that deserved (…and here Tåsan read the word: demanded), respect. Overall, the ISA was a consortium of business individuals who needed the kind of protection they themselves could not provide, so they created it. They created the IGC and empowered it with the capacity to perform on ISA's behalf.

The IGC quickly grew in size and scope and took on the expanded responsibilities as directed by the ISA. The organization became the peacekeepers, conflict moderators, and ISA emissaries around the mapped universe, developing customs and courtesies designed to provide stability among ISA member corporations.

Fortunately, Tåsan's instructor taught the class with the flair of an excited storyteller, making the history more real and by far, more interesting. Tåsan felt separated from the IGC's history by the mere fact that at least five generations of time disconnected him from its beginnings but the antics and enthusiasm of his instructor helped relieve much of the boredom.

It got much more interesting for Tåsan when the class moved into the IGC's modern history. This was where Tåsan paid closer attention, figuring that it had more bearing on the manner of his current and future interactions within the IGC and outside of it, while on duty.

Two of his other Quad One classes, Biquaternion Mathematics of Quanta Mechanics and Advanced Verbal Skill and Strategy were heavy on study and class participation. Tåsan thanked his fortunes that these were Quad One classes only, although he took pains to learn and understand the Quanta Mathematics because he saw where the studies would progress into a future class in propulsion.

The final Quad One class, and one that would be included in seven of the eight quads of Tåsan's officer training, was misleadingly titled Physical Training. It was, in practice, a boot camp of cardio, endurance, and strength. There was a definite class start time but the end time was nebulous at best. It ended when the instructor said it ended and at times, seemed unpleasantly cruel. Tåsan took to calling the instructor "Relentless" as the most apt description of the man and his style. Yet, it was sincerely meant as a compliment.

As the quad crept closer to its conclusion, class assignments became a little more difficult and grade point averages a little more critical. The pace of the first quad, for Tåsan, foretold of what was to come: Hard work, discipline, and the way of the IGC. Nothing less would do.

But just as the quad was coming to an end, so would begin a one-week break and Tåsan was looking forward to it. He planned to go home and was glad that he didn't have to travel too far. He sent comm's to a couple of his friends expressing a desire to get together for a pulse rocket race along the Flats and received enthusiastic replies.

Three days before the break, Tåsan ran into Castell between classes and arranged to meet him later that afternoon at The Commissary for a mug of ale.

• • •

"Castell, over here!" called Tåsan as he stood and raised a hand to indicate his location.

The Commissary was full but Tåsan had managed to locate a small table in the center of the bustle after he stopped at the counter to order two ales.

The two foamy brews stood at the ready and when Castell was close enough to see them, he smiled and said, "Ahh, thank you! Nothing better after a tough week," and took his seat opposite Tåsan.

"I took the liberty," waving a hand to indicate the two brews, "thinking that I would be able to persuade you, if you were to decline, by using my uncanny abilities of verbal strategy." Tåsan widened his eyes and side glanced at Castell, waiting for him to get the joke.

"Yes, Tåsan, that may have worked if I had not also had to take the same class," Castell said as he reached for the chilled brew.

The two friends lifted their mugs in an easy salute to each other's health and took nice big gulps, tasting the slightly bitter liquid as it passed over their tongues.

Tåsan asked, "How are your classes going?"

"Good. I'm doing well and believe my scores are up but I'm looking forward to the break. I've gotten used to the pace of the classes but that hasn't made it go any more easily." Castell took another sip from his mug. "How about you? Everything good?"

Tåsan lifted his eyebrows into an expression of guarded optimism, "Yes, everything is fine. My scores are good, I'm happy with them." And changing the subject, "What are your plans for the quad break?"

"Oh, I'm going home. My family is excited about a visit with me. They have many hundreds of questions about my studies and life in the academy as well as a deep curiosity about Naiad Five. I'm scheduled to shuttle out immediately after my last class," said Castell and followed up with the same question for Tåsan.

"Same. Going home, although it's only a short ride for me. I was going to invite you to stay in Merula with us, my parents would be more than happy to have you."

Castell said, "Thanks, that sounds tempting but I'm afraid my family has already made plans."

"The offer stands. Maybe for the next quad break. Think about it. I'll introduce you to some of my friends. It'll be fun," Tåsan said.

"Okay, ask me again next quad, and speaking of which," Castell pulled his e-pad out of his pocket and touched the screen before continuing. "Received an e-version of my Quad Two schedule about an hour ago." He turned his device so that Tåsan could see it.

"Oh! Look at that," Tåsan said after looking closely at the short list of classes displayed on the small screen. "We're in the same Advanced Analytics class with instructor Vonnit," and dug out his own e-pad to reference his class schedule. "I'm also on for Statistical Distribution of Geometric Axioms and the ever present Physical Training, too."

Castell remarked, "Looks like another heavy work load is in store for both of us." He fell silent for a moment as he absentmindedly turned his mug in a lazy circle.

Tåsan glanced at Castell's face and wondered what he might be thinking. Castell's features gave no indication, which led Tåsan to guess that his thoughts weren't negative and possibly private, so let it pass.

At length, Castell spoke, "I'm starting to wind down from the day. The ale is definitely helping. I think I'll say good evening and go to my quarters," and gave a wan smile.

Tåsan said, "Yes, it's getting later."

Both Tåsan and Castell stood up and picked their way between tables and empty chairs as they started for the front doors.

Once outside, Castell turned to Tåsan and said, "I may not see you again before the break. Have a great time off and we'll meet again next quad."

Tåsan had gone down three steps and turned to Castell, "Have a fast shuttle and a nice break!" and raising his hand, added, "See you next quad!"

~

Tåsan's quad break went as he had predicted: Too fast.

There were several outings with friends that were particularly fun, and lots of time with the family. Tåsan hadn't realized how much he missed his family until he was on his way home from the academy. He had thought that since the training center was so close he would have opportunity to see family and friends throughout Quad One, but that wasn't so. The academy was all consuming, leaving no free time.

Tåsan made the most of his time off, which included times when he did nothing at all. It was during one of these times when he was sitting on the back balcony with his feet up looking at the vista and drinking a cold frostie, when Stellanova joined him.

"Tåsan, may I intrude?" she asked, hesitating in the doorway.

"Absolutely!" smiled Tåsan. "Pull up a chair."

The two sat quietly together for some time looking at the landscape that lay before them, letting their thoughts settle down.

The Sulac residence overlooked a wide, undeveloped stretch of land that ran for several milia in either direction. The scape was dotted with large, very old Methusel trees and at certain times of the year covered with Monarda flowers and blossoming Choke Berry shrubs.

45

Stellanova spoke softly, breaking the silence, "Remember when we were little, we would play at Disguise-n-Hide out there?"

Tåsan said, "Yes, I would always win because you would become distracted by this Muscari flower or that little Niognat bug. I would always find you!"

"I know," said Stellanova, "I loved to pick flowers for mother and we would often come home all scratched up by Choke Berry thorns!"

"Yeah, those little cuts would itch for days," agreed Tåsan.

Stellanova smiled at the memories. After a moment she said, "Hey, I got high score for the Eros dig-site habitat project you helped me with."

"That's great!" said Tåsan.

"Professor said it was very forward thinking and well planned. Said I may have a future in advanced terra-forming." Stellanova beamed with pride.

Tåsan said, "You still have a way to go before graduation, try to keep your career options open for as long as you can."

"Yes," said Stellanova, "but I like what I'm doing. It's hard not to focus on it right now."

The conversation was interrupted by the call to supper.

As Stellanova and Tåsan got up from their seats, Tåsan touched Stella's arm. She turned, bright-faced and expectant.

"It's all about the options," he said.

• • •

It was becoming more unusual for the entire Sulac family to sit down to a meal together.

Arron had attained his instructor's degree in Advanced Spatial Mathematics and had relocated to a cluster of mini-dwellings on the far side of Merula as a convenience to his classroom and office. Tåsan was away at IGC Training and while Stellanova was still at home, the demands of her education left her little time for family nicety. Many times she would come home, grab a fast bite and retire to her room to work or study.

Rebetta and Amans were fulltime careerists, which meant long days and exhausted nights.

Tonight was special. Tonight, everyone was home.

Rebetta had put together a wonderful meal of roasted wild

Cracidae with brown nut breading and a creamy brassica, daikon, and skirret side. Stellanova made a wild Choke Berry crumble for dessert and Amans opened a chilled bottle of Lingdon Práxus. Arron and Tåsan, possessing very limited cooking skills, set the table and were on task to clear and wash the dishes after the meal.

Amans raised his glass and addressed the family, "What a pleasure it is to have everyone around the table again!"

Smiles lit each face and consents filled the air. Amans continued, "I think it would be nice if each of us were to say a few words about our achievements since we last sat together as a family. Arron, would you mind starting?"

"Not at all, father. Let's see...after graduating, and I'm still happy to say...with honors, I was accepted for the position of Level One Tenure at the Naiad Five Institute of Technology for Higher Learning. Everything moved at a blur for about a quad as I found near-campus housing, moved in, started my instructing position, developed class materials, and stumbled my way into a workable routine. I think that about sums it up."

"Thank you, Arron," said Amans, and addressing himself to everyone said, "Let me speak for your mother and myself. Rebetta has an exciting new project starting next week. A new 'substance', for lack of a better word, has been collected from one of the asteroids that follow the planet Jahved Tuk in its orbit. She's leading a team that will investigate what it is and how it may be employed. There may be a 'Rebettavite' in our future."

A smattering of congratulations punctuated the news.

Stellanova exclaimed, "Oh, mother, that's wonderful news!"

Rebetta smiled, a little embarrassed and a soft blush rose to her cheeks. "Thank you, everyone, but it may be a bit early for compliments, especially if this substance turns out to be nothing more than antiquated guano with limited applications." After dabbing at her mouth with her napkin, said, "Amans, tell about your new assignment."

Amans put his fork down and cleared his throat before speaking. "Oh, yes. The ISA has initiated a new alliance with the peoples of Thorium 4 and have assigned the IGC, and in turn, me, to broker cooperative agreements with at least a dozen prominent business leaders representing everything from mining uridium-8 for export, to importing materials and technologies for the internal manufacturing of goods."

Stellanova asked, "What are the people of Thorium 4 like?"

Amans thought for a moment, and then answered, "Physically they are pleasing to look at. Most are tall, somewhat slender with skin the color of copper. They all have eyes the color of gold with small black pupils. They're very modern in their dress, as far as I can tell, having only vid-comm'ed with their business leaders to this point. I think I'm not wrong in my initial assessment of their business prowess: they're sharp and quick."

Tåsan asked another curious question, "Isn't it true that Thorium 4 has actively avoided interactions with the other planets in their own system as well as outside galaxies?"

Amans answered, "Yes. Preferring to keep to themselves, they've managed to live in secrecy but are finding their planetary isolation is limiting them. It's my job to help them into inter-galactic commerce without the attendant growing pains of trying to do it without IGC guidance."

Arron had started to clear the dishes and Tåsan followed his lead, leaving the glasses and several pieces of tableware behind.

Stellanova had brought the berry crumble and another set of small plates to the table and set about placing a tasty portion on each and passing them around.

Rebetta took a taste and said, "Stella, this is very good! Did you use real cinspice?"

Stellanova smiled at the compliment. "Yes, and a dash of sweet sallow to tone down the bitterness of the Choke Berries."

"Good call, Stella, it's just about perfect," said Arron before he took another forkful.

Amans said, "Stella, tell us about your recent quad at university."

"There's not much to say", said Stellanova. "I've loaded my schedule with classes and spend endless hours in study and work. There's not enough time for outside fun, although I did manage to attend a lecture on terra-forming by Jonat Serrit early in the quad." Stellanova stopped to scoop another bit of dessert before continuing. "He's widely recognized as the current expert in Terra-Forming Biomechanics. It was very interesting."

Arron asked, "How are your scores?"

Stellanova said, "Very high. I'm actually finding that's the easy part since I'm still excited about the studies. It's time management that sometimes alludes me."

Arron added, "Well, that's life at university."

Rebetta said, "You'll learn to flow with your time as your studies wind down. Right now, everything is so new to you, but you'll get better and find it easier."

Stellanova nodded her agreement and became still as she thought about the advice.

Addressing Tåsan, Amans said, "Tåsan, I'm so curious to know how you find the IGC officer training program. Tell us about your Quad One adventures and something about what's in store for you later on."

Tåsan started, "All the quads have physical training. Mega strength and endurance fitness routines that push hard. Some muscle somewhere always aches. Quad One studies start at the bottom with Quanta Mechanics Mathematics and Verbal Strategy skills. These are work heavy but I'm managing to stay with the classes. There's one class in Inter-Galaxy Command Standards and I've found it mildly interesting at first, with all its dates and wars and treaties, but noticed that as IGC history became more contemporary, it also became more fascinating."

"How do you mean?" asked Amans.

"Well, there's writings on many of the known planets, their people, business dealings, and the like, that are well-written, informative pieces. Very helpful material. There's also an earnest attempt by dozens of IGC officers to round out the various descriptions by writing of psychological observations they had made while dealing with any of the above subjects. They address phobia, angst, the use of non-committal or inflammatory speech, anxiety, mood, general behavior disorders, and in some cases, an all-binding patriarchal society. All these footnotes, if you will, add a very colorful overlay to the peoples or individuals that the IGC has interacted with. This part of the class really managed to spark my interest. The outward ceremony and the inward psychology. Treacherous as a land explosive!"

The family sat quietly, looking at Tåsan. He took a quick glance around the table at the mixed emotions that played across each face and wondered if he hadn't said too much.

Tåsan looked at his father, and not being able to read his thoughts, quickly offered, "Next quad is more mathematics and analytics. Oh! I've made a friend. Castell Brann. He's from Astor. I'd like to invite him to stay here next break. Would that be okay?"

Amans said, "If it's alright with your mother, it's certainly alright with me. What do you think, Rebetta?"

Rebetta smiled, "We'd love to meet your friend, Castell. Please invite him with our sincere welcome."

• • •

The hour was late and the table was clear.

Arron had left for home some minutes ago and after Stellanova had suppressed a third yawn, Rebetta made their good nights and they both retired.

Tåsan and Amans had withdrawn to the great room after Tåsan challenged his father to a game of Parudi Rule. Amans poured two glasses of Tradorian Berrywine while Tåsan set the boards and distributed the avatars into two teams. They sat opposite each other and began to play.

The game was several moves in and it was Tåsan's turn. Amans sat watching his son's face and remembered back when Tåsan had first played Parudi Rule. How he concentrated over every move and was so very pleased when he won the game. It was much the same now, although the exuberance of youth had been tamed into the beginning of a mature statesman. Amans saw a bright future for Tåsan in the Inter-Galaxy Command.

"May I give you some advice?" Amans said.

Tåsan looked up from the game and said, "Absolutely," and reached for his glass of wine.

"You'll go far in the IGC if you use this time to study hard and keep out of trouble." Amans leveled a look at his son in an effort to silently communicate his meaning.

Tåsan said, "I do study hard. I study all the time. As a matter of fact, with all the study, there's no time for trouble. The next two quads are sizing up about the same way." He leaned back in his chair but couldn't fully relax and studied his father's face. Was there something behind the simple words of advice? Tåsan had not given his father cause to warn about trouble so why now the concern?

"Father, is there anything in particular that worries you?" asked Tåsan.

Amans was thoughtfully silent for a long moment and Tåsan could see he was choosing his words carefully. Finally he spoke.

"You have a penchant for excitement almost to the exclusion of reasonable thought." Amans paused and leaned forward for emphasis, catching and holding Tåsan in an intense gaze, then continued, "It would be a shame and a disappointment if you were to do something foolish just as your officer studies were commencing."

Tåsan could only sit with his now confused and jumbled thoughts. *"Has he heard something? What was to hear?"*

Amans added, "Think of this small observation as a father's concern for his son's future. I'm sure that if you temper yourself and learn the IGC way, you'll have a long and distinguished career ahead of you."

Tåsan thought to respond but Amans spoke first, "It's late, son, and I have an early morning tomorrow. I concede my play of Parudi Rule but beg a rematch in near future." Amans rose to his feet and Tåsan followed.

"Good night, son."

"Good night, father."

After Amans left, Tåsan sat with his thoughts for a time before he, too, retired to bed.

~

In written form, Quad Two looked to be easy, with only two classes in addition to the ever-present Physical Training. But actually it was all together different.

The Statistical Distribution of Geometric Axioms course was laden with study and tests and more study, and the instructor proved to be a very rigid teacher. On day one, he announced "The Rules". Do all the assignments correctly. Make all deadlines. Pass the course. At the end of this succinct speech, he smiled a wry smile and said, "Simple," then began lecture one.

The Advanced Analytics course was, in comparison, easy in that the subject was not new for Tåsan. He loved problem solving and had honed his analytic skills early on. Amans taught his children the use of logic as a way to think clearly and to proceed with confidence. What made the class more enjoyable was that Castell Brann was also there and they frequently teamed up in class discussions and over homework.

After one particularly rousing discussion on the hypothetical evolution of techno-assist starship propulsion as applied to guidance and stability, both Tåsan and Castell composed papers that earned them top scores for the assignment. To celebrate, they met that evening at The Commissary.

The two friends found a table at the windows that had a view of the campus center, had ordered small plates and Cirrus Ale, and were waiting for it to be brought out to them.

"I still can't believe that our papers rated top score," said Castell.

"Finally our genius is being recognized," replied Tåsan, punctuating his statement with an obvious grin.

Castell was still chuckling and shaking his head in amused disbelief when the food and ale arrived. They lifted their glasses and Tåsan said, "Enjoy it while you can, my friend, our fame may be fleeting in the quads to come."

"Hear, hear!" said Castell in agreement.

After they drank to their inspired partnership, both went to work on their food. After a moment of quietude, a sudden shout from the center of the room caused them to freeze mid-movement and turn their attention to the ruckus.

Two recruits had jumped to their feet and were shouting angry words at each other. One pointed a finger into the other's face, which clearly the recipient did not like so he made to swat it away. The owner of the finger, his anger more heated, had yelled, "Don't you lay your hands on me," and swung a fist, punching the other in the face just below the eye. This momentarily stunned the man, who quickly recovered and punched back, sending the first man stumbling backward where he fell against a table and went down to the floor.

Tåsan had dropped his fork and jumped to his feet. His immediate thought was to intervene in order to stop the fight. Three steps later, Tåsan found himself closer to the two combatants but now unsure of what he would be able to do once he was in the thick of it. The first man had picked himself up off the floor and assumed an aggressive stance, ready to strike back.

Immediately, six uniformed IGC security guards were on the scene. They separated the combatants and escorted them out. Once outside, they were put into two separate vehicles that then drove away into the darkness of the night.

The Commissary was in stunned silence until, almost at once, everyone recovered their voices, filling the air with loud conversation.

Tåsan made his way back to his table, sat down, and with a slight look of stunned confusion looked over at Castell and asked, "Where did the uniforms come from?"

Castell said, "Out of nowhere. The entire scene from start to finish, couldn't have taken more than one minute."

"Efficient," said Tåsan.

"It never occurred to me that there was any kind of law enforcement for the academy."

"Neither to me. It's almost frightening, in a way." Tåsan sat quietly with his thoughts, clearly disturbed by what had just transpired.

Castell asked, "What motivated you to jump up and get involved? You were awfully quick to decide a course of action."

Tåsan ran his fingers across his brow and faintly shook his head as he spoke, "A split-second thought to break them up made me react, but was quickly replaced with the fact that, acting alone, I couldn't have accomplished it. Fortunately, the authorities solved the dilemma."

Eventually the Commissary settled down and Tåsan and Castell finished their meal and the last of their ale. They paid their bill and walked the fifteen minutes back to Res A. Once they reached their building they said their good nights as each repaired to their own quarters. Tåsan had a bit of class work to finish up and Castell had an early morning.

~

The remainder of Quad Two completed in a blur of study and tests. Just before the break, all trainees received their Quad Two scores along with their Quad Three and Four schedules.

Castell accepted Tåsan's invitation to stay on Naiad Five with Tåsan's family and he was looking forward to it. It was such a relief to Castell that he not have to complete the fifteen hour shuttle home and another fifteen hour shuttle back, although from the looks of his schedule, he wouldn't have another opportunity to visit home for another three quads of the solar year.

Tåsan's family enjoyed Castell's company, especially Stellanova, who plied Castell with questions about Astor. Her curiosity got the better of her. What was the terrain like? Were there mineral and quartz deposits to be found in their mountains? What kind of life forms existed at the bottom of their seas? Eventually Tåsan had to ask her to confine her questions to the evening mealtime. She was much too enthusiastic in her queries so, please, give it a rest.

Tåsan enjoyed introducing Castell to some of his friends and spending a little time playing tour guide.

Castell fell in love with Merula's architecture and arts. He was suitably impressed with the discrete blend of art and science, with both disciplines represented in equal parts throughout Merula. He was especially interested in the art history museum and gallery located in the heart of the city. It was built a short five years after Merula was established in 29076.1. It had been expanded and improved over time but retained much of its original architecture.

Two days before the break was over, Rebetta managed to prepare a nice dinner meal in honor of Castell's visit. Amans was to work very late so would not be at table, neither would Arron as he was very busy at his work as well.

Rebetta, Stellanova, Tåsan, and Castell sat down together and relaxed over a hot one-dish meal. When everyone was finishing up, Stellanova brought a kettle of hot tea and four mugs to the table. As she portioned the tea, she asked Castell if she might ask him one last question.

"Castell, please tell about Astor and its twin, Lux, specifically their peoples, their ties to each other, commerce, weather and all. It's so unique that two planets travel together on a single, fixed orbit. Also, I'm curious about Lorantu Dau, your shared science station that travels in coordination with both planets. How did that come about? What kind of science is done there?"

When Stellanova ran out of steam, she sat quietly and as she realized she hadn't asked one final question but closer to ten, she lowered her eyes and started to blush.

Castell smiled at Stellanova, remembering his own unrestrained curiosity when he was her age.

"There's a lot to tell about Astor and her twin Lux. You should be able to research their early histories through your own librariums as several noteworthy volumes have addressed the subject. If you can't find those particular missives, I can send you one or two to get you started."

Castell talked for a few minutes about how the peoples of Astor differed slightly from those of Lux. For instance, speech patterns and inflections are more subtle for the Luxonians. Another distinction, he noted, between the two would be the civil celebrations observed during the solar year. While many observances are common to both planets, each has their own Founding Day, for instance. Other than that, Astor and Lux are like family, with all that that connotates.

"Astor and Lux did not think there was anything significant about sharing an exact orbit course until we moved out into the galaxy and realized how unique it was," Castell remarked. The discovery gave rise to immense studies and theories and for a brief period, fear and superstition. However, cooler minds prevailed and fortunately for both peoples, gave birth to Lorantu Dau, the crowning achievement of the two joined planets and societies.

Castell stopped talking and lifted his mug of tea, took a sip then continued for another brief moment.

"Lorantu Dau is a science station of merit. It was named after a renowned biosyst from Astor's capitol city, Kijani. He is credited with the discovery of Dau-morph, a double-celled mold capable of producing Fermi gasses. Doctor Dau donated much of his personal wealth to the establishment of the research lab." Castell paused a moment before continuing. "I'm sorry. I sound like a text book."

Stellanova's face brightened, "Not at all, it's fascinating!"

Castell smiled, "Then I'll just conclude with this...Lorantu Dau has two large sections connected together by a large structure that serves as a corridor that provides crew quarters and galley and storage as well as flight engineering and its related necessities. The two large science stations at either end are very large and host any number of long-term studies as well as current tests of interest. Lorantu Dau represents Astor and Lux at their best."

"You've made me very curious about hearing more," said Tåsan and turning to Stellanova, "How about you?"

"It's very compelling and I think I'll reference your planet's history further, Castell. Thank you for sharing."

Rebetta remarked, "I had occasion to visit Astor just after graduation to attend a seminar on bioluminescence of trilopods, being held in Oswedor. I didn't have much time to explore the city due to schedule constraints, but was impressed with how modern the architecture was and how open and friendly the people were."

"Things haven't changed too much in the past few years," said Castell. "Maybe now, you could visit once again, as my guests. I could show you all our hidden treasures, those not ordinarily noted in the tourist literature."

"That's a very tempting offer, Castell, one I may take advantage of," replied Rebetta.

Castell raised his mug and nodded in appreciation, "Here's to trusting that you will."

• • •

The next day, Tåsan and Castell spent the hours being lazy. They packed a few things to prepare for the short trip back to the academy, sat on the back balcony, got up at some point to take a "wake-up" jog along the open space behind the house, relaxed on the balcony again, and at the end of the day, ate chilled leftovers before retiring, each rather tired from their day of doing nothing in particular.

"Two quads from now, I'll think back to this day in total disbelief that it ever happened," said Castell.

"Yea, in light of the two quads already gone by, it does seem like a dream," added Tåsan.

"Hope the thought of it isn't too painful when we're back in physical training."

"I'm going to have to run a few extra milia to get back into shape. Fortunately, I didn't succumb to too many second helpings," joked Tåsan.

"I'm afraid your mother's cooking is too good. I see at least fifteen hard run milia in my future," said Castell.

Tåsan added, "We're due back at the academy tomorrow, I'm going to suggest an early start so we should prepare before the night's out. We've already said our goodbyes so can leave at first light, if that works for you."

"Perfectly. I'll be up and ready," said Castell.

"Okay. Then with that...I'll say good night and will see you in the morn."

~

Quad Three. By the end of the first day of physical training class, Tåsan had sworn he would never have another helping of berry and nut crumble as long as he lived. However, by the end of the week, he had shed the pounds and felt fit enough to think, *"Well, maybe just a small helping wouldn't hurt all that much."*

The class in Navigation started out familiar but progressed quickly to an intermediate then to an expert level of study and practice. It went far beyond the monitoring and controlling of a craft's movement. It delved into celestial observation, inertial nav and various rad systems, and even included wayfinding, or as Tåsan took to calling the subject, "Intuitive Nav."

Tåsan's flight simulation instruction went well enough, he thought.

Trainees were to play multiple roles of commander, pilot, co-pilot, navigator, and those of other bridge crew positions. They would be part of a virtual crew played by holograms that were enlivened with a convincing artificial intelligence interface program that could mimic their crew positions and seemingly act and react in random variables.

All the simulations took place aboard a variety of ships but confined to very realistic-looking command centers. Officers in training need not be concerned with the rest of the ship. It would respond as ordered, so was excluded for the sake of brevity.

The actual simulations varied from fairly simple, like docking with a satellite station, to relatively difficult, as in taking skillful action or the correct course.

Professor Cullen gave Tåsan a brief introduction, explaining to him what types of situations may occur and what he may expect. "You will be scored on how well you handle each flight position and your interactions with others while performing in that capacity."

Tåsan nodded his understanding.

Professor Cullen continued, "My role is to observe. I may interrupt the simulation at any point if I have a comment or I perceive a teachable moment or if I see you struggling with any aspect of the simulation."

"Thank you, sir, that's very clear," responded Tåsan.

"Good. Shall we begin?" asked Cullen.

• • •

The days ticked by and so did the number of sims. In the role of commander, one episode came up where Tåsan was required to respond to a distress call originating from the void of space. After the sim played through, Professor Cullen made a point of telling Tåsan that he scored an excellent for that category. He had proceeded with caution and employed sound IGC protocol. "Well done, Tåsan."

Tåsan changed roles to that of pilot, a position he felt very comfortable in.

The sims continued in progression and Tåsan flew through each one with ease, but on the seventh day as pilot, an unexpected turn of events presented itself.

Seemingly out of nowhere, the ship was being bombarded with space dust that caused intermittent interference with the comm and some of the sensors. There followed shortly, a cascade of events that seemed to overwhelm the crew of the command center. The virtual navigator was shouting about combustible clusters of meteorites and the virtual science officer was reporting a biomass, with the capacity to harm the ship's outer hull that had changed course and was closing fast.

The virtual commander had ordered Tåsan to make a token evasive maneuver but it had been an inadequate move. The dangers were multiplying and still closing. Panic laced the virtual commander's voice as he yelled to Tåsan to, "Get us out of here!"

Tåsan took a calculated risk and spun the ship sharply to the left, firing the starboard engines almost to full, then rocked the helm from one side to the other and as he let up on the starboard engines and rammed the port engines to life. Out of the corner of his eye, he saw the virtual commander tossed backward and tumble, arms flailing, onto the floor, landing on his virtual butt while the momentum of his fall splayed his legs wildly up into the air. Tåsan dismissed the act as overblown and summed it up in one word, "*Puhts.*" The craft jolted left then again to the right before Tåsan fired the engines simultaneously and shot past the cluster of meteorites at 14.8 rads/sec, clearing the vector. He then slowed to a speed distance of 1800 milia/hour and when his station was secure, Tåsan looked to the virtual commander and said, "Orders, sir?"

The sim immediately stopped and Professor Cullen spoke, as he approached Tåsan, "That was very interesting. Tell me, what were your first thoughts?"

Tåsan answered, "I felt the confusion and panic from the crew was a bit premature. I didn't think the situation warranted it. I thought to monitor the dangers using the motion sensors, maybe detect a pattern."

"Okay," noted Cullen, "Then what?"

"As the panic rose, I thought I had missed something and was checking my instruments but holding her steady. When the commander raised his voice and ordered our hasty exit, I used the forward visuals to guide the ship out of the traps...fast." Tåsan looked at Cullen.

Cullen was stroking his chin, in thought, then spoke, "Tåsan I'm going to mark this portion of your sim training as complete and we can move on to the co-pilot portion. And, Tåsan?"

"Yes, sir?"

"Well done."

• • •

As Tåsan prepared for his final flight crew sim, he could only think that he was more than ready to be done with simulated flight. He felt that while the sims were somewhat instructional, it still wasn't real flight. He looked forward to his next quad when he would fly real craft in actual space.

In this sim, Tåsan would perform as co-pilot whose main duties would be navigation and communication but who would also act as pilot or commander in dire circumstances.

Tåsan joined the virtual crew already at their stations and as he took his chair, the sim displayed a scene in progress. Immediately, Tåsan noted that they were in deep space, the Allodial Expanse, on a heading for the Rayten Galaxy some 10^3 parsecs from their current position. Everything was steady. There were no blips on any of the displays.

Suddenly, most of the bridge monitors lit up in warning while an insistent alarm rhythmically pulsated in tandem with the blinking blue lights emanating from the ceiling.

The commander listened carefully as the pilot relayed information from his console. "An unmarked ship has appeared directly off our bow. It's a large Class-P ship, origin and intention unknown."

"Co-Pilot Sulac," the commander charged, "Hail the ship. Demand identification."

"Aye, sir," responded Tåsan, his fingers busy at the comm. Addressing the ship he said, "This is the Sim Pro A17, identify yourself, we await your comm."

There was a moment of silence as the two ships hung effortlessly in the void of space. Quiet and serene.

POW! The ship fired a round from its forward weapon that streaked toward the Sim Pro's starboard nacelle, barely missing it but grazing the hull as it passed.

The bridge crew erupted into a panic. Everyone was shouting. Tåsan was at his controls, sizing up the intruder ship and looking at its attitude when he heard the commander announce, "We are no match for a Class-P ship. My decision is to leave this area of space immediately. Co-Pilot Sulac, set a course and get us away from here!"

Tåsan turned in his chair to face the commander and said, "Sir, I believe we should stay in proximity and notify the IGC to send backup."

The commander leveled a look at Tåsan. "My order was to get this ship out of here. What didn't you understand about that?"

Tåsan let the snipe pass but pressed his point. "We're smaller, lighter, and more agile than the Class-P." He heard the hard edge to his voice but didn't stop. "I can out maneuver her, sir. Call the IGC for backup."

The commander had stood up. Tåsan could see the anger rising behind his eyes and saw the commander set his jaw in a clench as he stepped forward.

"You are to pilot this ship away. Now!"

"No sir!" shouted Tåsan. "Your actions are irresponsible. Your course will lead the ship into direct danger from the intruder. I will not be a part of that!"

POW! Another grazing blast from the Class-P, this time taking out a sensor camera on the Sim Pro's prow that eliminated several monitors and knocked everyone off balance.

Tåsan looked to the pilot and commanded, "Send an urgent message to IGC – request fast assistance."

The pilot looked stunned and caught in indecision.

Tåsan barked, "Now!" Shaking the pilot to action before taking flight control and moving the ship closer to the Class-P where he knew it would be very difficult for it to fire on them again. He then ordered tactical to fire a forward blast, targeting the Class-P's nav guidance probe, all the while moving the Sim Pro closer to the Class-P's hull.

Just as the Sim Pro fired three successive cannons, that took out the Class-P's navigation probe and crippled one of its secondary engines, the big lights of the Sim Pro's bridge came up, causing the virtual crew to slowly faze into transparency, leaving Tåsan alone on the Sim bridge.

The simulation had concluded.

Tåsan sat back in his chair, now aware of the tension that was slowly draining from his shoulders and arms. And then it hit him. His actions were insubordinate. Tåsan felt he had done all the correct things to save the Sim Pro and in his thoughts, defiantly defended himself to that end.

Then Instructor Cullen appeared. He stood silently looking at Tåsan as the moments ticked by.

Feeling very uncomfortable under Cullen's gaze, Tåsan stood up and faced him, assuming the posture of attention. And waited.

At length Cullen spoke, "If I hadn't witnessed it myself, I would never have believed you capable of such an act of disrespect for lines of authority as set forth by the IGC."

Tåsan stood erect, staring straight ahead, listening.

Cullen continued, "The duties of a co-pilot are clear and are

61

only expanded beyond that definition in cases where the commander and the pilot have been incapacitated in some way. Neither of those things happened but somehow you felt it your duty to defy orders and take control." Cullen stared at Tåsan. "Defend your actions, Lieutenant Sulac."

"The commander's actions would have placed the Sim Pro in immediate danger. The Class-P could easily have overtaken us as we ran away," Tåsan placed an inflection on the words "ran away" before continuing, "They had already shown that they were willing to fight. The commander should have called for suggestions before concluding the best and first (another inflection) course was to run. Sir."

Instructor Cullen had listened quietly as Tåsan spoke. After a quick moment of continued silence, Cullen took a half step closer to Tåsan and calmly said, "I will have to write this up. It will become a part of your training record." Cullen stood looking at Tåsan, studying his face, and wondering at his thoughts. "This will leave an indelible mark on your record, but I will add that had you been in the role of captain, your course of evasive and defensive actions would have been the best possible decisions to make…under the circumstances."

Tåsan moved his gaze to Cullen's face. He was relieved that he did not see hostility or animosity. "Thank you, sir. I'll remember this."

Cullen almost laughed out loud but held himself steady. *"There's no end to the surprises pulled by first solar year trainees."*

"You're dismissed, Lieutenant."

~

Neither Tåsan nor Castell went home during the break between quads. They were to prepare to relocate from the Firmus Opulentia academy to an off-world base on Erontu where they would spend quads four and five completing intensive in-flight training on a multitude of different fighters and star cruisers.

Tåsan sent an e-comm to his family to explain why he wouldn't be home on the break and had arranged a cam meeting with his sister Stellanova, just to see her happy face.

"How's university life treating you?" asked Tåsan.

Stellanova smiled, "Keeping me very busy. This quad is

engineering-centric...lots of tectonic stress analysis, mathematics, materials chemistry...you know...basic stuff. How go things with Admiral Tåsan? Are you running the academy yet?" and gave Tåsan a bemused look that made him laugh out loud.

"I'm working on that part."

"How's Castell?"

"He's fine. We're sharing classes in the next two quads: Propulsion, and Computer and Ship-wide Engineering, as well as Navigation and Armaments. Looking forward to it. I'll tell him you said hello and have more questions for him."

Stellanova blushed in embarrassment, "Well," she chided herself, "maybe one or two."

"Hey, Stell, next quad I'm flying a Class-N, I'll send you pictures of the bridge."

"Tåsan, we're going to miss you. When's your next break?"

"Not until the week following Quad Five. The next two quads will be slammed. I may not be able to send e-comm's for quite some time but rest assured, the IGC is taking good care of me." Tåsan added, "I should get moving, things to do and all. Take care of yourself and tell mother I love her."

"Okay, Tåsan. I might worry about you a little. If you can sneak a fast word, I'd appreciate it. Say hi to Castell and love to you, Tåsan. Take care!"

Bink. The e-comm ended and the monitor went blank.

~

Erontu is the second largest planet in the Niles system but orbits closest to the sun. Its ancient civilization was one of the first to join the Intersolar and Space Alliance, eager to increase the market for their newly expanding main commerce: the manufacturing of large inter-stellar craft.

Taking advantage of the alliance, the IGC brokered an agreement. They would create and maintain a flight-training base on Erontu in exchange for limited use of many of the craft being manufactured there. Thus, Jacamarici Lor began operations.

The trip from Naiad Five to Erontu took four days. Trainees were told not to expect too many conveniences, quarters would be tight, and movement generally limited. There would be scheduled flight instruction held in a cargo bay so all trainees were to keep their note pads at the ready.

The days passed quickly enough and soon the transport ship had completed its descent through Erontu's atmosphere and was sailing over the landscape toward Jacamarici Lor.

Tåsan and Castell had taken jump seats next to one of the bulkhead viewing windows and sat watching the topography as it slowly slid by far below them.

Castell spoke in a low tone, "It looks rather desolate."

"Yes," answered Tåsan, "but looks can be deceiving. My father once told me that many creatures thrive in the hostile environment of Erontu's backcountry. He told of one particular invertebrate, a Teropt, that lurks at dusk and whose bite causes severe illness and hallucinations and if not immediately treated, death comes quickly."

Castell was listening but the more he heard of the dreaded Teropt bug, the more skeptical he became. "Are you sure your father wasn't telling you a tall tale? Something to scare you just a bit or with the intention to spark your imagination?"

"Well, if you knew father, you'd know he's not given to flights of fancy." Tåsan turned his gaze back out the viewing window. After a brief moment he said, "Wish I had my pulse rocket. I'd love to ride the terrain, see what it's made of."

Castell pulled his e-pad out of his pack and sat thumbing through the displays until he located the one he was looking for. "There doesn't seem to be much free time allotted to us during our flight training. Looks to be one day off every two weeks." He turned the screen so Tåsan could see it. "I'm going to bet we spend it sleeping...not on a pulse rocket."

"Now that's a shame, although sleep is good, too."

Castell pointed out the window, "There's Jacamarici Lor."

Both watched as Jacamarici Lor, just then a small point on the horizon, grew in perspective until it dominated the view out the window.

The base seemed massive against the relative emptiness of the terrain that stretched for milia all around it.

From their vantage point, Tåsan and Castell could see jet ports and landing pads that dotted the area, several control towers, and dozens of land vehicles scurrying about the field. Most of the buildings were located around the perimeter and all were connected by elevated walkways and cordoned off from the wilds by a transparent shield fence only meant to keep uninvited backcountry creatures in their own territory, not the IGC's.

The transport slowed until it hovered over a pad and made its gradual and graceful landing, coming to rest on its strut pads with a small but final shudder.

All the trainees disembarked the ship and followed a clean cut Tech Class III as he led them through the field and up to one of the outer buildings. When the stragglers had caught up with the front of the group, now standing in loose formation in the building's foyer, the Tech spoke, "Welcome, Officers, to Jacamarici Lor. This will be your home for the next two quads. Your lodging assignments are posted here," pointing at a notice board to his right, "along with a base contact list. You've all received your training schedules and classes will begin tomorrow. In the meantime, it's suggested that you familiarize yourselves with your immediate surroundings, reference a base map to locate your training areas, and read all the cautionary materials located in your quarters, regarding the local vertebrate and invertebrate wildings that inhabit the area."

Tåsan looked at Castell, who was standing close by, and nudged him slightly with an elbow. When Castell glanced over, Tåsan raised his eyebrows and nodded toward the Tech, to underscore his last statement.

Castell let out a small puff of breath and smiled as he nodded in return.

The Tech had continued, "Generally, your movements around the base are not limited but Operations has asked that you stay alert when in the vicinity of flight ops." Pausing for a brief moment, the Tech looked over the faces turned his way, then finished his address, "If there aren't any pressing questions, I'll leave you to yourselves."

There was a brief silence while everyone waited for any queries to be made, and hearing none, the Tech said good night and made his way from the building.

Meanwhile, the group of trainees filtered around the building locating their rooms and those of their friends.

65

As it turned out, Tåsan and Castell were quartered in the same room along with two other officer trainees, Darrian Adaams, third year medical from Eros and Wyn Flann, an ensign trainee from Sador. After informal introductions, everyone busied themselves stowing their gear and getting their bearings.

Tåsan stood for a moment at the window. Their third floor room faced the wild backcountry that filled the view as far away as the horizon. It was rocky with outcropped low cliffs and fairly deep crevices and ravines that appeared to have been carved by water, although they were now dry and filled with prickly-looking low shrubs that hugged the bleached soil.

Each floor had a large center room along the hallway that filled the building space to the left and right. These spaces were outfitted with low tables and sitting areas arranged for trainee relaxing or study. One set of windows faced the side of the complex that viewed the constant activity of flight ops while the other set of windows, in contrast, viewed the desolate backcountry.

This is where Tåsan and Castell found themselves a half an hour later, surrounded by small groups of trainees, excitedly talking with old and new friends. Both had their e-pad schedules out and were in the process of comparing their classes against the base map when Darrian Addams approached them with another trainee in tow.

"Hello roomies," said Darrian, interrupting Tåsan and Castell's mild concentration. "This is my friend, Dea Sún, we know each other from our medical studies on Lux. Dea, this is Tåsan Sulac from Naiad Five and Castell Brann from Astor."

Smiles, handshakes, and greetings passed between them.

Castell asked Dea, "Let me guess, you're from Thorium 4?"

Tåsan would have guessed that, too. Dea was tall and willowy with copper colored skin and striking golden eyes.

Dea answered, "Yes and thank you for the compliment of recognizing that. It's unusual to meet someone with knowledge of Thorium 4 since as a people we're only just now joining the Intersolar and Space Alliance and taking advantage of what the Inter-Galaxy Command can offer."

Tåsan smiled, "Welcome!" and looking around at the small group added, "Let's believe that the next two quads are a benefit to

66

us all!"

...

Early the following day all officer trainees were gathered in the training field for a one-time, ten minute welcome speech given by the base commander. Following the brief interlude, the trainees had less than five minutes to report to their first class. Fortunately for Tåsan, he was already in his classroom because his first class of this quad was Physical Training.

Following this, he would meet up with Castell for their ship-wide engineering class and after the mid-morn meal break, start up again with a highly technical class on combat systems.

The Quad Four class that Tåsan was really looking forward to was the advanced pilot training class that put the classroom aboard actual craft, out in actual space.

Very heady stuff. And Tåsan couldn't wait.

By now, the routine of being a part of the IGC Officer Training Program was well practiced; almost a matter of course and Tåsan did not take it lightly. He was determined to make the most of it and found, to his mild surprise, that his resolution had only been slightly tempered by the excitement of learning new systems and meeting new people.

The engineering class syllabus outlined a very comprehensive program. All ship-wide systems including life support and all sub-systems, computers and AI's, and all Command Bridge engineering functions would be covered. Huge amounts of study and long nights were most definitely in Tåsan's future. It helped that Castell was also in the class. They were a good team, bouncing ideas off of each other and able to clarify vague or esoteric doctrine or terminology.

The first class of the afternoon, the combat system as used on various craft, started at a moderate rate. There were upward of forty trainees in the classroom that made it a fairly large group. The instructor had announced that the course was highly technical and required an in-depth understanding of all the systems as part of the ultimate goal. It was not enough to be fully versed on each system. One must meld the technical aspects of the systems with a portion of intuition that comes as part of the decision-making process. The class would cover combat systems and tactical strategies.

The mid-afternoon class was the advanced pilot training that Tåsan was really looking forward to. The first few craft were fairly well-known to Tåsan and as the evaluator sat in the co-pilot's seat observing, Tåsan took the 4-seat Hopper and the Class-N ships through their paces, scoring high marks in all required categories of flight and control.

As the class progressed through the days, the ships advanced in size, crew compliment, and mission type.

All ambassador missions were carried out using Class-A ships, either a twelve-crew escort or a thirty-crew cruiser. The ship's systems were essentially the same but weaponry was minimal. Trainees were chosen at random to ensure a fresh mix of personalities and although all ship's stations were assigned, frequent switch-ups meant all crewmembers had ample opportunity at each station. For Tåsan, it was all about the bridge crew and the command.

The Class-C fighter proved to be a bit tricky. It was a six-crew ship that the IGC routinely used for mild to moderate law enforcement. It could carry up to ten combat operatives and their gear and was equipped with displacement charges and air-to-surface missiles. It was a serious piece of machinery and required precise piloting skills. Tåsan scored high on his first run as pilot when the scenario changed from monitoring a hostile group of land-bound ruffians to a short distance chase and capture of a pulse rocket rider who lobbed a rocket at the fighter before hastily leaving the scene. Tåsan maneuvered the fighter in and around the terrain, dropping combat operatives into strategic positions before initiating a "stand-off" with the pulse rocket rider giving the operatives time to capture the perp. No one was hurt and the incident was cleared in no time.

A little more than half way into the quad, the trainees were introduced to the IGC's Class-C interceptor, the *Deidae*. What a beautiful ship. It was a twenty-crew ship meant for long-distance travel with the capability to support up to fifty combat operatives, hauling their gear and enough provisions for travel and deployment of durations up to one quad in length. The IGC found this vehicle handy in times of civil unrest where peacekeeping and negotiations would need time to play out.

As fortune had it, Tåsan and Castell pulled bridge crew duty together and they were very glad to be sharing command.

One by one the bridge crew reported for duty and assumed their stations. Tåsan was pilot and in command, Castell was ship's engineer, four other trainees reported in and after introducing themselves, took their stations and settled in.

Tåsan had begun his pre-flight checks and was in comm with systems support when his co-pilot entered the bridge and took her position at the station adjacent to Tåsan's.

"Commander Sulac, I'm Lieutenant Alyss Brannick, your co-pilot on this mission." Alyss had shifted in her seat to face Tåsan and offered her hand.

Tåsan turned to Alyss and smiled in greeting. For a brief moment he hesitated as he looked at her, his breath caught in his throat but his mind raced. She was slender, well toned, and had long, dark auburn hair and eyes the color of blue cobalt, lit from within with the light of smoldering embers.

When Tåsan realized he was staring at her, he quickly recovered and reached to take her hand. "Welcome aboard, Co-Pilot Brannick. Ready for the adventure?"

"Yes, thank you, sir. Let's make it a good one."

Tåsan liked that, it made him smile. He watched Alyss for a few moments as she turned to her console and began her pre-flights and he wondered about her background, what had brought her to the IGC, and was curious to know what her IGC career plans were. "*I'll make a point of asking her about that later,*" he thought.

With the *Deidae* pre-flights completed, Tåsan received the "go" from ground ops and using the bridge console, announced, "On my mark, lift and burn," and hesitated the briefest of moments as his eyes darted across the bridge noting that all personnel were fully engaged before commanding, "Initiate."

The *Deidae* slowly lifted from the pad and rose to the Zone of Demark before the thrusters ignited and the ship swiftly moved forward.

"Heading and target, Commander?" queried Alyss.

Tåsan responded, "Our training assignment is to investigate a report of unrest coming from the mining community of Ictus on the far side of the Thanda Meriki mountain range. The Gealt Mining Company has formally accused a group of miners with disruption of commerce and have requested IGC intervention."

Alyss spoke, "Course set, destination in forty five."

"Very good," answered Tåsan, then called over to Castell, "Flight Engineer Brann, what can you tell us about the Thanda Meriki territory. The bow-cam shows a vastness with little change."

Alyss addressed Tåsan, "Pardon me, sir. I know a great deal about Thanda Meriki. Erontu is my home."

"Our fortune! Please," said Tåsan, his face bright with expectation.

"Geo history teaches that when our solar year system was first being formed and Erontu still a young planet, stray asteroids would break away from their stationary orbit around the sun and head straight for Erontu, and with great force, strike the area we now call Thanda Meriki. This went on for several millenii until the asteroid belt stabilized and the bombardment stopped. Very little flora grows there due to the very high ironite content in the soil left by so many asteroids. The fauna is a collection of rugged creatures well adapted to the harsh terrain."

Here Alyss stopped speaking and Castell took the opportunity to say, "Our introductory materials on Erontu mentioned invertebrates along with a warning."

"A well-founded warning, too," said Alyss. "Travelers into Thanda Meriki should carry medical aids with them but the best practice is to use cautionary measures against needing them, like camp barriers and whatnot."

Tåsan asked Alyss, "Have you trekked into Thanda Meriki?"

"On a few occasions," answered Alyss. "My father is a leading biophysicist with the University of Erontu. He's an avid Thanda Meriki enthusiast and took me with him on several minimal trips into the outback."

Just then a soft click emanated from Alyss' console that brought her to attention. "There are three ships approaching from port side. Approximately two vectors out."

The communication officer called out, "Hail sent, no response as of yet."

70

Castell spoke up, "Ships are identified as Class-N. They appear to have been modified to include increased engine power and cargo capacity."

Tåsan listened to the reports then said, "Take all cautionary measures until their intent is known and they answer our hail."

"The three are assuming an attack position," Castell said.

"Evasive maneuver Low-flight One," said Tåsan. "Stay close. Let's try this by the book."

All stations came to alert and a ship-wide comm was issued to warn all others that the ride might get a bit rough.

"Status," Tåsan called out.

One of the three ships broke formation and sped toward the *Deidae* in an act of attack, swooping left, right, up, and down as it tried to maneuver close.

"Static charge the chrysoberyl shields, Co-Pilot Brannick," Tåsan ordered, "Ready us for a fight."

"Aye, sir," Alyss acknowledged as her fingers slid effortlessly across her flight panel.

"Flight Engineer, when I get us into position, fire a warning cannon but be ready to fire again on my command."

Tåsan took flight control and moved the *Deidae* to intercept the rogue Class-N. Just as he turned the ship into range, Castell fired a shot close to the Class-N's bow causing it to rock violently to starboard.

The communication officer spoke, "We have comm, sir, putting it through now."

Tåsan said, "Good. Apparently we woke them up."

The comm from the Class-N filled the bridge. Loud laughter was heard from at least three, maybe four persons. "Woo hoo, that was close, you IGC mongrels!" said one voice. "Yea, where'd you learn that? From daddy?" taunted another. Laughter again along with hoots and jeering noises.

Tåsan shook his head and said out loud, "Sounds like a drunken frat party gone bad." He sat for a second, thinking.

Alyss said, "The other Class-N's have moved away, they're out of range and moving steadily."

Tåsan said, "Open the comm, please."

"Comm open, sir,"

"This is Captain Sulac of the IGC Interceptor *Deidae*. You're interfering with IGC business."

The response was more laughter and a loud belch.

Everyone on the bridge fought to suppress their laughter but stayed on task. Lesson One was never underestimate opposing persons or situations.

Tåsan responded, "The IGC will not tolerate your continued impediment, nor, I might add, will your fathers."

The comm line was silent.

Tåsan continued, "Notification has been sent and I'm sure you will be hearing from them, I'm guessing, sooner than you would like."

The comm line churned with mildly panicked but muffled voices, "Oh man", "We should leave," and "Move it, Jer!"

Alyss said, "They're changing course and speed…away."

Tåsan watched his console for a moment then said, "Resume course to Ictus."

The bridge crew settled down and routine ops resumed.

Alyss said, "Fifteen minutes to Ictus."

"Thank you, Co-Pilot Brannick," said Tåsan. "In the meantime, what can you tell us about that nasty little outback bug called a Teropt?"

• • •

The exercise at the Gealt Mining Company went well. When the grievances from the miners and from management had been aired, the solution was simple. There was no need to deploy combat operatives as their presence alone brought both sides to the negotiation table. The disturbances stemmed from increased production without the balance of increased labor. When it was settled, everyone was happy and after a short amount of time, the *Deidae* lifted off and started the return trip to home base.

Tåsan was fast becoming an accomplished negotiator. He was good at evaluating a situation and forming a solution to a given problem. His natural strategic skills, whether at the flight controls of a ship or leading discussions to reach an agreement, would propel Tåsan to greatness. Even he was starting to believe this.

~

The remainder of Quad Four was hectic. Combat weaponry and

tactics was all inclusive and the tests were more and more difficult as the quad approached its conclusion. Computer Systems came easier for Tåsan, stemming from his interest in AI and command functions although the class was by no means simple. Still, for Tåsan, the flights taken aboard the various models of escorts, cruisers, fighters, or interceptors always excited him. It gave him the opportunity to work from all of the various command specialties and to interact with many different trainees learning a little about each one, their strengths and their decision-making processes.

He was able to work with Castell on several of these flights. Castell and Tåsan were becoming close and trusted friends. Their friendship flowed steadily forward seemingly without effort. They appreciated each other for what they had in common as well as their differences. Tåsan headed into command and Castell was advancing into ship's engineering. Still, they found time to enjoy each other's company.

To Tåsan's delight, he and Alyss Brannick shared at least eight bridge crew assignments together. He watched her as she performed the required duties of whatever station she had control of and was impressed with her strengths and abilities. He took note of her exceptional skills as pilot and co-pilot and in talking with her, found that her real joy was as pilot. She loved to exercise each ship to know what it was capable of, to take it through its paces, to push its limits. She also loved to fly fast and true. Alyss felt herself come alive as pilot. She was very good at the other bridge stations and excelled at combat tactics and command, but it was as pilot that she found her passion.

Slowly over the course of Quad Four, Alyss became friends with Castell and Tåsan. They formed a study group to help each other prepare for assignments and trusted the performance evaluations that they gave to each other on assignment completion. The two friends were now three.

Just before the Quad Five schedules were released, notifications were sent to all officer trainees telling of a special credit survival course that would be held during the one-week quad break. Trainees that elected the course would be transported to an unknown location in the Thanda Meriki and were to find their way back to Jacamarici Lor, the flight-training base. To earn the special credit, they must return before the week was done.

That evening, Alyss met with Castell and Tåsan in their quarters. They sat comfortable enough, relaxing from the day's activities, drinking tea and munching crunchy fried dough balls that Castell's mother had sent to him.

"They're called Jimacones. It's a family recipe," explained Castell. "Handed down through at least four generations. I'm not exactly sure what's in them."

Alyss stopped mid-bite to look more closely at the edible, her face showed her concern.

Castell noticed her hesitation and said, "Mother isn't ready to give up the secret. She guards it like an Astorian fire bug guards its lair."

Both Alyss and Tåsan stared uncomprehendingly at Castell.

"It's a vicious invertebrate capable of aggression," he offered by way of an explanation.

"Ah," said Tåsan then popped one of the tasty balls. "The secret ingredient isn't fire bug, is it?"

"I truly don't know," said Castell. "Mother has promised to pass the recipe on but hesitates to do so when asked. Something to do with my wild younger years."

Alyss and Tåsan busted out laughing. Castell was about the most "un-wild" person they knew. He was always calm and approached everything in a studied and technical manner. If his mother thought him wild, Tåsan wondered about others from Astor.

Castell blushed red at the ears with embarrassment.

After the moment had passed, Alyss spoke, "Okay. Are we going for the extra credit quad break course? I've already told my father I was considering it."

"I'd like to," said Castell. "Shuttling back and forth to Astor is a time commitment, leaves almost no time for relaxing."

Tåsan said, "My family is busy with their work and study and most of my friends are away at university or busy in their careers. There's no real reason for me to go home on this break."

The three sat quietly for a half minute, thinking to themselves. A click of the door handle roused them as Darrian let himself in.

His study group had finished up and he was famished. He helped himself to a frosty and flopped down on his bunk. "Hey. Whadda you think about the extra credit survival course? I've gotta say, I'm intrigued."

Tåsan answered, "We've been thinking about it."

Castell added, "Wonder if they would let us four be a team?"

Alyss said, "We can ask." Looking around at the others, "Are we in?"

Smiles and excited talk erupted among them all as they chattered at once.

Above the noise, Alyss called out, "I'll send the request!" and reached for her e-pad.

Three
Forces of Value

Three days later, e-messages about the special credit survival course were released. Alyss' team request had been considered and approved. She, Tåsan, Castell, Darrian, and a fifth person, a third year medical student, Tao Vu, were to report to flight deck eleven in the hour following their final Quad Four class. They would begin the weeklong course at once.

Darrian sent a text to his teammates suggesting that they meet in the third floor observation lounge early that evening for a meet and greet and to discuss strategy.

Tåsan and Castell had just taken seats next to Alyss and Darrian, who had arrived ten minutes prior.

"Hello, hello," said Tåsan as he flopped down into an overstuffed chair opposite Alyss, who smiled and nodded her greeting in return.

Darrian spoke, "Glad you could make it. I know everyone's busy with final exams so we'll keep this meeting as short as possible." He looked curiously around the lounge, "Has everyone met Tao Vu? Oh, here he is now."

The group looked up at the approaching team member. He was tall and muscular without being bulky. His face was angular with high cheekbones and framed by the slightest variation in skin tone that appeared to darken as it disappeared beneath a thick shock of shoulder-length dark brown hair. Tåsan noticed that Tao Vu's eyes appeared to be light brown as he looked directly at you but changed dramatically to green when he glanced away.

Darrian rose from his seat and extended his hand in greeting. "Ah, Tao, glad you have come. Please let me introduce the other members of the team. Team, this is Tao Vu from Jahved Tuk."

Handshakes, greetings, and smiles welcomed everyone to the newly formed survival team.

Castell moved a chair closer and Tao thanked him as he sat down and tried to get comfortable.

Darrian said, "In my excitement about the survival course, I put together a very preliminary outline of what we may need to prepare. My intention was not to assume a leadership role, only to make the best of our time."

Everyone nodded and Tåsan said, "Show us what you've come up with."

Darrian quickly e-sent his outline to the team. It listed several sections including camping essentials, food and water calculations, and mapping information such as star charts and topography maps. He then asked, "Suggestions?"

Tåsan looked to Alyss. "With your experience of the Thanda Meriki outback, would you guide us on some of the more obvious hazards we may encounter and give your recommendations on how to avoid them?"

Alyss leaned forward, "I can do that. I'll expand on Darrian's outline as version 2 and send it along."

Castell added, "I'll work the calculations for weight and quantities. We'll have to consider which supplies are absolute, which are possible, and which may be considered a luxury on a survival trip. We have to backpack everything so we need to be careful. Version 3." And looked at the others.

Tao spoke, "I'll fine-tune the star charts. At home, I was an amateur stargazer so I know my way around the skies. The skies above Erontu are probably organized much like those above Jahved Tuk. It should simplify our navigation decisions and save us on time. Version 4."

Darrian snapped his fingers with a sudden realization. "I forgot to account for a few essential med supplies. I'll look at that closer. Version 5."

Tåsan had been listening closely and as the others talked about plans a thought occurred to him. "We should consider the possibility that our electronics will not serve us in the outback or that the course stipulations may not permit them."

Sounds of assent murmured among the group. "I'll look into

this and let you know," Tåsan said, and added, "I'll make a fast study of the topography of Thanda Meriki and make notes about various distances from Jacamarici Lor and possible routes of return. I'll also make a list of the tools we should consider. Version 6."

Darrian, smiling and nodding at the team progress said, "How about two days of outline revisions and research and we meet back here There's less than one week remaining before we're to report for the course and time is not our friend right now."

~

Flight deck eleven was noisy with lift-offs and landings as many of the trainees rushed to catch off-world shuttles for their quad break back home.

Tåsan, Castell, Alyss, and Darrian stood in a group outside flight ops, rucksacks at their sides, idly watching the growing frenzy. As more and more trainees completed their final classes of the quad, the crush of bodies crowding the ops decks filled it to capacity.

Tao managed to spot the team and forged a jagged path around and past the crowds until he reached them and with a sigh of relief, dropped his rucksack at his feet and smiled. "My last class was on the far side of the center. I had no idea all this would be going on but I made it!"

Tåsan said, "This has all started up within the last five minutes. It's starting to make the survival course look like the better option," as he gazed unbelievably around at the seemingly chaotic scene.

A half minute later a uniformed pilot approached the team. "Are you survival course volunteers?"

Darrian and Alyss both answered, "Yes," at the same time.

The pilot asked, "Is everyone here and ready?" And hearing assent from everyone said, "Okay. Please follow me. We're taking my escort, *Trusted Companion*, waiting on flight pad E27A, that direction," pointing a few meters away.

Once inside the escort, the team stowed their gear and took their seats.

The co-pilot stepped into the cabin and welcomed them aboard. "As you are aware, you will be transported to an unknown location, hence the viewports have been covered. We've been instructed to fly in random patterns so you will not be able to build an accurate mental image of the direction out." He smiled a warm but knowing smile and said, "So, my advice for you all would be to sit back and relax…it may be your last chance to do so for the next week. Good fortune to you all." He gave a small salute as a way of saying goodbye and stepped back through the bulkhead to the flight cabin.

"Okay. Good to know," said Tåsan.

Darrian said, "My mind is still reeling from my final exams. I could use a quiet rest, myself."

Tao added, "I'm exhausted from late-night studies and think I'll try to catch some sleep. If you will forgive my poor company." And adjusted his seat and wriggled himself into a comfortable position.

Castell had pulled a hand-printed guide from his jacket and sat, head down, scanning the index and thumbing the pages.

Tåsan looked over at Alyss and asked, "How about you?"

Alyss shrugged her shoulders and answered, "I'm not that tired. Actually, I'm feeling quite alive with the anticipation of this next week."

Tåsan looked around at the others who were quietly keeping to themselves then looked back at Alyss. "Let's move to the galley, make some tea, and relax. Co-pilot's orders."

The galley was two stations aft and was nicely appointed. The two quickly found mugs and tea and had the water heating in the radwave in no time.

Taking a seat at the galley table and sipping at his tea, Tåsan said, "You're our Thanda Meriki expert. Are you concerned about our mission?"

Alyss did not hesitate in her answer, "Yes, I do have concerns. My father never took me too far into the rugged outback. I had asked him to, several times, but he always replied that it was no place for a small child. I'm sure he was as right as I am sure, that as a child, I might have danced off a cliff, so to speak."

Tåsan remarked, "Childhood exuberance."

"Exactly."

"What's your biggest concern?"

79

"I think it would be all that is unknown. We can learn from pictures and maps but it's a poor substitute for the real thing." Alyss looked pensive for a moment then said, "It's not the things you can see, like mountains and ravines and thistle. It's the things you can't see, like the flowing sands that can swallow a whole company of travelers and then shift and change location as it moves endlessly throughout the region." Here she paused and looked at Tåsan.

He was somewhat stunned at this small bit of information.

After a moment, Alyss added, "Not to forget our little Teropt bug."

"Yes," said Tåsan, "as if shifting sand isn't enough. Seems everywhere we may step, there is danger."

"Now you're seeing the true Thanda Meriki," concluded Alyss.

Tåsan and Alyss passed the next few minutes in easy conversation.

At one point, they shared private thoughts about their childhoods. After a brief account of his spirited activities and growing up on Naiad Five, Tåsan was mindful of Alyss' story...

Alyss grew up on Erontu. Her mother had died when Alyss was very young and her father, whom she adored, raised her. She can barely recall her mother's actions or words, fading into buried memories, year by year, but Alyss can still see her mother's face, alive with love. Alyss was a rambunctious, but not an unruly child. Curious, seeking, and for the most part, her father indulged her. She attributes her father with instilling in her a compelling attitude toward learning and curiosity and a strong work ethic that she maintains led to her successes.

As a young adult, Alyss excelled in education and hobbied in mechanics. It all seemed to come easy for her.

Alyss loved the Thanda Meriki Range almost as much as she loved to accompany her father on his outings. "You know he is a biophysicist with the U of E, right?" There was always something about uncontrolled nature that Alyss could not resist.

"I remember one time, I think it was during the height of mid-season, father and I had been camping and moving through the wildlands when we stumbled upon a hidden verdant tucked deep within a rift in the dry undulating landscape. It took an hour to

80

climb down a rocky crag to reach its floor. I was beyond excited and father was so sure that he would find a rare and at that time, an unknown species of herbaceous perennial. He said that he would name it after me, that he would name it Alyssaceae. We stayed two days. Father found several rare plantlets growing there but did not find the elusive Alyssaceae. He still looks for it, you know."

Alyss could not wholly grasp the nuance of teen society and after a very short time, did not pursue it. Instead, she immersed herself in the study of space flight and the operations of various flying craft.

"You know, Alyss," Tåsan spoke softly, in a low tone, "This tells me so much about the person you are now."

"It does make sense. Everything is built on a good foundation."

There was a moment of quiet between the friends and when they had finished their tea, washed and stowed their mugs and rejoined Darrian, Tao, and Castell in forward ship.

A soft warning signal came through the overhead speakers; the team was to prepare for landing. Castell roused Tao, who noticed everyone buckling in so did the same. *Trusted Companion* set down with an easy lowering onto the strut pads and the sounds of the engines winding down resonated through the bulkhead.

The pilot stepped through the flight cabin door just as the all-clear signal sounded. "I trust you enjoyed the flight? I've put us down on a flat plateau about three thousand meters above the valley floor. I'm giving you the one advantage you may encounter out here: a flat area where you may camp your first night and work your bearings and plan your route." Calmly looking from face to face, the pilot then said, "I'll meet you outside. Don't leave anything behind or consider it gone."

It took the team a minute or two to get their jackets on and to retrieve their rucksacks. Once outside, the pilot and co-pilot joined them.

The pilot addressed them. "Have you got everything?"

Nods and yesses.

"Good. We'll be taking a lower space route back to Jacamarici Lor so it wouldn't do to note our departure direction."

The co-pilot chimed in, "Essentially, your survival starts now.

Good fortune to you all," and offered his hand.

"Yes, good fortune. We should see you in one week," said the pilot, who also offered his hand.

Trusted Companion lifted up and was away and the team members were left standing in a loose group, looking around at their surroundings.

Tåsan asked, "Any suggestions as to where to camp the night?"

Castell offered, "Closer to that rock outcrop," pointing, "may offer protection from winds that may come up."

"Okay," said Tåsan, "Let's head for the outcrop."

As they walked, they talked.

Tåsan said, "We'll make camp and while we still have light, check ourselves and survey the topography and compare it to our maps. First things first…let's see where we are."

Castell added, "Thanks to the IGC, we're all in our top physical condition. We should be able to make thirty to thirty-six milia a day, giving us a range of up to…," scrunching his eyebrows together in thought, "three hundred twenty four milia."

Darrian spoke, "Barring any obstacles or injuries."

Castell replied, "Of course." Then said, "My calcs were based strictly on the one week time allotment and our ability to cover distance."

"I wonder if the IGC would put us somewhere in the Thanda Meriki that was far outside the expected completion time of one week?" asked Darrian to no one in particular.

"I would hope not," answered Alyss. "The terrain alone will slow our progress in places."

They reached the low rocky outcrop and shed their packs. Alyss and Castell climbed to the top of the outcrop and stood looking into the distance that lay all about them. Alyss was looking through her digi-lenses, idly saying what she was seeing.

"There's a distant mountain range almost…," consulting the distance meter on the right side of the lenses' field of view, "sixteen milia in that direction." She lowered the digi-lenses, glanced at Castell, and pointed.

Castell held a journal open to blank pages and had drawn a crude map of their immediate surroundings and was drawing in jagged mountains and noting the distance as related by Alyss.

Alyss resumed scanning the area even as Castell pulled a hand-held Directional out of a jacket pocket and waited for it to steady its readings. It worked by triangulation of the sun, the user, and the object it was pointed at. Its failing was that it did not work in the dark. "The Directional indicates that the mountains lay west of our position."

Alyss and Castell carried on for another half an hour before climbing down and rejoining the group.

Tåsan had configured the tent into a lean-to. He assumed it would be all the protection required for this night. He stowed the rucksacks off to one side and had started to clear rocks and debris from the area in front of the lean-to when Alyss and Castell appeared.

Alyss observed the camp setup then started to help by clearing rocks and flattening the grainy soil with her boot.

Castell addressed Tåsan, "We have a crude map of the immediate surroundings. When Tao gathers his star findings tonight, we should have enough information to compare with the maps and charts we've brought."

Tåsan asked, "Do you think it'll be enough to establish the direction back to base?"

"Yes, at least that's what I'm anticipating."

Alyss had stopped clearing rocks and now stood with her hand shading her eyes, looking off into the distance. Tåsan stepped to her side and faced the same direction, watching and quietly listening.

"There's a storm in the distance. I'm trying to note its direction," said Alyss.

Just then, Darrian and Tao returned from their sortie into the scrub, their arms full of dried branches and dried leaf kindling that they then unceremoniously dumped into a heap.

Excitedly, Darrian spoke out, "We won't hurt for fuel. The area is extremely dry." Then pulling a small wrapped cloth from a pocket, addressed Alyss, "Would you happen to know what these are?" showing her a small collection of dark blue berry-like objects.

"Oh, yes," remarked Alyss after looking closely at the berries. "These are the un-ripened flower buds of the Schaduo shrub. Don't eat them, they'll make your stomach hurt for days."

83

Darrian's face fell from the excitement of a discovery to concern as he let the berries fall from his hand to the ground. "Ah," was all he could say.

Alyss addressed the group, "There's a storm forming to the north," glancing at the lean-to, "It won't bring rain, the region isn't due for rain for another two solar years, but it may bring wind-whipped soil and dust. Storms here always mean static discharged lightning strikes, too. Maybe we should take precautions this night."

"Good idea," said Tåsan. "Tao, give me a hand?"

They quickly reconfigured the lean-to into a tent area providing about four square meters of enclosed space and made to move the packs inside.

Tao retrieved his journal and busied himself in review of the star maps he had brought. "I'm going to try to get organized while there's still daylight. Easier on the eyes."

Tåsan and Darrian had ducked inside the tent and set up the fire pit and arranged the packs to its outer wall perimeter.

Alyss and Castell grabbed armloads of dried branches and moved them inside as well.

It didn't take long for the camp to be organized and the group to start to settle down. Darrian had hydrated a pot of vegetables and roots and had also thought to make a pot of tea, both of which were simmering on the fire pit.

The light had faded to darkness as the day ended calmly.

Alyss set up the exclusion barrier around the camp and had scoured inside the perimeter for any interloping critters, carefully ejecting the few she found. A brief note to the group alerted them to the location of the low fence so they would not accidentally stumble into it during any nighttime excursions and Tao easily stayed within the area during his survey of the stars.

An hour after darkness had fallen, Tao came back inside, announcing that he had had a wonderful viewing, was a bit hungry, and would fine tune his notes in the morning.

Darrian was already asleep and Alyss lay on her bedroll, watching the fire as it glowed red embers, her eyes half-closed with weariness.

Tåsan and Castell talked in hushed tones as they discussed

what they thought the morrow should look like.

Less than thirty minutes later, the fire had been banked and everyone was asleep.

The storm moved off to the east, missing the camp entirely, taking its lightning and the fading sounds of thunder with it.

• • •

The morning meal consisted of nutri-cubes, tough little cubes of compressed grain sweetened with dehydrated berries and the juice of the Tehoa root. One can boil it down into a mush or gnaw on it as you move through your day.

The team decided to forgo any meal preparations in favor of breaking camp and readying for the day's journey.

Castell and Tao sat together, heads bent, comparing notes as Tåsan, Alyss, and Darrian disassembled the tent and perimeter fence and stowed all the gear. Alyss took an extra moment to erase any trace that they had been there. Her father had taught her respect for the outback. He had told her that the outback did not belong to them; they had no right to leave boot prints all around in total disregard for the natural inhabitants of such a wondrous place as Thanda Meriki. And she agreed.

With the work completed, everyone sat quietly as Castell and Tao finished their discussion. The silent moments ticked forward.

At last, Tao spoke, "I think we've got it. Overlaying my star map with Castell's topography and in comparison with the maps and charts we brought with us, we now know where we are."

Castell quickly added, "We're confident that we're within a milia of this location," tipping this map for everyone to see and pointing to a remote spot.

Darrian, Alyss and Tåsan had gotten up and moved closer for a better view.

"And Jacamarici Lor is here," Castell added.

"That direction," Tao said, pointing south. "Approximately three hundred twenty five milia."

Castell said, "We travel southward for one day then navigate east across the Sand Sea before turning south again."

Tåsan had been reading the map and listening to the men relate their calculations as he formed an overall plan in his mind's eye. When the conversation hit a lull, he spoke.

"Good job," looking first at Castell and then at Tao, "Very impressive work." Then gesturing to the map he now held in his hand, continued, "We'll need to average thirty-six milia a day to cover the distance, however, this is a survival course so we should assume that our progress will ebb and flow with the terrain. Now, while we're still strong, we should push to cover as many milia in a day as we can. I see at least three physical features that will require our attention: the Sand Sea, the foothills and ravines along the Makara mountain range, and a nasty stretch of swamp-like land that we will have to cross because it looks too large to skirt."

Alyss spoke up, "Night camp could be kept to a minimum to save time. I suggest we eat nutri-cubes as we travel and keep the main meal simple." And thinking for a brief second, said, "We should only travel during the light. Night travel is too hazardous. Also, a host of outback denizens prefer the cool of the night to the heat of the day."

Tåsan looked around at his team. "Shall we start?"

Everyone immediately stowed their notes, fastened their jackets, and shimmied their rucksacks onto their backs, adjusting the buckles for a snug fit.

Almost without a word, the five started south, quickly finding a pace that was comfortable but fast. It would be a slight downward hike off the plateau and across a fairly flat expanse before reaching Tåsan's first destination: the edge of the Sand Sea, some forty-two milia away.

Talk among the team was animated at first with Alyss sharing what she knew about several of the more notorious insects she had experience with, Castell recalling some outback facts about topography, and Darrian and Tao talking about their chosen careers in medicine and where the IGC would take them.

Tåsan listened and joined in where he could but his attention was focused on the trail. He had taken the lead as a matter of course and was intent on making the trail as succinct and trouble free as possible.

After five hours of hiking, Tåsan called for a fifteen-minute break. Castell sat down on a flat rock and started to untie his boots.

Tao said, "Better not do that, Castell. If your feet swell up, you'll never get your boots back on."

86

"Oh," responded Castell, rubbing his ankles, "Thanks, in that case I'll wait."

The team resumed the hike and as the sun moved across the bright cloudless sky, conversation faded until the group moved in virtual silence. Four hours later they reached the outer edge of the Sand Sea where they would camp for the night.

Tired but not exhausted, the team put the camp together very quickly and had gathered fuel for the cook fire before the light faded.

One by one, as the tasks were completed, they flopped down on bedrolls or sat around the fire as they wound down from the day.

Tao had taken his sextant out into the darkness to verify and record the night stars and Castell busied himself updating his topography notes. The two would have a lively conversation when Tao returned.

Before the night was done, the team would discuss the following day's plan. How far could they expect to get, what dangers would the Sand Sea present, and how could they mitigate them. Alyss contributed very valuable information about the Sand Sea.

"The sands flow like liquid through the landscape. No one knows exactly why the sand moves or precisely how it moves. It remains a mystery. However, it's possible to predict the shifting movement of the sand by observing the insects and small vertebrates that scurry at the moment of shift. They run to avoid being caught in the tides that will suck them down into the roiling sand. We could also observe any hunting birds, if present. They take advantage of the vertebrates' panicked retreat. Hunting is good when the sands shift."

Tåsan asked, "How much time do we have from the moment the insects panic to when the sand shifts?"

"Some insects are more sensitive to the changes in the electro-cellular movements of the ground and start their retreat maybe five minutes sooner than other, less fortunate ones," Alyss answered.

Darrian asked, "Do we follow the insects? Are they reliable predictors of solid ground?"

87

"Yes, for the most part," Alyss chose her words but added, "Somewhat."

Tåsan asked, "Do we have an alternative?"

Alyss answered, "There are islands of solid granite that the sands flow around. Some can be large areas. I would rather rely on our ability to visually locate land bridges that, at times, connect the granite outcrops and use the insects as a failsafe. Plan B, if you will." She stopped for a second and gazed at the faces turned toward her and shrugged in response.

Castell said, "The Sand Sea runs from the Makara foothills to a far distant point to the east. Too far to go around. And from what I've read, the foothills are not your average rolling hills. They are treacherous rock formations easily given to landslides and sinkholes. I would prefer to take cues from insects than be overtaken by a rockslide."

Tåsan considered all that was said, then spoke, "Our course is through the Sand Sea. Assuming that our steps are sure, we should complete the distance in one day and make camp on solid ground on the other side." And hearing no comments, said, "We'll start as soon as the dawn arrives."

• • •

The five stood together a few scant meters from the edge of the Sand Sea and regarded the relatively flat silica that stretched before them. The entire area was dotted with towering pinnacles some tall and pointed, others low and plateaued. No one spoke. A large patch of ground, off in the distance, suddenly started to violently churn, rising in waves and spewing plumes of sand several meters into the air. After several minutes, the land calmed and once again appeared serene.

Darrian picked up a stone and gently lobbed it forward where it plunked to the surface of the sand with a soft plop before sinking immediately from sight.

Tåsan spoke, "I think walking sticks are in order. We may need to probe for solid ground as we step."

Five minutes later, long, thin sticks in hand, the team once again stood at the edge of the sand. The ground quivered before them.

"There!" exclaimed Alyss, pointing to where she had noticed a

88

shift that revealed a land bridge that moments before had been obscured from view, covered by sand.

Everyone turned their attention toward the granite outcrop and newly revealed bridge.

"Keep watching," guided Alyss. And soon enough, the sand gently churned and the bridge disappeared.

"Right," said Tåsan, addressing his team. "We won't be able to plan too far in advance as we run from pinnacle to pinnacle. We've one day here, let's not make it any longer than we need to."

And as if his words had been heard beyond the group, the sand at their feet started to agitate and accompanied by a low rumbling sound, swirled into rough-looking eddies that slowly uncovered a bridge out to a wide, tall granite spire.

"Step lively," called Tåsan as he moved quickly forward, followed closely by the others.

They made the first outcrop without incident and within minutes another bridge opened up and off they went, barely making the next outcrop before the sand swallowed their track. As they hurried to gain hand and footholds, and climb safely upward, they soon realized that this granite outcrop had splintered stone formations that cut and nicked their hands. None of this was serious enough to stop their forward trek, but Castell found it annoying enough to wrap strips of his jacket lining around his hands in an attempt to avoid further injury.

The morning progressed much the same way as it had started. Everyone rushed across temporary bridges, scrambled up out of harms way, and at more than a few uncomfortable times, clung to precarious outcrops, nervously looking for the next bridge.

It didn't take long to realize that many of the inhabitants of this sandy wasteland also took refuge on the granite outcrops and were aggressive in their determination to not be displaced, especially by humanoid intruders.

Tao found, to his annoyance, that his lower legs, just above his cinched boots, were getting bitten and that the bites were stinging hot.

Darrian, too, was starting to suffer an overload of bites and took one nasty sting to his left jaw line before losing his patience. "Okay, that does it," he declared. "The next hospitable pinnacle we climb up on to, we take a break and I will perform a bit of first aid." And flicking at a flying something-or-other that had landed on his sleeve, huffed loudly with impatience.

"We're due for a breather," said Tåsan, scanning the changing terrain around them.

"How about that one?" asked Alyss, indicating a granite island about forty-five meters away. It was flat and wide and easily several meters above the roiling sand.

"Looks like a good one," agreed Tåsan. Then talking to the others, "Next opportunity, we head for that pinnacle."

Quietly they waited for the sand to part once again. They balanced uneasily on shallow stone ledges trying to reposition themselves for the next rush forward. Everyone stayed alert.

And as Tåsan called out, "Go," the team jumped down and stepped lively.

Halfway to their next mark, a guttural rumble sounded from beneath the liquid sands to either side of the bridge. Darrian, Castell, and Tao, following several steps behind Alyss and Tåsan, hesitated at the sound and stood wide-eyed looking around.

As the sand slowly started to churn and the cavernous sound of thunder rose, a host of insects swarmed up and out of the quiet sands at the bridge's edge, clearly panicked.

Alyss shouted, *"Run!"* Shocking the men to action.

As fast as they could, the five ran toward the relative safety of the granite island.

The sand eddied and churned and started closing in across the bridge. Castell suddenly went down, emitting a loud painful cry as his ankle twisted under his weight and he slammed down to one knee, taking a blow to his hipbone as he collapsed into a pile.

Darrian and Tao, immediately at his side, yanked him up, and bracing him by his arms, pulled him forward at a breakneck pace, all the while, the liquid sand churned into a huge whirlpool, spewing sand and rocks in every direction and issuing a deafening roar like that of a wild beast.

Reaching the slight climb up the jagged rocks to safety, Tåsan seized Alyss and propelled her upward before turning to the three men coming steadily along. He ran the seven paces back to them and grabbed hold of Castell and with fresh energy yanked the small group faster.

Sand was blowing through the air stinging their eyes and lashing their faces when they reached the granite outcrop and wrestled Castell up just as Alyss dropped a guide rope down to them.

Several agonizing minutes later, the team, high above the angry sands, had gained the summit and lay panting and exhausted where they dropped.

Darrian quickly recovered himself and went to Castell. "Let me have a look at that," unlacing Castell's boot as gingerly as he could without causing more pain. Tao had retrieved his med kit and knelt down beside them.

"This is going to hurt," Darrian said to Castell, who nodded his understanding and braced for the jolt.

Darrian got the boot off and was lightly feeling for breaks and talking with Tao. "Nothing seems to be broken but I'm concerned that the tendons may be wrenched out of place and a very dark contusion is starting to form. Soft tissue swelling isn't far behind."

Tao nodded and opened the med kit. "Well need to stabilize the ankle," and glancing at Castell, asked, "Are you in pain?"

"Some," answered Castell, "I think my ego is as bruised as my ankle. What the heck was that? I ran like a newly hatched ornith!" Frustrated, he lay his head down on the gravelly granite. "Just don't cut my foot off," Castell said, half joking.

Tao handed Darrian a container of liqui-splint that he immediately applied to Castell's foot, ankle, and lower leg. The gel went on cold but within minutes, warmed up and hardened into a sturdy support.

Tao helped Castell take a mild opiate, tipping the container of water and telling him, "It'll help manage the pain but won't interfere with your cognitive abilities," adding as mild humor, "assuming you still have them."

Castell rolled his eyes and nodded in disbelief at his big show of clumsy running skills. "All that phys training...for nothing."

Tåsan and Alyss had been standing nearby, watching and listening, and very concerned for Castell.

Darrian stood up and said, "He'll be fine with a short rest," and gathered the supplies he had scattered about for their return to the med kit, then added, "The liqui-splint has a local analgesic for short-term and a hot/cold cycle to reduce edema."

Tåsan just stared at him, waiting.

"Okay," Darrian said, "a mild pain killer and hot/cold for swelling."

"Ahh," smiled Tåsan, "*Nooow* I know what you're talking about."

Darrian nodded then said, "Let's give him about an hour. He should be somewhat better by then."

"How about nutri-cubes and water for lunch," Alyss announced, handing a cube to Tåsan and one to Darrian before going to Tao and Castell, who lay sprawled out, foot elevated on a large rock, gently snoring.

When he awoke, Castell announced that he was feeling much better and after munching his nutri-cube, got up and clomped around on his liqui-splint'ed ankle declaring that he felt ready to continue.

Darrian had applied chromistra to everyone's bug bites while Castell had slept and now did the same for him.

"That feels nice, took the sting and itch out of all of them. Thanks, doc," smiled Castell, in relief.

And then they were off.

The next pinnacle was low and pointed and the team had to cling precariously to sharp formations and shallow toeholds for what seemed an eternity until the sand opened up and a nice wide bridge appeared.

Tao made certain that Castell trod along before him. He thought to keep an eye on him and help if needed. At the next granite spire, Tao was steadying Castell because he had faltered as he started to climb.

Tåsan and Alyss had already made it to a flat ledge about halfway up and were peering over the edge watching Darrian, who was almost with them, Castell struggling with footholds, and Tao behind him, still standing on the bridge.

"You need to pick it up," Alyss called out.

"I'm sorry, can't find a foothold big enough," complained Castell in his futile effort to climb up.

Tåsan tugged Darrian up onto the ledge and was about to go

over the edge, back down, to help Castell if he could but Alyss lightly touched his arm to interrupt. "There's no room for you to maneuver next to him. It would help more if you guided his steps from here."

Tåsan looked at her for a brief moment and changed his mind about going over the side. "Castell, try a little to your left, that's it," as he knelt down and leaned over the side. "Now pull yourself up to that rock sticking out just above your right hand," he encouraged.

Castell's progress was slow.

Tao had just lifted one foot up to aim for a toehold when quick as a flash, the sand belched upward, over the bridge, and sucked greedily at Tao's other foot. He threw himself against the sharp, angled granite slope, and dug his fingers in and grasped at the scant, tiny ledges with all his might.

Alyss gasped in alarm and held her breath as she made sense of what she was looking at, far below. Immediately, she dug the rope she carried, out of her pack and quickly looked around for a place to tie it off. There was nothing.

Tåsan was calling down to Castell, shouting orders regarding where to grip and where to step, trying to keep the panic from his voice.

Alyss had made a loop in one end of the rope and turned to Darrian. "There's no place to anchor this end. You're the anchor," and looped the other end around his chest. "Brace yourself. I'll help in a minute."

Darrian sat down and placed his boots against the jagged edge of the ledge and encircled one hand with spare rope as he leaned back ready to brace himself.

Alyss stepped to the edge and looked over. Castell had made it over halfway up, another few hardy pulls and he would be up. She threw the rope down the cliff side, past Castell, to Tao.

Tao had struggled in vain to free his foot and could feel himself being slowly torn from his position, his fingers refusing to let go in spite of the deep cuts they had sustained.

"Tao! Put your arms through the rope. We'll help pull you up!" Alyss shouted.

Tåsan leaned way over the side and grasped at Castell's pack straps until he snagged one and started to pull, gritting his teeth with the effort. Alyss shot to his side and reached over, grabbing a handful...of what? It didn't matter. She flexed and pulled and together, she and Tåsan pulled Castell up and on to the ledge.

Immediately, Tåsan gripped the dangling rope and Alyss bent over the edge to look at Tao. "Are you ready?"

"Yes!" Tao shouted up, anxious that they should hear him, exhaustion robbing his lungs.

Alyss tugged at the rope, tightening the loop around Tao's chest. She turned to Tåsan and Darrian and commanded them to, *"Pull!"*

They strained against the forces that held Tao only to gain a mere centimeter or two.

"Again!" ordered Alyss. And again they pulled.

Tao felt his foot would rip off but in mere moments it started to slip free of the sand's grip.

"Again!"

With a sudden jerk, the men liberated Tao and he swung free at the end of the rope, able at last to ease his grip and flex his numb fingers. He was so grateful when he reached the ledge that he hugged everyone and thanked them profusely for saving him.

Darrian took a look at Tao's wounded fingers and made straight for the med kit and bandaged them. "Not too deep but we'll want to guard against any infections."

"Thank you, friend, for everything," said Tao as he lightly touched Darrian's shoulder in sincere friendship.

Tåsan interrupted, "Is everyone alright?"

"Yes," answered Darrian. "Everything is as it should be."

"Good. That's good," Tåsan said before continuing, "We can't stay here. We have to move on while it's still light."

Alyss had climbed a meter or two further up to get a better look at their surroundings. She didn't want any more surprises on this day. When she saw all there was to see, she climbed back down. Her last step was to jump down to the ledge. She then spoke to the men.

"Thank our fortunes, gentlemen. I see solid ground about ninety meters off to the south-east." Alyss stood grinning from ear to ear looking at her tired, dirty, torn-up, and bandaged buddies.

One more heroic push saw the team through the final meters of the Sand Sea. For good measure, Tåsan pushed them another milia before locating a suitable campsite and declaring the day done.

Grateful to be done with unpredictable sand and nasty stinging insects, the team happily put camp together and quieted for the evening. Tonight would be a hot meal, hot tea, a warm bedroll, and a deep sleep.

• • •

Dawn came too early but in spite of that, everyone roused themselves and broke camp.

The team stood together for a moment before donning their packs and beginning the morning's hike.

Tåsan addressed them, "Hard to believe we've only been out here for two days. Seems like so much longer." He looked at all the visible bandages and for one brief moment, felt that the word "survival" may have a larger connotation than they first thought. "Today we follow the Makara foothills around to the east and then due south. We have allotted three days of travel to this section of the journey and need to average about thirty-seven milia per day to stay on track. This may task our physical endurance but I strongly encourage everyone to push through. We'll stop as needed, patch what we can, but keep a thought for the schedule."

Castell said, "Agreed."

Alyss said, "Ready."

Darrian said, "Forward."

Tao said, "With fortune's speed."

Tåsan smiled, "Let's go."

The team hiked due south until they reached the Makara foothills and noticed their gentle change of direction as the hills pushed out to the east.

When close enough to clearly observe the terrain, it became obvious why trying to cross the hills was out of the question. The hills continuously formed as the stratigraphy from far below pushed upward, that in turn caused large jagged, spontaneously formed boulders to be torn loose from above and tumble down into heaps of sharp angular foot traps. It resembled a quarry that stretched far up the mountainsides.

The path the team took ran a hundred or so meters outside the tumbled boulders along the valley floor but was only better in the loosest sense of the word. The way was strewn with enough boulders to make it hazardous in places and enough large rocks to hinder a quick pace.

The air was filled with the sound of low rumbles as the ground slightly trembled and large concentrations of stone, far up one of the mountains, broke loose and crashed violently down to join the expanding quarry along the base.

One such episode caused the team to stop and watch as boulders violently tumbled and dust rose high into the air. Tåsan was sure he felt the ground beneath his feet shudder.

After hours of hiking, the team came to the edge of a ravine that blocked their path.

Tåsan asked Castell and Tao to follow it to the east for a couple hundred meters to look for a way across.

"I'll go this way," pointing west, "to look for the same. Only two hundred meters then come back. Alyss and Darrian, take a load off. We'll be right back."

Tåsan was the first to return. "There's nothing that way except steep drops and more boulders. I trust it looks better to the east." Tåsan sat down next to Alyss and accepted the water jug she offered.

Tåsan, Alyss, and Darrian sat quietly. Darrian had found a place on the ground where he could comfortably lean back on his pack and lay, eyes closed, face to the sun.

Moments later, Castell and Tao returned. "There's a crossing about one hundred ten meters from here," said Castell.

"It looks to be solid enough," commented Tao. "We pelted it with large rocks to test it."

Castell said, "It's still standing."

"Okay," said Tåsan. "Take a ten minute break and we'll go east."

Half an hour later, everyone stood at the one-meter wide footbridge that crossed the ravine.

Tåsan spoke. "We'll go across one at a time so we don't put too much stress on it. While it looks sturdy, it may not be."

Alyss had removed the length of rope from her pack. "We should rope team across in case there's a problem."

Five minutes later, everyone was lashed together with enough space between to allow only one person on the four-meter long natural bridge that spanned the ravine.

Tåsan took the lead. Going was slow at first as he cautiously picked his way across, with heightened senses and fully aware of every footfall.

Castell next and then Alyss. As confidence in the strength of the packed dirt and stone bridge rose, the team moved a little faster. By the time Darrian and then Tao came across, footsteps were almost normal.

All had made it across and were untying the rope lead that bound them when there arose a groan from the bowels of the mountains that froze everyone where they stood. Momentarily. Just as they turned their wide-eyed gazes to the mountains, the ground shook with such intensity that each of them were knocked to the ground unable to get back up to their feet for several seconds.

They sat sprawled in a heap watching as the ground on the other side of the ravine heaved upward and slammed back down with such force that it completely disintegrated the bridge the team had just crossed over.

It took one nanosecond for the team to react to the collapsing bridge before they scrambled to their feet and ran to put distance between themselves and the ravine.

The ground subsided in its temblor as the air became eerily still. Off in the distance, rockslides tumbled and clouds of dust rose up to be carried off by the high atmospheric winds.

No one spoke. They just looked at one another, brushed the dirt from their clothes, and walked on until it was time for the mid day meal break.

"Say," asked Darrian, "has anyone else heard rustling sounds in the underbrush as we've walked along?"

"Yes, now that you mention it, I have," said Tao.

"What do you suppose that is?"

Alyss answered, "The Rocky Flats are inhabited by dozens of types of creatures. My guess is that you're been hearing the startled moves of the Spiny Muroidea. A large, fearless rat-like animal with sharp teeth and a ridge of sharp spines down its back.

Truly nasty, determined little creatures. Capable of doing a great deal of damage."

Castell said, "So we won't neglect to erect the camp fence tonight."

"Speaking of which," said Tåsan, "we're about eighteen milia from that campsite. We should move steadily on."

Shortly thereafter, the terrain smoothed out in places, affording a quickened pace. The team decided they would push on as far as they could and made an extra five milia before dusk dictated the end of that day's hike.

• • •

Starting each morning quickly became a routine. With each team member consistently taking responsibility for one or more of the tasks, the entire campsite was disassembled, packed up, and the site returned to its natural state in less than thirty minutes, and each person fully packed and hiking as they munched on their nutri-cubes.

In places, hiking was single file as they picked their way along through boulders and thorny shrubs. In other places, they could hike in a loose group and look up and around at their surroundings.

Darrian and Tao were side-by-side on a wide, flat part of their tramp when Darrian nudged Tao to get his attention and pointed off to his left.

Tao looked in the direction indicated and frowned.

What they saw, a mere five meters into the boulder dotted, dry shrubbery, were a number of Spiny Muroidea, maybe a dozen, some hiked up on their back haunches, others perched in the branches of the thorny shrubs, but all of them intently watching the team as they hiked past.

Darrian turned to Tao and said, "It's almost as if they were calculating something. They stare with such intensity."

Tao said, "They're very disturbing. It's hard to guess what they're thinking, what they might do."

Darrian replied, "We'll have to trust that their natural instincts are to be aware of their surroundings and that they were only curious and cautious."

They walked on for several more paces before Tao added,

98

"We're making an assumption, of course, that they were not sizing us up as dinner."

Darrian puffed out a breath, "There's a thought," and glanced back, over his shoulder for one last look, but the sharp-eyed pack of Muroidea had disappeared back into the underbrush.

• • •

The mid-day break was short. A ten-minute rest, little gulps of water, and back onto the southeast track around the Makara foothills.

Tåsan was in the lead, picking the trail as it changed from clusters of tumbled boulders to that of flat, fairly uncluttered stretches more easily traversed.

Alyss followed a step or two behind. "There's a storm brewing up behind us. It appears to be catching up."

Tåsan slowed and turned to look, stopping completely as he faced northward.

The others stopped and turned, too.

"It does look to be gaining on us," Tåsan said. "But does it pose much of a threat since it carries no rain?"

Alyss answered, "True, rain is not due for another two solar years, but storms like this could always stir up dust and stones and damage depends on its wind velocity."

The others were now grouped with Tåsan and Alyss.

Castell said, "The non-rain storms are known for the discharge of static lightning."

Tåsan said, "Noted. Let's push forward but keep an eye on the storm and look for a place of shelter, just in case. We still may make camp without incident."

Over the next hour, the wind picked up and the skies in front of the churning dark clouds behind them, turned gray. Tåsan called out, "Let's pick it up a bit." And the team increased their pace.

Behind them, bright flashes of white and blue built in the dark mass and violently discharged downward into the terrain. The crackling sounds as the lightning shot through the air and the muffled boom as it struck Erontu's surface was building in intensity as the storm moved ever closer.

Looking intently for a rock shelter of sorts, Tåsan scanned left and right, but he took only brief glances back to make sure his team was still with him noting appreciatively that they kept with his pace. Suddenly, the scent of smoke reached his nose and Tåsan abruptly stopped and scanned the distance.

"There," shouted Castell, pointing behind them, at the dark storm. When all had turned, he yelled, *"Fire!"*

That word shot fear through everyone, straight into their bones. A lightning strike had touched off a wild fire that the wind was pushing forward at an alarming speed.

Tåsan shouted, "Follow me!" and took off running as fast as the rocky ground would allow.

The team was in a mad dash to get as much ground between them and the fast-moving brush fire that threatened to overtake them.

In his rush, Tao thought to run around a large boulder that lay in his path and stepped off to the right. As he cleared the boulder, his footing seemed to dissolve and he found himself tumbling in a free-fall, his mind unable to resolve the situation, until, with a sudden breath-robbing thud, Tao realized he had hit bottom. He lay stunned, trying to catch his breath as a sharp pain started to crawl up his left leg. As his eyes focused, Tao became aware of two things: he had fallen into a ravine and he had probably broken his leg. His first reaction was disappointment in himself for being so clumsy and then he was a bit angry at his predicament.

Immediately, Darrian and Alyss' faces appeared in the crevice opening above Tao.

"For fortune's sake, are you alright, man?" called Darrian.

"Oh, no," replied Tao, "I seem to have damaged myself."

Castell was now looking over the side as well, "It looks to be about three meters down."

Tåsan, looking down through the opening said, "Sorry Tao," then asked, "How bad are your injuries?"

"I think I've broken my leg bone," and the doctor in him started to feel the part of his leg that was starting to go numb. "It hasn't broken the skin but the trauma is severe."

Alyss was eyeing the storm and said, "The wind has shifted to the east, taking the fire with it. For now we seem to be safe," and under her breath, "whatever that means."

The smoke-filled air around them started to clear as the storm continued eastward.

Darrian said, "I'll go down and stabilize Tao's leg and check him over."

Tåsan said, "We can lower you down on the rope and bring you up, one at a time, the same way."

And it was done.

Darrian worked on Tao's leg for fifteen long minutes as the others waited impatiently above. Finally, he called out, "I'm going to truss Tao up into a sling around his rump and up under his arms, around his chest."

Tao allowed himself to be manhandled as Darrian made the rope secure.

Darrian called up, "Okay, ready. But carefully!"

Tåsan, Castell, and Alyss grabbed hold of the rope and started to pull Tao up.

All the while, Darrian guided the effort, "Easy, easy," and "That's it."

Eventually Tao was out of the hole and sitting precariously on a large rock, his leg bound in liqui-splint, propped up in front of him.

As soon as Darrian was hauled up, he strode to Tao's side, a look of deep concern on his face.

"Is he okay?" asked Tåsan.

"Will he be alright?" asked Castell.

"He's as fine as he can be for tumbling into a ravine and breaking a major leg bone." Darrian leaned in to look closer at Tao, gently widening one of Tao's eyes with his thumb. "He may have a slight concussion. He needs rest."

Tåsan said, "We can't stay here, it's unsafe," and looking to the southeast, "Castell, you and I will scout ahead, look for a campsite." And addressing the others, "We'll be back shortly. Rest for a moment."

Castell and Tåsan doffed their gear and left to search out a site that would not pose too many problems. It needed to be flat, away from obvious hazards, and close. Just such a site presented itself about a half milia further on and they returned to the group within thirty minutes.

101

"We've got it," said Tåsan. "A short distance on. Will Tao be able to make it?"

Darrian and Alyss had fashioned a sort of crutch out of a fairly sturdy piece of wood and had secured Tao's leg between two branches to give it further support.

Darrian answered, "Yes, but not too quickly and not too far."

Tao was exhausted by the time camp was up and the dinner meal was on the fire. He took a weak sedative, complaining of a mild headache and fell asleep almost as soon as he lay down.

Darrian spoke to the team, "I'll keep an eye on him. If he wakes, I'll give him some cold stew and check him, but I think he will be alright after a good sleep."

A wave of relief washed over Tåsan, Castell, and Alyss as their fears and concerns for Tao started to subside.

• • •

In comparison, the next day went very well. Hiking was slowed due to the rocky ground, but the southeast trek gave way to a more southern direction that served to bolster the mood of the group.

Tao slept off his headache and happily noted that his vision had stabilized and that he felt good, although he still couldn't put full weight on his leg. He dispensed with the crutch but kept the leg supports..."Just in case."

At mid-morn, the team stopped for a rest under the sparse, flowing branches of a Betula tree that crossed their way. The shade offered relief from the full sun and cloudless sky.

Darrian sat down next to Tao, who had plopped down on the ground so he could stretch his leg out flat. Unfastening the ties that secured Tao's torn pant leg, Darrian peered at the liqui-splint, touching it here and there.

"Can you feel this? Does it still pain you?"

"It's more tired than painful," answered Tao. "Is the splint holding?"

"For the most part, but I may shore it up along the edges." Darrian looked closer, "The swelling is down and the fiery red coloring has subsided."

"Will I live?" joked Tao.

"You had better!" Darrian looked at Tao with feigned surprise, "Don't ruin my reputation before I even have a chance to get one!"

102

Castell was standing up on a boulder, facing south. He had his Directional out and held the optics close to his eyes as he scanned for a suitable object for triangulation.

Tåsan and Alyss had found a nice place to sit, their packs were off their backs and Tåsan, who had removed his jacket, was sprawled out on a large boulder and taking sporadic gulps of water from his jar.

Alyss had untied her boots and was busy re-tying them for a tighter cinch. "My legs are getting sore from walking on all this wobbly stone."

"Yea, I'll be glad to be done with this. Shouldn't be much more. We're starting to leave the Makara Mountains," Tåsan said.

A muffled rumbling made everyone turn and look into the distance. A huge rock avalanche, high up the side of a mountain, had let go and hundreds of enormous boulders crashed their way downward, throwing dense clouds of gray and brown dust high into the air.

Tao said, "From here, that truly is a spectacular sight."

"One I'm not likely to forget too soon," added Tåsan.

Castell jumped down from his observation perch and stood now, making new notes in his journal and consulting its previous pages. He stood long enough to get everyone's attention, although he, himself, was unaware of it. Quietly they watched as he read and considered and recorded the new data and performed calculations as only he could.

Finally, Castell looked up. "I've spotted what looks to be the beginning of the Thanda Meriki Fen. Rough guess is fifty-two milia."

This wasn't surprising news to anyone.

Almost as an afterthought, Castell added, "It's called, Fen Mortis. Fen of Death. It's the only consistent source of water for the whole of Thanda Meriki."

This *was* surprising news and caused more than one raised eyebrow among the travelers.

After a moment with that thought, Tåsan said, "We should push on."

The last twenty milia of the day passed without incident. The more the Makara Mountains receded into the distance behind them, the less rocky the trail became and that afforded a more sure footing and a slightly quicker pace, especially for Tao who still walked with a painful limp.

Having no direct episodes to deal with during the day's hike, gave the team a chance to recover, somewhat, and mealtime around the cook fire was relaxed and the company convivial.

Tao removed the stick supports from his leg and tossed them into the fire. "I don't think I'll need these any longer. My leg feels well enough." He loosed his pant leg and started to examine his leg. "The liqui-splint is still holding but may not be needed."

Darrian watched as Tao peeled the splint off to reveal the break. "The liqui-splint did its job well. The trauma is nearly healed."

Tao's leg was whole again with barely a trace of injury at all. "I'll sleep without the splint and test this in the morning," he said as he flexed his leg and bent his knee to unknot the muscles.

Tåsan said, "We only need to make thirty-two milia tomorrow. We can afford to slow a bit, if you need, Tao, but the further we can go, the better."

Alyss offered, "We've been out here for five days. That's past the half way mark. I, for one, feel pretty good about that," and smiled.

Tåsan said, "We've done well in spite of what the Thanda Meriki has thrown at us."

"Yes," said Darrian, "it could have gone so much differently."

Castell raised his mug of tea to the group, "Here's to tenacity."

"And to extra credit for surviving!" joked Tåsan, who laughed with the others and drank from his mug.

"Hear, hear!" said Tao.

• • •

The next day, the team made the thirty-seven milia, including five into the Fen, before finding a high and partially dry area large enough for the tent and the exclusion barrier.

Mealtime conversation was sparse as everyone was more interested in eating than talking but as the warm food hit their bellies and they started to relax, chat soon followed.

"Alyss," said Tåsan. "What are the secrets of Fen Mortis?"

Alyss considered the request. "There's a tale handed down

104

from old Erontu. Many generations old. As old as Fen Mortis.

"It tells of a beautiful maiden named Annatae who lived in a village now long abandoned and decayed, that once stood at the edge of the Fen. She had long, dark flowing hair that she adorned with flowers and wild dancing eyes the color of jade that flashed when she laughed.

"All the young men of the village became love stricken at the sight of Annatae but her grandmother forbad her marry, always muttering of danger and heart-break. Eventually, stories about Annatae circulated among the villagers. There were dark and mysterious things about her that were hinted at in hushed tones.

"One particularly love stricken young man, named Rivand, was determined to win Annatae for himself but he was a very shy man and could only watch her from afar, trying to screw up his courage to speak to her.

"One night he couldn't sleep and left his hut for some air. Eventually, he found himself at Annatae's hut, standing across a small distance in the shadows, hoping for a glimpse of her when suddenly she appeared outside her door. She hesitated as she looked through the darkness straight at Rivand with sadness and pain before turning and walking in the direction of the Fen.

"Her look shot fear into Rivand's heart and he receded further into the shadows, afraid and unsure but he couldn't help but to follow her as she crossed into the Fen to almost disappear among the Salix and sedge. He followed her for some time before coming to a clearing, lit only by the full moon. Here he hid himself and watched Annatae, as she stood motionless, looking up at the moon for what must have been minutes and minutes until she started to sway as if hearing music.

"Rivand could hear nothing but the buzzing of night insects and the wind through the rushes.

"Annatae's dancing became more and more frantic as the seconds ticked by until eventually she seemed a blur, spinning and throwing her arms wildly about.

"Rivand's fear was so acute, he could hear the blood rushing in his ears and feel his heart pound in his chest, but even as every fiber in his being was telling him to run, still he stayed. Still he watched.

105

"Annatae's manic writhing turned her into a ghostly image that rose up into the night air and as she spun, she transformed into a giant bird as long dark wings unfolded to take the air. Annatae, in the form of a large dark beast, hung in the air, looking at Rivand for a long moment before throwing back her head and sounding out in a most painful, sorrowful way before disappearing deeper into the Fen.

"Rivand, overcome by fear and confusion, fainted to the ground where he stood.

"He awoke the next day in his own bed, unsure of how he had gotten home or of what he had seen the night before. He trusted that it had only been a dream but as he roused himself, he noticed his arms scratched and bitten and felt a bruise on his cheekbone where he had hit his head on a rock as he slumped to the ground in a faint. He knew it was real. It was not a dream.

"For the full of his life, Annatae only ever looked at him with sorrow and sadness in her eyes and it always made Rivand turn away in shame and pity." Alyss fell silent and gazed into the fire.

No one spoke.

"There is a moral to the tale," she said. "Only bravery can enter the Fen and emerge victorious. Anything else is less and will only shame the effort."

...

This day's hike began thirty minutes after dawn but it soon became clear that "hike" was the wrong word to describe exactly how the day shaped up.

To take his mind off of the toil of traversing through the Fen, Tåsan played a word game with himself. *"We're not exactly stomping...the soil is too sticky for stomping. Stomping connotates slapping ones boots down hard to make a deep thud kind of sound...(slap)...Aye, these rotten little biting insects!...This isn't a jaunt. Too long to be a jaunt, and too little pleasure...Are we marching? Nooooo. Can't march all bent over pulling your feet out of mud and steadying yourself as you climb up mushy inclines...(slap)...I guess it could classify as an excursion if by excursion one meant expedition...(slap)...Nope. Not an expedition..."*

The Fen was so much more different than all the other terrain of the Thanda Meriki. It was wet. Too wet. The soil was soaked so

106

full of water that it created a bog. And the water was so high in mineral content as to make it undrinkable. Alyss had warned that this water could cause heart palpitations and shortness of breath. Darrian supplemented that notation by adding that those were the immediate symptoms pointing to the onset of respiratory failure. "So please don't drink any of it," he had said.

Because of the mineral water, the Fen supported a variety of grasses, sedge, and poa and hydro-trees like Salix and Alnus that grew in rifts along ridges and that followed some deep underground current.

Dotted among the grasses were oval-leafed plants that held beautiful five-petaled flowers high above the leaves.

Alyss couldn't contain her excitement when she spotted the vivid pink flowers among the grass in their path. "Castell! Have you ever seen a carnivorous plant?" she called out.

Castell stopped his trek. "No, I haven't. Carnivorous you say?"

"Yes," Alyss confirmed. "Look at this." She carefully picked at the grasses that surrounded the plant she wanted to examine. "This is a butterwort."

Castell leaned down to look closer and reached out his hand to touch.

Alyss made a quick "wooh" sound that caused Castell to pull back his arm in alarm. She laughed and that made Castell laugh at her humorous chide.

"It won't bite you, but your finger may damage the leaves, reducing its ability to capture its prey," Alyss said.

Castell said, "I hope it's eating these little flying stingers." (slap) Adding, "There's plenty to go around."

The others had walked on so Alyss and Castell did not linger but sought to catch up.

A seemingly long while later, Tåsan called for a break, having found an area littered with boulders that offered dry places to sit.

After a quiet few minutes, Tåsan said, "Okay. I've been giving this some thought." Everyone looked at him. "What we're doing here is slogging."

Alyss started to snicker and could only shake her head at the absurd comment.

Darrian, who looked at Tåsan in a mixture of amusement and

107

thoughtful consideration, said, "I agree. This is a drudge in the true sense of the word."

"Slogging," said Tao, "is an apt description. I believe I've heard my footsteps making that exact noise all morning."

The conversation calmed until all that could be heard was a low buzzing of insects among the tall grasses, the three-noted song of an unseen avian, and the occasional slapping sound of hand against skin.

"We should move on," said Tåsan. "I think the insects have found us again."

The slog concluded about an hour before dusk when a raised and fairly dry campsite came into view. The tent was pitched, the exclusion fence erected, and enough dry twigs collected for a nice fire pit. There was definitely a hot meal in their future.

Castell took advantage of the waning daylight to update his journal and took extra care to draw a close approximation of a carnivorous butterwort plant, complete with a flying bug caught on a sticky leaf.

Tao spent a few minutes during the early evening to observe the night sky and, likewise, updated his journal.

The others took time to sort through and organize their rucksacks, taking note of their supplies.

When the meal was ready and with everyone gathered together, the chatter naturally favored the day's hike and what might be expected for the following day.

"We've been out here for seven days," said Darrian as he passed the jar of chromista to the others after first dabbing his bites and welts with the sticky goo.

"That means we only have two more to go!" exclaimed Castell.

Tåsan said, "It's been a hard pull and we should be very proud of ourselves, but," he emphasized, "let's not get cocky. There's still almost fifty milia to go and we shouldn't let our guard down now."

Castell said, "I can say, with certainty, that we have adequate food supplies to see us through."

"How about water rations?" asked Tåsan.

"It'll be close but I think we'll be okay."

Alyss offered, "We have one more night camp. If everyone can stand it, we could forgo the hot meal, saving that water for the hike."

All agreed.

...

"Dawn seems to occur earlier each morn," Tåsan said, rubbing the sleep from his eyes and pulling himself up into a sitting position.

Alyss and Tao were already awake and outside the tent. Darrian was trying to wake up and Castell started to move around in his bedroll, clearly not wanting to get up.

"Two more days, men!" Tåsan called. "Up and at it!"

"Oh, the bones are tired," lamented Darrian. "But the day awaits."

Disassembling the camp went a bit slower owing to the sore bones and aching muscles but moved along, as it should. The rucksacks were collected off to the side, out of the way, as Alyss unbound the exclusion fence, the men started to extinguish the nightfire and bring down the tent.

The shrill sound of a snarling animal fight brought everyone to alert with Alyss the first to see what was happening.

A pack of Muroidea, maybe ten of them, were fighting over one of the rucksacks that they had managed to drag two meters toward the brush before being stopped by a group of four reed felines that challenged ownership.

"Hey!" yelled Alyss in a futile attempt to scare them off. "*Hey!*"

Castell and the others had stopped what they were doing to come front and center.

Tåsan pulled the utility knife from his belt and took a step toward the fray, yelling and waving his arms as he did so.

Two of the reed felines flinched and looked his way, sizing him up. The other two were busy harassing the large rodents, trying to claim the rucksack, but the rodents outnumbered the felines and confused the scene by swarming around the pack in many directions at once. One large Muroidea managed to flick its tail, catching a feline across the ribs, making it bare its fangs and loose a growl as it stepped back in reaction.

Tåsan cautiously advanced, still yelling, and was joined by Alyss, who had picked up a large rock in one hand and a stick in the other, that she held up defensively.

The four reed felines quickly surmised their defeat and bound into the tall grass as stealthily as they had first appeared.

With the felines gone, the Muroidea returned their attention to the rucksack, pulling it in their teeth and pawing it with sharp claws.

Castell re-emerged from the tent with a flaming stick he had pulled from the smoldering fire pit and now stood with Tåsan and Alyss, slowly advancing on the hissing, snapping pack of rodents. As the distance closed, half of the rodents turned as if to defend their find, snarling and baring their teeth.

Tåsan pitched forward with a war cry, followed by Castell, who wildly brandished the fiery stick. Alyss was one half step behind, emboldened and menacing the Muroidea with her stick weapon.

Several of the rodents scurried into the grass, leaving four to do battle, which they did. One rushed Tåsan, grabbing hold of his leg and sinking teeth into flesh. Tåsan let out a yelp of pain as he slashed at the beast, deeply cutting it across its shoulder, drawing blood. With a snarl, the rodent turned to limp toward the brush.

Alyss was pounding another rodent, forcing it into a retreat when as a last effort, the thing lunged at her arm, scratching it badly, before it jumped back and ran away.

Castell had swung the smoldering stick, catching one rodent across its snout, causing it to screech and flail as it backed away in surprise. Seconds later it fled, taking the one remaining rodent with it.

Darrian and Tao had stood, frozen, staring gape-mouthed at the predicament, unsure of what to do. The snarling and hissing encounter had ended before they realized it.

Tåsan, Castell, and Alyss stood dazed and panting as they looked around at the battlefield and then at each other.

Alyss stood cradling her right arm, bright red blood seeping through her grasp. The slashes thrummed with pain but when her eyes lit on Tåsan's torn pant leg, now soaked with blood, she let out a gasp. "Tåsan, your leg!"

Tåsan was standing, bloody knife in hand, chest heaving from the skirmish, looking at Alyss and Castell, and taking a mental inventory of the scene. The rodent he had gashed managed to limp

110

for a scant meter before falling dead and now lay still and blood encrusted. The rucksack lie torn and spattered with mud and blood but on first glance, was still functional. Tåsan made a note to look closer but his thoughts were interrupted by Alyss' shocked observation of his leg. He looked down.

"Yea. Kind of hurts," Tåsan said then took a step toward a boulder where he thought to sit down.

Darrian was at his side, offering to support Tåsan's steps and Tao was rummaging through his pack for the med kit.

As the team started to calm, their muscles loosed the tension of combat and they were able to determine the situation with more clarity. For the short-term, Darrian assessed Tåsan's injuries and Tao ministered to Alyss as Castell kept a wary eye on the perimeter, and the rucksacks in particular, lest the marauding rodents return.

"These are deep wounds," said Darrian as he inspected the gashes and punctures along Tåsan's lower leg. "You're going to need stitches."

"Alyss!" Tåsan called, "Are you okay?"

"Yes," she answered. "The scratches are drawing blood and are starting to throb with pain, but my fingers still work so I'll be fine."

Tao spoke, "A few stitches, derma-med, and bandages. She'll be fine in a week and none the worse."

Alyss smiled, "Thank you, Tao." And looking over at Tåsan, "And you?"

Darrian answered, "This is bad. The damage is deep and has to be cleaned and the bleeding staunched. If there's no further damage, I'll pack the wounds with anti-viral, stitch them up, slather derma-med on them, and bandage them up." Turning to Tåsan, Darrian said, "I know you won't follow doctor's orders, but ideally you should stay off that leg for two days, maybe three, to let the stitches and medicine work."

Tåsan just smiled. "Well, doc, you know we've got deadlines to keep and extra credits to collect."

Darrian tsk'ed at the comment but before he could retort, Tåsan said, "Sew it up good. I'll be fine."

An hour later, the battered and bandaged team headed out. Darrian made Tåsan distribute most of the weight out of his pack to the others, to "lessen the stress" on his leg.

Tåsan was determined to make up for lost time by hiking the majority of the remaining fifty milia on this day. His leg, packed with meds, was doing fine so he set a brisk pace. As brisk as the Fen Mortis would allow.

The team mustered their strength and their wills to the task and stepped lively, but by the time the mid day break came, rest was sorely needed.

Alyss' arm had started to throb again and everyone was covered in insect bites and losing energy.

Castell passed around half rations of nutri-cubes saying, "It should help us get to the end of the day and won't deplete our rations by too very much."

Everyone rubbed chromista onto their cuts and bites and Tao checked Alyss' bandages and had her swallow a small pharma pill to ease the pain even as Darrian looked after Tåsan's leg, changing the bandage after packing the wounds with a fresh layer of meds.

Castell took advantage of the break to use his Directional to figure out how far they had come and how far must they still go. "We've done almost eighteen milia," he said to Tåsan.

"That means another twelve or fifteen before nightfall."

Castell said, "That may be optimistic."

Tåsan said, "What do you mean?"

"Well, the terrain has been fairly smooth and relatively flat. In spite of the wet ground, we've made good time so far. But looking ahead," Castell gestured briefly to the south, "I can see the beginning of a Carr."

Tåsan stood up and looked southward.

Castell continued, "Within a Fen, a Carr is very waterlogged. Our footing will be slowed dramatically. Carrs support a vast number of trees, unlike what we've experienced so far."

Alyss joined the conversation. "Carrs are unique in that the soil is full of plant debris and clay making it very fibrous and highly hydrophilic. Castell is right. Our pace may be slowed. We may not get as far as you would like."

Tåsan pulled his Thanda Meriki map from his vest pocket and unfurled it for study. Alyss came to his side so that she could look, also.

A moment passed. Then another. When Tåsan was satisfied, he looked up. "The Carr is too big to go around. We have no choice but to go through," and added, "I may have been a little zealous in my estimation of the milia we should cover but I'm going to wait on voicing any revision until I see what this Carr is all about."

Castell said, as he looked around at the others, "If we can make twelve milia by the end of the day, we will be out of Fen Mortis. Back on dry land."

Tao said, "That's a good goal, one I would be happy to try for."

Either energized by the burst of nutri-cube proteins and saccharides or by the promise of leaving the marsh and its violent nature behind, the team made fair time as they ventured into the Carr.

The ground was very soggy as Castell forewarned, but was covered with grasses and sedge that provided a buoyant path.

The Carr was crowded with tall, very old trees. There were thick, mottled Ash, with roots sunk deep and large numbers of Laurel in stands that followed a path only the trees knew. Here and there, Wild Malus in displays of large red flowers and dark green leaves that hid the truth...deep thorns and rancorous fruit. Everywhere grew clumps of carex and sedge and the drone of insects was continuous.

Tåsan, keeping a faint eye on his team as he watched for exhaustion, found the way less dangerous than he had feared, but troublesome just the same. The flora prevented walking. Each step had to be chosen, each leg lifted up and carefully placed so as not to slip down soggy inclines or trip over large tangled tree roots. After several milia, Tåsan's leg was aching; the meds had clearly worn off.

Alyss gritted her teeth against the never-ending shin bangs and thorn nips to her fingertips, determined to put the Fen Mortis and its perilous Carr behind.

Tåsan swallowed down his leg pain in his intent to not cause further delays.

The team sputtered steadily along for eight very wet milia when suddenly, Darrian's foot slipped as his step tore out a clump of grass and skimmed out from under his weight. In a panic to try to save his balance, he spotted a tree limb close by and thrust out his hand to grab at something stable, but was shocked when the saving grasp produced a horrific pain that shot through the palm of his hand. He let out a cry that stunned the others from their fatigue.

Tåsan called out, "Darrian! What happened?"

"Oh, I reached to steady myself but managed to impale my hand on a very large thorn."

Alyss had gone to him. "Darrian, you need to pull that out, now. It's from an Acantha tree, it's loosely called Thorn of Fire because it will burn with pain."

Darrian took hold of the thorn and pulled as fast as he could, sliding the seven-centimeter spike from the palm of his left hand. "Yeow!"

Tåsan spotted a small raised mound just ahead and ushered everyone on. "We'll take a break over there."

Darrian grasped his palm, plugging the puncture holes with his thumb and index finger as Alyss helped steady him the few paces to the grassy mound.

Tao and Darrian, with their heads bent together in concentration, worked to clean and bandage the wound.

Alyss stayed near watching, but after listening to them discuss Darrian's injury, decided they knew what they were dealing with so went to join Tåsan.

Castell was looking closely at an odd little bit of moss clinging to a tree trunk and making notes in his journal.

As Alyss approached, Tåsan nodded in Tao and Darrian's direction.

She glanced back at them then turned to Tåsan, "He'll be fine but the injury will vex his hand for awhile. They're being very doctor-like, excited about troubleshooting and recovery and the like." Alyss plopped down next to Tåsan. "How's your leg?"

"Seems okay. A little tired."

"How much longer do you think we've got out here?" asked Alyss, almost afraid to hear the answer.

Tåsan looked up at the sky, trying to determine the hours left in the day. "Maybe five milia."

"My decision would be to make one last push, to put this behind us," Alyss said, fatigue creeping into her voice.

114

Tåsan got up and went to Darrian and Tao, just then finishing the bandage. "Five milia, men. Can you do it?"

"To dry land?" asked Darrian. "You bet I'll make it," answering himself.

Tao smiled and nodded.

And off they went.

Five milia, dry land, and a bedroll...nothing better.

• • •

Day nine. The last day of the duad and the last day allowed for the completion of the weeklong survival course. It was an hour past dawn when the team, one by one, awoke to the new day.

Darrian's hand was still sore and the puncture holes were inflamed to bright red welts. Tåsan's leg was healing, but slowly. Alyss' arm was aching but looked better. Tao was starting to limp on his recovering broken leg, and Castell looked like a spotted abnormality from all the insect bites and if that wasn't enough, his ankle was stiff.

Tåsan, still bleary-eyed from sleep, looked from one friend to the other to the other, and laughed. "We are a sight to see, that's for sure."

"We have managed to slowly degenerate during this trip," said Darrian.

"During this *survival course*," corrected Castell.

Alyss volunteered, "Thank our fortunes this is the last day...we're running out of bandages!"

• • •

The sun had passed its zenith when Jacamarici Lor came into view, rising out of the glare of the buff-colored land to stand stark and modern and lively. Just the sight of it gave energy to the step and lightened the load.

• • •

The pilot and co-pilot of the *Trusted Companion* reported to the observation room for their briefing. They were on stand-by, waiting for their survival course volunteers to make it back before the final hour. If the volunteers failed to return at the appointed time, *Trusted Companion's* mission would then be one of search and rescue.

An hour and many minutes later, a message floated over the

115

inter-communication line reporting that the group of intrepid survival volunteers was approaching from the north. They were roughly three milia out, all were present, and should arrive at the base within three quarters of an hour.

Trusted Companion's pilot notified his crew that flight plans had changed, that the craft was to be returned to stand-by mode and then they were dismissed. He and his co-pilot decided that they would wait at the base parameter to greet the returning volunteers.

They were the first new faces Tåsan and his team had seen since they had been dropped off at the high plateau three hundred twenty-five milia ago.

The pilot and co-pilot walked out a few meters to meet the team, smiling and raising their hands in salute.

"You're the first group to return," smiled the pilot, "and early, too!"

The team looked ragged and dirty and well worn from their week in the Erontu outback but stepped as lively as they could in response to the welcome home and the smiling faces.

"The first group?" asked Tåsan.

"Yes. Two other teams went out, although to other locations in the Thanda Meriki. They have not been seen, yet."

The co-pilot added, "There's still an hour to go so they may make it, in any case, rescue flights are ready."

"We've saved you a flight out?" Tåsan said with a raised eyebrow.

"So you have," said the pilot. "I suppose we owe you an ale for that!"

Tåsan said, "I'll trade it for a bath and a hot meal."

"Done!"

• • •

"What a way to end solar year one of Inter-Galaxy Command Officer Training," mused Tåsan. *"Who would have thought a week in the Erontu outback could have taught so much...I've learned a few things about myself. I'm a bit surprised that facing the new and unexpected each day did not stress me as much as it could have; working in a team, this team, was very satisfying...the problem solving alone was worth it; I feel that my contributions to the course were valuable and welcome. Where but in the outback would I ever see liquid sand, steep ravines and giant*

116

snarling rodents ever again?" The thoughts gave Tåsan pause and he shook his head in mild disbelief as though it was all a dream. *"I think my skills in leadership may have improved, too. Fortune would favor me if when father hears all about it, he would take as much pride in my accomplishments as I do."*

Four
Fortune Smiles

The Quad Five class schedule could be summed up simply as: Physical Training, Propulsion Engineering, and Class-W Ships.

Tåsan was very excited at the prospect of being part of a bridge crew and that of pilot in particular, on the IGC's fleet of Class-W's. All were specified as conflict resolution and designed for long distance flight. There were the vast Battle Class-W's with a one hundred and twenty crew, Starchasers with a two hundred crew, and Stratos Class beauties with an impressive four hundred and thirty crew. All were outfitted for time and distance and could transport and sustain a large contingent and their supporting gear.

The Propulsion Engineering class was designed to be an electronic communication system accessed on e-pads. It required the trainee to review class materials and submit assignments as outlined by the "instructor," a hybrid system of circuits and artificial intelligence. This type of system didn't allow for a verbal exchange of thoughts or ideas. It was a straight up course to be learned and passed.

On the first day of Quad Five, Tåsan received his class assignments. He was to report to the Starchaser *Terebellum* as Commander for the first half of the quad and then transfer to the Stratos class ship, *The Garnet Star,* for the second half. The propulsion studies and physical training would be provided for on ship.

Tåsan could barely tap out a message to his friends for all the excitement he felt. He had scarcely touched the "send" connect when two messages streamed in. Alyss messaged that she was assigned to *Terebellum* as pilot and Castell messaged that he was assigned to *Terebellum* as Flight Engineer. What were the odds!

Tåsan immediately invited his friends to join him in his quarters for a small celebration to cheer their good fortunes. Minutes later the three stood together, arms locked, jostling each other, smiling and buzzing about the prospect of living and working aboard a Starchaser.

Castell said, "I think my longest flight ever, was with my family. We were on a working holiday for my father. I couldn't have been more then five solar years old. It took two days to go from Astor to Sador and I clearly remember being quite miserable."

Tåsan clapped him on the back, "Cheer up! Things have improved dramatically since your father's family vehicle."

Alyss, in her jubilance said, "A Starchaser!" The smile on her face and the light in her eyes was shining. "I can't wait!"

Tåsan said, "I've built up such fantastic ideas about serving aboard Starchasers and Stratos, I trust they don't disappoint."

Alyss asked, "Your father is an IGC officer, he must have been assigned to Class-W ships. He never mentioned life aboard?"

"No," said Tåsan. "He's a very conventional kind of officer. His focus is always on duty and regulations. He never talked about...amenities...if you will. Didn't feel they were necessary."

Castell said, "Well, my initial research of Class-W's didn't reveal any real details about recreational benefits, but I think since the Class-W's are long distance ships, there has to be something besides duty to occupy ones time."

"Yes," said Tåsan, "there's Propulsion studies and boot camp."

Castell and Alyss gave little laughs. Alyss added, "IGC's motto is: Reliability, Valor, Excellence. So there's that."

Castell said, "That almost seems like a bonus!"

Alyss stood for a second looking at her friends. "Gentlemen. I have a lot of preparation to do before we report to the *Terebellum* tomorrow morning, so I'll say good night."

"Okay, Alyss, see you aboard ship," said Castell.

"Good night."

• • •

The *Terebellum* sat at the ready at the edge of flight pad W401A, its smooth, dusky gray metal surface, luminous in the early morning hour. Light shone from almost all the bulkhead view ports as

119

support and maintenance crews completed flight prep and began their pre-ops checklists.

Tåsan located his quarters easily enough. It was a single, two room space with a desk, a bed, a bath, and not much else. After stowing his gear, he reported to the bridge as ordered.

Taking his position at Command, Tåsan quickly scanned the controls at his fingertips and then looked around the bridge, guessing at the functions of the various stations arranged strategically around the space. He noticed several bridge crewmembers were already at station, intent on their pre-flight checkouts, and thought to introduce himself.

Tåsan approached a crewmember, "Co-Pilot, welcome. I'm Commander Sulac," and extended his hand in greeting.

The co-pilot stood in formal style at being addressed by a superior officer. "Thank you, sir. I'm Lieutenant Nikliss Hywell," and took Tåsan's hand. "I'll be your co-pilot on this mission." Nikliss smiled a warm and friendly greeting.

"Excited to get going?" asked Tåsan.

"Yes sir," answered Nikliss. "And very happy to be here."

Tåsan saw right away that Nikliss Hywell was from Jahved Tuk. He had the classic features, the high cheekbones and light brown eyes that turned green when he turned his head.

Tåsan said, "I see you are from Jahved Tuk. I'm from Naiad Five."

Nikliss responded, his voice lowered in respect, "Yes. Seems we're both a long way from home, sir."

"Yes and all the better for us. I've met one of your countrymen, Tao Vu. Do you know him?" asked Tåsan.

"Yes. Our paths crossed during Quad One Quanta Mechanics and again during Quad Three Sims. Nice man. Good officer."

"Well," said Tåsan, "he's assigned to Medical for this mission. Maybe you will meet again."

"I'll make a point of it. Thank you, sir," said Nikliss.

"Let's have a good flight." Tåsan smiled and nodded to Nikliss and turned to step away. That's when he noticed Castell had taken his station at Engineering and smiled to him in greeting just as Alyss took her pilot's seat and he smiled to her, also.

Tåsan slowly paced about the bridge, observing the crew at

work and familiarizing himself with station set-ups and display output. Eventually he found himself observing the navigator. He knew right away that she was from Cimtun 8 in the Hedorrion Galaxy. Her long thin arms shown the faint color of Lapis Lazuli and when Tåsan introduced himself, her moss green eyes flashed with excitement.

"Navigator, hello," said Tåsan. "I trust I'm not interrupting. I'm Commander Sulac."

"Greetings Commander. I'm Major Shú Vit Fisk," and she stood up in formal style.

Tåsan motioned for Shú Vit to sit back down. "Major Fisk," glancing at Shú Vit expectantly and leaning a bit closer, "Is that correct?" and hesitated, waiting for her answer.

"Yes, sir, perfect."

"Thank you," smiled Tåsan. "I'll let you get back to work, then. Good flight, Major."

"Good flight, Commander."

Alyss called out, "Commander. Control is signaling that we have been cleared. We may begin when you are ready."

"Thank you, Lieutenant Brannick," said Tåsan as he regained his chair at Command. "Flight Engineer Brann," Tåsan called out to Castell, who was intently looking at his displays.

"Yes, Commander," replied Castell. "All ships systems check and report ready."

Tåsan touched the comm icon on his control pad, took one last look around the bridge and said, "On my mark, lift and burn. Up to the demark zone." And leaving the briefest space, enough to take in one breath, commanded, "Initiate."

The *Terebellum* lifted from the flight pad and rose with grace, smoothly upward, leaving Jacamarici Lor far below.

Tåsan said, "Navigator Fisk, set our heading for the Outer Stars," and to Alyss, "Slow and easy for now, while we review mission orders."

The mission was routine. Fly to Sador's moon, Eriop, to complete a check on a family owned quarry operation, the Hatzeg Affiliation, who happened to be a well-connected ISA member, whose main deliverables are pure quartz rhodinite and granite. After which, *Terebellum* would await further orders.

Tåsan spent most of his duty time shadowing the other bridge disciplines, learning the stations and getting to know the skills of his crew.

Several days into the routine and rather slow moving mission, Tåsan decided to pilot the starship and took the controls, inviting Alyss to sit in Command.

"Let's see what the *Terebellum* is made of." Tåsan pushed the throttle open and watched, excitement climbing, as the indicator moved steadily on, registering a rate of velocity upside of the normal range. When the ship was clearly hurtling through open space, Tåsan abruptly changed direction, putting the craft into the equivalent of a sideways slide, then powered the port side thrusters as he steered to starboard, rocking the vessel into a neat one hundred and eighty degree spin before guiding the movements to a full stop.

The *Terebellum* hung in space.

"Okay, now we know a little more about the maneuverability of an IGC Starchaser," declared Tåsan, a smile broad across his face. "Lieutenant Brannick. Let's see if you and Co-pilot Hywell can manage a figure eight. What do you think, Lieutenant Hywell? Care to give it a try?"

The next thirty minutes were possibly the most interesting of the entire four weeks worth of starship training. Tåsan, Alyss, and Nikliss took turns putting the ship through some very interesting actions while proving that their piloting skills were indeed, adroit.

When not on the bridge, studying Propulsion, or running the punishing on-board par course, Tåsan, Alyss, and Castell, joined occasionally by Nikliss and Shú Vit, made use of the communal area where they could listen to music, play games of strategy, read, or sit with friends.

It was during one of these rare times that Tåsan learned a little more about Nikliss Hywell.

"I've never been to Jahved Tuk," said Tåsan. "Tell me about your home and what brings you to the IGC?"

"Jahved Tuk, you may already know, has a permanent asteroid belt at its equator. It's very lovely on most clear evenings and can attract throngs of lovers and tourists. Many poems and songs have been written about the mystery and the beauty of so many objects slowly tumbling about the night sky." Nikliss reached for his mug of tea, cooling on the table at his elbow. "Of course," he continued, "it's all a nightmare for spaceflight and periodically, a small asteroid will get bumped and chipped and plummet down to the planet. The entire equator is full of craters and scars. Hah! If you ever get the chance to visit, don't miss that particular show."

"Growing up there, you've seen it so much you probably don't really see it any longer," said Tåsan.

"It is a marvel, but you're right, I look past it now." Nikliss sipped his tea. "My home is in the north, closer to the sun pole. I'm from the capitol city, Magnus. It's a huge, very modern city. Full of life. Very busy."

Tåsan had been listening closely and could almost picture city streets bustling with activity. It made him a little homesick. "Does your planet have one economy or many?"

Nikliss thought for half a moment, then answered, "There's many independent and family run businesses. Mostly agrarian and industrial businesses whose main clients are each other. It keeps things in balance. But to be honest, it was too small for me. My interest has always been in Space Science and the call for pilots on Jahved Tuk is very limited. So..." Nikliss spread his arms to encompass all that was around him, "Here I am!"

• • •

Soon enough, the training flight time on the Starship *Terebellum* came to an end. The mission, that of checking in with the Hatzeg Affiliation, took all of ten minutes. It consisted of a very polite communication with the head of Hatzeg security who assured *Terebellum* that all was fine.

As a way of finalizing the training period, a small semi-formal ceremony was held in cargo bay Epsilon. The evening had been declared "uniforms only" and almost the entire ship's compliment attended.

Tåsan and his bridge crew stood in a group several meters from the makeshift stage that had been erected at the long end of the bay. Their talk was innocuous and rambling as they waited for the ceremony to begin.

Out of nowhere, Castell nudged Tåsan's arm and said, "Hey, look," as he nodded toward the stage in order to direct Tåsan's attention.

The Starchaser's Training Supervisor, Captain Atelli was standing with three other IGC officers, softly chatting and smiling at the proceedings.

"Isn't that your father?" asked Castell, causing Alyss, Nikliss, and Shú Vit to turn and look.

Tåsan looked closely. "Yes, that's him."

"Did you know he was here?"

"No. He never said a word."

To a smattering of light applause, Captain Atelli stepped up to address the assembly. After a brief introduction, the Captain proceeded to recognize various crewmembers, inviting them up to the front and presenting some with awards for good conduct and for others, he gave achievement medals. Several minutes passed, when without further hesitation, Captain Atelli launched into a sort of speech touting the precision and skills of the first shift bridge crew.

Alyss leaned over and whispered to Tåsan, "Wasn't that us?"

Tåsan was just as surprised as Alyss. "Yes. Shift one bridge. Yes."

Nikliss and Castell turned to the others with huge smiles shining across their faces. Shú Vit put her hands together and almost did a little dance she was so happy.

As invited, they stepped forward as Captain Atelli announced that they were to receive commendation medals, not an award loosely handed out. After the medals were affixed to their uniforms, all turned to face the assembly, who clapped and gave good cheer to the crew.

Captain Atelli declared the ceremony concluded and everyone started talking at once.

Almost immediately, Tåsan turned to look to his father, but Captain Sulac had already left the stage and was retreating through the crowd in the company of the other senior officers.

Tåsan looked after him, but Amans Sulac never looked back once. Tåsan hid his disappointment and confusion but was quickly swept up in the celebration that filled cargo bay Epsilon with the sound of laughter and high spirits.

• • •

The next morning came fast and the trainees were hectic as they jammed their belongings into travel cases in preparation for the next training phase. It was time to transfer to one of the IGC's crown jewels: a Stratos Class-W ship named, *The Garnet Star.*

Stratos Class ships were too massive to berth on any of Jacamarici Lor's flight decks. Instead, they were docked at Brenton Kae, residing outside the Niles Galaxy at a fixed point to its sun. Brenton Kae was a massive space station that was host to the IGC, who operated a huge repair and maintenance operation taking up a full one third of the station. The other two thirds played host to the commerce surrounding smaller craft traveling from one place to another. There were rooms to let, restaurants, services, and entertainment as well as housing for the workers and merchants who operated the establishments. Management oversight was provided by a cooperative of Brenton Kae citizens.

All trainees and their travel cases were assembled in Loading Dock E² Portage-A according to rank and they stood in perfect lines and rows, waiting for transport. As the *Terrebellum* slowly approached Brenton Kae, *The Garnet Star* filled the view screens throughout the loading dock.

Tåsan couldn't get enough of the view. *The Garnet Star* was a massive ship that gleamed of silver and gray and wherever the ambient lights touched the outer hull, the protective chrysoberyl shields reflected gold and orange and opaque quartz. The ship was wide and sleek and dotted with view ports, almost all lit with activity. It was a study in beauty and dynamics.

Tåsan became aware that he was holding his breath in anticipation and excitement and inwardly smiled at his reaction.

His thoughts were interrupted by the announcement that the docking and orderly disembarkation process would commence in fifteen minutes. Stay sharp.

Tåsan had been assigned to Bridge Crew Aleph, sharing the clock with one other crew, Daleth. During the hours when he was not on the bridge, he was to keep up a physical training schedule and sleep. After that, his time was designated personal time but, and the Quad Five schedule stressed this point very clearly...if performance declined in any way, censure would be given. You did *not* want a censure. Ever.

125

...

Aleph's bridge watch would start at 018.20, four hours from now. *The Garnet Star's* corridors were a bustle of activity with crew moving between assignments, trainees locating quarters, and friends trying to find friends.

Tåsan, Alyss, and Castell agreed to meet in the central shared area after stowing their cases and getting their bearings. Tåsan messaged Nikliss and Shú Vit that if they had a minute to spare, they should join them. Shú Vit agreed but Nikliss begged pardon, he was meeting up with Tao Vu but would take advantage of a re-invite at a later time.

The friends managed to converge on the shared area at about the same time and found chairs just ahead of the crush. They exchanged particulars about the shuttle ride from *Terrebellum*, the location of their quarters, their excitement at being on *The Garnet Star*, and to be part of the experiences to come. When the animated chatter died down and the friends started to relax, the conversation naturally wound down, too.

Shú Vit had been sitting quietly when she spotted a friend among the crowd and called out as she stood up to hail him. "Mason, over here!"

Mason stood above average height with long pale hair, tied back with a woven thong. His eyes were the color of dusk. His smile was friendly and he looked relieved to see Shú Vit among the mass of strangers crowding the communal area.

Mason smiled and waved as he tried to thread his way through the throng. When he reached the group, Shú Vit turned to her companions, "This is my dear friend Mason Trang. He's assigned to Aleph crew as the Communication Officer." She put a hand lightly on his arm, "Mason, let me introduce Commander Sulac," gesturing toward Tåsan.

The men clasped hands in greeting and Shú Vit continued, "Lieutenant Brannick, Pilot and Ensign Brann, Engineering, Aleph crew. Everyone, this is Tech Class I Trang, Communication."

Tåsan said, "Nice to meet you. Grab a chair and join us."

After Mason was settled, Tåsan spoke to him, "You know we're going to be curious about you so let me start. I'm from Naiad Five. Alyss Brannick is from Erontu, and Castell Brann is from

Astor."

Mason smiled and said, "I'm from Crosus, one of the two moons of Titus, largest planet in the Hedorrion Galaxy. Neighbor to Cimtun 8," glancing over at Shú Vit.

Shú Vit added, "Mason and I met a few solar years ago during a conference on 'System Network Inter-Connectivity As It Applies To Control and Sub-Systems of In-Space Transport.' It was held on Titus."

Mason said, "Our common bond was that we didn't know any of the other attendees."

"And we've stayed in touch since then," said Shú Vit.

Castell leaned in just a bit. "Crosus. Not much is known about the moon Crosus. Is it an independent? Or is it tied to Titus?"

"You could say a bit of both," answered Mason. "Our terra was formed by accident some seven billion years ago when Crosus was held close to Titus by its strong gravitational pull. So close, in fact, that both were enveloped by the same atmosphere. That was, until a dwarf planet, Eris, drifted by and interrupted their dance by pulling Crosus away."

Castell asked, "And Eris is now the second moon?"

"Correct," answered Mason, "and a barren and battered place of not much interest. As to commerce, Crosus mainly mines metals and minerals highly sought after for use in terra-forming processes. In contrast, Titus's main commerce surrounds the University complex that stands as a centerpiece to all things Titus."

Tåsan asked, "Is that where you were trained in Communication? On Titus?"

"Yes. I attended Elo-Technic University and soon after graduation, applied to the IGC and was accepted as Tech Class III but worked my way to Senior Tech Class I during my first three quads."

"Quite an accomplishment, you should be proud," said Tåsan.

Alyss glanced at her e-time and said, "Oh, we've only an hour before Aleph shift begins. I need to stop by my quarters to pick up a few things. I should go," and stood up. She smiled at Mason and said, "We'll see you on the bridge," and stepped away.

One by one, the others followed suit.

• • •

The bridge of *The Garnet Star* was bright, wide, organized and full of energy. The large view screen, displaying several windows along its breadth, showed views of all the bustle of activity about the outer hull, several of the other non-IGC ports of Brenton Kae, and a steady stream of operations status reports.

Several Aleph bridge crew were already at station, including Castell, when Tåsan stepped from the lift and took a moment to look around. All the sims and tech manuals couldn't have done this bridge justice.

Command was center and central. To either side of the wide, ergo chair were system access screens within easy reach. The view was perfect. All could be seen from Command.

Alyss stepped from the opposite lift and with confident steps, crossed the bridge to Flight Control.

The next few minutes were a controlled chaos as Aleph crew reported for duty and Daleth crew gave turnover and left. Tåsan had assumed his position at Command and was watching the ops status stream by his screen, noting that, steadily, all systems were coming online and completing checkout and verification in preparation for flight.

Tåsan was deep in concentration when he became aware that the ambient noise levels had dropped dramatically. Curiously, he looked up from his screens, noticing that Nikliss and Alyss were trying, subtly, to glance at a bridge member who had stepped from the power-way lift and was threading her way to the Tactical Systems station.

Alyss tapped out a cryptic message to Tåsan, ((ref brdg man AI sys.))

Tåsan scanned the manual reference and from it, surmised that highly classified labs operated by the IGC had been working for years to integrate artificial intelligence into IGC Stratos Class ships, with a focus on Tactical Systems. As a natural progression of the work, the AI interface could be transferred, not only from discipline to discipline, for instance from Tactical to Engineering, but from ship to ship. Modifications would undoubtedly need to be made, but once done, AI transfer was a matter of course.

Tåsan looked up incredulous of what the manual stated and with what...no...with who...he was looking at. He thought he

128

knew about artificial intelligence. AI was a big part of his personal interest and as a hobby he regularly made AI system mods to his pulse rocket. But nothing of what he knew compared to this.

Her name was Annis O'hAirt and her rank, Major. By the ribbons and tokens she wore on her jacket, a well-honored Major. She was tall, Tåsan guessed six or so centimeters taller than himself. She wore her hair back in the Osanti style but Tåsan could see that it was long auburn hair with ruby highlights that framed her face. Her eyes were pale gray with dark gray flecks that made her look rather imposing.

Tåsan found her most interesting feature, one he could not help to muse over, were the visible circuitry that showed here and there along her skin. It was not obvious. It did not blink and pulse. Rather, it was like art. Subtle. And Tåsan thought it added to her appearance. Almost balancing her out.

At her breastbone, a large star garnet implant gave off the perfect six-pointed asterism glow that shone with her every move. Annis had the implant, an unusually dynamic AI power source, decorated with the movement of precious metal, gems, and a surround of boron that glistened in its blackness. The implant was made to look like an exquisite and very delicate piece of jewelry.

Alyss had gone over to Tactical and the two were engaged in conversation. Tåsan observed that both women were talking in low tones presumably carrying on introductions and not much else. Major O'hAirt's eyes were alert and her smile subtle but warm. Alyss gave a small laugh at something the Major had said, extended her hand in salutation and returned to Flight Control.

Tåsan could not let it go. His curiosity was eating at him almost to distraction. He pulled up Major O'hAirt's personnel file.

The idea that artificial intelligence need not be subject to the ship bound restrictions of panels, screens, and data bases was the natural progression of a complex theorem that AI could be robust and free of the status quo. The main focus of experimentation and testing was strengthening the IGC's tactical advantages, so study naturally led to the integration of biology and advanced collaborative robotics. Thus the idea of an "Annis O'hAirt" came into being. Specifically, there were several hybrid humanoid-robotic living beings that had been redefined, one for each IGC

Stratos Class-W ship in the fleet.

Tåsan quickly scanned the file...the science of Major O'hAirt was fascinating. She was outfitted with a universal meta-luristic tracking device capable of long-range comm. One of her eyes contained four digital-spatial lenses: telephoto, infra R-B-G-Y, high-res, and macro-scope to detect at a sub-atomic level and frequently used for electronics inspections. Tåsan was envious. How many times had he wished for an eye like that? Hundreds? He read on. The digi-eye could record, compare, interface with other systems, and had steady-cam capabilities. Tåsan was going to look into this. He thought, *"Wouldn't that be spectacular to have on a wild pulse rocket race!"* Further, Major O'hAirt had several implants, one among them gave her the ability to move very quickly, another, the ability to access situations, interface with ship systems at a moment, *and* she was multi-lingual. Her enhanced brain had expanded memory functions as well as classified technologies and the garnet at her throat was a seemingly eternal power source that could recharge through a highly classified form of osmosis.

Annis O'hAirt's psych profile was included in the pers file. This piqued Tåsan's interest because after reading about the science of her, Tåsan had been thinking of her as a sort of machine, but the term "Psych" was only used in reference to humanoids, right? Well, there was only one way to find out. He read on...

The psych evaluation at the end of the file was very interesting. It said, "Major Annis O'hAirt is fully self-aware. She understands exactly who she is, her capabilities, and her limitations. Her understanding of esoteric concepts such as trust and friendship has remained unchanged throughout her conversion process and she is happy to be exactly as she is: Annis O'hAirt assigned to Tactical, currently an officer on *The Garnet Star*. No further evaluation is required at this time."

Tåsan closed the file but his mind had raced forward, *"I'd like to set up an exercise of sorts for my bridge configuration, something that will allow me to observe the crew at their stations as individuals and how they handle inter-communication in times of high-alert. Something for me to think about."*

...

130

Alyss touched her comm pad and said, "Aleph Bridge, we've been cleared for flight. At your mark, Commander."

Tåsan responded, "Very good Lieutenant Brannick. On my mark, lift and burn." And hearing no exceptions, "Initiate."

The Garnet Star gently cleared the now retracted moorings that moments ago held her secure to her berth at Brenton Kae. Data streamed across the view screens as the chatter between the dock crew and ship's engineering monitored and communicated *The Garnet Star's* graceful and exacting departure.

Smoothly she sailed upward and away from Brenton Kae reaching the instructed coordinates that situated *The Garnet Star* among the outer stars on the edge of the Allodial Expanse.

"Our mission," announced Tåsan, "is to patrol the Allodial Expanse between the Niles, the Hedorrion, and the Rayten Galaxies. We're to monitor shipping lanes and in general, be aware."

"Captain," spoke Mason Trang from his place at Communication.

"Yes, Mister Trang," answered Tåsan.

"Are you able to add detail to the order, 'be aware'?"

"The mission orders do not provide detail but I'm sure they have the fullest confidence in our ability to add dimension to such a statement." Tåsan stood up and took a step forward and addressing the entire bridge, continued, "My own interpretation would include monitoring short- to long-range sensors for activities or objects, using track-and-map methodologies, and building a three dimensional display of all inputs." He glanced around the bridge, adding, "I believe we should use this time to exercise our station capabilities and identify limits…real or perceived."

Thinking to give everyone a minute to consider what he had just said, Tåsan lightly stepped to Alyss' side at Flight Control and stood quietly watching the data displays.

"Sir," Shú Vit spoke.

"Yes, Navigator Fisk," replied Tåsan turning to look in her direction.

"I would like to program several Nav scenarios that would cover various situations that may be encountered including evasive maneuvering and a few defensive moves. If that meets your criteria, sir." Shú Vit looked expectantly at Tåsan.

"Perfectly, Navigator Fisk," smiling, Tåsan added, "Any others?"

The next two minutes were filled with creative dialogue, best guesses, interdependencies, and plans. Tåsan was more than pleased; he was excited by what he heard and very proud of Aleph crew. He regained his seat at Command and watched his data screen as several proposals gathered on the status window. He was pleased to see that no one had overlooked the true mission in their zeal to set *The Garnet Star* through her paces. The main view screen, at the head of the bridge, reflected their true course through the Allodial Expanse, complete with shipping lanes and private transports, and all associated comm, flight plans, and manifests that usually attended "business as usual."

• • •

The shifts that followed were at times, routine to the point of redundancy and were, truthfully, fully automated. Taking advantage of such times, the Aleph bridge crew strengthened their bonds of trust and appreciation and frequently fell into playing a game of, "What Would You Do?" where someone would invent a plausible situation and the crew would answer for their stations. The predicaments ran from the absurd to the sublime.

One scenario suggested that a freak mining accident on one of the outer asteroids turned a four-dram megadrile into a nasty sixty eight million kilogram slime-exuding monster. In their haste to cover up their horrible mistake and avoid awkward questions by the IGC, the mining company towed the thing into space and pushed it into the general direction of the Allodial Expanse, hoping it would just "go away." Instead, Aleph bridge crew detected it. So. Game on.

The majority of Aleph bridge time was spent in standards with routine monitoring of shipping lanes and encounters with citizens on travel or company transports that happened to be in the same space as *The Garnet Star*.

During one of these lackluster moments when everything appeared to be in order, Navigator Shú Vit Fisk noted an irregularity and reported it to Tåsan.

"Sir, I've detected an anomaly at the outer edge of my sensor range," said Shú Vit as she adjusted and focused her detectors for the extreme distance. "It's a ship of unknown origin."

Tåsan's attention was on the large view screen. "Are you able to tell us anything about it, Navigator Fisk?"

A brief moment passed and Shú Vit answered, "It's approximately one point two five times larger than our Class-W. It does not match any of our database records for size, class, or compliment."

"Ah," said Tåsan. "An unknown." In response, Tåsan stood up and rocked on his heels, considering the situation. "Bridge," addressing everyone, "what can we tell or conclude about that ship?"

Shú Vit spoke first. "It has slowed its approach. We could conclude that they have detected *The Garnet Star* and have taken notice of our near presence, since we're the largest ship in this vector."

Tåsan nodded.

Alyss spoke next, "Sir."

"Yes, Lieutenant Brannick."

"At this point I may make the assumption, based on size and configuration, that we would be able to out maneuver the vessel."

"Aye, sir. There's a good doubt that a ship that size could complete an effective evasive maneuver in a direct confrontation, most likely it is armed for defense," said Nikliss Hywell.

"And," added Castell, "we must conclude that they are successful in their encounters, wherever they may have been since we've never engaged a vessel of this type before in our space."

Tåsan said, "Good points, all." And taking a moment to consider what he had heard, continued, "Change course to intercept but move slowly, we don't want the Captain of that ship to misinterpret out intent. Charge the chrysoberyl. Ship wide Alert Level III. Let's database this ship, and Mister Trang?"

"Yes, sir," responded Mason as he shifted to face Tåsan and come to attention.

"Do your best to find an unsecured comm and send out an innocuous greeting with an invitation to introduce themselves."

"Yes, sir."

"Everyone. Stay alert." Pausing briefly, "Here we go."

Alyss turned the ship and started forward at a cautious pace. She could feel her adrenaline starting to rise and her focus sharpen.

Bridge chatter had all but ceased and Tåsan took his seat at Command, his eyes steady on the view screens, taking it all in.

The unidentified alien vessel hung in space. For some moments it stood still and quiet. Mason Trang could detect no electro emissions that would indicate the transmission of comm signals, nor could Castell Brann detect any evidence of propulsion ions. Except for the forward lights that dotted the surface, the ship appeared derelict.

The Garnet Star had slowly closed the parting distance by several thousand meters when the alien ship suddenly swung about, startling Aleph crew with the suddenness of the move.

Tåsan commanded, "Steady, everyone, steady."

The only sound on the bridge was the low murmuring of Mason Trang's voice as he repeated the outgoing comm of introduction and invitation, sending it in several languages.

"Major O'hAirt, do you have anything yet?" inquired Tåsan, his eyes still on the view screen.

Annis replied, "Sir, while the ship is unfamiliar, I have found that its appearance faintly resembles that of our Battle Class-W's, outfitted for distance and conflict. Their forward defenses may be formidable but it's my opinion that we hold the advantage of maneuverability and tactical design."

"Very good. Thank you." Tåsan stood up as his nerves tingled to alert. "Alert Level II, please." Tåsan's voice was calm and controlled even as his mind raced. *"Wonder where they're from and why are they here? Passing through? Lost? Reconnaissance? And if so, what are their final intentions?"*

They were now close enough to the ship to have it clearly displayed on the view screens. It was sleek and dynamic and to Tåsan's mind, made for long voyages at high rates of velocity. The markings along its sides could not be referenced in the IGC's database and gave no logical indication of what they might mean. Tåsan supposed it was the vessel's identification, which meant it could be part of a larger fleet. Not just a lone reed feline.

"Sir," Mason said, interrupting Tåsan's line of thought. "I've

134

picked up an odd comm on channel zero-point-zero-eight. I'll put it through."

Tåsan listened to his earpiece for a brief moment, long enough to detect a repeat in the pattern, then directed the comm to the bridge system so all could hear it. After the fourth repeat, Tåsan asked his crew, "Any recognition in the pattern or phrasing?"

Mason responded, "The translator found two sounds akin to 'you' and 'greet', embedded in the sound stream. It's on the data screen, now, sir."

The two words floated by on a loop display, separated by incoherent blurbs. Tåsan tapped his control panel and studied the results. "There's no inflection of stress that would belie aggression. So it's either confidence or sincerity." Tåsan unconsciously touched his chin as he fell into a sort of deep concentration.

The two ships faced each other across an empty space. The comm loop played softly above the hum of the electronics and as *The Garnet Star* pulsed slowly forward, Aleph crew held quiet and steady.

Tåsan broke the tense silence, "Open channel zero-point-zero-eight, Mister Trang. I'll have a word with the visitors."

"Open, sir."

Leaning forward into the tense moment, Tåsan found his voice. "I am Commander Sulac of *The Garnet Star*. As representatives of the Intersolar and Space Alliance, we greet you." Tåsan fell quiet and waited a moment or two before interrupting the comm channel with a mute signal from his control pad, then said aloud, "Let's display my greeting on a loop display next to theirs. I'm interested in seeing both cadences."

The two loops, when seen together, seemed almost to match in rhythm and inflection.

Tåsan gave a short huff of satisfaction. "A cautious but sincere first greeting liberally laced with the appropriate amount of nerves." And in the next moment, "Good." Switching comm zero-point-zero-eight out of mute, Tåsan spoke to the visitors once more. "You have entered ISA space, an alliance of three galaxies and the Allodial Expanse that unites them."

Mason immediately set the translator to work, transmitting Tåsan's words in several languages.

135

Tåsan continued, "You have come a great distance. To pass through without a proper introduction could be to your disadvantage." Tåsan tapped the comm mute and spoke to his bridge crew. "Hold the ship steady at fifteen vectors, send a brief noncommittal message to IGC Command about our visitors, and stay ready for Alert Level I. I've issued an ultimatum they will not be able to avoid. They may choose to answer with either words or with protons."

Alyss sat with her hands poised on the flight controls in expectation of moving *The Garnet Star* quickly into defense flying from the steady position they now held. Her eyes focused on the view screen, her nerves tingly with anticipation. She glanced briefly at her co-pilot, Nikliss Hywell.

Nikliss caught the movement and glanced back, giving Alyss a broad smile and a slight nod, before returning his attention back to his own controls.

Both ships held their positions, the silent standoff and near frozen scene punctuated only by the slightest puff of vapor as attitude adjusters fired along both hulls. The moments passed into minutes and threatened to post the hour when a crackling was heard throughout the bridge.

Tåsan sat forward as he came to alert and finding a deeper need to focus, stood up.

« Citizens of *Garnet Star*, we greet you in apology for comm delay in order to locate common language. We are visitors to your space therefore unknown. »

Zero-point-zero-eight fell silent. Tåsan took the opportunity to speak, "We are curious about your travels and would like to learn who you are and your point of origin, among the many other friendly queries that we have."

« Understood. We are Vellosians. We come from far beyond your stars. A very long way. »

"What brings you to this quadrant? What might you be looking for?"

« Opportunity. »

This gave Tåsan pause. The word "opportunity" without any qualifiers attached to it could mean anything. He furrowed his brow in thought and stood watching the view screen waiting for the Vellosians next move and formulating his own. And in a briefest of moments, all was clear to Tåsan. This was no different than playing Parudi Rule. The objective of the game was to use skill and strategy to capture all the game pieces and win. The Vellosians thought only to not tip their hand, thereby losing control of their situation but Tåsan thought to tip it for them.

"The citizens of the ISA are always interested in new opportunities in commerce and trade and would welcome the chance to negotiate with new partners." Tåsan hesitated for a brief instant to emphasize his next point. "But don't let their smiles and affability fool you, they are fierce in their determination of ownership and gain." And changing to a lighter tone, "The ISA expects all new visitors to engage in a productive dialogue and would like to extend an invitation to meet. Now would be most convenient."

Tåsan tapped the comm into mute and stood smiling to himself. *"Well, if that doesn't pry any information from them, nothing will."* He addressed the bridge, "The decisive moment is upon us, Aleph. Stay sharp."

"Sir," spoke Mason Trang. "A message from IGC Command. They're sending *Celestial Hook* and *Watcher*, two nearby Class-C Interceptors and will standby for further word from you."

"Thank you, Mister Trang," replied Tåsan as he stood still waiting for the Vellosians next move.

Eventually it came.

« IGC *Garnet Star*. Thank you for kindness. It surprises us to receive such a definitive greeting and in the name of the citizens of Vellosi, and the crew of *Salvificus*, we accept the invitation and trust that it becomes a mutual and beneficial alliance. »

"This is good news indeed!" exclaimed Tåsan. "Transmit your ship's manifest and compliment, and stand by to receive coordinates of a vector of space belonging to the Niles Galaxy. The IGC will provide an escort and on behalf of the citizens of the ISA, welcome and thank you. You will not be disappointed."

Tåsan disconnected from comm zero-point-zero-eight. "Mister Trang, talk to the two Class-C's, trans my conversation with the Vellosians to the IGC, and post the records to my station."

As he stepped once or twice to move his body and to stretch

137

the tension from his legs, Tåsan found himself close to Major Annis O'hAirt's station.

Annis looked up from her controls and smiled as she said, "Impressive negotiation tactics, Commander Sulac. The ISA may have just been handed another galaxy."

That particular point had escaped Tåsan's notice as he was far more focused on the immediate...not stumbling into a shooting match with newcomers. He gave a thoughtful little tilt of his head and said, "Huh, that sounds much more impressive than my risking the destruction of their Stratos Class-W, doesn't it?"

Mason Trang's voice interrupted, "Sir, the Interceptors have arrived and would like a word."

Tåsan answered, "At my comm, Mister Trang, thank you," and turning to Annis, "Excuse me, Major," adding, "Maybe we can talk again when there aren't so many distractions."

"Aye, sir."

• • •

Aleph bridge worked steadily to clear the Vellosian ship for transit through the Allodial Expanse to a vector nestled in the outer stars adjacent to Naiad Five where they were to hold steady and await the arrival of *Shadow Warrior*, another of the IGC's Stratos Class-W's. Both ships would work out a comfortable agreement concerning all the details of meeting for the first time.

Tåsan requested progress reports as to how the situation played out. He could not remember ever hearing about the arrival of aliens into ISA space and was very curious about how negotiations would develop.

The *Salvificus* manifest listed some five hundred fifty crew and seventy-two non-crew and a cargo hold full of the most unusual and odd items, from rocks and minerals to art and gemstones, and most everything in between. Tåsan scanned the list with mild curiosity. In short time, he tapped out a message to Alyss. ((Dried hopping-beetles? Could there really be a market for that?))

Alyss messaged in reply, ((I didn't read past the entry for a fifteen point seven keras gem, The Red Vulpes. I've always thought The Red Vulpes to be a myth since no one has ever actually seen one.))

Eventually, *Salvificus*, accompanied by the two Interceptors, set out for their destiny, leaving Aleph team to wind down from the thrill of their alien encounter and slowly resume standards.

That evening as Tåsan, Alyss, and Nikliss grabbed a break together in the common area, they naturally reviewed their day.

Tåsan asked Alyss, "You mentioned a mythology regarding a gem on the Vellosian manifest. Can you tell me more about that?"

"The Red Vulpes. Yes, I was surprised to see it listed. I had always thought it was imaginary. Made up for story telling, you know...that rare, expensive, elusive thing just out of reach. Something to long for...to dream about. I never for a moment thought The Red Vulpes was real. And the Vellosians have a fifteen point seven keras stone with them!" exclaimed Alyss.

Tåsan and Nikliss thought about what Alyss had just told them. Nikliss said, "It may be destined to join a rich Sadorian's collection, to be locked away from sight."

"Or," offered Alyss, "it will adorn the finger of his fifth and most beautiful wife!"

Tåsan said, "Changing subjects, what were you two thinking during the tense moments of standoff, before their translators caught up?"

Nikliss said, "I was ready for it. I was formulating flight scenarios in my head."

"So was I," offered Alyss. "I thought first of rushing them to scatter their firepower and counted on Major O'hAirt to disable their weapons and maybe their maneuvering thrusters, leaving them basically, powerless."

"I thought that might be your main position," said Nikliss, "and was ready to play it to that win. Failing that, I thought a good follow-on might be to set about flying a pattern of Nip-N-Hit."

"Yea," agreed Alyss, "we should code a combination of both into the sim and practice together."

"Good idea," said Nikliss, smiling at the thought.

Tåsan said, "I trust the IGC won't find fault with our performance. Technically, we're still in training."

"Oh, you wait and see," smiled Alyss, "You're going to get a big fat reward for your performance. The Red Vulpes has got to be worth many hundreds of thousands of tenges, alone!"

"That *is* a lot of levy to the ISA's coffers," nodded Tåsan.

"And feathering for the IGC's comfort," added Nikliss.

Just then a Tech Class III stepped up and addressed them, "All Aleph crew members are to assemble in Stor-Deck F by order of Vice Admiral Caoin. My apologies, sirs, but you only have ten minutes," and gave a practiced salute.

Tåsan gave an easy salute in reply and turned to his companions, "Here we go." Then added, "It'll take the full ten to navigate the passages and ladders. Shall we?" rising from his seat and indicating the way.

• • •

All Aleph crew were assembled forward, followed by a group of IGC instructors and administration persons, and grouped around the storage deck's perimeter were a lot of the ships personnel. Tåsan could only guess that a full one third of *The Garnet Star's* compliment were present.

Vice Admiral Caoin stepped forward and spoke.

"I'll get right to the point so you can return to your work and studies with all haste." Vice Admiral Caoin shifted his weight and took a long look around at the expectant faces all turned his way. "I am here to bestow Meritorious Medals of Honor on Aleph bridge crew for their adroit and expedient handling of an alien encounter."

A cheer went up among the onlookers but quickly died down once the Vice Admiral continued his speech.

"This is a record day for the Intersolar and Space Alliance as it has gained knowledge of civilizations beyond our system, promising a profitable future. The IGC stands to benefit because that space and those civilizations and those ventures will all be in our charge." Caoin cleared his throat to regain his point, then continued, "This is indeed a record day." Then pausing briefly, "Aleph bridge crew," addressing the small band of IGC trainees standing before him, "I hereby honor your actions by granting each of you Meritorious Medals for your teamwork in the alien event, hereafter to be referred to as The Vellosian Encounter."

A senior IGC instructor was already pinning medals to Aleph's uniform lapels and Caoin continued, "In addition, one of Aleph crew stood out among the others. Lieutenant Sulac please step forward."

140

Tåsan was taken aback and hesitated a split moment as he tried to reconcile the words just spoken with his name being called. He took two quick steps forward.

Vice Admiral Caoin stepped toward Tåsan. "In recognition of your quick and decisive actions, you are hereby awarded the Admiral's Citation," pinning another medal to Tåsan's lapel. "Congratulations...*Commander Sulac.*"

Tåsan smiled and snapped a salute and after it was returned, they shook hands and all Tåsan could recount afterwards were the loud cheers and the hardy slaps on the back as well as warm hugs from Aleph crew as they gathered around him laughing and dancing for joy.

Later, in the quiet of the evening, Tåsan sent a message to his family sharing the news. Within minutes Rebetta and Arron responded with cheers and congratulations, swiftly followed by a heartfelt salutation from Stellanova. As the minutes ticked by, comm from Tåsan's friends streamed in and he tried to respond to each of them in turn. An hour ticked by and then another and still there was no word from his father. Amans Sulac had not acknowledged his son's very big, very significant achievement.

• • •

Alone in his quarters, Tåsan was feeling pretty good about the day's activities and his accomplishments. He was glad that bridge duty was recorded because it provided a record that corroborated his Commander's Log.

Then it started. It always started. The doubts and second-guessing that crept in whenever Tåsan was feeling good about something in particular or things in general.

Should he have consulted higher ranking, more experienced personnel before making the decision?

Could he have done something differently to produce a better outcome?

Would he be viewed as reckless or worse, inept?

In the past such thoughts had served to put Tåsan's ego in check. He felt that if he rode too high, he would fall too far and strove to avoid an overinflated sense of self. So why, after many years of self-discipline did he continue to tear away at his pride?

"I'm so tired of this. It's the same old thing again and again," Tåsan

thought. Then like the decisive drop of the other shoe, it hit him.

"Father." Tåsan could feel the disgust well up in his chest at the mere mention of that word. He shook his head slowly once and then again, his thoughts slowed to a crawl as he remembered back to his childhood…

Tåsan had studied for a school test he was to take the following day. He reread the lesson. Twice. He worked the problems until late in the evening. In the classroom, the next day, he concentrated and answered all the questions with confidence. He submitted the test, receiving the scored result within minutes. He had missed one answer. This threw Tåsan into confusion, he could not understand how he could have gotten one wrong and was hurt when he found that he knew the answer, it was just a transcription error.

That evening when he presented the test score to his father, Amans looked up from the e-pad screen and stared at Tåsan without speaking for what seemed an eternity. Tåsan was uncomfortable under Amans' gaze.

"'You should have done better,' was all he said," remembered Tåsan.

He sat, now angry, wrestling with the memory thinking that he should have said something. He should have defended himself.

And there it was…again.

• • •

After the excitement and celebration of The Vellosian Encounter, the remaining days of Quad Five wound down in a series of routines and mechanical habits, until all of a sudden, *The Garnet Star* was back in berth at Brenton Kae with IGC maintenance assuming control and all the trainees queued up for transport ships that would return them to Firmus Opulentia, back on Naiad Five.

Tåsan was a little melancholy over having to leave *The Garnet Star*. He felt as if he had found a home on the ship, a real purpose, his "calling" if you will, and leaving seemed as if it was being taken away from him. Tåsan dealt with these feelings by promising himself that he would command a ship such as *The Garnet Star* in the near future and that he would do whatever it took to make that future a reality.

The trainees had one day back at the academy to prepare for the quad break. Tåsan stashed his travel cases in his quarters,

142

checked his e-pad for messages, and thought to sit in the shaded landscape across from his building to breathe the fresh air. He sat, viewing the bustle of the other trainees as they scurried about their duties and preparations and thought to comm Darrian, Castell, Alyss, and Tao and ask them to join him.

Twenty minutes later, the small group of friends sat together in the shade of the large Methusel tree talking about their plans for the quad break.

"Oh," lamented Castell, "I'm not looking forward to the shuttle ride home, but I'll be happy to see my family. I haven't been home for three quads."

Alyss asked, "Will you do anything special while you're home?"

"No, not really," replied Castell, "But I do have some wonderful stories about surviving snarling Muroidea and if I time them just right, I will be able to entertain my parents for days."

Tåsan said, "I don't envy your ride home, it makes me thankful that I'm already here. I am so ready for pulse rocket rides and my mother's parsit stew!"

"I catch my shuttle at first light and should be home within a half day. Not too difficult of a ride," said Alyss. "I may spend the time reviewing my Quad Six class materials."

Darrian had been stretched out on the thick mat of grasses that thrived in the shade of the tree, seemingly asleep. "My break is scheduled from the moment I arrive home until the moment of my return."

"Anything interesting?" asked Alyss.

"Yes, as a matter of fact, I'm attending a four-day seminar on Advanced Neurobiotic Interface Techniques as Applied to Memetics and Transcranial Stimuli. I'm very excited about this."

There was a long moment of silence, awkwardly noticed by Darrian, who then sat up to look at his friends. Noticing the blank looks on their faces, he shyly said, "Too much information, right?"

The small group laughed and Tao tossed a small pebble, teasing Darrian and making him flinch a bit. Smiling, Darrian tossed it back, asking, "How about you, Tao?"

"Oh, it's too far to travel to my home. I'll see my family after graduation. For this break I'm staying with friends and cousins, or some such connection of family, on Sador. Sador and Naiad Five will be in alignment so the trip out and back will be mercifully short." Then added, "Nothing planned but I suspect mischief will spontaneously occur, knowing my cousins as I do."

The group fell quiet. For a short while, all that could be heard was the muffled far-away sounds of the academy and the slight rustle of a wind across the top of the shade tree.

Tåsan spoke, "Friends, I don't know how the final quads will be able to top the last two," then stood up.

Alyss, Castell, Tao, and Darrian followed suit. Soon the friends were in a loose circle facing each other.

"Make the break count," said Tåsan, "I expect good stories from each of you and will strive to add to the pending revelry, myself." Tåsan extended his hand, palm down, to the center of the group and Alyss did the same, placing her hand on top of Tåsan's. With understanding, the others did the same.

"Friends...together," said Tåsan as he swung his arm upward.

"Friends, together," echoed his companions.

Five
Seeds of Darkness

Tåsan took his time riding home. He was in no real hurry, everyone would be working or away and he would be going to an empty house. Not the best of homecomings.

He made a detour out onto the Cirrian Flats and smiled with pleasure as he rode over the rough stony surface. He rode to the top of the Phyllite Cliffs and shut down his racer. The view from the cliffs was really quite grand. Merula sprawled out in the distance, its clean lines and pleasing shapes drawn across the skyline. From here, Tåsan could make out the tallest of the trees and clumps of park greenery and he could guess at the location of the Sulac residence as well as make out the spires of the university. The familiarity of the scene was comforting.

Tåsan sat down with his back against a rock, still warm from the sun. He relaxed and leaned back and let the sun warm his face. Taking a deep breath in and letting it slowly out, Tåsan's thoughts drifted along. First he thought, with amazement, at the number of new craft he had flown and commanded, then fragmented memories of Thanda Meriki crowded past. Finally, Tåsan took a moment to appreciate his IGC friends and found he had developed a real fondness for them as well as a deep respect for their talents and technical skills. He took pride in the knowledge that he was friends with and equal to persons who excelled in their fields.

Then a dark thought intruded on his reflections. There had been no comm from his father. Neither for the Quad Four commendation medal, which he was actually present for, nor the truly prestigious Admiral's Citation medal for the now famous Vellosian Encounter. If anything were to move Amans Sulac to tap out a comm, even a terse, straight-to-the-point, no-adjectives-

145

necessary comm (the words jolted through Tåsan's mind), it would have been the Vellosians, for crying out loud!

Tåsan scowled at the thought and felt an anger start to rise. With a half-thought, he picked up a dirt clod and wrapped his fist around it and squeezed it until it burst into dry soil and fell from his hand. Tåsan sat staring at his dusty fingers. *"I will not slip back into my childhood desire to please father. If he will not recognize my successes, then to him, neither will I."* A strange sort of calm came over Tåsan as he rubbed the fine soil from his hand and brushed it from his pants. *"Father's approval may never come. I may never be an equal in his eyes but by the fates, and in spite of him, I will thrive and I will succeed."*

With his anger pushed aside and his mind set, Tåsan got up, brushed again at his clothes, took one last look at the vista, and strode to his racer.

• • •

Tåsan's visit home had its share of downtime as his family were all busy with work and Stellanova was, as usual, busy with classes and course requirements. Dinner was usually rushed as family members dashed in late, grabbed a fast bite, and rushed away again.

On Tåsan's third night home, Stellanova took an extra handful of minutes to sit with him over a cup of tea.

"It's so wonderful to have you home for a few days, I've missed you," she said.

"I've missed you, too. There's so much for us to catch up on, so let me start…how's university treating you?"

"Very well. I only have to finish this solar year and next and I'm done. Maybe sooner if I ply my schedule with more classes. Can you believe that? I almost can't imagine life without coursework."

"Studies getting harder?"

"Not so much harder than more time consuming. Work is more complex so takes more time," thought Stellanova. "How about you, Tåsan, collect any more medals?" Stellanova tilted her head and tried not to laugh as she gave Tåsan an innocent look.

Tåsan laughed, "They missed giving me the 'I Rule' medal but they're probably saving it for next quad…to spread the wealth out,

146

not to spoil me too much." Tåsan idly turned his mug in circles, smiling, then asked, "What are you doing for fun these days?"

Stellanova was quick to answer, "Oh, I've met a boy. Tezzo Maluki. We've dated a couple of times and we have fun together. He's taking me to a party tomorrow night. His dad owns a cabin down by the lake. We're going to meet friends there. I think it's someone's birthday."

Tåsan cocked an eyebrow and said, "Soooo…you've met a boy, eh?"

Stella blushed and laughed lightly at the embarrassment of it. "Yes, and he's nice."

Tåsan patted her hand, "As long as he's nice."

They fell silent, not really thinking too much of anything when Stella yawned. Looking a little surprised, she said, "I'm sorry Tåsan, but I'm going to have to go study. I have a mid-term tomorrow and a paper due in the afternoon. Let's catch up this weekend!" and reaching for their mugs, stood up and went to the kitchen.

Tåsan followed. "This weekend would be good. I'll say good night, then. Good study!" and he hugged Stellanova and kissed her forehead before she trundled up the stairs and was gone.

• • •

The next afternoon, Tåsan was relaxing with a cold frosty, reading a local dispatch that had popped to his e-dev, a short missive about a new levy that was being considered, when Stellanova burst through the front door full of excitement and in a rush. The energy of her sudden appearance caused Tåsan to put down his reading and see what was up. He found her in the front entry trying to divest herself of course books and shopping bags, her face flushed with anticipation.

"What's the hurry?" asked Tåsan. "Why all the commotion?"

"Oh, hello!" said Stellanova, a little out of breath, "My date will be here in half an hour, I have to rush to get ready."

"Did you bring me a present?" asked Tåsan, trying to sneak a peek into one of the bags.

"Nope. I've got a new outfit to wear tonight, and I've got to get moving, Tezzo will be here any minute!" Stella scooped up the bags and in a blur, was gone.

147

Tåsan smiled at her quick departure. *"Was I ever that excited for a date at her age?"* he asked himself, then answered, *"Nope. It has to be a 'girl thing'."*

A little past the hour, Tåsan's reading was interrupted again by a rumbling out front that got louder as it approached. *"Sounds like a clumsily modified Hopper; the plasma burner vents are missing, and the fuel ports are too big."*

The noise grew louder.

Thrumble rumble rumble rumble... thrumble rumble rumble rumble rumble...

Just then Stellanova burst from her room and danced down the stairs, calling out, "Mother! I'm leaving now!"

Rebetta's voice echoed from the back of the house, "Ok, have fun but don't be too late!"

"Ok, mother, good night!" Stellanova replied and stopped to grab a coat before charging to the door.

Tåsan managed to call out, "See you later," before Stellanova was out the door. He stepped to the window just in time to see Stella hop into the front compartment of a sleek, shiny black, two-seater Nebula 80E, its Avabird wing-like door slowly closing, and the thundering twin engines roaring to a higher v-charge. Two seconds later the Nebula had raced down the way and was gone.

• • •

The evening was rather slow. After a light meal, Amans and Tåsan played a round of Parudi Rule and sipped a rather vintage distillation called Valunde. It was from Metamere, one of the planets in the Rayten Galaxy.

"This is favorably smooth, father," said Tåsan after a tiny sip of the amber liquid. "Thank you."

"You're welcome," said Amans. "It's a gift from the Ards Colrane Distillery, a new member recently joined to the ISA. They sent several casks as a thank you."

"A very nice fringe benefit," said Tåsan, smiling.

Amans looked steadily at Tåsan for a long moment. Long enough for Tåsan to notice and for a thought to zip past, *"Is he about to lecture me...again?"* But Amans did not respond, much to Tåsan's relief. He was in no mood to be chided for an innocent comment.

Soon enough, the hour became late and Amans and Tåsan retired.

Tåsan lay on his bed in the dark until he drifted off to sleep but awoke to quiet steps on the stairs and the hushed closing of a door down the hallway.

"Oh, Stella's home." Tåsan glanced at his e-pad and noted how late it was but didn't muse over it too long. He remembered his own university days with humor and understanding, rolled over, and went back to sleep.

• • •

The next morning, Stellanova missed the morning meal but did make an appearance for the mid-noon meal. She looked rather pale and nervous, avoiding eye contact and conversation.

"Honey, you don't look so good," said Rebetta. "Are you feeling unwell?"

"I'm fine, mother. Just out too late and maybe the food did not settle well with me," said Stellanova. "Maybe I'll stay in for now and rest a bit."

"Yes, I'll bring some tea up later," said Rebetta, "You go rest. Take care of yourself."

"Ok, thank you, mother." Stella got up from the table, avoiding Tåsan and went up to her room.

Tåsan looked at his mother, concern furrowing his brow. "Do you think it was the food? She looked anxious."

"I'm sure she'll be fine. Probably ate something disagreeable, that's all," Rebetta offered. "She'll be fine."

Tåsan wasn't so sure. After helping clear the meal dishes, he went up to Stella's room. He hesitated before knocking, listening for sounds that might tell him what Stella was up to. No sound escaped through the door. Tåsan knocked.

"Yes?" Stella's soft voice acknowledged the tapping.

Tåsan entered and closed the door softly after him. Stella was curled up on her bed holding a stuffed doll to her breast. She looked as if she had been crying.

Tåsan moved her desk chair to the bedside and sat down, looking at his little sister. "It wasn't the food, was it?"

Tears threatened to well up in Stellanova's eyes. "No, but don't tell mother or father!" she quickly added.

149

Tåsan asked, "Don't tell them what, Stella?"

"Oh, Tåsan," cried Stella in anguish, covering her eyes and sobbing into the doll.

"What, Stella? Tell me what's wrong," leveled Tåsan trying to sound serious but not cross.

Stellanova's sobs began to soften and her breathing became more regular. Eventually she took her hands from her face and looked at Tåsan.

"Last night at the party, Tezzo handed me an ale. I told him I didn't want one. I wanted to dance first. He insisted, saying that I wasn't going to be any fun, that maybe he should have brought another girl instead of me. To show him I could be a fun girl, I drank the ale but then started to feel dizzy." Stella wiped her nose, then pleaded, "Please, please don't tell mother, Tåsan! Promise!"

Tåsan said, "I promise, Stell," and prompted her to continue.

"Everything seemed hypnotic and out of focus. I began to get scared so I started for the washroom but was so dizzy that Tezzo had to steady me but instead of helping me to the washroom, he guided me outside saying the night air would help. *(sniff)* I don't know what happened next but all of a sudden, I was laying on a pile of blankets and Tezzo was on top of me, his hands pawing at me, his face centimeters from mine, the smell of him in my nostrils."

Tåsan sat motionless. Stella could see the anger behind his eyes.

"Please, Tåsan," Stella said, looking at her brother.

He shot his hand up to stop her next thought and said, "Then what happened?"

"I pleaded with him to let me up and struggled against him. I screamed, 'No Tezzo, let me go!' Tezzo knocked me back down, back onto the blanket pile and put his hand over my mouth saying 'What's the matter, Stellanova, aren't I good enough for you?' and laughing at me. I couldn't breathe! I thought I was going to die, Tåsan!"

Tåsan could feel his muscles tighten all along his spine and could feel that his jaw was clamped down hard. "Then what happened?"

"My friends Jyn Iso and Fredah Chion had been looking for me

150

when they heard me yelling from the back shed and pushed in the door. They punched and kicked Tezzo to get him off of me and took me out of there and put me in their cruiser. Jyn said I was acting like I had been poisoned with some sort of pharma. They stayed with me until I recovered enough to bring me home. *(sniff)* It was very late. I hope they didn't get into trouble over it."

Stellanova dabbed at her eyes and wiped her nose and then dared to look at Tåsan. He had quietly listened to everything Stella had said, taking mental note of all the names.

"But you're alright now," said Tåsan.

"Yes, thanks to Jyn and Fredah."

"You need to get yourself together. Mother thinks you ate something that has upset your stomach. Just keep with that and don't worry, you're fine, nothing happened," soothed Tåsan. He rose from the chair and moved it back to the desk. "I'll see you at dinner. And Stell?"

"Yes?"

"Don't worry, everything will be fine."

• • •

Tåsan left the house after dinner, saying he was going to meet friends down at The Game of Twenty public house out on Kranon. When in fact, Tåsan had found the contact information for Jyn Iso and had made queries about Tezzo Maluki. What could she tell him...not much. Where did he live...didn't know. Where did he hang out...at The Game of Twenty, out on Kranon.

Tåsan was sitting at the bar, periodically taking a sip from the Cirrus Ale he had ordered over an hour ago. It had gone warm but he barely noticed. Instead, Tåsan was focused on the front door. Jyn Iso had given a vague description of Tezzo Maluki...tall, well built, dressed nice. Could be anyone. Tåsan knew it would be difficult but he couldn't stand by and do nothing. The look on Stella's face as she told her story. So much anguish, so much pain, so much humiliation. Tåsan steeled his resolve and took another sip of warm ale just as the front door swung open and lighthearted greetings went up amid a small group at the far end of the bar.

"Hey Tezzo! Finally made it!"

Tåsan took it in. Tezzo Maluki raised a hand to his friends and called out, "Hello!" and joined them, laughing and slapping one's back, nodding and giving a half-hug to another. Very jocular.

Tåsan watched.

Tezzo was offered a drink but turned it down with a smile and a few words that made his friends toss back their heads in laughter.

And Tåsan watched.

After a few minutes of chatter, Tezzo made to leave. He gave a rowdy farewell and smiling broadly, stepped to the door and was out.

Tåsan had tossed a few tenges on the bar and was three steps behind. He caught the door as it reached its jamb and pushed it open. A quick glance about the lot and there was Tezzo, walking to the fast, loud, shiny, black Nebula, its running lights already ablaze in the night.

"Hey, Tezzo!" Tåsan called out in a good approximation of a friendly voice.

Tezzo stopped mid-step and spun to greet who it was that had just called his name, his broad smile and expectant look slowly fading as he came to realize that he did not recognize the man striding toward him.

Tåsan did not slow his step as he closed the distance between them. Tezzo started to flinch away as he realized that the stranger was not going to stop but Tåsan quickened his pace so that he caught Tezzo by the front of his jacket before he managed to turn away. The force with which Tåsan overpowered Tezzo took him off balance. The two men moved quickly…Tåsan pushing forward and Tezzo skidding as he tried to balance his steps as he was pushed backwards.

Through clenched teeth Tåsan hissed, "I'm Stellanova Sulac's brother."

Tezzo's eyes widened in fright just as he stumbled backward and fell onto his back. Tåsan quickly straddled his chest, pinning Tezzo's arms at his sides.

Tåsan had a hank of Tezzo's hair knotted in his grip and pulled Tezzo's head up as he said, "How do *you* like being powerless?" Tezzo started to answer, fright dripping from his voice but before the words could leave his mouth, Tåsan hit him square in the face, drawing blood from his nose and splitting his lip.

"If you ever, *EVER!* bother Stellanova again, I will find you, and if you ever, *EVER!*" shaking Tezzo's head by the knotted wad of hair coiled around Tåsan's fingers, "speak of last night or this night to anyone," Tåsan punched Tezzo again, widening the split in his lip and causing Tezzo to cough on his bile. "I...will...find...you." Breathing in short hot breaths, Tåsan loosed his grip on Tezzo's hair as he dropped his head, hearing it thump on the hard ground. "Is that understood?" menaced Tåsan.

"Yes," whimpered Tezzo, blood spattering across his face.

Tåsan got up off of Tezzo and stood looking down at the pathetic excuse for a male, controlling an overwhelming desire to drive his boot into Tezzo's side. "Good."

Tåsan started to walk away but stopped. His anger was a red-hot fire in his brain, he had his teeth clenched tightly together and felt like a wildman. He turned.

Tezzo was holding his head in his hands and had managed, in his agony, to roll to one side and pull his knees up in an effort to stand.

Tåsan walked back to the prone body and with all his might, drove his boot into Tezzo's ribs, hearing to his satisfaction a *crack* followed by a low wailing sound escaping from Tezzo's bloody mouth.

• • •

Later that night, Tåsan knocked on Stellanova's bedroom door and smiled when she opened it.

"Stell, I wanted to tell you that everything is fine. You don't have to worry about Tezzo Maluki any longer."

Stellanova started to say something but Tåsan hushed her. "We'll talk another time. Rest. Relax. Everything is fine."

• • •

For the remainder of the break Tåsan fully expected some sort of blowback regarding that night at The Game of Twenty pub house. Pleasantly, there was none. He did not speak to Stella about what happened and after she saw his bruised and nicked knuckles, she avoided the subject of Tezzo Maluki altogether.

Tåsan rode back to Firmus Opulentia with a clear and open mind.

Six
Steady On

Quad Six promised to be interesting. Tåsan's course in Fighter Craft Design allowed each trainee to work with two other trainees on a project that would be due one week before quad completion. Immediately, Tåsan teamed with Castell and Alyss before anyone else scooped them up. His other required courses were the ever-present Physical Training and a leadership course that focused on Tactical Decisions, Search and Rescue, and Emergency Procedures. Tåsan was looking forward to the design study with excitement and a heightened sense of confidence.

As the quad wore on, the Fighter Craft Design project was what truly held Tåsan's interest. While the academics of leadership was a necessary subject, it lacked creativity and contained a lot of class lectures and written essay assignments. And what can be said of boot camp? It was boot camp.

But Fighter Craft Design. Now that project was worth losing sleep over.

...

"We've finalized most of our requirements, the high level ones at least," said Tåsan.

Alyss agreed, "We have our concept drawing but we should start compiling the main schematic before we find we're pushed for time."

"Okay, then we'll need to talk about each requirement," said Castell, "and the build process so that we put together our final paper in that order."

Alyss looked through her notes and spoke, "I've started on our proposal and will hit on a long list of descriptors such as agile, fast, stealthy, efficient, durable, long-distance, pretty…"

"And aggressive," interjected Tåsan.

"And using the appropriate amount of aureation," said Alyss. "After all, it's a proposal. We have to assume the point of which is to sell our ideas and designs."

"So," Castell asked, "we should address this to the IGC, to reach further than the classroom?"

"We can use the IGC as the target audience," said Tåsan, "but, honestly, we should look even further than them." Tåsan looked from Alyss to Castell and back, then added, "Without being too mercenary, of course."

Castell sat quietly, eyes downward, a slight smile moving across his face, clearly having a moment of introspection.

Alyss flashed a wide grin at Tåsan and nodded in agreement.

"Alyss, your descriptor list could be used as section headers, just over a nice piece of concept art before we launch into the related technology," offered Castell.

"Good idea, each section could show a different ship design, to highlight the flexibility of our ideas. Broaden its appeal to as many buyers as possible," said Tåsan.

"Absolutely," said Alyss.

Castell crunkled through a few papers but not finding what he was looking for tapped his e-dev awake and busied his fingers. "Ah, here it is. I've put it in a file." Scanning down an entry or two, his eyes steadied out as his voice summarized, "The Fighter should have no more than three crew: a pilot/navigator, weapons/tactical, and a control. I see this as flexible, that one person could do all the functions, or two could manage just fine, but three is ideal, especially in difficult situations." And thumbing past a few more pages of data, added, "I've drawn a rough diagram of how I see this working," and tipping his e-dev toward Tåsan, who took it and looked at the picture displayed there.

Castell's drawing had the pilot center with weapons and control side-by-side just behind, making the seating configuration compact. All the controls were located appropriately but could be reconfigured to the number of bodies present. Very flexible,

Tåsan had handed the e-dev to Alyss who was studying it very closely. "I've been working on a canopy design that would fit well with what you've got," Tåsan said. "It's soundproof so comm can be clear and exact, but what I've spent most of my time on is the capability of this canopy to display dimensional images. I've created three options. No images, just a view of real space in any direction. A combination of dimensional images layered with real images, to fill in details. And full-on dimensional imaging of the immediate surroundings, a flight course from one point to another, some other scene altogether, or any such visuals as desired."

"Flying blind but not really," said Alyss.

"Exactly."

Alyss handed Castell his e-dev, "Impressive work." She sat back to unwind her legs, then said, "Two requirements have occupied my thoughts. The first concerns pilot controls. I've been working on a system that produces hyper-responsiveness to pilot commands. I think I can integrate touch sensitive receptors to the hand-helds that will quickly...hyper quickly...and accurately interpret a range of data and put the craft to it. I've layered voice-activation into it, if that function is desired. It's borderline intuition, I envision it to be that fast and exact." She handed a schematic to Tåsan.

Tåsan said, "I can't wait to fly this machine. This is going to be an easy sell."

"My other idea, and I want to bring it up for your thoughts and a near-future discussion, is this: the power supply should be modeled after Major O'hAirt's. A small, powerful, nearly infinite, electrical source." Alyss quickly added, "I know that Major O'hAirt's power supply is super secret, high level, classified technology, but I believe we can approximate it, or propose it like we know what we're doing."

Alyss smiled at the guys, watching their faces reflect their thoughts.

Castell said, "Very thought provoking. Yes. I'm already looking forward to that discussion."

The team fell quiet. Tåsan was reviewing his notes and work and trying to make sure he had covered all his subjects and Alyss was sitting, looking off into nowhere in particular, tapping her e-dev stylus on her chin, apparently working on a technical point and lost in thought.

Castell said, "I've thought about the flight suits. Well," he hesitated, "enough to have a partial list of req's."

Tåsan and Alyss turned their attention to Castell and he continued, "It should have advanced physio-monitors that also regulate body chemical requirements to keep the occupant's physical condition at optimum performance...for short, controlled periods. Completely programmable. It should morph to zero-grav and zero O2 conditions immediately, protecting the occupant and alleviating the need for user control. It should be super light, advanced material with automatic helmet/gloves/boots that activate when conditions dictate or via user control, and lastly," added Castell, "communication is built in." He looked at Tåsan and then at Alyss. "It goes without saying."

"Fascinating," said Alyss. "I've just thought of two more things. It should carry concentrated food/liquid tabs...for those long moments of free-floating in space, and total comp capability, independent of the ship."

Castell made a note, "Perfect."

"We've made a huge start," said Tåsan. "Let's say we take two weeks to detail our ideas and to create the associated schema and begin to build the sections that will be included in our final."

Castell added, "I'll talk with Darrian about the physical aspects of the suit, get his ideas on miniaturization and so forth."

"We should also come back with a list of lesser ranked requirements," said Alyss. "We've got the big pieces but need the supporting pieces to make it real."

The trio agreed to meet in two weeks at the public green next to the academy café where they could work and relax with few distractions or interruptions.

• • •

"This was a good idea," said Alyss. "The day is perfect, not too hot, very comfortable."

Tåsan proffered a box and smiling said, "I took the liberty of bringing food and drink. Nothing too fancy," hiking the box up onto his shoulder, adding, "Where do we want to camp out?"

Castell waved an arm, "How about that table over there? Shade and quiet."

After the team had set up and settled down they got to business, each as eager as the other to progress their project.

157

Tåsan started, "This meeting should be the last formal meeting we plan to hold after today. We need to work on the final paper in order to submit our thesis on time."

Alyss said, "I've actually finished two of my entries and have posted them to a folder on my e-dev: APFL, start-code protected, so use SfF2+gO. Files are text with pic enabled formatted. And..." Alyss held up until both men looked up at her, "...tell me what you think!"

"Right!"

Castell said, "Along those lines, I spoke with my sister last night, told her about our paper and she got quite excited about doing the conceptual drawings for us. She's an accomplished artist, you know, currently between inspirations, and she sparked to the idea right away. I gave her a false deadline of three weeks thinking to scare her off, more or less."

"Did that work?" asked Tåsan.

"No. Quite the opposite, really," replied Castell. "She's sure she can do it with little or no problem, doesn't want remuneration, and sent this," tilting his e-dev, "early this morning."

Tåsan shared the screen with Alyss and after she got a good look, declared, "Your sister is brilliant!"

The screen was filled with a stylus and pixel drawing of a sleek, shiny rocket with contrasting metal fixtures, dynamic features, swept back airfoils, and artistic markings all along the body that made the entire craft look amazingly realistic.

"She says she can come up with a number of various craft types and looks and their possible accoutrements. All we have to do is list 'em for her," said Castell.

Alyss asked, "Would it be okay if I spoke with her? I have several ideas, myself."

"Absolutely. I'll send you her contact info." Castell looked to both Alyss and Tåsan, "So, she's in?"

"Yes."

"Definitely."

Tåsan said, "How about this. The craft is manufactured of self-healing space-frame alloys that can withstand up to 7.825E forces with very little interference to flight stability."

Castell asked, "Is that a real thing?"

158

"Yes. Sort of," said Tåsan. "There's a metal mining company out in the Ultimet Adob here on Naiad Five that has been experimenting on the tentu strength of alnico. Long story. But, I'm sure a query from a curious student might yield a general statement or an overview, nothing that would give away trade secrets."

"Also, the craft must have short- and long-range capabilities," said Castell. "No need to always be up close and personal."

Alyss added, "Easily upgradable. Main purpose is air and space but I propose an easy conversion to short-term underaqua as I see that capability being a desirable upgrade."

"I've come up with a pitch," Tåsan said with a smile, "and it's this. Cost is irrelevant...because 'This Is What You Need'. The startup number of Shadow Fast Fighters is set at fifteen. Some months in, and per contract, an additional fifteen will be shipped, with upgrades and replacements at regular intervals thereafter."

"And maintenance, don't forget to mention maintenance and our knowledgeable team of experts," said Alyss.

Castell was smiling with humor and a smattering of credible disbelief but nevertheless, added, "Swear all the buyers to top secret secrets. This new technology stays the intellectual property of the IGC until we say otherwise."

• • •

The final thesis titled, "Shadow Fast Fighter Craft, A Proposal, A Design, and Beyond by T. Sulac, A Brannick, and C. Brann," was submitted a little before the deadline and to the complete satisfaction of the authors, who immediately resumed study on their other Quad Six courses.

The quad was winding up and the IGC academics instructor had compiled a long list of subjects he was sure to include on the course final...*in three weeks.*

There was very little time for socialization and this seemed also true for the entire academy. Everywhere one looked, trainees sat alone or in small study groups with heads bowed to their e-dev's or scribbling notes into databases. The pressure was on.

• • •

And now it was done.

Tåsan had sat for four hours taking the final exam for Admin

159

Part I of IGC Academics. The questions on Tactical Decisions were lacking in finesse, or so it seemed to Tåsan, but he answered in the way of the classroom. Answers for the Search and Rescue portion of the test as well as the Emergency Procedures part contained equal parts intuition and process due to the everchanging definition of the word: emergency.

Overall, Tåsan felt he had done well and had no doubts as he dropped his completed test file into the instructor's Quad Six folder and emerged outside the hall into the bright, warm noon.

Tåsan had barely taken a dozen steps when his e-dev chimed. It was Alyss. Could he meet her under the Methusel tree in ten?

• • •

"How do you think you did on ol' Ginty's final?" asked Alyss.

"Pretty well. I'm confident that I side stepped one or two of his tricky questions on tactical," answered Tåsan.

Alyss said, "Apparently those are called 'silent bombs'. You're sure of your position right up until you receive your course grading, then you're sure that you don't."

Alyss' e-pad chimed and she looked at its screen. "It's a notification about my Quad Seven schedule," and tapped the read icon.

Tåsan flipped his chiming e-dev open and said, "Mine, too."

"Oh look, I'm in Raiook's Negotiations, Law Enforcement, and Administrative course," said Alyss.

"Which time?" asked Tåsan.

"Early, first AM timeslot."

"Hey! So am I!" said Tåsan. "Maybe we can team up or at least study together."

Alyss smiled and nodded.

"I'm not going home on this break. We only have two more quads to finish and we're out. Graduated. I'm going to use the time to review. I hear that the academy exams are tougher than…well, tougher than a Spiny Muroidea intent on stealing a rucksack," said Tåsan, giving Alyss a sly smile and waiting for her reaction, which quickly came.

"Oh," she exclaimed, unconsciously touching her arm, "Then we had better use caution and carry weapons!" Adding to the conversation, "Many of the instructors are offering short-course lectures designed to refamiliarize trainees with, I guess, course highlights. I'm interested in the simulation brush-ups that are scheduled for two days only."

"Those are the thirty-minute fast runs, aren't they?" asked Tåsan.

"I believe so."

"Maybe we'll meet along the way."

"Or I'll see you Quad Seven day one!"

• • •

Which came fast enough.

Tåsan was glad that his Admin Part II class was first up on his schedule. His only other course for this quad was Physical Training that started exactly one hour after his morning class and ran for three and a half grueling hours.

Quad Eight was for testing, rigorous testing in all of the courses the IGC prescribed for trainees. Physical Training, a staple part of every quad, administered its final exam throughout Quad Seven. It was not for the faint.

Strength, flexibility, stamina, cardio endurance, and agility were tested with lift and carry, crawl and climb, long distance runs, weights, treads, and more runs.

There were eight par courses that when accessed in order, increased in level of difficulty by a denary factor of ten. Each trainee had three chances to complete each course to the prescribed time, failing that, reduced ones final grading.

At the end of each day, Tåsan was completely exhausted but rallied long enough to complete the daily workload from Raiook's Admin Part II course and cram in some refresher studies of the courses he had had many quads ago.

Weekends were spent in study but Tåsan made a point of connecting with friends and colleagues for meals and quick breaks to grab a tea or to take short walks to stretch out and limber up.

"It's important for morale," he would say, "to know that we're all in this together."

• • •

The break that followed Quad Seven was spent in study, more study, endless study, late nights, and early mornings. Eventually, everyone who was still on campus resembled sleep-deprived psy-

161

patients on an irreversible trek to an untenable position.

One quad to go.

~

Quad Eight was as exhausting as every IGC trainee had feared. Each final exam was a full four days long with the only aspect worthy of the slightest hint of joy being that there was only one course exam per week.

As the weeks marched on and more tests completed, time could be found for a slower pace of study and relaxation. Many of the trainees caught up on sleep. Tåsan chose to keep up his physical fitness routine.

On many of the non-exam days, Tåsan would go for long runs. His favorite circuit was an irregular ellipse around the Firmus Opulentia base. It was rough and rocky and gave a good workout. Tåsan took to taping his ankles for support after his first run out. He had lost his footing as he scrambled over loose rocks and almost tumbled into a briarberry shrub. As it was, he scratched his arms up pretty bad in an effort to keep from falling.

By week nine, Tåsan's schedule was relaxed enough that he found full days that could be his own.

"Alyss, grab your mag boots and a heavy jacket and meet me out front in a couple," Tåsan spoke into his vid comm.

Two minutes later, Alyss appeared at the doors of Res D and with a huge smile, hopped and jumped her way down the steps to the street. "What's all this?" she said barely containing her excitement.

"Today's the day I teach you to ride," smiled Tåsan.

He stood between two pulse rockets. One he had borrowed from a friend, the other was his.

"Which one is mine?"

"Take mine, the red one," said Tåsan, holding out a helmet to Alyss who popped it on her head with no hesitation and straddling the bike said, "This is fantastic!"

Tåsan pointed to the ignition, "Starter," then pointed again, "Throttle", and again, "Hydraulics and reverse power with an AI assist." Tåsan was very proud of his pulse rocket, every system tuned and modified, worthy of special note.

Alyss said, "Thanks!" She snapped the ignition on and held the hydraulics in check as she slowly twisted the throttle until the rocket increased its rads and sat screaming and trembling beneath her. She turned to Tåsan, smiled slyly at him and laughed at the look of confusion across his face. She called out, "See you!" as she sped away, headed for the main gateway.

Tåsan recovered from his moment of astonishment and shock and hurried to fire up the other racer and catch up with Alyss, who had cleared the gateway and was speeding eastward. It took five harrowing minutes to catch her.

"Well, well," said Tåsan through his vid comm, "I should have known you could ride. How did I not know that?"

Alyss laughed, "My first transport was a used, very unreliable Scoot 510. It broke down constantly so out of necessity I learned how to repair it. Finally I sold it for an ATR 3 and the rest is history." And jumping thoughts, "Where're we going?"

Tåsan answered, "Along the top of the Phyllite Cliffs. There's a remarkable view and a copse of Elder trees several milia out. Follow me." Tåsan sped away with Alyss close behind.

The ride was extraordinary. Tåsan and Alyss pushed the rockets to their limits as they raced along the flats, dodging spires of rock and hurtling over and around stone and rock outcrops. At one point, Alyss had moved ahead and Tåsan could see she was hugging the racer close as she tore through the landscape, seemingly unafraid. He could hear her through the vid comm making sounds of appreciation as she successfully maneuvered a tight spot and heard her suck in and hold her breath as the racer launched skyward to clear a particularly massive boulder, letting out an "Alright!" as she regained her terra track. She was probably the best pilot he had ever met. Tåsan knew that Alyss was something special.

The copse was shaded and cool and it was good to stop riding for a time to enjoy it.

Tåsan retrieved two water flasks from his pulse rocket's side storage and carried them to where Alyss had found a fairly comfortable spot. They sat in silence for a few moments, gazing around at the trees, wild grasses, and sage that made up a small island amid the dry and crackling scape that surrounded it.

In time, Tåsan spoke. "We're more than halfway through Quad

163

Eight. In just a few weeks we'll be fully-fledged IGC people. It's almost unbelievable."

"When I first started at the academy," said Alyss, "and tried to look ahead, down through the quads, I couldn't really see the end. All I really saw was two solar years of work and study and stress and study."

"You said 'study' twice," smiled Tåsan.

"I probably should have said it twenty times!" laughed Alyss.

"I know what you mean," said Tåsan. "It's been a long haul, for sure." And after a moments thought he added, "But I feel good about what I've accomplished. I feel ready for what's to come next."

"Well, first up is the grad ceremony, that is, after grades are posted. I'm looking forward to that. We could use a nice ceremony to mark the end of academy pain and the beginning of IGC life and career."

Tåsan said, "As tough as the past two solar years have been, there's been some saving times, ones that I'll remember fondly for a long time."

Alyss smiled at the thought, recalling her own memories. "I'll be forever grateful for making new friends," she smiled as she looked at Tåsan.

"Without saying," agreed Tåsan, "Along with our first command of a real ship, *Terebellum*. Now that was a sweet ride!"

"Loved putting it through its paces," agreed Alyss. "I was actually a little surprised we weren't disciplined after the way we flipped and sped our way across two vectors."

"I heard later that the auxiliary crew loved it!" said Tåsan. "Said it was the best time they had had in over six flights out."

Alyss said, "Yes, but was it better than the one week in the Thanda Meriki outback?"

"No!" exclaimed Tåsan, "Nothing will ever surpass that in terms of sheer terror and stress," he joked. "What I *will* take away from that experience though, is a deeper appreciation of my friends and the value of teamwork."

"What I liked the most about it all," said Alyss, "was coming to a deeper understanding of the team as individuals. Being able to observe, in detail, each person's skills and diverse approach to situations and problems."

Tåsan added, "And here's something else....there were no arguments among us. At *any time*. And there could have been. There were plenty of opportunities along the way. I think that's an awfully good 'tell' about us as a group."

Alyss thought about it for a while. "It *is* a good 'tell'," and added, "I trust that we will all team again after graduation. It would be a shame if that wasn't so."

Tåsan took another gulp of water and looked around although his thoughts were not far away. As he recapped the flask he said, "Let's ride on for a time. Several milia further on, there's a cut-through to the east that will take us over to the Ardent Preserve side. The view from up here is wholly spectacular. The soil is rich in pyrite and rudimentary carbon and under the bright light of day, it appears red but then as the wind changes, it shimmers yellow."

"I'd like that," said Alyss.

"There's another copse located to the south-east where we can stop. I've brought tea and fruitlets along with some sweetbreads."

"Sounds good," said Alyss, "Thank you."

Tåsan and Alyss readied themselves and rode on, this time slowly, to enjoy the ride and take in the experience.

~

The energy levels in Res A were ridiculously high as evidenced by a large number of trainees hollering out to friends and laughing uproariously up and down the hallways.

Final quality point averages and granted duty classifications were being posted to trainee e-dev's and one-by-one, trainees were whooping it up.

Tåsan was in his quarters, door open, organizing his travel cases. Often one trainee or another would poke his head in, shout greetings, and dance off into the amicable fray.

"Hello, Tåsan," said Castell as he helped himself in and started to sit down. "There's quite the commotion out there. Have you received your finals, yet?"

"No, not yet," answered Tåsan, "I expect so, any minute. You?"

Castell pulled his e-dev out from his hip pocket and twiddled a couple of icons then offered Tåsan a view. "Yes, and I'm very pleased, I've made Major! I'm now Major Castell Brann, Engineering." Castell stood back up smiling, his eyes bright with excitement. "You may shake my hand," he said in mock exaggeration.

Tåsan was delighted and clasped Castell's hand and thumped him on the back and said, "Good news! Good for you!" Just as Darrian rushed in the door, flushed with delight.

"I've made Major! Major!" he said a little out of breath. "Medical *and* surgical!"

The men all smiled and their happy voices mingled in their excitement when suddenly, Tåsan's e-dev chimed an incoming message. Everyone froze; Tåsan held his breath as he retrieved the device and read the screen.

The men waited. Tåsan looked up, almost unwilling to believe his eyes.

Darrian said, "Out with it, man, what's it say?"

"I've made...Commander."

"Oh, that is great!"

"It's what you've wanted!"

"Congratulations!"

Alyss burst in, "I've made First Lieutenant, Pilot!" She was so happy that she was bouncing on her feet, unable to stand still. "Pilot!" she cried out.

Darrian looked up from his e-dev, "Tao made Major Medical, too! He's waited for this...but not too patiently!"

• • •

The celebration continued well into the early evening with much of it now centered in the main study area in the center of the residence. Many graduates (they're no longer trainees), brought food and drink to share with the other residents. By this time, the noise and energy levels had wound down and Tåsan sat in the company of his friends, talking about their futures.

"I so want to be assigned to either a Battle Class-W or a Starchaser," said Alyss.

Nikliss Hywell had joined the group shortly after their arrival and hearing Alyss' statement, asked, "Why's that?"

"I think they maneuver with more agility than other Class-W's," she answered.

"Possibly, but the Stratos class, while larger and perhaps less agile, have speed and stamina on their side."

Tåsan joined in, "A Stratos class could easily be retro'ed to take on sortie attack fighters whereas the Star's lack the necessary space. But let's say space was found, by...I don't know...eliminating the recreations..."

Groans and oh-no's followed, clearly that was a bad suggestion.

Tåsan laughed then pressed his point, "...The Star's could not make up for it. Fuel efficiency and morale would decrease exponentially. The Star's would run out of fuel and their crews would riot. It's a simple process of physics and a lack of enthusiasm."

Alyss just smiled and shook her head, Nikliss became distracted by his e-dev, and Tåsan declared that he had won the discussion.

Darrian ventured, "I like having my final grade and my rank but not knowing my commission is really bothersome."

Alyss said, "I know what you mean. IGC protocol dictates that commissions are announced at the ceremony."

"Then I'll have to wait," said Darrian, "but it's bothersome."

"Speaking of ceremonies, are your parents attending?" asked Alyss

"No, too far to travel right now," Darrian answered. "Yours?"

"My father," she said, "and I can't wait to see him." Adding, "He's so proud of me, I should think he might pop!" She looked over at Tåsan and nodded as if to ask, "Yours?"

Tåsan offered, "My family will be here, well, not my father, he's busy with something. I want to introduce everyone to my mother and sibs. You will love Stellanova...just ask Castell!"

"She's full of energy," Castell said, smiling. "I enjoy her enthusiasm for just about everything."

As the hours ticked on, more and more graduates drifted away from the hall until finally, the friends realized how tired they were and how much work they still needed to do before the graduation ceremony took place...*the day after next.* Graduates were required to clear their quarters before attending the ceremony.

"I've too much packing to do," Nikliss said. "I must go. Will

167

see everyone later," and standing up, raised his hand in salutation.
"Good night."

Seven
Upward Lift

Cirrian Auditorium was a blaze of lights and a crush of activity as families arrived and graduates rushed about greeting friends and escorting visitors to the viewing balconies.

Tåsan had found a place on the steps outside the main entrance where he could watch for the arrival of his family. He had nervous flutters in his stomach and wished he hadn't drank that last cup of tea.

At last Rebetta, Arron, and Stellanova arrived at the drop-off space in front. The family's Hopper eased up to a stop and Stellanova burst from the door and started up the steps, her face bright and animated, her voice almost a song.

"Tåsan, Tåsan!" she called, waving excitedly. "Hello!"

Tåsan smiled and started down the steps to meet Stellanova half way and wrapped his arms around her in a hug. "Hello, little sib," he said.

"I am so happy for you," Stellanova spoke softly into his ear, "and proud." She leaned back to look into his face, "Are you happy, Tåsan? And excited for your future?"

"Yes, Stella, I think I am."

Rebetta and Arron joined the small family reunion moments later. When they reached Stellanova and Tåsan, Rebetta exclaimed, "Son, what a day this is for you. You've made your father and me so proud."

"Yes, Tåsan," said Arron, "Good work, in the top of your class no less, and an Admiral's Medal. Who knew?" he joked, clasping Tåsan's hand in greeting.

They laughed and jostled each other and Tåsan said, "Well, Arron, it was the only way I could top all of your

169

accomplishments. I had to do it!"

Grinning, Tåsan took Rebetta's hand and wrapped it in the crook of his arm. "Let me show you to your seats. The ceremony will probably start in about twenty minutes." And he led them through the main doors.

• • •

Tåsan stayed with his family for a brief moment but as the auditorium started to fill up, he felt that he needed to gain his position on the main floor before it was too late.

Sitting between Alyss and Darrian, with Castell next to Alyss, Tåsan was feeling pretty good. He looked smart in his dress uniform and polished boots. He almost hadn't recognized himself after putting his jacket on. The ornate medals that shone from his chest looked so surreal to him, he had had to take a closer look.

The friends sat quietly, nervously waiting to hear about their futures. Slowly the auditorium calmed and conversation hushed in anticipation. A brief instant later, Major Sedwik took the stage.

"Officers, graduates, visitors, and IGC attendees, welcome. I am Major Alide Sedwik and I am the officer in charge of IGC Academy Internal Affairs." Major Sedwik paused as he looked across the auditorium, a faint smile playing across his lips. When the faint applause died away, he continued.

"Today's Inter-Galaxy Command is built on a strong foundation that began some 2743.89 solar years ago. The organization is older than the formal establishment of Merula, itself. But just as Merula has grown from the wild and unkempt small town that it was into the shining example of modernistic society it is today, so has the Inter-Galaxy Command grown from the original vision held by our founder, A. J. Padue, and his few like-minded associates, that is to say, from the crude beginnings of wild justice to the refined, burnished, disciplined, and highly respected organization that it is today.

"The IGC has well over 400,000 officers, technicians, and specialists who work together to keep IGC agile and influential and we're looking forward to adding this graduating class to its numbers.

"The IGC takes responsibility for the safety and security of its member citizens very seriously. That goal is reflected in the rigorous training of our officers and the fast, efficient, cutting-edge standards we strive to uphold.

"The graduating class of 31822.14 have exceeded IGC expectations. We set before them hard work, an in-depth education, peak physical performance requirements, and an unerring appetite for improvement of self and the Inter-Galaxy Command, and they have delivered by breaking long-standing endurance records and by raising the graduating point averages to new heights...which will be much to the dismay of future incoming recruits."

A smattering of laughter made Sedwik pause and look up from his notes.

Continuing, "Noteworthy accomplishments, all. But one particular incident stands out among them: The Vellosian Encounter."

Alyss nudged Tåsan's leg with her knee to communicate her growing excitement and to punctuate Sedwik's mention of the Vellosians. She sat, eyes wide and smile bright as Sedwik continued.

"For those of you unaware, the Vellosians arrived out of deep space and were first encountered by *The Garnet Star* and more specifically, by the Aleph crew who were on duty at the time. (Alyss knocked Tåsan's leg again) To make a long story short but not to diminish the importance of such an encounter, Inter-Galaxy Command has secured trading rights with the Vellosians and have accepted them as the newest members of the Intersolar and Space Alliance."

Here a great wave of applause and approving cheers went up throughout the auditorium and Major Sedwik stood proudly as he waited patiently for the noise to subside before he went on.

"I can't tell you all of what that means but will venture this: great things lay ahead for the IGC. (applause) After careful consideration, it has been decided that Aleph crew should continue into their first commission, together (Alyss knocked Tåsan's leg again but this time, Tåsan pushed back, sharing her excitement), under the mastery of Commander Tåsan Sulac."

The auditorium burst into whoops and whistles and those nearest Tåsan clapped him on the back and reached to shake hands. Tåsan was absolutely floored!

Major Sedwik could scarcely be heard above the noise calling for everyone to settle down and come to order. When the room had quieted again, he said, "Well. I'm glad we made the right decision. (light laughter) As reward for conduct that led to increased prosperity and a promise for greater recompense, Commander Sulac, First Lieutenant Brannick, First Lieutenant Hywell, Lieutenant Fisk, Major Brann, and Technician Class I Trang," Sedwik looked up beaming at Aleph crew, "Your first commission will be aboard *Ari Arcturus*, Inter-Galaxy Command's newest Stratos Class-W ship. You will rendezvous with *Ari Arcturus* on Brenton Kae in less than two weeks. All particulars will be transmitted to your e-dev's in good time.

"Meanwhile, to you as well as to all graduating officers and specialists, I say this...the academy has provided you with a solid foundation upon which it is expected that you will build a sound and valid career. The IGC is the backbone of the Intersolar and Space Alliance. Without us there would be no order. Without us there would be only chaos. Follow the rules, follow orders, be responsible, and contribute.

"Thank you," concluded Major Sedwik before taking a step back and leaving the podium even as the house lights came up and excited conversations reached a state of uproar.

Tåsan stood and turned to find his family in the balcony waving and clapping and raised his hand to return their salutations and motion to them that he would join them soon.

~

The *Ari Arcturus*.

IGC's most ambitious purpose to date and Tåsan embraced it wholeheartedly.

His quarters were afore ship, large, well appointed and fitting of the Commander. When Tåsan stepped through the entry, he stood for a moment taking it all in, committing it to memory.

A wide array of windows dominated the main sitting area and presented a view of the forward travels of the ship. Off to one side, the sleeping quarters, the other, a sort of small, efficient galley. The main area was furnished for casual sitting but could be reconfigured for work with ease.

Tåsan's excitement was palpable and threatened to overwhelm him. He had to remind himself that he had earned this, he deserved to be here.

A soft chime sounded in Tåsan's aural implant.

"Sen-dev on," said Tåsan, shifting his attention to the incoming comm. "Yes, Alyss, I'm in my quarters." Tåsan moved to the bulkhead windows. "Yes, whenever you're ready." The view was crowded with riggers and lights and drifting puffs of vapor as maint-bots and technicians hurried to ready the ship for its scheduled embarkation. Its maiden voyage. "Sen-dev off."

Tåsan went to his sleeping quarters and there he found, at the foot of the bed, his three travel cases. Gingerly, he opened the one holding his wardrobe and began to stow the articles in their proper places, taking care to set aside the officers uniform that he would wear on bridge command.

After the last piece of clothing was put away, Tåsan showered and changed and was standing by the windows ready, when Alyss pressed the wi-comm at the door announcing her presence.

"Open," said Tåsan. "Hello! Come in!" he smiled as Alyss took a step forward.

"This is fabulous," she said as she looked around Tåsan's quarters, "I think the architects knew the importance of keeping the Commander happy."

"It *is* pretty nice," said Tåsan.

"It's *very* nice," agreed Alyss.

Tåsan stepped away from the windows. "Bridge?" he asked.

"By all means," smiled Alyss and she turned toward the door.

Down the hall and around the corner, the Commander and his Pilot ran into their ship's Engineer.

"Hey hello, hello!" called Alyss as they neared the lift.

Castell turned, "Hey! There you are!" smiling. The lift doors slid silently open, "Just in time," he said.

"First day on a new bridge, in a new ship, with a new mission," said Tåsan. "I have a really good feeling about this!"

In a fast moment, the lift delivered them to the bridge and all three stepped out, paused, and looked around with what could only be described as transcendent joy.

The bridge was wide and perfectly luminated, its working

spaces were stepped-down, as any good command theatre would be. There were several large bulkhead view windows across the front, all separated by a variety of comp-screens that were busily displaying aspects of the ship. The running stations faced forward and the research stations ringed the bridge at its periphery. Command was optimal with a view of all.

Alyss made a happy sound as she looked across the bridge, "Oh! It's Annis!" and quickly stepped in her direction.

Castell smiled and Tåsan exclaimed, "Well, I'll be." Both men followed in Alyss' wake.

The three gathered around Annis and she shook hands with Alyss and Castell in turn, even as everyone smiled and happily greeted her.

Tåsan took her hand and said, "I see it's First Lieutenant O'hAirt, congratulations!"

Annis said, "Yes, thank you, sir. It was your brilliant handling of the Vellosian Encounter that propelled my promotion. And it was the affinity and trust of this crew that prompted my request for immediate reassignment to the *Ari Arcturus*."

Alyss had caught sight of Annis' new stone. "You no longer have the garnet?"

Annis touched the beautiful red and yellow splashed blue stone at her collarbone. "The garnet belonged to *The Garnet Star* and is now worn by her current AI Tactical. This stone, a blue Bloodstone, is what I chose for myself and is mine as long as I am assigned to *Ari Arcturus*. It belongs to the *Ari Arcturus*."

Alyss leaned closer to get a better look, "It's beautiful. Are those real?"

A faint, candid laugh escaped Annis' lips, "Yes. The Bloodstone is surrounded by Sangoshi druzy and together with the black diamonds they form the celestial phenomena Valorous Atundi. Altogether it represents strength, courage, and vitality, all of which I see for *Ari Arcturus*."

Alyss smiled, "What a nice sentiment."

Tåsan said, "I'm very pleased that you are aboard, First Lieutenant," and looking at her and the others, "If you will excuse me, we have a first journey to prepare for." Tåsan smiled and gave a small nod then headed for his first official command with the

IGC.

~

"Lift and burn" came the command and the *Ari Arcturus* rose gracefully from its berth and lifted flawlessly to its Zone of Demark in an even and steady rate.

Their mission is to travel to coordinates adjacent to quadrants of both the Niles and Rayten Galaxies and to move across the Allodial Expanse monitoring for unidentified ships.

"Initiate" came the order and *Ari Arcturus* moved out with hardly a quiver. Engines low and steady, movement certain.

The bridge crew was engaged with their stations and Tåsan was thoroughly engrossed with the ship's vitals. It seemed to him that the current settings barely registered on any of the data displays. He furrowed his brow and he thought for a moment then had an idea.

"Bridge crew," announced Tåsan. Everyone came to attention. "A simulated condition has come to my notice. A band of privateers have been reported, most coincidentally, in the exact sector of space we are now headed to. There are three ships of unknown model and origin that appear to be swarming and attacking ships of value and harassing those less fortunate, and there are several disabled ships muddling the area. The privateers are reported as heavily armed and fairly ruthless and we've been tasked with straightening it all out."

Tåsan stood up. "First Lieutenant Brannick."

"Aye, sir," Alyss turned and looked expectantly at Tåsan.

"I know you're curious about the flight and proficiency of this ship."

"Yes, sir."

"And I know that the remaining bridge crew would like to make a thorough verification of their stations." Tåsan raised his brow to look around the bridge for verification and found everyone, to a member, smiling at him. "First Lieutenant Hywell."

"Yes, sir."

"Ship-wide Alert Level III, please."

"Aye, sir, Alert Level III," responded Nikliss as his fingers danced across his stations icons.

"First Lieutenant Brannick."

175

"Sir?"

"When you are ready," Tåsan paused.

"Yes, sir?" queried Alyss, her excitement building, her fingers hovering over her flight controls in nervous expectation.

"*HAZE THE HIDES!*" Tåsan called out, the words barely spoken when the ship thrust forward and the view through the bulkhead windows accelerated to a blur.

~

Patrolling the Allodial Expanse around the Rayten Galaxy was, for the most part, uneventful with long stretches of routine broken only by a passing transport from the Niles Galaxy making its way to a delivery point on Jahved Tuk or possibly Zetta Ma.

It was during one of these times that a classified message came in from IGC Headquarters.

The bridge crew had been layers deep in a game of "What Would You Do?" employing strategies and virtually pushing system limits when the comm announced the message.

Technical Class I Mason Trang noted that the IGC messaged Commander Sulac, First Lieutenant Brannick, and Major Brann and labeled the communiqué as confidential. Mason sent notification to their stations but did not call out that he was doing so. He watched the three as they engaged their comm's, looking for signs so that he might guess at the message contents.

After reading through the comm, Alyss turned to Tåsan, her face lit up with delight. Tåsan looked up, wide-eyed and smiling, first at Alyss and then at Castell, who was showing his clear satisfaction, then back to Alyss. Tåsan motioned that Alyss and Castell should stand up and when they did so, he spoke.

"Everyone. It is my extreme pleasure to tell you that the Quad Six fighter craft team design paper submitted by First Lieutenant Brannick, Major Brann, and me, variously titled 'Oh, We'll Never Get This Done On Time' to 'We May Yet Have A Shot At This' but in the end, appropriately titled 'Shadow Fast Fighter Craft,' has been awarded special merit by the IGC." The bridge crew raised their voices and clapped their congratulations and when he could, Tåsan continued. "There's mention of design consultation and build oversight and there seems to be a bit of a brouhaha in the works. They're promising delivery of fine foods so that a

176

celebration can be held to mark the occasion. All of which I will share with you."

Murmurs of assent sounded across the bridge.

"The IGC is considering putting Shadow Fast into production sometime within the next two to five solar years," Tåsan smiled, he was so surprised and happy. "Why do I feel like I'm a new father!" he blurted out to everyone's amusement.

There was a monetary compensation that came with the special merit distinction. A sizable one that Tåsan quite naturally collected to his personal account back on Naiad Five. He had no real plan in mind, other than the normal dreams of a young man starting out in life. He would leave it for another time.

Later that evening, Alyss, Castell, and Tåsan were together in Tåsan's quarters having a small celebration. Drams of Astorian liqueur were raised and Tåsan made the first acclamation.

"To us, my friends! Who could have known that a design requirement would lead to such a great reward?"

Alyss spoke next, "Fortune favors the brave!"

"As said on Astor," Castell smiled, "Sarafe du tenuous pitkás. To honor the effort with happiness," and raised his glass to his friends.

In unity, the three friends touched glasses and drank. Castell hastened to fill the drams once more before making himself comfortable on the settee under the windows. Alyss sat across from him and Tåsan flopped down into an overstuffed chair adjacent to them both.

"I was a little thrown by the award of 150,000 tenges," said Tåsan. "I had no idea that the IGC could spend like that." Tåsan looked at Alyss. "What are you going to do with your award?"

Alyss sipped her liqueur and thought for a moment. "My first thoughts were crazy. Acquire a new jet bike or a flashy, red, twelve vig astro cruiser."

Castell interjected, "Ohh, those are very nice."

Continuing, Alyss said, "They are, aren't they? But then I calmed down. I think what I'm going to do is put it aside until the time comes for me to acquire an expanse of land and build my home." She sipped at her liqueur again. "How about you two, any plans?"

Tåsan said, "I haven't given it much thought. As long as the IGC takes care of me, there's nothing I really need right now." He placed his dram on a side table, then added, "I guess I'll save it and see."

"Well," Castell said, "I wouldn't mind having a personal Shadow Fast Fighter."

The friends laughed at that and Tåsan said, "You're going to need at least one hundred more special merit awards for that!"

"Then," Castell downed his dram, "I had better get to it," and stood up. "This has been quite a day, hasn't it?"

"Yes it has," said Alyss as she, too, stood up.

"Again, thank you, friends," said Castell, "With you two it was possible."

"Friends," said Tåsan.

Alyss smiled at them both as she stepped to the door. "Friends."

• • •

Later, as Tåsan sat alone, lights low, and watched as stars slowly moved past the view windows, he thought about how fortunate he was to have found such true friends, to have won a place in the IGC, to command a Stratos ship, and now to have an account of value. It was almost enough. Almost.

~

Life aboard *Ari Arcturus* took on a quality of familiarity and routine.

Tåsan fell into a sort of happy rhythm of bridge duty, vid recording his log reports, his almost daily work-outs in the officer's gym and on the expansive par-course, and his self-allotted weekly social time.

This day, Tåsan was on bridge duty, he had been studying star charts for this sector of space but was taking a short break, chatting with First Lieutenant Annis O'hAirt, when a message from the IGC Council came through: The Vellosians are threatening to quit the Intersolar and Space Alliance over an issue of ownership.

After hearing the message, Tåsan turned to Annis, his face suddenly serious. "Seems the Vellosians are very unhappy with what the ISA is proposing for a partnership and are alternately saying that they will either quit the ISA and leave or will operate

178

as independents."

Annis said, "The ISA will never agree to that."

"They've announced an impasse," said Tåsan, "but are working the issue in spite of the stubbornness that each side is displaying. They've decided that the best immediate course of action is to withdraw and regroup. For now." He stood looking at nothing in particular.

Annis watched him for a moment, then spoke, "And the ISA is looking to you to come up with a solution?"

Tåsan gave a small sad smile, and spoke, "Basically, yes." He took in a breath then gave a sincere smile. "They think I might know something they don't since I was the one who originally brought the Vellosians to the table."

"And do you?" asked Annis.

Tåsan was following a thought then looked at Annis. "I just may," he said and returned to Command where he pulled up the complete records of the Vellosian Encounter and spent the next hour reading through the negotiations report and thinking. At last, he came to a conclusion and began to compose his proposal to the ISA Member Committee.

> : 31839.54
> : Regarding Vellosian Trade Negotiations,
> : After careful consideration of all the recorded meeting discussion and communication with and to or from the ISA Board of Trustees and the Vellosian Representatives, I am confident that if the following recommendations are pursued, in earnest, by both sides, the current stalemate that has stalled progress toward a rewarding partnership, will soon be ended.

The document went on to describe a gross misunderstanding that was built out of the language barrier that existed and in spite of the best of efforts to alleviate this barrier, have unwittingly fueled confusion and rancor beyond need. An expanded linguistics team must be assembled to correct the idiom as fast as possible.

The mediation venue must be moved immediately. The use of ISA corporate, while suitably impressive, does not offer a neutral backdrop nor does it lend to the comfort of the Vellosians. Meetings should be moved to the Niesus Resort at the edge of the Niles Galaxy.

Tåsan knew the Niesus Resort was the playland of the rich and the richer. It was opulent and accommodating and would give the Vellosians a clear understanding of what could be possible once they were in a business relationship with the ISA.

One last provision was outlined. The ISA must hold forth an accord. They must offer an incentive. Tåsan proposed that the Vellosians be given preferential choice of at least one exclusive trade opportunity. It could come with a time limit, of say, one solar year, but it should be a good trade opportunity that involved giving them both buy and sell options. It would underscore possible future trade openings and excite them to continue with the ISA, it would help to build Vellosian confidence in their negotiation skills in a new system, and it would be the right thing to do.

Tåsan read, adjusted, read again, modified, and refined, and when he was satisfied that the document was clear and complete, sent the proposal to the ISA, and replicated it to the IGC and to his log files. When his comm reported delivery and receipt complete, Tåsan sat back, his mind still turning the situation over and as his thoughts slowed, his confidence came up. He was satisfied with his position and smiled to himself. This was better than the best game of Parudi Rule.

~

Tåsan hadn't seen Darrian Adaams, or Tao Vu for that matter, for a handful of weeks and thought it was about time. He sent a comm asking if they could spare a cup of tea, that he would be in their area momentarily.

Darrian responded right away, ((Absolutely! Tao is on next shift so is unavail, but I've just put a pot on the heat. No better time!))

As Lead Medical Surgeon, Darrian took possession of the *Ari Arcturus* medical facility with great enthusiasm. His first commission aboard a new ship gave him the opportunity to leave his mark and he couldn't have been happier. His organizational skills and determination turned the medical section from a mere

180

facility into a premier complex. Besides the expected Preventative, Emergency, and Surgical sections, Darrian added a multi-part Research Facility, thereby expanding medical's presence and importance.

On this day, Darrian was catching up on his log entries and had felt the need for a quiet break from his workload, when Tåsan's comm came in. It would be a welcome diversion and it would give him the opportunity to give Tåsan a quick tour. And to impress the Commander with all the Chief Medical Officer's changes and improvements could only help.

The "tour" was short and as Darrian led the way to his office, he continued the conversation, "I'm very excited about progressing my study of robotic AI circuitry as interfaced in humanoids. I feel it's a wide-open field, right now."

"Well, it looks like you may have the infrastructure here to do just that," agreed Tåsan, taking a seat in one of the two cushioned chairs that stood next to a small table off on one side of Darrian's office.

Darrian immediately brought two cups and a hot pot of tea from the small galley and poured two full portions. "Can I get you something to eat? I have fruitlets."

"No, thank you. I just want to spend a moment catching up with you."

Darrian sat opposite Tåsan and smiled. It was good to relax with a friend. He had been so wrapped up with organizing his labs that he hadn't had time for anything else.

Tåsan spoke. "So, tell me, how have the crew adjusted to life aboard a Stratos Class? Any measureable effects?"

"No," answered Darrian, "although in the start there were a rash of personnel reporting headaches. But that seems to have passed." He sipped his tea. "How about you? Are you feeling the stress of Command?"

Tåsan smiled, "Nope. Absolutely love command."

"Are you maintaining a regular exercise schedule?" asked Darrian, leaning forward in slight concern and peering at Tåsan's face for signs of fatigue.

"Relax, Doctor," joked Tåsan. "I'm doing all the right things." The look on Darrian's face prompted Tåsan to add, "Promise. If something changes, I'll bring it up."

"Okay."

Tåsan said, "Tell me about your thoughts on the future of robotic interfacing. You know that I'm a willing audience."

Eight
Under The Apex

The days seemed to rush past. Even in the throes of routine, Tåsan could find something to fill the void. He studied ships systems and schematics, and reviewed department and station log reports, wishing to stay abreast of maintenance trends and problem solving. But his main interest, the one he always made time for was his passion for Astrophysics. Tåsan wanted to understand and use the guiding principles of inter-planetary and inter-galaxy energies to boost the strategic capabilities of *Ari Arcturus*. His part-time hobby was working with engineering in the development of an intelligent mechanical interface that would gather the energy of space, interpret its mass, and introduce it to the boron drives in steady coordination with their power consumption. He took to calling his passion, Spacial Propulsion.

Tåsan could be found in Engineering with Castell. They are immersed in the discussion of various compounds and their capacity to store space energy.

"Out of these three, it seems that osmium, with its quantum level of .76 has the most potential," said Tåsan.

"Yes," agreed Castell before adding, "but it doesn't quite meet the eigenvalue energy absorption requirement necessary." Castell tipped his e-pad toward Tåsan to share his notes and equations.

Tåsan studied the data, his brow furrowed in concentration.

Castell had a thought. "Maybe if we add a quantity of…"

"Commander." Announced a Class II Tech. "Pardon the interruption."

Tåsan turned, "Yes?"

"Incoming from the Bridge."

"Thank you."

« Commander Sulac, we have a situation in progress. You're needed on the Bridge. »

"Thank you, Mr. Trang. I'm in route. Please transmit situation specifics to my aural, and copy to Major Brann." Turning back to Castell, Tåsan motioned toward the doorway and said, "Shall we?"

...

The tension on the Bridge was obvious to Tåsan the second he stepped from the lift. As he assumed Command, he took it all in. Alyss and Nikliss had their heads together in discussion, Shú Vit was adding detail to her tracking dimensional, Annis was studying her various inputs, and everyone was on station and alert.

"Bridge crew," Tåsan called out and the ambient chatter fell silent as attention turned toward him. "Navigator, set course for sector T-one-A7, speed optimum. ETA?"

Shú Vit hurriedly entered the coordinates and answered, "Less than ten minutes."

Tåsan's orders were concise. Alert Level I, ready weapons, standby combat troop and two dozen Deployable Conversion Modules (DCMs), all stations prepare for any degree of response but above all...

"Stay calm, be alert. This is not a test," concluded Tåsan.

The crew of *Ari Arcturus* had received a missive from IGC Command apprising of the facts surrounding a distress call made by *Starlight*, an IGC, thirty-crew Class-A cruiser, only a short while ago.

Starlight had been deployed to Zetta Ma on an ambassadorial mission three days prior. They had successfully negotiated a trade agreement with a local mining conglomerate that would make available large quantities of iridium to manufacturing communities of the Niles Galaxy. *Starlight* was leaving Zetta Ma and had just reached its Zone of Demark when it was fired upon by a Class-C interceptor and that was partnered with two Class-N ships, apparently armed with, as yet, unidentified weaponry. *Starlight* took evasive flight and was given chase. They managed to comm their coordinates and their extreme distress before all comm ceased. *Starlight* has no armaments. *Ari Arcturus* was ordered to the scene to evaluate and rectify the situation...with all haste.

As all stations came to stand-by alert, Tåsan received further intelligence from IGC that he relayed to the bridge crew.

"The privateers responsible for the unwarranted attack on *Starlight* are calling themselves Liberty Fighters and declaring that the IGC are imperialists and that they, the Liberty Fighters, will battle the IGC at every step. Not too much is known about the group other than they have claimed responsibility for various other acts of piracy in this sector of space. It's assumed they are from Zetta Ma and may be disgruntled cast-offs from the local unions or a bunch of ruffians with nothing else to do. Either way, they've proven their worth."

Tåsan stood, "Let's test their battle savvy. ETA Navigator?"

Shú Vit responded, "We're two minutes out. Current sensor data is streaming. We've got visual."

The compiled dimensional flashed onto the main comp screens.

"Lieutenant Brannick, take us in. Target the interceptor."

"Aye, sir." Alyss descended out of rad drive less than four vectors from the interceptor, barely slowing the ship as she quickly closed the distance.

The interceptor fired a handful of sub-proto rounds that were deflected by the energized chrysoberyl coating protecting *Ari Arcturus'* hull from harm.

Tåsan's voice came through, "Disable it."

Annis fired a series of protowaves that vaporized one of its nacelles. Instantly the interceptor lost speed and started to spin uncontrollably. As Alyss brought the ship about, Annis loosed two proto bursts. The first one blasted one of the Class-N's with a boracite explosive that blew a hole in the guidance system array and the other stained the hull with hematite, marking it for further IGC search and detection.

Alyss banked *Ari Arcturus* sharply to port, targeting the other Class-N, who had made an appreciative distance back to the planet in its hurried retreat.

Annis took a shot but it missed.

Shú Vit announced, "They're through the Zone of Demark, we are not able to follow." And looking to Tåsan, "Sir, your orders?"

Tåsan responded, "Notify Combat Services to be ready to deploy twenty four DCMs as soon as we've slowed our approach and connect me with DCM Leader Emis."

Tåsan instructed Leader Emis to direct the Deployable Conversion Module team in pursuit of the run-away Class-N. He was to apprehend the privateers but not to the detriment of any troop members. Use force if necessary.

Ari Arcturus swooped into position and slowed quickly just as the twenty-four DCMs surged out of bay AE17-a.

The bridge comp screens recorded the DCMs as they dropped from the ship and lit their thrusters. Each single-solder DCM aligned to the fleeing Class-N and began pursuit.

The Class-N headed straight for the Zetta Ma outback at a terrifying speed, fueled by fear and with no apparent thought to its safety.

Several nolans into the atmospheric flight, the Class-N suddenly dropped altitude and tried to lose itself in the canyons and pinnacles that crowded the terrain. The craft banked left and right, dropping down only to suddenly shoot up through a hidden fissure in its attempts to out maneuver and lose the DCMs that pushed ever closer.

One by one, the DCMs converted from their space rocket configuration to the terrestrial pulse rocket mode used for fast travel across land.

Tåsan listened intently to DCM Leader Emis direct his deployment and watched the comp screens as the action unfolded.

Sensors showed the Class-N blip closely followed by the twenty-four DCM blips. Suddenly, in the middle of its reckless dash across the outback, the Class-N blip halted and ten smaller blips swarmed out and away in several different directions, leaving the Class-N as derelict among the boulders and brush.

Technical Class I Mason Trang transmitted this detail to DCM Leader Emis who immediately issued orders.

Tåsan watched as the twenty-four split into teams of two and three and race after individual targets.

The bridge crew was silent as they watched the comp screens and witnessed the battle unfold. Over the course of eleven minutes, each DCM team eventually overtook their quarry, the final showdown ending either in peaceful surrender or badly, in a hail of weapons fire that in the end left one trooper and three privateers dead. Leader Emis reported two emergencies and requested shuttle assistance in the transport of prisoners, adding that the able-bodied troopers would transport back to *Ari Arcturus* by way of their DCMs.

When the troopers were back onboard and the privateers secured, Tåsan met with Leader Emis in bay AE17-a where he was making an inspection of the damaged deployables for his report.

"Let me ask you about the privateers," said Tåsan.

"Yes, sir," replied Emis.

"Did they strike you as professional mercenaries or do you think they were more representative of disgruntled union workers?"

Emis thought for a second or two, then answered, "I would say that the leaders possess a level of expertise that they could have picked up through law enforcement training. Maybe a stint in a local police force. That type of thing." Emis ran his fingers across his cheek as he continued, "That being said, I think most of them are followers and wanna-be's. They made rookie mistakes and some acted like frightened children when looking down the barrel of our cid-shot blasters. Not too professional."

Tåsan lowered his voice. "I'm sorry you lost a man. Did you see it happen?"

"Thank you, sir. Trooper Hardain was a good man. Five years with the IGC and two with me." Emis looked down at the floor and took in a deep breath to catch his thoughts. "I arrived at the scene already in progress. Hardain and his partner had two of the perpetrators pinned down among the rocks. The perpetrators were firing their weapons wildly." Emis shook his head. "Shots were flying in all directions and I believe that Hardain took a hit that glanced off the granite rock face that he had taken cover next to. Unfortunate."

Tåsan nodded his understanding and held his last question until Emis looked up at him with new focus. "What can you tell me about the deaths of the three privateers?"

"They were clean kills, sir. My men acted professionally and appropriately," Emis replied.

"Yes, I trust that was so. Thank you, Leader Emis." Tåsan lightly touched Emis' shoulder to communicate his empathy then said, "Well. I'll leave you to it then," and turned to walk away.

"Thank you. Sir," Emis called after him.

• • •

That night as Tåsan lay abed, he tossed and turned in an effort to clear his thoughts, finally falling into a haze of fitful sleep.

I feel something is watching.

SNAP!

Tåsan came to alert and focused his attention in the direction the noise had emanated from. He slowed his breathing and sharpened his hearing. Nothing. Nothing. Then there it was. A low growling sound fluttering in the underbrush. A warning that pricked fear straight into the center of Tåsan's head and shot adrenal into his muscles.

Tåsan froze for one brief moment as his mind clicked.

GRRRRR...

It was closer now.

Before he could put words to his thoughts, Tåsan turned and ran in the only direction he thought was safe...away. As he fled, the terrain seemed to close in on him, slowing his flight. Branches slapped his face and thorns grabbed at his clothes and tore at his skin. His progress slowed but the fear gripping his chest started to creep into his throat, choking his air. He struggled, clawing at the brush and gulping for breath. As the underbrush grew more dense, Tåsan felt that it was consuming him and his fear focused on a new threat, one that could bury him, kill him, leave him lost forever.

It was all Tåsan could recall. The threat was real, the fear palpable. An unseen adversary had clearly communicated a warning. But what was it? It did not reveal itself. What was the danger it warned of? Itself? The underbrush? Myself?

Tåsan mused over several possibilities but could not find a satisfactory explanation. It had no meaning and of itself it made no sense.

• • •

Two days later, *Ari Arcturus* was ordered to Brenton Kae, where an Inter-Galaxy Command Court of Justice had been assembled to conduct a hearing on all matters related to the *Starlight* incident.

The list of *Ari Arcturus* crew being ordered to give deposition looked like a Who's Who, and not surprisingly among the names was Commander Tåsan Sulac.

> : 31972.1
> : Commander T. Sulac
> : Regarding *Starlight* Episode
> You are to appear before the Inter-Galaxy Command tribunal where you will be deposed as to your participation in and your knowledge of the actions carried out by the *Ari Arcturus* personnel in regard to the *Starlight* Episode of 31970.48. You will report to Magistrate Adrobach. Details to follow. In accordance with IGC policy N3E.1F, you are prohibited from discussing this matter with any person either verbally or in writing until such time as you are formally released by decree.
> Signed, **B.R. Matorios**, IGC Legal Council

Tåsan read the official notice three times, each time looking for a small slip in the language that might give him some sort of leeway to talk with any of the others on the deposition list, or really, any who weren't. But the third time through and a fast glance at Reg N3E.1F, pretty much summed it up: don't do it.

For two days, as *Ari Arcturus* underwent maintenance and systems testing, Tåsan stayed to himself in his quarters, his mind thoroughly going over his orders, his actions, and his observations of the entire *Starlight* Episode, until his mind swam with the enormity of detail it encompassed.

• • •

Inter-Galaxy Command appropriated a large room on the sunstar side of Brenton Kae and arranged a raised dais for five magistrates, had placed a witness chair before that, provided furniture for council, legal, and reference go-fors, and set dozens of chairs for watchers and observers beyond that.

Magistrate Adrobach had been appointed Judicial Leader and would be supported by four additional magistrates who would provide discussion and opinion as necessary.

As soon as *Ari Arcturus* had docked, the *Starlight* Episode deposition process began and orders to appear flowed steadily out.

Tåsan was to appear before Magistrate Adrobach at 1387 hours on 31979.0. Today.

As Tåsan made his way to the tribunal room through the halls of Brenton Kae, he felt confident and assured that he was in command of the facts and could answer any question put to him regarding the *Starlight* Episode. As he entered the passageway adjacent to the courtroom, Tåsan was surprised to see Alyss seated outside the doors. She smiled as he approached but said nothing in the way of a greeting. Tåsan was about to say hello when one of the court doors opened and a clean-cut cadet, carrying an e-dev, stepped out and addressed Alyss.

"First Lieutenant Brannick, they are ready for you now."

Alyss rose, gave a meaningful glance in Tåsan's direction and disappeared through the door.

The cadet tapped at the e-dev and gave it his full attention for a handful of seconds before looking up at Tåsan. "Commander Sulac, please take a seat. You are the next deponent." He looked quickly at the closed court room doors and added, "Make yourself comfortable, there may be a bit of a wait." He smiled and asked if could get Tåsan anything. A water, perhaps?

"No thank you, cadet. I'll be fine," replied Tåsan and watched as the cadet quietly let himself back into the court room.

Fifteen minutes plus one hour later, Tåsan was momentarily startled as the court room door suddenly swung open with a loud swoosh as the cadet led Alyss from the room. "Thank you, First Lieutenant Brannick. You will be notified of the tribunal's decisions as soon as they are filed." And turning to Tåsan, "They are ready for you now, Commander."

Tåsan searched Alyss' face for any hint of what was to come but found that her eyes did not give anything away. He was curious to note that her jaw was clamped tight, as if guarding against any words that threatened to escape.

Inside the room, the cadet motioned to the witness chair, stark in its solitary position before the judges. Tåsan nodded and strode across the room, his steps echoing in his ears through the silence. He stood before the chair, his back straight, and his eyes taking in the scene.

Magistrate Adrobach spoke, "Commander Sulac, please be seated."

Tåsan sat down, keeping to the erect posture appropriate for the situation.

"We would like to start with your account of the events of 31970.48," spoke Adrobach. "Take as much time as you need. My fellow magistrates," said Adrobach nodding to his right and again to his left, "and I would only interrupt your narrative for clarifications or to ask pertinent questions." Adrobach busied his fingers on a large e-dev that occupied the space in front of him, adding, "Your deposition will be recorded and IGC Legal is standing by in case of need."

Tåsan wondered if that was for his need or theirs.

"You may begin when you are ready, Commander Sulac."

Tåsan adjusted himself more comfortably in the solid unyielding chair, and leaning back, took in a steadying breath and began.

"I became aware of a situation involving *Starlight* ambassador mission when I received an urgent notification from IGC Control stating the *Starlight* and her crew were in jeopardy and instructing *Ari Arcturus* to respond. We were to rectify the situation," began Tåsan.

Magistrate Adrobach inquired, "Were there any guidelines provided by IGC Control, other than to 'rectify' the situation?"

"No, sir." Tåsan hesitated, his eyes on Magistrate Adrobach, who waved a stylus in front of him to indicate that Tåsan was to continue.

"My first thoughts were to protect *Ari Arcturus* as we were headed into an unknown situation and to be prepared for what we might encounter upon arrival. I ordered a Level I Alert..."

Adrobach interrupted, "A Level I Alert is very extreme. You felt it necessary to bypass levels III and II and go straight to Level I?"

"Yes, sir. Due to the un-quantified nature of the situation, I felt we should approach it well prepared. Fully aware."

"I see," said Adrobach. "Continue."

"When we reached sector T-one-A7, *Starlight* was in evasive maneuver and dodging proto-fire from the unidentified

191

interceptor. *Ari Arcturus* dropped from hyper-speed and sought to stop the attack on *Starlight*. We disabled the interceptor by vaporizing its starboard nacelle…"

"Vaporizing?" asked the magistrate seated at the far end of the bench.

Interrupted, Tåsan's thoughts pulled up as he voiced the answer, "Yes, sir," and then waited, watching the magistrate who gave no acknowledgement of the answer nor did he indicate continuance.

So, Tåsan went on, "With the interceptor out of action…"

"But was it 'out of action', Commander? With only a nacelle destroyed, wouldn't an interceptor still be capable of continued fire power? Couldn't it still have been a threat?" queried Adrobach.

"We left the interceptor spinning out of control, seemingly unable to maneuver. It *may* have been able to loose a protowave but in its unstable flight, could not have clearly targeted anything. I assessed its threat level close to nil." Tåsan could feel his heart pick up its pace and his thoughts fly, *"Are they insinuating that I should have destroyed the interceptor?"*

"Continue," said Adrobach, his attention on his e-dev.

"As we came about, *Ari Arcturus* targeted the closest Class-N and fired on its guidance array and marked it for further search and seizure by IGC backup." Tåsan hesitated in anticipation of queries or clarification requests.

And one came. "Was that your considered choice of action?"

"Yes, sir. Considered and carried out," answered Tåsan before he continued, "The second Class-N was undertaking an escape. *Ari Arcturus* quickly surmised that that Class-N was headed to Zetta Ma's uncharted outback in an attempt to evade capture."

"How was this surmised?" asked Adrobach.

"By their straight, unswerving flight path, sir," answered Tåsan.

"So…no guesswork or assumptions?" asked the magistrate to Adrobach's immediate left.

Tåsan turned his eyes to the man. "No, sir. No assumptions were made."

"Thank you."

"You may continue your narrative, Commander," added Adrobach.

"I ordered a detachment of DCMs to stand-by..."

"DCMs?" asked a magistrate. Looking to the other judges for help.

Adrobach looked down the dais and quietly spoke to the judge, "They are one-man vehicles. Deployable Conversion Modules." The judge nodded his understanding.

"And I instructed DCM Leader Emis," continued Tåsan without waiting for permission, "to pursue and seize the Class-N and to capture all privateers." Tåsan again shifted in his chair and continued. "With all consideration for his troopers."

At that, all of the judges and Magistrate Adrobach looked up from their notes and silently stared at Tåsan. He took it as a signal to continue.

"DCM Leader Emis displayed capability as an officer and was in control of the situation he was faced with. I have respect for his discernment and his command."

"I'm sure you do, Commander, thank you."

Tåsan was starting to realize that he was slowly moving away from a recitation into a defensive mode. The attitudes of the judges were becoming more obvious as time ticked past. He was not merely reciting a narrative of the *Starlight* Episode, he was defending *Ari Arcturus*. He was defending himself.

"Amid the hazardous and very dangerous chase through and around the natural granite outcroppings and sheer cliffs, the Class-N instantly halted. My initial thought was that the Class-N had crashed owing to their erratic flight throughout the treacherous Zetta Ma outback. However, the immediate departure and scattering of her crew was evidence that there was no crash and this intel was immediately comm'ed to DCM Leader Emis who took decisive action."

"And would you detail that action, Commander," spoke Adrobach.

"Yes, sir. DCM Leader Emis ordered his troops to divide into pairs and follow the quarry deeper into the outback. Which they did."

"Did you agree with Leader Emis' decisions?" another

193

magistrate spoke up.

"Of course I did. I do," corrected Tåsan. "Leader Emis is an experienced officer. He has been awarded medals of honor by the IGC for merited behavior in the line of duty. I have no reason to doubt his abilities." Tåsan could hear his heart beating and started to breathe rhythmatically in an effort to slow its pace. He could feel his anger starting to come up and fought to push it back down.

"Where were you at this time, Commander?" asked a judge to Tåsan's left.

"I was on the bridge of the *Ari Arcturus* watching and listening to the situation on the planet's surface as it unfolded." Tåsan watched the judge as he scribbled something across the face of his e-dev, finally acknowledging the answer and motioning Tåsan to continue.

"The pursuit had changed from one chase to ten and the troopers measurably closed the distance. Within heartbeats, several of the flights had ended as the privateers, no doubt, realized that escape was futile." Tåsan took a breath. "One by one the flights ended in this manner until there were but three groups still on the run. We watched, from the bridge, as all three pursuits ended but not in immediate surrender. Laser blasts and sidearm fire was reported and at the end of the assaults, when all chases had ended and all arms discharges had ceased, three privateers were dead."

Tåsan focused his thoughts. He found that in the telling of the *Starlight* Episode, it was rather difficult to say aloud...

"We lost Trooper Hardain in the last confrontation with two privateers who in their panic, were firing everything they had in a last effort to gain some sort of advantage. Trooper Hardain took a ricochet. He died almost instantaneously." The room was silent. "I did not know Trooper Hardain personally but understand him to have been a committed IGC trooper of good character, well liked."

The magistrate to Adrobach's left asked, "What part or parts of your decisions throughout the entire situation might be attributed to your inexperience as a Commander?"

Tåsan was stunned. He had not anticipated that his command would be put to question. "I believe that no part of any of my decisions could be attributable to inexperience. I did not come to this Command with little or no training. I have logged several hundreds if not thousands of flight hours at Command and in other capacities." Tåsan's anger was heating up. He fought to control it. "I stand by all my decisions and those of my crew. I did not second-guess myself then nor do I now. Does that answer your question?" His jaw clenched. "Sir."

The magistrate just shrugged his shoulders and looked to Adrobach.

Magistrate Adrobach was slouched back in his chair, elbow propped on the chair's arm, resting his chin in the palm of his hand, looking at Tåsan. Just looking. The seconds ticked by, the courtroom silent. Suddenly, he took his hand away from his face and as if coming out of a daydream, shoved forward and sat up. "Right. Well, we've heard enough for now. We assume that in the interim between then and now, you have observed all IGC protocol, filed your reports, and carried on with our summons. Is that correct, Commander Sulac?"

"Yes, sir. It is," Tåsan said. *"Is this over?"* he wondered.

"Then you are dismissed."

"Ah." Tåsan stood up at attention.

"You are reminded," Adrobach added, "that you are still under summons until tribunal decisions are filed. Cadet, show Commander Sulac out."

"Yes, sir," Tåsan said as he snapped a salute which none of the judges answered.

The cadet, e-dev to his chest, motioned for Tåsan to move to the door, but quickly stepped just ahead of him to open it and hold it open so Tåsan could step through unencumbered.

Tåsan's thoughts ran fast, *"What the hell just happened there? The judges were either hostile or addled. Do I have anything to worry about? And should I be talking with Legal?"*

Outside in the hallway sat Annis O'hAirt looking very much alone, waiting her summons.

She got to her feet and nodded to Tåsan. "Sir," she said as a greeting.

Tåsan barely uttered, "First Lieutenant O'hAirt," as acknowledgement before the cadet hustled Annis through the courtroom doors with no further notice of Tåsan.

Tåsan, standing alone, in a long, very quiet, very vacant

195

hallway, was very much disquieted by what had transpired during that last, (he checked the time) ninety eight minutes.

"I can't decide if that was protocol or a farce. I'm going to have to defend myself but to who? And by what means?" Tåsan walked slowly back to docking ramp 2-7E.B and boarded *Ari Arcturus* wishing to take refuge in his quarters to think it through. *"Oh, fortune, stay with me, maybe I should ask father..."*

• • •

Tåsan allowed himself one day to think and rethink and brood about the *Starlight* Episode and his court experience. He turned it over and over in his mind, questioning his command and his court narrative.

In his command, he was sure he had done the right thing at every step. He reassured himself that his restraint in the use of force was ethical and of the correct amount. He gave the privateers every chance of surrender and only used force at their provocation. Subsequently, the captured privateers, who under IGC interrogation, had given information that pointed to a larger network of dissidents harboring deep resentment toward the IGC. That was of some value. Right?

In his debrief, he felt that all of his answers had been forthright but, he admitted to himself, he became increasingly agitated as time passed, under what seemed to him to be an intensified amount of thinly disguised anger and skepticism from the magistrates. Maybe he could have done better at controlling himself and maybe then, he could have answered more thoroughly. He was sure Magistrate Adrobach would then have been satisfied. Wouldn't he?

Halfway through his ruminations, Tåsan's head started to ache. To ease the tension in his shoulders and neck, he decided to take a break and do a ship-side workout thinking that a hard and fast par-course and a steam shower would go a long way.

And it did. Returning to his quarters, Tåsan composed a message to his father, briefly outlining his dilemma and asking for advice.

Within an hour, it came...

((To be an IGC Officer requires strength of character
and a moral fortitude far above the ordinary

196

citizenry. The IGC will ask a lot from their officers
and one must either step up or step back.))

Tåsan read the message slowly and deliberately. *"Succinct and to the point, leaving me in a quandary...yet again...and all too typical."*

• • •

The Commander's bridge crew moved about *Ari Arcturus* in a fog, each of them still reeling from their debriefing by the Court of Magistrates. To calm their thoughts and emotions most busied themselves in maintenance and checkouts of their stations as *Ari Arcturus* was still berthed at Brenton Kae, under orders. She would not be ordered back to commission until the court's final decisions had been made known.

Within days, notification of final decisions had been messaged to everyone involved, copied to IGC Command, and written to the IGC official classified catalog.

The IGC tribunal had found the actions of *Ari Arcturus* acceptable upon condition.

> : 31997.37
> : IGC Petitioner v. *Ari Arcturus*
> : Official Finding and Final Record; Inter-Galaxy Command Archive
> : *Starlight* Episode; Date 31970.48
> Overview
> *Ari Arcturus* rescue of *Starlight* with minimal damage and/or loss from privateers concluded in the capture and eventual prosecution of said privateers.
>
> Findings of Fact
> ◦ IGC *Starlight*, concluding a mission on Zetta Ma (Rayten Galaxy), was put upon by privateers. Unarmed and outnumbered, *Starlight* sent a distress comm. (docs 15.7-84D)
> ◦ *Ari Arcturus* ordered to respond; ensuing actions. (docs 87G-472.9)
> ◦ Record of events. (docs 727.ef – 1489.7)
> ◦ Dispositions available by High Command order on a need-to-know basis only. (docs 1591Ze – 7026.i9)

Opinions

Magistrates combined opinions are as follows:

∘ *Ari Arcturus* flight and bridge crew acted responsibly as ordered and are to be held indemnis.

∘ While the loss of a trooper is regrettable, said loss occurred during a live mission and in uncontrollable circumstances (ie. Act of Terrorism). This court holds no IGC personnel directly responsible.

∘ According to IGC Article Hv71-8CS, Command Structures, it is the opinion of all magistrates that allowing for his inexperience, Commander Tåsan Sulac acted to the best of his ability given all circumstances under current consideration.

Conclusion

(1) That consideration be given to providing IGC Class-A ships some sort of armaments, (2) These and future privateers be dealt with in the harshest sense of the law, (3) That *Ari Arcturus* be returned to service, and (4) That Commander Sulac resume his post and that a Letter of Record be added to his permanent file.

Signed, The Honorable, *Adrian Adrobach*

Tåsan was on the bridge studying and expanding his Spacial Propulsion theory of energy conversion when his command console chimed an incoming message. In the background he heard several other e-dev chimes indicating a wider distribution. It was the formal notification that all tribunal briefs had been filed to the official record. It was followed by a copy of the court summary.

There was a deafening silence throughout the bridge as most of those present were focused on the newly delivered missive.

Tåsan looked up from his console and glanced about the bridge. His crew was very quiet, barely moving, and most of them looked stunned and emotionless. He spoke.

"So. It's done. I don't think this is the time or place for reactive discussion, so please, carry on with your duties and carefully consider what you've read. Save you thoughts for personal conversation, among friends, on your private time."

Quietly, everyone returned to their duties. Almost immediately, Tåsan's e-message chimed. He glanced at its small screen, noting that the sender was Alyss.

((My qrtrs. 2615 hrs. I hve 130-yr brandy.))

Tåsan smiled and looked up. Alyss was turned in her chair, facing him. He thought, *"Alyss, my dear friend,"* and nodded his assent.

• • •

Alyss poured a second drachm and placed the decanter on the low table that occupied the space between the comfortable, softly padded chairs that she and Tåsan had settled into.

Tåsan had just finished the retelling of his session with "the gang of magistrates" as he now referred to them, and could again feel indignation rise in his chest. "I feel an almost desperate need to complete the record," said Tåsan as he reached for his brandy, "to fill in the details so that there is a complete understanding of my command actions."

"But will there be a complete understanding?" Alyss asked. "In light of what you've just said, I truly doubt it. It almost sounds as if the magistrates were guiding the investigation to a predestined end."

They sat quiet for a moment. Tåsan's brow furrowed in concentration. He looked up. "Tell me about your deposition. Was it anything the same?"

"Somewhat, yes," answered Alyss. "At first they focused on my piloting skills asking questions like, 'Was that a considered move?' and 'Was there any input or discussion from the co-pilot?' It started to annoy me. I felt they were trying to undermine my actions."

Alyss sipped her brandy and continued, "Then, just as I was reaching a point where I might have said something regrettable, they became silent and busied themselves with their e-dev's. All I could hear was a cacophony of stylus nibs tapping at e-dev screens." She shook her head at the memory. "Then the line of questioning changed. Suddenly they were very concerned with you. 'Did I agree with your orders?', 'Did you seem nervous or distraught?' That type of thing. I tell you, I was past being annoyed, I was quickly being moved to anger. It was all I could do to keep my answers direct and my breathing under control."

"I know what you mean. I'm sure my irritability shown across my face," added Tåsan.

Alyss went on, "There was a moment when the questioning stopped. I had come to a natural pause in my narrative and fully expected a barrage of questions but none came."

Tåsan listened intently.

"The magistrates looked distracted. Each of them looking at their e-dev and shifting in their chairs. All except Magistrate Adrobach. He sat, head slightly bowed, staring at me. Hard. It was unsettling to say the least."

Tåsan said, "Yes, he did that to me, too. He was either trying to intimidate us or read our minds."

"Or determine if we were lying. Fabricating the whole incident," Alyss countered. "At least that's what I felt. More brandy?"

Tåsan tipped the last drops onto his tongue and held his glass out so Alyss could fill it without getting up from her chair.

"There were additional questions, mostly inane, then Adrobach declared the session completed." Alyss smiled and gave a slight chuckle, more to herself than as an exclamation. "He was so abrupt that it actually startled one of the other judges who jumped in his chair a bit."

"Is that when you came out into the hall?"

"Yes and when I saw you, I very much wanted to talk with you." Alyss looked down at her hand holding her glass, remembering the time. "The next few days were very lonely."

"Yes," agreed Tåsan, "I gave myself one day for reflection and a smattering of self pity."

Alyss watched Tåsan as he stared at the amber liquid in his glass. At length he spoke. "I concluded that I did nothing wrong, nothing lacking in discipline or character. As a matter of fact, I ran over several different scenarios, all with various outcomes."

"And what did that tell you?"

"That none of the other scenarios ended any better. There was not one scene that was more acceptable than my own decisions and actions were. In fact, all were worse." Tåsan sat forward and looked at Alyss. "Basically, I was right and I stand by my command."

Alyss nodded her head in agreement. "Good. Because as Commander, if you had been wrong, then you've led your entire bridge crew into the wrong and I, for one, know that my actions during the *Starlight* Episode, were calculated and ran true." She tipped her small, stemmed glass to catch the last drops of the one hundred thirty year old brandy then put the glass down with a clink.

Tåsan moved to pour more into her glass but Alyss held her hand up to stop him. "No thank you, I'm good."

"Alyss," Tåsan said.

"Yes?"

"I still feel strongly compelled to compose a written communiqué that clearly articulates my actions throughout the *Starlight* Episode. As a defense. And if for nothing else, a follow-up to be filed in my permanent record."

"For posterity?"

"Fortune knows I'll need it."

"I would only caution this, Tåsan...be very careful with your words. There are egos about, that have no limits. Do not tread upon them or you may find yourself, not understood, as you desire, but defamed and reviled...all to be filed in your permanent record."

• • •

Tåsan could not let it go. He tried to occupy his mind with other things, but the more he ran from it, the more the memories of the hearing intruded. Finally, a small handful of weeks after the final judgment of the *Starlight* Episode had been filed, Tåsan sat down and put stylus to screen and fingers to pad and began his personal defense.

It was not difficult to round out his description of the events as they had unfolded that day and he resisted adding a jab or two about not being allowed to complete his telling of the affair due to Magistrate interruptions. It was, however, a painstaking process to seamlessly integrate explanations of his thoughts and logic into the facts of the entire event. This part occupied his nights for several weeks.

Then it was on to a discussion of the Magistrate's in-court

conduct. Tåsan was obsessed over the wording in this section of his discourse. He juggled between his perceptions and the magistrate's demeanor that at times seemed leading while at others seemed disinterested, that still at other times, hostile and arrogant. Tåsan tried to describe their attitudes without insult.

This was not as simple as writing one's truth. Tåsan found that for every paragraph he wrote, it took an hour of wordsmithing to smooth down the emotions and accusations that had crept into his writing.

Tåsan prepared himself for the closing argument of his document. The Magistrates conclusions. Their final and official proclamation. The part where he tells them that they're wrong, their judgment flawed.

Tåsan put his determination in check and slept on it for two nights and turned his thoughts over and over again for two days. On the third evening, with his mind still set, Tåsan began composing his conclusions.

He found it took a long while to clearly articulate his objections to being referred to as inexperienced. Tåsan sited his IGC record to date: he was exemplary in his admissions résumé and academy training, even going above IGC standards at times; he garnered praise and monitory awards for his innovative thinking; he won citations and medals of merit; he brought untold opportunity to the ISA through the Vellosian Affair while…yes!…in a command situation. So how? How can he be viewed as inexperienced?

He felt the official record should include his counter-points and his conclusion: that he acted professionally and in the only manner possible in this set of circumstances. He was sure any number of the other IGC officers would have done the same.

Tåsan put his stylus down, pressed the 'save' function, and scrolled back to the top to read through his arguments once again.

After a final edit and a 'save', Tåsan formatted the file for transmission. He pushed back from his writing table and stood up, noting that his legs were a bit stiff. It was then that he realized he had been sitting for five full hours. The clock showed the hour now past 2750 and he was to assume Command in four hours.

Tåsan stood looking at his e-dev screen unsure of a new feeling of apprehension that slowly started to prick at the edges of his conscience. He knew he was right, he knew he was clear. After a brief unexplained hesitation, Tåsan leaned over the back of the chair and touched the 'send' icon.

Nine
Gliding

Ari Arcturus ran, more or less, by the book. Days blended together, one after the other and time combined into weeks.

There were minor interruptions to the dull sameness of traversing the Allodial Expanse between the Rayten, the Niles, and the Hedorrion Galaxies. The only incident worth notice was a confrontation between two merchant ship captains, both of which seemed to be headed for something important when an argument between the two captains escalated past social decorum to an ostentatious display of "I'm right and you are not."

One of the ship's Comm Ops had the good sense to message *Ari Arcturus* of the angry situation in progress and Tåsan ordered her to respond with all haste.

After a few minutes of listening to each captain complain about the other and throw wild accusations of treachery and backstabbing back and forth, Tåsan interrupted the unproductive discourse.

"Gentlemen!" Tåsan shouted at the vid screen, shocking the captains into silence. And with his voice lowered and civil, "I've heard enough, thank you," staring at the images of the men on his screen. "It's all too clear that we have a miscommunication that has led you both to this place of impasse."

One of the captains started to object, "If you are insinuating…"

Tåsan held up his hand to halt the speech, "Enough, Captain, please let me finish."

The disgruntled man squirmed to turn sideways and motioned for Tåsan to continue.

Tåsan went on to explain that, as he saw it, the problem started with a vague comm originating at the corporation both captains were doing business with. *Ari Arcturus* had contacted said corporation and straightened it out. "The updated and unambiguous comm has been transmitted to your consoles. And now, gentlemen, you will cease your hostilities or the IGC will be forced to take a more direct approach to this arbitration."

Tåsan sat quietly watching the two men as they worked this bit of dialogue through their minds, finally coming to the conclusion...accept the outcome or be drawn into a long and unprofitable IGC hearing.

"Do we have your agreement?"

Both nodded and talking over one another, created a jumble of words that added up to an apology.

Tåsan dropped the comm, leaving them to their renewed, slightly guarded amity.

After taking a minute to review and approve the text of the situation, Tåsan returned to his notes and development of his Spacial Propulsion theory.

• • •

The next day, as Tåsan sat his bridge command, Tech Class I Mason Trang forwarded an IGC comm that had blipped across his message queue. The Vellosians and the ISA after quads of negotiation had finally reached a trade agreement. The Vellosians were so excited and happy with their two solar year contract that they were holding a celebration at one of the most exclusive accommodations the Niesus Resort had to offer. All IGC top ranking officials were invited. The IGC had attached a list of names of those authorized to attend.

Tåsan's name was not among them.

• • •

The following week an informational IGC message landed in the queue. *Bright Torch* had been assigned to meet and escort a group of delegates from Thorium 4, in the Hedorrion Galaxy, on a mission to Sador, the outer planet of the Niles Galaxy. Or more specifically, to Eriop, Sador's moon. The delegates were to meet with those from Sador to work out a trade agreement whereby the Thorium 4 officials seek to trade quantities of uridium-8 for Sadorian minerals and metals. Very important. *Bright Torch*, a twelve-crew escort ship, is to be accompanied by a small armada of other Class-A escorts that will be determined later.

The jewel of the IGC, *Ari Arcturus*, was not mentioned.

• • •

An IGC message queued up. *Ari Arcturus* was to respond to a request for assistance made by a large space barge stranded in a sector of the outer stars of the Rayten Galaxy. *Ari Arcturus* was to assist in repairs of the barge's guidance system so it could resume its course.

• • •

Troubling thoughts started to take root in Tåsan's mind. At first he put his questions and doubts off to an overactive imagination probably brought on by seemingly endless days of routine and well defined process.

Lately he wasn't so sure it was all due to his penchant for contemplative thought. There were specters in the wires.

• • •

The wi-comm chimed and Tåsan stepped toward his quarter's door saying, "Open," quickly followed by, "Hello! Come in and make yourselves comfortable."

Alyss and Castell came in smiling and stood for a moment as they greeted Tåsan.

"This is nice," said Alyss. "We haven't done this in some while."

"And to celebrate the rare occasion," said Castell, "I've brought a lug of Cirrus Ale," offering the container to Tåsan.

"Thanks," said Tåsan, "I'll get glasses. The dinner meal is heating so we have time to relax."

When the three friends were seated and enjoying the ale, conversation moved easily through a variety of topics. How was the day? What are you working on? And on it went until it was time to sit at table.

Tåsan brought a large, low-sided bowl from the galley and set it down in the middle of the table. "It's a replication of my mother's parsit and serra grain stew." And looking at Castell, quickly added, "You'll have to forgive my pale attempt. I was never allowed to cook after I managed to damage mother's kitchen with an exploding bean cake." Then glancing at Alyss, said, "You don't want to know." And shook his head as he took his place at

206

the table.

The stew was ladled and the glasses filled and so the three settled down.

"I'm curious to ask," said Tåsan, "How do you find life aboard *Ari Arcturus*?" He looked from Castell to Alyss, who glanced across the table at each other.

Castell sort of wiggled his fingers at Alyss as he nodded and said, "You go first, please."

"Okay," Alyss said as she lowered her spoon and wiped her mouth. "So far I find this assignment...prestigious but lacking in adventure. It's one thing to have a brand new *Ari Arcturus* but it's quite another to use it." Alyss reached for a brown grain muffin and continued, "We should be ordered out past our known borders. We should explore, not patrol shipping lanes and energize stalled cargo ships." She stopped and looked at Castell. "How about you, Castell?"

"Well," he began, "speaking as a ship's engineer, I find life aboard *Ari Arcturus* to be stimulating. The science and technology that has been combined to create such a ship is endlessly fascinating."

"But the study of such extraordinary technology would eventually come to an end," said Alyss. "Then what?"

Castell looked at Alyss as if she had just said something in an unknown language. As he considered her words, a faint look of confusion clouded his face. Then he answered, "I would hope that that time never comes but if it should, I'm almost sure I would become nervous at not having something to occupy my attention."

"So you would be bored?" asked Tåsan.

"Yes," considered Castell. "I would be bored."

The three ate stew and sipped ale for a few quiet minutes before Alyss said, "And what about you, Tåsan? How do you find life aboard *Ari Arcturus*?"

"I love this ship," Tåsan replied as he set his nonic of ale gently on the table. "I find it, as you both do, reputable and fascinating. Commanding *Ari Arcturus* feels natural to me." Tåsan hesitated before continuing. "It's life in the IGC that I find more difficult to navigate."

The friends just looked at Tåsan and waited.

"Have either of you noticed lately that *Ari Arcturus* is passed over for some of the better assignments?" Tåsan looked to his friends. "Or am I imagining that?"

"There was that ambassador convoy, but really, how important is a trade agreement?" asked Alyss. "It might have been more a matter of circumstance…not assigning the IGC jewel to a menial task, and all of that."

Castell added, "We're experiencing a slow time right now, that's all. It may pick up soon and we'll find ourselves knee deep in alien encounters and bonusable offenses."

Alyss and Tåsan smiled at Castell's not-so-subtle humor but Tåsan added, "I trust fortune that you're right. Maybe I'm being overly sensitive since the *Starlight* Episode, but I feel something is going on behind my back."

Tåsan felt a bit foolish as he heard the words he spoke to his friends. It did sound a bit reckless so he thought to steer the conversation away from his growing suspicion of IGC intentions, especially since he did not have proof of such a thing.

"Are you two up for a game of Parudi Rule?"

~

And in the telling of it, I was on a small rise overlooking a vast expansive horizon. It was daylight and the sunstar shone bright white. I looked at my hands but they didn't seem to be mine, they changed, slowly turning long and slender. Even as I wondered at that, the changing light made me look up. I caught a glimpse of a dark cloud that roiled and shifted and grew. I became fearful and thought to run to my home in Merula. Surely that was safety and security. I felt that if I could get there, all would be well.

I took two steps forward and knew with all certainty that all was not well, all would not be well. There were forces gathering and a voice had told me that as many forces as could fill the dark space would watch and calculate and devise.

Part of the distance to Merula now seemed hostile and unsafe. The dark cloud expanded to cover the warmth from the sunstar and as I watched, seemed to throw dark sinuous arms outward, threatening to envelop all.

I knew that escape was impossible and hiding was futile. I knew it would find me, I knew it would tirelessly search until it found me.

So, I bent the knee before it. Where there were words without form there was now fear. I cast my eyes downward and waited.

"You are among, not of. For that, there is payment."

Fright bid me not look up, except that I did.

"Dare!" boomed across my awareness and I cowered smaller, my breathing hard and fast.

"Because I must," I replied. "Because I must."

~

Time moved slowly during the following weeks and life aboard *Ari Arcturus* seemed to move in a sort of slow motion with the ever-present appearance of routine. While on bridge command, Tåsan tried to liven things up with periodic games of "What Would You Do?" but noted with concern, that his crew were slowly losing interest in playing. Or more precisely, the drill scenarios were lacking a spark of creativity and the fun of the game was starting to resemble habit.

Tåsan spent his off-duty time honing his Spacial Propulsion theory and working on detailing several aspects of his Shadow Fast Fighter craft as it moved closer to actuality, but neither of those ventures fully occupied his attention, for pricking at the boundaries of his concentration was the nerve racking sensation that circumstances were moving against him. He was able to hold his thoughts in check while his attention was focused on some task or another but as soon as he sat back or took a breath or changed projects, they would rush forward again.

After a particularly frustrating time trying to adjust a ratio of zanthii to tetrahedrane intended to maximize engine thrust and sensor detection, Tåsan had had it with his lack of concentration and stopped working for the day. He sat quietly in his quarters looking out the view windows watching the outer stars of the Niles Galaxy slowly move across his line of vision. It was time to stop busying himself with diversions; it was time for problem solving.

It seemed to Tåsan that his worries and suspicions began with his first significant command decision involving the *Ari Arcturus'* pursuit of the privateers in what had been long ago classified as the *Starlight* Episode, along with the subsequent court fiasco, and most definitely, with his memorandum-to-file outlining his defense explanations. Yes. That's where it started. He was sure of it. The subtle change in assignments, the exclusion from IGC ceremony, the lack of IGC communication. Tåsan felt it all.

Thinking to improve the situation, Tåsan sent a communiqué to IGC ranking officers at Command Headquarters requesting that they assign the *Ari Arcturus* to explore beyond the known space of the tri-galaxies, to use their resources to expand their boundaries. The lag time between when his request was sent and when the IGC responded was so lengthy that Tåsan had started to doubt the comm had been received. The implied castigation of the official response was hurtful. No, the IGC was not supportive of Tåsan's suggestion. This was not the time to risk valuable resources and personnel. Request denied.

Tåsan waited another length of time and tried again, this time requesting that he be allowed to host a gathering of top Intersolar and Space Alliance corporate leaders to spotlight *Ari Arcturus* and impress them with the ship and her crew with the implication that they might want to finance an expansion of their limited boundaries, thus mitigating the expense to the IGC. Request denied.

And all the while, it appeared to Tåsan, the assignments that came to *Ari Arcturus* were becoming less noteworthy and sometimes downright menial.

Frustration, and its attendants insecurity and dissatisfaction, grew daily. Tåsan became concerned with his career future. He was used to adventure and challenge, neither of which were evident in any of the assignments since the *Starlight* Episode. Things couldn't go on like this much longer. Tåsan knew the situation was affecting his concentration and performance, feeding his frustration into a passion. And it was affecting his crew. Tåsan understood that if the plight of *Ari Arcturus* could not be remedied, things would go from bad to worse.

Tåsan watched the stars roll past his view windows. He had time-lined the problem but it remained unsolved.

"Oh fortunes, I can not find my way out alone."

Tåsan pulled his e-pad closer and tapped open a comm-line

210

and began his message. ((Salutation father. May I have a portion of your time to discuss a dilemma that I find myself confronting? At your convenience, of course.))

• • •

Tåsan sat passively listening to his father.

Captain Amans Sulac's voice emanated clearly from the vid-screen, "I've listened patiently to your dissertation and have to tell you two things. First, that your *Starlight* Episode document outlining your so-called defense was poorly received. The IGC takes great pains to find facts and come to fair and just decisions and they dislike junior officers questioning their work. My advice is to never...*ever*...do that again. Second, you are wholly wrong in thinking that there is any kind of conspiracy designed to discredit you. The IGC simply does not work that way. Take my further advice seriously: Quit this line of thinking as it will only disquiet you and affect your command. You need to prove your abilities and the best way to do that right now is to stand fast and wait for your time to come as I'm sure it will." Captain Sulac sat staring at his son, waiting for a reply.

Tåsan's thoughts ran fast but he managed a slight smile.

Captain Sulac continued, "A career in the Inter-Galaxy Command is a long-term commitment, Tåsan. You want everything too fast. You must learn patience and you must learn self control."

Tåsan said, "Thank you, father."

"I have a pressing schedule I must attend to," and paused. "Is there anything else?"

"No, father."

"Good," said Amans. The vid-screen went black.

211

Ten

Descent Into Conformity

((Father. I appreciate that you took the time out of your busy schedule to speak with me. Thank you for your advice. As always, there is wisdom in your words and I have taken your advice under due consideration. I find valuable guidance that I trust I can apply to my own career with the same unyielding determination that you have always shown in yours. I will strive to be a better person and an excellent IGC officer.))

One quad has elapsed since Tåsan sent the carefully worded apology to Amans Sulac. As usual there was no acknowledgement from his father but Tåsan took that as a good sign. Apparently he had done something right for a change. After a week of anxiously waiting for a word, Tåsan put the affair behind him and renewed his commitment to his IGC career.

The first thing Tåsan did was to put his distrust of IGC conduct and his suspicion of an IGC vendetta against him under wraps. He had no doubt that the IGC was waging a subliminal disciplinary action against him for his daring to question their authority and decisions. He just didn't have proof and until he did, Tåsan thought it wise to keep his eyes and ears open but his thoughts to himself.

As the weeks passed, Tåsan did notice that the assignments given to *Ari Arcturus* had increased in frequency but to his dismay, not in importance. They were dull and routine and most of them not worth the boron it took to power the engines but Tåsan carried them out with all the professionalism he could muster.

For a short amount of time, Tåsan buried himself in IGC's Command manuals reading about codes of officer conduct, meeting protocols, laws guiding decisions, regulations regarding written entries, the adjudication process, and every other rule or law the IGC saw fit to record. Tåsan sincerely tried to apply himself to the rules and the rules to himself.

And still the inconsequential assignments slipped in, one by one but never amounted to anything more than patrol duty.

Tåsan soldiered on and for a short time longer, managed to distract himself by burying himself in protocol.

Eventually, Tåsan had to admit that he was in a constant struggle with conformity. And in turn, conformity was sucking the joy out of his job and the spark from his creativity. It was maddening. One day he's plodding through seemingly fine and the next, fighting the urge to throw it all away.

Tåsan could not find a comfortable middle ground.

• • •

Ari Arcturus had been out on patrol for almost five quads when ordered to Brenton Kae for routine maintenance and inspections. The prospect of a shore leave seemed to revive ship personnel and Tåsan noticed that the crew became more animated with anticipation. He, too, was looking forward to the down-time that shore leave offered and thought that it would be good to relax his IGC standards if only for a short time, to return to his previous care-free self.

Tåsan had risen early in his eagerness to disconnect from his routines and explore his more amiable nature and found he was looking forward to walking the passageways of Brenton Kae once again. Just off ship, he stopped at the wide view ports and stood gazing at *Ari Arcturus*, the hugeness of her filling the dock to its capacity, watching the maint-bots move methodically over the hull, scanning with macro ability, detecting all and the least flaw and setting about to repair it. He watched suited technicians float from one sensor array to another, hook up test devices and hang motionless in the moments that followed to analyze data, then move to the next and the next. Tåsan was always a bit awe-struck at just how much work went into Starchaser and Stratos class ships to keep them moving at their top precision. A fact sometimes lost when Tåsan called *Ari Arcturus'* technology into play.

Tåsan watched, mesmerized, for the better part of an hour then thought to move on. He really hadn't had much of an opportunity

213

to explore the for-profit side of the station. His first time here, he boarded *Ari Arcturus* and did not disembark again until summoned to testify at the travesty of a trial where men masqueraded as arbiters.

Tåsan forced those thoughts from his mind and took a deep breath to steady down and then walked on. *"Not today,"* he thought.

The corridor connecting the IGC to the rest of Brenton Kae terminated at an upstairs promenade that overlooked a huge central plaza that was bright and colorful and filled with movement.

As Tåsan stood taking it in, he could feel the happiness rise in his chest even as thoughts of the IGC receded to the background. With a lightness of step, he boarded the redi-lift that would take him downward, right into the middle of it all.

The sights and sounds of Brenton Kae were stimulating and Tåsan thought how different it was from his life aboard ship where routine was the norm and noise and excitement usually meant trouble.

At noon meal, Tåsan found a table on the concourse and ordered a small plate and a mug of ale from a very amiable waiter who had then disappeared through the doors of the tratoria, only to reappear a brief moment later holding a tray swaying over his head as he wove his way though the obstacle course of other tables already filled with raucous customers. With a flourish, the waiter set the ale in front of Tåsan and was about to say something when his attention was diverted, and calling out a greeting to someone sitting far in back of Tåsan, ran off smiling and chattering, leaving Tåsan and his ale in peace.

As Tåsan sat, sipping his brew and watching the flow of the market street, he was struck with how multiplanetal Brenton Kae was. He heard at least five other languages than his own and from the crowd could pick out visitors from Astor, Erontu, and Titus.

In time his small plate arrived and he munched his fare and finished his ale and sat quietly amid the chaos and wondered of the lives of the denizens that passed through Brenton Kae.

Tåsan spent the next handful of hours wandering the markets doing a bit of window shopping and occasionally stepping inside a shop to more closely look at the wares. As the hours ticked forward, Tåsan noticed that the lighting of the station, or at least the part he was now traversing, started to change. It moved from bright yellow to a lower intensity hew tinged with light orange and Tåsan soon realized that the station was simulating a dusk effect. He looked at his e-dev and noted the late hour and thought to message Alyss and Castell to invite them to join him for an evening in Brenton Kae's nightlife.

...

A third round of drinks stood in front of the friends, amid the debris of several small plates and a basket still holding a half dozen uneaten grain muffins.

Alyss had plucked a muffin from the basket and was tearing small pieces away with her fingers before popping the bits into her mouth. She sat passively, half listening to Tåsan and Castell's serious discussion of tangible data displays and how they could be miniaturized.

"But what would the hardware application look like?" stressed Castell.

"It might look like," Tåsan responded, "a physical pop-up screen one fifth the size of my e-dev. The array could be lined up either horizontal or vertical and be called on demand."

"Well, yes, I suppose that would be one way to utilize a new technology," mused Castell.

Tåsan was about to say something else when Alyss cut in, "Okay. Enough shop-talk," and indicating the frosty drinks standing at the ready, "A toast."

With glasses raised, Castell and Tåsan waited expectantly for Alyss to say something.

"To our future," she said, "to fortune and dreams," and with a smile to her friends, raised her glass.

When the toast was done and the three had fallen quiet, Castell spoke, "I dream some day to be a very distinguished Engi-mec with deep tech intelligence and a way with words."

Tåsan and Alyss watched Castell's face for signs of anything further to come and in short moments, he continued. "I may even become a master of writing with several of my papers used as required study at University." Castell took a sip of his drink. "I'm

215

looking for my subjects among the great number of details of *Ari Arcturus* and the elusive solutions needed for Shadow Fast." Castell sat back, "It's a big undertaking," and looked at Alyss. "How about you? What are your dreams?"

Alyss shifted in her chair and thought for a bit before speaking. "My dream for my future lacks the precision that yours does, Castell, but if I were to put it to words, it may simply be this. I desire success and satisfaction in my career. I aspire to stay true to myself." She glanced up from her drink and continued, "That's the esoteric side, If in reality I also acquire a vast stretch of land, build a sprawling residence, and live simply while contemplating my next career, well, all the better for me." Alyss raised her glass to Tåsan. "It's to you, friend, what do you dream of?"

Tåsan had listened as Castell and Alyss spoke of their imagined futures of good fortune and personal happiness and while he too, wanted those things, his thoughts ran contrary. "My desire is to command interstellar ships, to explore what lays beyond our star maps." Here Tåsan hesitated as negative thoughts of the IGC crowded into his mind. "I'm not confident that those dreams are possible. I seem to be in a perpetual struggle against unseen forces where my choice of career is under constant question." Tåsan hesitated and nervously raised his glass to drink the bittersweet liquid it contained.

His friends sat silent.

"The main question now, and one I ask myself quite often," Tåsan continued, "is, do I have a career with the IGC at all." He sat staring at his glass, "It's very confusing."

Alyss leaned in and lightly touched Tåsan's wrist. "Your situation may only be current and that with time, may resolve, in which case, all your worry has done is to age you."

"Look to yourself," added Castell, "for your dream. The IGC may simply provide the means, not the result."

"You are both right, of course," Tåsan said. "And from this moment," he smiled, "I will find a way to navigate through."

"Hear, hear," Castell said and tapped his glass on the tabletop to underscore Tåsan's resolve.

• • •

Time aboard *Ari Arcturus* passed in much the same way as it had before...slowly and filled with uninspired assignments. Only one unusual point had arisen: a small ceremony to mark the two solar years since the initial launching of *Ari Arcturus*. The occasion was marked by the distribution of a small, quartz commemorative that noted the launching date along side the IGC logotype.

Tåsan had tossed his into a drawer, dismissing it as a meaningless longevity award of little value.

In the quads following shore leave, Tåsan threw himself into the further development of his pet project, Spacial Propulsion, finding it a welcome diversion even if his concentration was interrupted periodically by menial ship's assignments.

In spite of assignments that lacked integrity, Tåsan still enjoyed his bridge duty for no other reason then he was in command and among peers, his friends.

This day's duty found Tåsan hours deep in ship's manuals, refamiliarizing himself with schematics and modifications. His head was starting to swim in a sea of data and explanations and engirythms and he realized he wasn't absorbing as much as he should, so he sat back and let his gaze float around the bridge.

After a very short time, Tåsan stood up and slowly made his way to Alyss' side. "Everything in order, Lieutenant?" he asked.

"Yes, sir," she replied. "We're following a random course from vector 827F1, here," Alyss pointed to a spot on her graphic rep screen, "in the Hedorrion Outer Stars, to here," drawing her finger in a jagged line across the map, "vector 35N1.8, on the far side of the Rayten Galaxy." Alyss glanced up at Tåsan. "That is, until something interrupts us, sir."

Tåsan took that as a joke and widened his eyes in delight. "Of course. Well," he said, "steady on, Lieutenant." And stepped easily over to Castell's station.

They nodded to each other in appreciative silence and Tåsan stood quietly observing Castell's monitors as they pulsed with ship's information. The constant rhythm of the engine's energy absorption rate, graphically displayed, shown as a sinuous never-ending line was slowly seducing Tåsan into a trance. He had to jolt himself awake and look away.

Tech Class I Mason Trang interrupted Tåsan's quiet commune. "Sir, an incoming message for you from IGC. It's marked private."

"Thank you, Mr. Trang. Please put it through to my sen-dev." Tåsan listened intently to the words as they sounded in his head.

"A message from Vice Admiral Caoin. Commander Sulac, I have the honor to inform you that you will be reassigned to Supĕrus Tacere where you, and three of your hand-picked, technically adept and personally trusted colleagues will begin development of the Shadow Fast Fighter. Reassignment will take place in one week. Enough time for preparation. Additional information will be communicated at a later time. These orders are highly classified and you may only discuss them with your designated assignees."

Tåsan was momentarily stunned but stood true. "Mr. Trang, please copy to my dev."

"Aye, sir."

With only an hour of bridge duty remaining, Tåsan sat Command and played the message again, then with barely a moment of hesitation, tapped out a message to Alyss, Castell and Annis.

((A confidential meeting, if you would. My quarters. 32150 hrs.))

• • •

Tåsan brought a pot of hot tea from the galley, poured four mugs, and handed them around. He took the next handful of minutes to explain why he had asked Castell, Alyss, and Annis to meet with him. It was a very short introduction, as Tåsan did not have any information other than that of Vice Admiral Caoin's brief message.

On the mention of Supĕrus Tacere, Castell immediately tapped a query of the IGC database on his e-dev and on return of the search spoke to the group. "The information is very sketchy, less that half a page, but basically Supĕrus Tacere is a top secret facility dedicated to the research and development of various IGC projects."

"And now the 'Shadow Fast Fighter' among them," said Alyss.

Annis added, "I know Supĕrus Tacere. It's where some of my AI circuitry and implant technology integration was developed. You won't find hardly a mention of it anywhere. The IGC guards against information going public. Even rumors are written on the wind. I doubt that many ISA personages are even aware of

Supĕrus Tacere."

Noting that no one had negative comments on the discussion so far, Tåsan asked, "Do any of you have reservations about being reassigned to this project? We may be gone up to one solar year." He waited.

"I would only ask a curious question. Would we return to *Ari Arcturus* after the Supĕrus Tacere assignment concluded?" spoke Annis. "Otherwise, I'm very much on board."

"Good point. I'll find out and let you know," Tåsan answered. "Castell?" he than asked.

"I have to marvel that our Shadow Fast is moving into reality. I have no reservations about helping that happen."

"Alyss?"

"I've got to say that the prospect of watching and assisting our concept become tangible," Alyss smiled broadly, "is very exciting."

Tåsan said, "I agree. And I'm so happy that you are all willing to commit to this. I can hardly wait to get started." He refreshed everyone's tea then continued, "We should meet again on the morrow, after bridge, to list preparation steps."

The conversation was animated and fractured and lasted a small part of an hour before the group started to break for the evening.

"Remember," reminded Tåsan, "top secret comm."

• • •

The week of preparation went fast enough. Tåsan notified Caoin of his new teammates and further orders of departure place and time were transmitted.

In short, four replacements were assigned to cover the posts that Tåsan, Alyss, Castell, and Annis would vacate for the next solar year. Tåsan didn't see why the relief personnel couldn't take over their assignments immediately, which left the team free to prepare for departure.

Alyss spent some time reviewing the details of Shadow Fast with Annis to ensure that she was up to point with the others.

Castell was spending an inordinate amount of time turning over his station to his replacement. So much so that Tåsan caught up with him in the corridor one afternoon and advised him to trust the engineer and wind it up.

For himself, Tåsan copied his personal research on Spacial Propulsion and his AI Robotics to an exterior port-drive, backed it up for a second copy, and deleted all trace of it from the ship's databases and archived holograms. It was his work and he intended it to stay that way.

• • •

The Class-A escort, that was to transport the Shadow Fast team to Supĕrus Tacere, met *Ari Arcturus* at the designated vector and departed as scheduled for the two-day flight to Eros.

The base, located deep in the wild lands of Eros' outback, was inaccessible by land and kept from detection by an intricate grid of sensor distortions that masked the buildings and flight field from view. Security was always on high alert and the space above the lands that surround the base for many milia in all directions, are off limits to all.

A freshly dressed cadet met the team as they disembarked the escort and led the way to a low, simply ornamented building where they would be quartered. Along the route, the cadet pointed out the café, the supply, and the building where the Shadow Fast development work would take place.

That evening in quarters, Tåsan and Annis sat together in the spacious lounge that faced the ever-busy flight field, decompressing from three days of travel and settling in.

"It's all very impressive," said Tåsan, his head turned toward the view, now seeing a small ship arriving at the far end of the field and small carts zipping out to meet it.

Annis was watching Tåsan and thought to herself, *"Even in his idle time, he's alert."* Then to Tåsan, "It *is* impressive and will be more so when you see our workspace tomorrow."

Tåsan turned to face Annis. "How long were you stationed here?"

"Almost four solar years," she replied. "My technology is very complicated."

"You must know all the secrets of Supĕrus Tacere," Tåsan smiled.

"Ah, yes," Annis said, "starting with Supĕrus Tacere being the biggest secret of all!"

Tåsan gave a quiet laugh and Annis smiled easily. "I'm very

pleased to be able to share this experience with you and Alyss and Castell," she said. "May I ask why you thought to include me?"

"For several reasons." Tåsan looked serious, "The main one being your precision of thought. And along with your familiarity with abstract concepts and problem solving abilities, I must admit it was a selfish choice on my part." Tåsan sat trying to find the words.

Annis was quiet and waited.

"This is going to sound mercenary, and I apologize in advance, I mean no insult," he sputtered.

"Honestly," Annis encouraged, "I won't take affront. I am curious to hear."

Tåsan looked at Annis for a long second and seeing only soft curiosity in her eyes, plucked up his courage and spoke. "I am devoted to AI but find that I am far deficient in my knowledge since learning of the technology that you bear." Tåsan tumbled onward, "You are so advanced, beyond what is taught at University or even by IGC...*and the tech is theirs!*...or yours," Tåsan lost himself in the enormity of the subject and thought to stop talking before he said something he couldn't un-say.

Annis had sat quietly amused at Tåsan's embarrassment. "You are an interesting being, Tåsan Sulac." Annis took a small breath and continued, "I have a curt description of myself that I use upon introduction that I will spare you the hearing of. Instead, I will converse openly and fully with you at any time about the technology of me," she smiled.

Relieved by her words, Tåsan said simply, "Thank you, Annis O'hAirt, that is extremely generous." And with a slightly embarrassed tone added, "Would this be a good time?"

Annis smiled as she shifted to a more comfortable position in her chair, "I was born on Erontu..."

Annis did not have many clear memories of a "childhood" other than a vivid recollection of her fascination with technology that quickly evolved to include what would become a life-altering love affair with the development and enhancements of Artificial Intelligence.

As a young adult, Annis found that she had an aptitude and an interest in logistics and how to overcome barriers to it. "It was like a puzzle that I was determined to solve." Soon her education and interests encompassed strategy and as she excelled in her education it became apparent the she was destined for a career that included anything technologically advanced and where else than with the IGC would she find opportunity to work with so many disciplines?

At the time, Annis was the youngest recruit in two generations to apply and be accepted into the IGC. As a result, she attracted special attention and customized training. Soon she added weapons and flight control to her ever-widening field of expertise and applied her puzzle-solving skills to the application of tactical strategies. Annis could be presented with an "obstacle" and quickly and seemingly without much effort, resolve an objective.

Annis had been with the IGC almost one solar year when she was offered the opportunity to work on the highly classified project of AI integration being conducted at Supérus Tacere. She was warned that it was experimental among other risk factors that she barely remembers hearing because she leapt at the chance as quickly as the IGC counselor stopped speaking.

It took all of one AI implant for Annis to realize that her full potential lay ahead. She spent the next four solar years advancing AI implant interfacing, bio-testing, and upgrading the technology that now enhances her physical body and mind.

Her free time at Supérus Tacere was her own and Annis eventually found a way to restore the energies that she freely spent in work and research. She used her multi-lensed digi-eye camera to its fullest extent, composing serene landscapes comprised of thousands of images of natural elements, such as stone, soil, leaves, insects, and the like, all stitched together to create a scene from her creative imagination. It was what she did to calm the streaming technological dialogue of her working mind, easing it down to rest and restoration. She was good at her art and enjoyed it immensely.

By the time Annis had finished her bio and answered all of Tåsan's questions, the time was very late and the friends were tired from the day. Soon they said good night.

• • •

The next quad was hectic almost to the point of chaos. The team was introduced to their dev center and set about outfitting it with long tables, designated spaces, specific tools, and information access as well as a project database.

For the project start-up period, Tåsan requested four cadets be assigned, one to each team member, to act as go-fors and do-ers. He figured that once the project moved from chaos to something resembling steady progress, extra hands would be invaluable.

Each team member took a Shadow Fast project aspect and set to work. By the second quad, it was very apparent that the work was setting the pace, that the level of complexity was deeper than anyone could have imagined in the beginning.

Long days and exhausted nights became normal, however, Tåsan insisted on periodic team meetings where members could present any problems or stick-points and discuss possible fixes. He made sure to have copious amounts of tea and a variety of small plate fare on hand as the meetings were not only for work, but for relaxation and would at times wind down into a rousing Game of Twenty or if time allowed, Parudi Rule.

During this period and for the quads that followed, the Shadow Fast Fighter project would be visited by base command and various other officers each desiring to know the progress, any difficulties, and as if on cue, would inevitably ask if the team needed anything.

Tåsan began to resent these visits as intrusions to be tolerated. They accomplished nothing other than to irritate him, but he kept in check and learned how to put on his "serious face" when in the company of base officers. They would show up unannounced, hem-hem this, nod approvingly at that, and spout IGC platitudes such as, "This work will bring honor to the IGC," or "Strength through superiority," or any number of other buzz worthy slogans. It all made Tåsan wonder just how anything got accomplished at all since being run by such frivolous, non-sighted men.

Late one evening as Tåsan sat with Castell in the quarters lounge, he breached the subject of how it seemed to him that most long-term career officers had lost their spark and wondered if it was the fault of the man or the fault of the IGC.

"Is there something within the IGC that eventually kills a man's drive?" he earnestly asked Castell.

Castell did not know how to answer. He just shook his head

and looked confused.

Tåsan noticed Castell's unease. "Oh, pay no attention to me, I'm over tired and am being ridiculous." But Tåsan knew he wasn't foolish in his assessment and re-dedicated himself to keeping his opinions to himself.

• • •

Toward the end of the last quad of the Shadow Fast reassignment, the IGC held a celebration in recognition of all the hard work that Tåsan, Alyss, Annis, and Castell, as well as their able assistants, had put into the startup, organization, and development pace of the Shadow Fast Fighter. The entire project was invited to the base café at 3750 hours on the evening of sol. Dress uniform required.

On the appointed evening, Tåsan slowly made his way from his quarters out to the byway that ran between four of the housing units and half-heartedly turned toward the base café. He could see it up ahead, ablaze with light and whether aware or not, he could not say, his steps slowed until he had stopped and he now stood in the evening shadows, watching the motions and animations of those already in attendance as they moved through the throng smiling and greeting.

Tåsan had not heard Alyss as she stepped up behind him, and was unaware that she was standing beside him until she spoke, "Hello, I thought *I* was late." She leaned slightly forward to look around at Tåsan's face. "Are you alright?" she asked.

Tåsan gave a small start at her voice, shook from his inattention and said, "Woa, I did not hear you, sorry. Yes, I'm fine," he stammered. "I was watching the celebration and started to dread going in." His gaze returned to the café windows but he made no effort to step forward.

Alyss said, "Well, I understand. Part of me feels the same way but another part of me wants to mark the occasion with a little pomp. Rub elbows with top secret guys, maybe leave them knowing who I am, what I'm capable of."

Tåsan smiled and glanced in her direction. "It's just that I'm unenthused at the prospect of standing around smiling and small talking."

"Look at it this way," Alyss offered, "For a couple hours of your time, you will be treated with respect, you will eat a good meal, probably better than we've had for three and a half quads, and," she looked at Tåsan and smiled brightly, "*and* you will sip the very best Lingdon Práxus that IGC tenges can buy." She slipped her hand around Tåsan's elbow and gave a slight tug.

He wrapped her hand into the crook of his arm and said, "Okay. I'll do it for the Práxus," and allowed Alyss to lead him onward into the jaws of IGC Muroidea.

• • •

The full sum of the celebration added up to this: The team received a small token award in the form of an odd-looking sculpture bearing the date, their rank and name, the IGC logography and a small embedded piece of rhyolite. And as Tåsan saw it, they were further insulted by the gifting of a five hundred tenges bonus. All this to the indulgent smiles and polite applause from ranking officers.

None of this helped Tåsan's attitude.

Eleven
A Fork In The Road

Five more weeks passed, the solar year ended, and for Tåsan, Alyss, Annis, and Castell, their work on the Shadow Fast Fighter and assignment to Supĕrus Tacere concluded. They would transfer back to *Ari Arcturus* but were first granted a two-week leave of absence.

Tåsan chose to go home to Naiad Five.

The homecoming was a joy made nicer by the absence of Tåsan's father and a welcome relief from the ever-present IGC and constant battle that waged in Tåsan's thoughts.

For three glorious days, Tåsan relaxed and caught up on family news. He messaged friends and even managed to hear back from one or two. He borrowed Romis' pulse rocket and took a long, slow ride along the Phyllite Cliffs only turning back when the fuel ran low.

Somewhere around day five, Tåsan summed up his days…he had been running away, trying to distract himself from what was concerning him the most: mistrust of the IGC. But it had caught up with him and it was time to deal with it.

Later that evening, Tåsan sat brooding on the back deck, drinking a Cirrus Ale, watching the light of day fade into a murky dusk, trying to organize his thoughts.

Rebetta had watched from the kitchen window and could tell that something was bothering her son and decided to talk with him. She took another ale from cool storage and stepped outside.

"I've brought you another," she said, offering the drink to Tåsan.

"Oh, thanks mother," he said, taking the bottle and setting it next to the other.

"I know something is weighing on your mind, Tåsan," Rebetta said, "I may be able to help." She looked at him expectantly.

Tåsan did need to talk about his darkening thoughts but wondered if talking with his mother was the answer. "I'm just feeling a little frustrated with how things are going right now," he said.

"In what way," Rebetta asked.

"In many ways, mother." Tåsan could feel his barriers start to fall. "The IGC has lost the spirit of adventure that used to drive command. I see now that many, if not all, top officers have fallen into a pattern of predictability. Everything is safe and if anything comes close to upsetting that safety, the response is fear." Tåsan took a sip of his ale and thought, *"I've tumbled to the truth of it. There's no going back now."* He continued, "There's fear of risk, fear of losing their pensioned futures, and what frustrates me beyond all annoyance," Tåsan said, "is their blatant fear of the youthful attitudes of *their* new recruits!" Tåsan could feel tightness in his chest and realized he had stiffened his back while he spoke and sought now to sit back and with an effort, calm down.

Rebetta looked at Tåsan's face and saw there the look of a confused child trying to work out a particularly tough problem. "Are you sure you are reading this correctly? That there is real fear among the officers in command?" She spoke softly. "Your father has never acted from fear, quite the contrary."

"I'm not speaking about father, he never speaks to me, anyway." Tåsan pushed on, "I'm referring to the attitude of complacency with the status quo and the rigidity with which they resist change. Both of which produce fear." Tåsan looked at his mother, almost defiantly, waiting for her to comment on his criticisms.

"I'm sorry, son," Rebetta spoke, "I had no idea that you felt this way. I think the only way I can help you is to give you some advice, the same I have given myself, and that is...contemplate your frustration with this problem and the answer is sure to appear." Rebetta leaned closer to Tåsan and her movement caused Tåsan to meet her eyes. "Don't do anything rash, but follow your heart." She said in summary and got up, kissed Tåsan's forehead, and stepped back inside leaving Tåsan to his thoughts.

And they ran away with him. *"Well, that didn't help to solve anything except to let off steam...I've upset mother...she's sure to tell father...that's all I need...Maybe I should leave..."*

Later, after an awkward and uncomfortable dinner meal where barely two words were exchanged with his mother, Tåsan retreated to his room and sent a comm to Alyss.

((Family obligation complete. How about you? Want to meet up?))

• • •

As fortune would have it, in its ellipse, Eros was an eight-hour flight for Alyss and a ten-hour flight for Tåsan, and would be, in one weeks time, within easy transport of Brenton Kae, where they would rejoin *Ari Arcturus*.

It was agreed. Tåsan and Alyss would meet in the small inclusive city of Caliah on the southward border of Delosi, Eros' capitol city.

They took rooms on the main street and spent their time walking the side streets looking for abstract eateries and sitting on benches in the central park, away from the constant noise and movement of the small city.

One late afternoon as they sat together in an outdoor café, Tåsan broached the subject. "Alyss, do you ever find yourself at odds with IGC convention?"

"Hmmm," she pondered the question then answered, "Yes, at times. I find IGC protocol a little stiff and I think they tend to rule by committee, which makes the system ineffectual."

"I find the endless routine a grind. I'm afraid it's taking a toll on me. The boredom of patrol is sucking the life from my spirit. And the conversations that I have with freight captains and service ships could be pre-written dialogue...it never varies." Tåsan shook his head in annoyance at the memory of all the regular checks that had been carried out in the past.

"Agreed," said Alyss, adding, "Travel from the Niles Galaxy Outer Stars to the farthest vector of the Rayten Galaxy can only be done a small handful of ways and I've managed to repeat those ways dozens of times."

They sat quietly for a moment before Tåsan gathered his thoughts, "When I think that this is my career, that I may be this

228

and only this for the majority of my adult life, I'm telling you, Alyss, I experience a sort of depression."

Alyss looked at Tåsan. She had never heard him talk like this before. It frightened her a bit.

"It's getting harder to shake it off," he added.

"I don't know what to tell you, Tåsan," Alyss said faintly.

"And that's been exactly my dilemma, Alyss. No one knows what to tell me, including myself. So there's no easy answer to my problem. It's one I will have to keep at until I resolve it. But," he looked at Alyss, her face pained with concern, "I appreciate your friendship and support."

Alyss tried to smile.

"And thank you for listening. It means a lot to me."

• • •

Alyss kept an eye on Tåsan and for several weeks made a point of, every so often, asking him if all was well. He always answered with a smile and a little joke that, yes, he was fine, don't worry. But she would see the black circles under his eyes and the furrowed lines across his brow and know that Tåsan was not fine. Not really. But she had to back off, to give him time, to stop smothering him with care.

• • •

Tåsan had been with the IGC for six, almost seven solar years when one day as he sat Command, another call for assistance came from a stranded craft that had lost an engine and now floated helplessly about the Allodial Expanse, drifting into Rayten Galaxy space.

Upon hearing the comm, Tåsan's frustration and anger boiled to the surface and before he could check himself, it all spewed out. "That does it!" Tåsan loudly exclaimed. "A Stratos Class ship is not a low-class space service!" In his anger, Tåsan had stood up as he continued, "You would think it would behoove the ISA to make a rule among their members…Keep Your Transports in Order!"

Tåsan became acutely aware that the entire bridge crew was staring at him, most in stunned amazement and others in shocked disbelief. He looked to Alyss, "Lieutenant," he barked, "you have the Bridge," and turned, strode to the power lift and was gone.

Back in his quarters, Tåsan paced. *"I am so sick of this,"* he fumed. *"The IGC is nothing. It's affected my thoughts and my attitude and now my command. I've put up with this for far too long."* Pulling a decanter from a shelf and a glass from the galley, Tåsan flopped down in his favorite chair, poured four drams of the golden green liquid, and took a huge mouthful. As the liquid warmed his tongue and his throat, finally settling into a warm ball in his stomach, Tåsan flexed his neck and shoulders to let go the stress.

"Let's sum it up," he thought. *"A succession of low pay raises, the never-ending onslaught of meaningless assignments, and my extreme unhappiness. Humph."* Tåsan almost laughed out loud, *"And now...anger."*

Tåsan sipped at his glass. *"I'd say this has just about played itself out. Time to do something about it."* He finished his drink and poured another then moved to his desk and pulled out his e-dev sending a comm to IGC authorities requesting a short leave of absence, followed by a comm to his family telling them that he would appreciate their opinions and perceptions on a matter of great importance to him.

$$\bullet \; \bullet \; \bullet$$

After talking for twenty almost non-stop minutes, Tåsan sat back and looked from Rebetta to Stellanova to Amans to Arron and back. No one spoke and the moments seemed to meld into a long continuous crush of silence.

Tåsan spoke again, "There isn't too much else for me to say."

Amans cleared his throat. "If you're looking for my favor in this matter, I will not give it," his voice steady. "It is my good opinion that you are throwing away a viable future, one you can count on. You are assured a place by Inter-Galaxy Command, one, I may remind you, that they have assured to you by providing the training..."

"Wait, father," Tåsan interrupted, "Are you saying that the IGC has bought me? Have done me a favor by bestowing me with a highly decorative career of patrolling a few vectors of shipping lanes?"

"What I'm saying is that the IGC has made a substantial investment in you," Amans' voice was hard and smooth, "and they are correct in expecting that you provide a return for that investment. That you demonstrate loyalty and trust that their

230

decisions are just." He stared, unblinking at Tåsan.

Stellanova spoke, barely above a whisper, "Tåsan, I had no idea you were so unhappy. It makes me very sad to think that you've had so much on your mind for so long." She absentmindedly twisted a small beryl ring round and round her finger. "Is there anything I can do to help?"

Tåsan heard the angst in her voice and noted the concern of her words. "Nothing other than your support, Stella. It means a lot and is enough for right now." He smiled a wan smile but turned his eyes to Rebetta. "I'd listen to your advice, mother, if you have any to give."

Rebetta took in a deep breath to steady herself. She had listened to what Tåsan had said, noting the conviction in his words and listened to the counter-argument put forth by Amans, noting the staunch IGC loyalty in his. Now she sought to find her own words. "In the beginning, starting with your admissions to IGC training, you burst with happiness and excitement at the prospect of experiencing something new and you applied yourself with whole-heart." She looked at Tåsan. "And it proved successful, your hard work rewarded you with a very good commission, the best of what the IGC had to offer a highly promising young officer. But now," Rebetta looked at Tåsan and with a bit of indulgence in her voice, continued, "...now that the thrill of newness and the initial excitement of Command has wound down, you find your days dull and boring. It seems to me that you have lost your way. I am sure that you will regain your path and find a positive answer through recommitment. Recommit, Tåsan, to your goals, to your strength, and to yourself." Rebetta fell silent.

"Thank you, mother," Tåsan said.

Arron had been leaning against the doorjamb with his arms folded across his chest, looking at Tåsan with what could be called mild disgust. He now interrupted, "It seems to me, Tåsan, that you have not thought this whole thing through. It's just as it was when we were children. You rushed off to each new experience, each new sensation as if it was the only thing on the planet worth doing until it lost its thrill and you turned your attention to the next thing and the next and the next." Arron had advanced a step into the room. "You are not a child any longer, Tåsan. My advice to you is

231

to grow up and consider your next step very seriously. Don't throw a perfectly good career away because you are now bored."

Tåsan sat for a moment staring at Arron, realizing that they had, indeed, grown apart. "As I was about to say, I have a lot to think about and when I find a solution to my dilemma, I will be sure to include you all."

Tåsan stood up, "I'm returning to *Ari Arcturus* tomorrow and will leave at first light. Thank you for indulging me with your time and your words." He smiled as best he could at his family and strode to the doorway.

"Good night." And he was gone.

Twelve
Declining Curve Analysis

Tåsan wrestled with the advantages and disadvantages of his staying with the IGC and applied the same logic to his leaving the IGC. The argument, never far from his thoughts, tilted one way this minute and tilted the other way the next minute. There were clearly good motivators for each side of the discussion that raged endlessly in his mind.

The IGC provided a career structure that could be counted upon. Tåsan could build it up to some level of greatness and maybe even get a Recognition installed in the vestibule of the Cirrian Auditorium. Wouldn't *that* be grand.

The alternative to the IGC and their structure with its expected sameness presented a much more indistinct picture. Tåsan knew his alternative choice was leaving the IGC and having to make it on his own. Several possibilities presented themselves rather readily. He could use his technical experience in test and research, he had knowledge of AI applications, and he could always employ his piloting skills. This seemed the most appealing to Tåsan as it played to his sense of control.

But before making any final decisions, Tåsan resolved to give the IGC one more opportunity to make things right.

He drafted a Letter to File clearly outlining his résumé highlights including, several of the more remarkable points: Prior educational high scores, IGC entry score of Lieutenant, top of all his classes, first team to return from a truly wretched survival course, Shadow Fast Fighter concept and start-up, graduated top of his class as Commander and assigned to the jewel of the IGC, and let's not forget the Vellosians.

Tåsan smiled and nodded to himself as he reviewed the high

points of his career...to date. He wondered how many more points he would have to make before the IGC reciprocated.

Yes. That was it. The IGC should make concessions. It was necessary as a motivator. Tåsan carefully considered what it would take to make him decide to stay with the IGC, and once decided, his Letter to File grew longer.

Tåsan asked that the IGC formally recognize him as an officer in good standing and accept his style of command without further question. There should be an apology for their unwarranted treatment of him in regard to the *Starlight* Episode. He wanted increased status for *Ari Arcturus* assignments, in essence, elimination of the ludicrous run-arounds now in effect. Tåsan wanted permission to explore space beyond the known star maps and last but not least, Tåsan wanted promotions and compensations in line with his accomplishments.

The final list of concessions was not long, nor was it impossible to effect. If the IGC could see their way to making it right, and to Tåsan's mind, do it in short order, he would easily decide to stay.

The Letter to File was sent according to IGC rules and regulations, addressed to appropriate officers and structured exactly as outlined in the "Officer's Guide to Written Comm."

Three days later came a formal response from Vice Admiral Caoin stating that the IGC denied any wrong doing in the treatment of Tåsan in his capacity as an IGC officer. Just the opposite: Tåsan had been treated more than fairly. Using IGC property for personal gratification is out of the question and requesting compensation for doing ones duty is beyond preposterous, it is absolutely absurd, not to be brought up again or a disciplinary action may be required.

Tåsan could see by the form and official seal following Caoin's signature that this letter had been appended to his personnel file. Another black mark upon his name and most likely another obstacle to achieving his career goals.

"*I expected as much,*" Tåsan thought.

• • •

: 34891.0
: Vice Admiral Caoin
: Regarding Letter of Resignation

: Commander Tåsan Sulac, currently of *Ari Arcturus*

Accept this as notification of resignation effective 34909.1. May the transition be uncomplicated.

Signed, *Tåsan Sulac*, Commander

Within moments of Tåsan touching the "send" icon, a message chimed to his e-dev. ((Your presence is requested at an officer's meeting to occur in two days time to review current situation status. Routing change transmitted to *Ari Arcturus*. Report to Brenton Kae Commander upon arrival.))

Tåsan reported to the Brenton Kae commander who immediately conducted him to a meeting room in wing 32FE. The commander showed Tåsan into the room and motioned that he was to sit at the foot of the long table that occupied the center of the space.

"You will be joined shortly by the others. It will only be a moment," the commander said, then closed the door behind him leaving Tåsan alone in the quiet room.

Tåsan stood looking around at nothing in particular and without much thought, moved to the view window to gaze out at space. He was roused from his thoughts when suddenly the door snapped open and several ranking officers filed in one by one led by Vice Admiral Caoin.

"Take your seat, Commander," said Caoin, "This panel hearing will now begin."

When all were seated and the shuffling of papers and clicking of e-dev's had subsided, Caoin, sitting at the head of the table, closely grouped by six other officers that Tåsan did not recognize, spoke, "This panel," he said as he opened his arms to indicate the men who sat at table to his right and to his left, "have been apprised of all recent communication received from you, Commander Sulac, as well as Inter-Galaxy Command responses. Furthermore, access to your personnel file was granted. After a cursory review by this panel," again Caoin indicated the men seated around the table, "it was decided that the IGC would keep this situation off the record, if, Commander Sulac, you would cease in your pursuit of your radical demands. If that were agreed to, the

235

IGC would be willing to overlook your transgressions, to let it go, as it were."

Vice Admiral Caoin stared emotionless at Tåsan and as Tåsan sat looking back at Caoin, he saw every head turn to face him, all with noncommittal eyes.

Tåsan collected his thoughts then spoke, "Sirs, I'm afraid I can not agree to your premise…"

Caoin interrupted, "In that case, Commander, this panel is now on the record." Caoin touched an icon on his e-dev then added, "You may now proceed with your comments."

"As you wish, Vice Admiral Caoin. On the record," Tåsan said. "I do not agree with your calling my requests for progress as radical demands. I did not invent any of my suggestions merely to vex the IGC, to agitate and upset IGC officers, or to bring disarray to my career. I truly feel that each and every suggestion holds intrinsic value and should be seriously considered by the IGC and acted upon. I will add, I have fully thought these requests through and all of them will benefit the IGC greatly." Tåsan looked from face to face and noted that not one of the officers looking at him seemed engaged, but he pressed on, "I truly do not understand IGC reluctance in this matter." Tåsan could feel his "stand and fight" reaction start to rise in his chest. "If the IGC were to implement just one of my enterprising ideas, for example, promote *Ari Arcturus* for what it was intended, a Stratos Class vehicle capable of much more than she's now assigned, the ISA would stand to profit greatly. You have to see that. It's that obvious."

The reaction from the panel was to click, clack on their e-dev's without recognizing that Tåsan had spoken at all.

"I want change, gentlemen," Tåsan summarized.

The room was quiet.

Finally Caoin addressed Tåsan, "What you are asking for is not acceptable at this time. All requests are denied."

"I am due a great deal more respect than this, Vice Admiral Caoin," Tåsan was almost furious. "I have accomplished more in my seven solar years with the IGC than most other senior officers have done in their entire careers. I come from a long line of distinguished IGC officers. That alone warrants consideration." Tåsan sat straight up in his chair and stared intently at Caoin. "I want change, sir."

Caoin glanced up at Tåsan. "On behalf of Inter-Galaxy Command, your letter of resignation is accepted."

Tåsan was momentarily startled by the abrupt decision but he was not altogether surprised by it.

Caoin continued, "Effective date 34909.1, you, Commander Sulac, will be decommissioned from the IGC."

Tåsan quickly gained his feet, shoving the chair out from behind him. "Fine," he snapped and strode across the room and out the door without a backward glance.

• • •

Ari Arcturus was ordered to remain in port at Brenton Kae until further notice.

When Tåsan returned to his quarters, after the meeting with Caoin and his silent minions, he poured himself a dram of Sadorian Vatted Malt and sat at his desk in front of his e-dev. The first thing he did was back up his files, including his IGC personnel file, to an exterior port-drive. Upon completion, Tåsan pulled up three pre-written comm's he had composed the night before.

The first comm was lengthy and addressed to Alyss, Castell, Annis, Darrian, and Tao. It was an explanation of the circumstances that had brought Tåsan to this point. He allowed for his personal friendship with these fellow officers by adding information about his observations and feelings in the matter and what had shaped his decision to leave the IGC. He wrote that this incident in no way affected his friendship with them and he was sure that he would see them again soon.

The second comm was addressed to Nikliss Hywell, Mason Trang, and Shú Vit Fisk and was much shorter since it lacked any description of the accumulated events but held a sincere note of thanks for their being a loyal and efficient bridge crew and if fortune held, Tåsan would run into them again.

The third comm was as succinct as possible. It was addressed to his family and simply said that Tåsan was separating from the IGC, he would not be coming home, and would contact them at a later time.

Tåsan read through the comm's, wordsmithed them just a bit

more, and when he was pleased enough, sent them out and away. It was then that he got up and poured another dram.

"Three days to go," he thought.

On the third day, Tåsan looked about his quarters. His personal belongings were stowed in his travel cases and stood ready for transport. All that was to be left behind was IGC property, including Tåsan's uniforms (hanging at attention in the wardrobe), the e-dev (scrubbed clean), and a few token awards Tåsan had received along the way. He remained unimpressed by them and felt that he didn't need such reminders of his time with the IGC. He could easily remember the good as well as the bad.

On 34909.1, Tåsan disembarked *Ari Arcturus* for the last time. Alyss, Castell, and Annis, in an unsanctioned ceremony, gathered at the port doors and saluted as Tåsan passed by.

He stopped in front of each friend, returned their salute and embraced them, whispering a private farewell to each before stepping through the port, thereby transforming himself from a decorated IGC Commander to an ordinary citizen on visit to Brenton Kae.

Part Two

A Clear
Entanglement

The night was still. The only sounds that cut through the blackness were the snap of contracting metal and the unmistakable sound of predator snatching prey out among the low brush. Dark clouds obscure the midnight stars just as dark thoughts transmute Tåsan's dreams into troubled nightmares.

> Deep gloom tugged at his boots, weighting each step heavier and heavier, pulling him down into the mire. Tåsan struggled against it and losing his balance, he looked wildly around for a handhold, but found none. Panic rose in his chest and he told himself that he still had time but deep within the subconscious recess of his mind, he knew that wasn't true. He knew he was caught. He could hear his life ticking, ticking, ticking.

Tåsan blinked awake with a start. It was still dark. It was only the middle of the night. He lay quiet, bringing his breathing to a measured rhythm and feeling his heart slow from its frantic pace in response.

"My nights are so far from restful," he thought, blinking against the dark. *"I could use one good night without dreams."*

Tåsan swung his bare feet out from under the therm blanket and stood up, sleep still a fog in his head, and plodded to the window.

The clouds had cleared, further darkening the night and turning the outer stars into a crystalline blanket that filled the visible horizon with glimmering specks.

"How did I come to this?" Tåsan abstractly asked himself before catching his thoughts. *"Ohhh,...It's no real surprise that I've come to this point, but I did think it would have turned out differently."* Tåsan rubbed at his eyes in an effort to focus his thoughts. *"Everything has been a struggle. University. IGC Academy. Father. Career entry. But didn't I persevere? Didn't I earn praise and commendations? Why wasn't father satisfied with my accomplishments? Why wasn't he proud? And where was my reward? Didn't the IGC reap the riches that I made possible?"* Tåsan turned from the window and stood peering through the interior darkness. *"Of course they did,"* he sighed, *"Then*

all I did was for naught. All it did was to bring me to this."

He stood motionless in the dimly perceptible light, his bare feet cold against the concrete. Looking to his bed, with covers twisted and pulled out, Tåsan let out a quick, low moan and thought, *"No. I can't face that just yet."* He turned and made his way through the space to his work area and switched on the illumination high above the long wooden table. A large industrial hood buzzed to life and Tåsan pinched his eyes closed against the harsh glare of the glowing carbon resistors as they roiled to life above his head.

As his eyes adjusted, Tåsan slowly opened them and mindlessly looked about, eventually he plopped down on the tall workbench stool and stared at the drawings and schematics that littered the wide surface. He had been designing an upgrade to the conversion chamber of the fuel thrusters that controlled pitch and roll. The last time he flew *Tempest*, he felt that she had not responded to inputs as quickly as he had wanted her to. He sat now, examining details, solving problems, and running scenarios through his mind.

Absentmindedly he reached for a forgotten flask of cold tea at his elbow and managed a large gulp before realization struck him. He would have to warm it up.

Tåsan lost himself in his drawings and when he finally sat back, highly satisfied with his improvement plans, he became aware of the sun streaming in through the high row of windows and only then did he notice that the hour had slid past morn.

His e-dev chimed and chimed again.

"Yes," said Tåsan, "I'm awake." He strode to the window and stood listening. "Yes." His eyes slid uncomprehendingly across the landscape. "Bring the boracite." His hearing became focused on the comm. "I have three detonators. QVs." A slight pause. "Bring as many as you have." Tåsan focused. "Okay. I'll see you in an hour." He stood tall to stretch his back. "Good."

A list of loose ends started to organize in Tåsan's mind... *"Full systems check, additional fuel rods, general ship and crew supplies, explosives, weapons...handhelds and trackers...armaments..."*

One
Bright Star

Tåsan kept very busy during the following three quads. He purchased a large piece of property just to the southwest of Merula. There was a warehouse structure in the center of the property that had once been used by a long defunct company that provided a shipping/receiving service. He turned the warehouse into a ship hangar and after upgrading all of the utility hookups, expanding the power connectors, and repairing the flight pad, Tåsan outfitted the hangar with commercial grade lighting, power lifts, and heavy tools. He designed the space as efficiently as he could and stocked the workbenches with specialized tools. He also built a floor above the hangar where he lived, providing for a full galley, a nice sleeping space, and a leisure space, if one called reading and research, leisure.

Tåsan also expanded the second floor to include a large, well-lit space that held long, wide, wooden tables where he could draft his upgrades and design his ideas.

But, Tåsan's main reason for the upgrades and expansions was his pride and joy...a used Class-C, twenty-crew interceptor he had named *Tempest*.

He gave *Tempest* a good going over from prow to stern. Everything shined, everything looked new, and everything was in repair. In short, *Tempest* was open for business.

Tåsan had been living off of his savings as he worked endless hours retrofitting thruster modules and increasing engine speed. He reworked the pilot controls to include Engineering, Comm, and Support, thereby giving over the majority of flight controls to the pilot's station.

Some weeks ago, Tåsan started promoting himself as a Pilot-to-

Hire business, which he named Corvus Space and in short order picked up a handful of regular clients who needed to be quickly flown between business meetings or shuttled off to personal obligations. Either way was fine with Tåsan. He was interested in building his business and growing his accounts. Tåsan was happy enough but the current list of clients was not sufficient to sustain the entire operation, including his hiring temporary employees to help staff the larger flights. He needed to increase his bottom line.

Tåsan threw some tenges into publicizing Corvus Space, and managed to attract several short-term contracts, sort of a one-time pilot for hire thing, and two new business clients that did help to offset some of Tåsan's expenses.

He threw a startup party, inviting a list of influential business leaders he hoped to impress. The hangar was cleaned, the tools polished, *Tempest* was gorgeous in all the spotlights, and Lingdon Práxus was chilled to perfection. All of which added another three regular clients and a tiny number of one-offs.

Still it was not nearly enough. Tåsan would have to puzzle it out quickly, before the slow months started up when he would have to let his three-man crew go and tighten the budget.

"Oh, fortune, that's a bit depressing."

$$\bullet\ \bullet\ \bullet$$

One warm afternoon when Tåsan was hands-deep in repair of one of *Tempest's* sensor arrays the sound of approaching engines signaled visitors. Tåsan quickly wiped his hands and stepped to the hangar doors. He stood, shading his eyes against the mid-noon sun, ready to greet whomever it was winding their way across the terrain leading to his business.

As the Class-N came closer, Tåsan recognized the pilot and in his joy, he thrust his hand upward and waved a greeting as he gingerly stepped forward.

The Class-N came to rest and the pilot door opened in a whoosh and out leapt Stellanova, her face bright with a smile, her voice full in her excitement.

"Tåsan!"

"What a surprise!" Tåsan caught her up in a hug and she clung to him. "Oh, oh, oh, let me look at you!" he said as he tried to hold her at arms length. "I think you've grown again at least the height of an Anuran lizard, although you're still better looking!"

"Oh, I don't know about that anymore," she blushed slightly but then smacked Tåsan on the arm and said, "Hey, I'm upset with you. You sent that cryptic comm all those many weeks ago then disappeared, and in all that time, Tåsan, no follow-up message? What was up with that?" she asked earnestly.

Tåsan was letting his embarrassment show and was starting to apologize, finding a string of excuses he knew weren't good enough.

"Are you angry with me, Tåsan?"

"Oh no, Stella, never with you. I'm sorry," he stammered, then steadied, "Let's go in, I'll make tea."

"Good, I brought sweet biscuits for us!"

Twenty minutes, three apologies, and two fast updates later, Tåsan and Stellanova sat together in Tåsan's galley kitchen sipping dark, black tea and chatting about the details of their lives.

"Tåsan, I have to tell you this," Stella said almost as an afterthought. "Father won't say your name out loud. He's still very upset with you for leaving the IGC."

Tåsan shook his head and nudged his mug. "That's nothing new."

"Listen, I understand your motivations and agree with you on almost all points. I'm not judging. But apparently father is. I think he's wrong, but there it is. Father is being father, he can't help it. Anyway..."

"Father is holding the world to his standards, his impossible standards," Tåsan said.

Stella just looked at him for a moment then continued, "Anyway, father won't speak your name, but I do. I wonder out loud how you are doing, I ask if anyone has heard from you. I do it in defiance, I do it to annoy him." She was smiling, "And it does. Hah!"

Tåsan laughed out loud and Stella joined him.

"He's acting like an adolescent," she summed up. Then looking about the large loft space, "This is grand. You'll have to give me a tour. And I'm dying to see inside your ship."

Tåsan smiled as he looked around. "It *is* slightly grand," he said with pride, "although it can get a little cold at night." He stood up and so did Stella.

"The two tenges tour, please," she said jokingly.

Tåsan held out his hand for the coins.

"I'll owe you," she replied flatly.

"Okay," said Tåsan, "We'll start with the living quarters." He stood still, looking at Stella, a smile creeping over his face.

"Alright," she said, "lead on."

Tåsan didn't move. "This is it," he said, sweeping his arm across the space to his left.

Stella looked around, her face blank. "This is where you live?" she asked in disbelief.

"Yhup. Sleep," pointing to a big bed, "wardrobe," pointing to his travel cases, "bath," pointing to a privy door and jokingly added, "You don't want to go in there," smiling wryly, waiting for her reaction.

And she scrunched her face in mock repulsion.

Tåsan said, "You've seen my galley. The rest of this space is where I work, when I'm not flying clients or working on the ship."

"Show me *Tempest*. I can't wait to see how the better half lives." She said.

• • •

Along about dinner hour, Stella left to go home ("Big paper due tomorrow. The Master Degree program waits for no one!"), but not before eliciting a promise from Tåsan that he would message or comm or contact her more often. It didn't matter: lunch, dinner, a walk, or just talk. And Tåsan agreed.

Just as she was boarding her Class-N, Stellanova promised to send him the contact information for two well-heeled seniors she knew at University whose fathers, she thought, owned companies in Merula and did business with off-worlders.

And with a wave and a smile, the Class-N fired up and she was toward home, leaving Tåsan to look after the craft as it climbed and sped away. He turned, looked at *Tempest* and caught his thoughts back up, *"One more mod to the number two sensor and I'll start on the re-circuit of the landing thrusters..."*

Two

Standing At The Bottom

Just as Naiad Five follows a path around the sunstar, so does commerce follow a predictable cycle of harried business transactions and deadlines followed by times of rest, relaxation, and no worries.

It was six weeks into the seasonal slowdown and on this particularly cloudless and cold night, Tåsan sat with his ledgers, his hands wrapped around a hot mug of tea, staring at the columns of numbers that represented his life.

Corvus Space was barely hanging on.

The income statement account glared off the page. Expenses outweighed the revenues by some forty five hundred tenges, which had to be taken from savings in order to stay afloat.

Tåsan looked hard at the entries, his eyes searching for a slip in the numbers to be corrected or any frivolous entry to be discarded...anything to make it all better. But it was not to be. The numbers were correct, the ledger accurate.

Tåsan rubbed at his forehead as if to wipe the memory of it from his mind. *"Bottom line. At this rate, Corvus Space will survive another two quads, maybe three if I economize. But then what? I have to figure this out now or the inevitable is merely postponed."* He got up and walked to the window where he stood looking out across a dark landscape, lit only by a half lunar that threw long shadows across the black terrain.

"What other services could Corvus Space provide? My core competency is of pilot and shuttle to business class leaders and directors in a hurry. What would they be doing if not in a hurry? Humph." Tåsan tsk'ed at his thought. *"They would stay at home, of course."* He walked back to his ledgers and stared blankly at the pages that

glared in the light and seemed to mock him with their starkness. *"What else can I do?"* he thought. *"I could provide pilot training but now I'm looking at another outlay of tenges for licensing fees and marketing that may not pay off. So, no."* Tåsan took his mug to the galley and poured another measure of hot water onto the already over-saturated tea buds. He returned to his worktable and flipped open his scheduler. *"This week nothing. Next week a run out to Lux and then..."* Tåsan flipped through his calendar. *"And then that's it for a set of weeks."*

Frustrated that his creative problem solving was not producing innovative results, Tåsan closed the ledger and closed the scheduler and moved aimlessly along the long wooden table until his eyes caught sight of a schematic of an interface he had been working on earlier in the week. As he scanned the diagram and its complex of interrelated components, the troubles of Corvus Space lost their strength, slowly fading into the background even as Tåsan picked up a drawing stylus and made a note in the margin about translating a power supply to its signal flow.

Soon he was lost in his engineering.

• • •

Tåsan watched as the sky turned dark and the sunstar's warmth withdrew. It had happened so fast that he wondered at the size of the storm that was coming. He felt that he must get away to safety and fired his pulse rocket up thinking to escape by outrunning it. He had just touched the booster when a shower of small rocks began to fall from the sky, pelting his hands with painful stings.

Tåsan saw that his rocket was damaged and knew that it would not make the distance. He abandoned it and thought to seek safety in his workshop in the hangar. The falling rocks had grown in size and were damaging all that they hit. As Tåsan ran wildly across the ever-widening distance, huge boulders pummeled *Tempest* where she stood, now flightless and beyond repair.

Tåsan's fear for his safety now changed to hopelessness. What was he without *Tempest*? His time, his effort, his pride...now all gone.

He stopped running, for what was the use? Standing

247

in the middle of his life's work, Tåsan watched boulders smash everything he had built and in their intensity, pummel the very ground he stood on into huge craters. As the terra beneath his feet fell away, Tåsan was swallowed into a darkness that he knew he would never recover from.

When he woke, Tåsan felt heaviness upon his heart. He lay quietly and pieced together the fragments of his dream, trying to make sense of it. He lay for a long time, finding no logic other than to conclude that it was some sort of premonition, a warning of what was to come. Accepting this as true, Tåsan rose and dressed quickly, seeking to put distance between him and the shadow he could not put aside.

• • •

The run to Lux was overwrought to say the least. His client, a highly successful and influential machine part manufacturer from Naiad Five, was demanding in his comforts aboard *Tempest* and exacting in his directions to Tåsan. He desired to be fashionably late to his big meeting, or more precisely, he wanted the meeting to wait upon his arrival so he had Tåsan hold at a distant parsec while time ticked forward and Tåsan burned more boron than necessary.

This client also made Tåsan wait long hours at the spaceport while he socialized over an extended dinner with colleagues. When he finally showed up, he was intoxicated and loud and particularly obnoxious in his unending diatribe describing his work associates and his horribly lazy son.

Tåsan burnt an extra measure of boron in an effort to return this magnate of industry to his drop-off point as quickly as possible. A recurring thought running through Tåsan's mind was that he was working way too hard for very little compensation.

Insult to injury…the client did not even grant a tip.

• • •

Tåsan slept off the annoyance of the previous day but woke feeling uninspired. He looked around his loft, thinking he should work on this or clean that but was not moved to actually do so.

Instead, he took his pulse rocket out for a long run, returning when his hunger overtook him. The ride managed to clear his head, except for one persistent thought: he's spending too much time alone.

While preparing his meal, a thought hit him, *"I think Tempest would make a great party ship."* Tåsan's thoughts gained speed. *"It's big enough. The central area could hold forty or so. I managed the start-up party in the hangar and that went well enough. I could market to corporate. Tempest could be booked for parties, award ceremonies, commemoratives, milestone celebrations, oh fortune, I may have just hit on something!"*

Flushed from the excitement his new venture presented, Tåsan sat in the galley and between bites, sent messages to his friends asking their whereabouts and if they were available to meet, say, in three days time at the distillery on Brenton Kae. Tåsan relaxed with the thought that everything may yet turn out all right. It was then that he finished his meal and turned his thoughts back to one of his favorite past times: AI Interfacing on a Macro-Bio level.

• • •

Tåsan sat among a group of his friends, smiling and talking above the din of the room. He had supplied the first round of Cirrus Ale and a variety of small plates and had watched for the opportunity to address his small band of friends, which in short time presented itself.

"Everyone!" Tåsan stood up so he could be seen. The faces of his friends from Naiad Five and the IGC all turned to look at him and the conversation levels dropped. "As the proud owner of Corvus Space, I am pleased to announce the launch of a new venture..." Tåsan looked to his friends, a mischievous and teasing smile broadening his face. He held his breath until many of the faces smiled back at him and then, "...Corvis Space Entertainment!"

Several of his friends called out, "Oh, that should be fun," or "When do we leave?" Around all could be heard small sounds of congratulations and joy.

"Tempest is available for corporate...or private..." Tåsan paused and tilted his head to give a rascally look to one of the guys who laughed in return, "parties. Several levels of sophistication are available and range anywhere from an elegant aboard ship affair to

a fast jaunt to the Naiad Five outback for an intimate open air meal." Tåsan smiled at his group. "Contact me for further details and I hope to hear from you soon!"

Tåsan leaned over and almost whispered to one of his IGC fellows, "Does the IGC still use hold number 8A2.F as a stash for their Práxus?" Hearing that they did indeed still have vast quantities of "gift" beverages on board *Ari Arcturus*, Tåsan asked would they miss four cases and if not, would his buddy be willing to procure the cases in trade for a flight service?

Chatter among the group was fast paced and excited but before it could quiet down Tåsan made another announcement. "I have something to add! As a gift to all of you present here tonight, Corvus Space is hosting a bargain priced introductory party to be held one week from tonight on Thorium 4. Get there any way you can or be at Corvus Space port one hour prior to party time and I'll give you a ride out and back. Complimentary food and four cases of Lingdon Práxus will be provided so you can 'Experience the Experience' and then tell all of your friends!"

Tåsan picked up his tankard and held it aloft, saying, "Here's to Corvus Space Entertainment, your party among the stars!" Tankards raised and clinked, "hear-hears" were shouted and laughter sounded. Tåsan called out, "Detailed information will be sent to you within a day, be sure to book early to ensure your place. And thank you!"

The gathering continued for another hour as slowly all of the friends left for the evening until the only one remaining was Alyss.

"You know you are not fooling me, don't you?" she asked, her tone even, her eyes scanning Tåsan's face.

"What are you talking about?" he asked through his mounting embarrassment.

"Corvus Space Entertainment is a plea for help. You are facing a tough time and this 'New Venture'," her voice emphasizing the words with irony, "is a sure sign that you are starting to thrash about for a life line."

"I'm expanding the business," Tåsan protested.

"You are losing your core strength. Never have I heard you say, 'I aspire to be a party planner and to pilot a party ship.' What I *have* heard," she emphasized more strongly, "is that you desire to be a leader and to be adventurous, not hold the heads of drunks and muck your beautiful ship after the frats have left." Alyss folded her arms across her chest, defying Tåsan to contradict her.

Which he did not.

He sat staring at the bottom of his tankard, knowing that Alyss had hit it squarely and hearing his situation summed up in those particular words was a little like hearing that you had failed at an important task. It hurt. Tåsan swallowed down his pride. "I have to do something, Alyss. Corvus Space is on a slow decline to failure. If I don't do something, I will be nothing. All of what I have done will be nothing."

"I understand and have sympathy, really I do," her voice softened. "Promise me that you will not devote all your time to entertainment, that some of your hard-earned tenges will be put into marketing your intelligent side, your technical skills." Alyss waited for Tåsan to respond. She could see the conflict of his thoughts play across his face.

Tåsan sighed as he pulled in a big breath. "I think I can safely promise that I will continue to push Corvus Space as a top service and try to expand its marketing so as to reach a better financial state." He looked at Alyss and tried to reassure her with a smile that he was serious.

• • •

The midnight run to Thorium 4 was a huge success for Tåsan. He cleared the costs and managed to show a profit and pocketed several hundred tenges in tips.

Within a week of the Thorium 4 party, another party booked in. The caller was arranging a party for fifteen to celebrate a new contract accrual. They desired a several hour ride through any available space, not caring where because the celebration was about the announcement and good times among colleagues. Would Corvus Space be interested?

Of course. Tåsan obtained the details and booked the party. He hired four temporaries to assist with the flight and one personable young Merulian to manage the guests, to see that the party flowed seamlessly.

After all the passengers were aboard, *Tempest* lifted up and rose to the Zone of Demark. Tåsan was pilot and the course

251

unimportant. He thought to fly a few hours out and a few hours back and set the heading for the Rayten Galaxy through the outer stars. This would fix the landing back at Corvus Space to about midnight.

On the fourth hour out, Tåsan thought to make an appearance at the party to personally welcome everyone to Corvus Space and to ask if they found everything to their satisfaction.

He was barely one minute into a smiling conversation with one of the attendees when he was interrupted by a loud voice at his back.

"Well, well, well. Look who we have here," the voice accused.

Tåsan turned in surprise. It took but one split second to recognize who had addressed him. "Tezzo Maluki," Tåsan tried hard not to spit the name from his mouth.

"Everyone," Tezzo raised his voice. "This is the brother of a university girl I dated once."

Tåsan held his ground.

"She spent the entire evening teasing me and when I went to collect on the promise, she withdrew the offer."

"The way I understand it, Maluki, you drugged her and then you forced yourself upon her."

"Is that what she told you?" Tezzo snarled in his anger and took a step forward, thrusting a finger in Tåsan's face. "She's a liar!"

Tåsan couldn't control himself. He hauled back and swung his fist, catching a fast and tight punch to Tezzo Maluki's left cheek that sent him flying backward through a couple partygoers before he crashed to the floor in a heap.

One of the ladies standing nearby knelt at Tezzo's side to comfort him, holding his hand and trying to help him to sit up.

Tåsan stepped forward and pointed at Tezzo, "We're returning to Merula, this party is over and I want you off my ship." He spun around and stepped deliberately to the bulkhead door, scattering partygoers as he went.

"You haven't heard the last of this!" Tezzo shouted at his back.

Tåsan set course back to Corvus Space at an almost frightening speed. He fumed, *"If it weren't for the witnesses, I would kill him!"*

• • •

It took two days and some hard pulse rocket riding for Tåsan to calm down.

Tezzo Maluki did not bring the law down on Tåsan but what he did bring was far worse. He brought ruin.

The next week, two clients cancelled. One was a party of thirty-five that had booked for an all-day cruise to Cimtun 8 and back and Tåsan stood to make a couple thousand tenges above expenses. The other was a regular client who filled Tåsan's schedule with business runs and tipped well. The cancellation message said that the client, "...had heard about some rather troubling behavior on Tåsan's part toward an onboard client," and "My company can't afford to be associated with such conduct."

Then came a blitz of messages with basically the same content but with a twist: each said they had been considering hiring Corvus Space but had changed their minds after hearing about a recent "incident."

Tåsan sat with his ledger, holding his head, thoughts barely moving as his eyes followed a short list of numbers down the page to their conclusion. Corvus Space would be flat in less than two quads.

An incoming message chimed on his e-dev and he picked it up and switched it on. "Corvus Space, how may we help you?" Tåsan listened. "Yes. We will be able to accommodate that on our schedule. What is the cargo?" Tåsan's stylus tapped along as the information was supplied. "And the delivery point is a private pad on Sador?" The caller confirmed. "Sador's ellipsis puts it two days out," Tåsan added. "Fine. Corvus Space will be at your field at 3715.8 hours to receive shipment."

• • •

Tåsan knew enough about mining equipment to know that what was in the shipping containers was *not* mining equipment but turned a blind eye. He was paid by a shifty-looking individual who claimed to have no information about anything.

Tåsan let it go. It was a job. It paid. What did he care.

The drop-off was uneventful and the shipping containers were loaded directly onto a small fleet of ground movers and hauled into the night.

Tåsan asked the field manager if he could recommend anyone

253

wishing to transport goods to Naiad Five, no reason the two-day trip should go unpaid for. And as fortune had it, yes, but the "goods" were limited and could Tåsan wait an hour while a few messages were sent.

The "goods" turned out to be a well-dressed Sadorian accompanying a large, fairly heavy travel case. He was not inclined toward conversation and at first meeting, handed Tåsan a small box of tenges and announced, "I require very little in the way of amenities and would prefer to be left to myself." Tåsan nodded his understanding and withdrew to the helm and only caught a glimpse of the Sadorian on the following day, totally focused on his portable technologies, head down and concentrating. Tåsan left him alone and upon landing at Corvus Space, watched the Sadorian lead his hovering travel case out to a waiting luxury transport and leave without further acknowledgement of Tåsan or Corvus Space.

Later that evening, over a chilled half-glass of Valunde, a smooth little distillation from Metamere, guaranteed to "reduce your daily stress" and, as he knew...cloud your mind, Tåsan opened the Sadorian's payment box to count the tenges. To say that he was shocked at the contents would only be partly accurate. Tåsan's eyes popped open and his jaw dropped, speechless at the sight: four neat piles of crisp, new tenges. Tåsan picked one of the stacks up and spread it out on the table in front of him. Unbelievable! The stack amounted to one thousand tenges, making the box worth four thousand. Tåsan had booked the Sadorian's flight at seven hundred fifty tenges. His mind flew the math...then a question slowly formed...what actually happened there?

Tåsan sat back and sipped his Valunde.

• • •

Over the next eight weeks, Tåsan had enough work to barely hold the bottom line but not enough to keep him from slowly sliding further into debt. Hauling trinkets and trash from one end of the galaxy over to the next and back, wasn't exactly where Tåsan had seen his career or his future end up.

Time for another serious conversation with himself.

He packed food and water and drove his pulse rocket far out into the outback. He reached a small copse of alder trees and parked his rocket. Sitting in a nice shady spot, Tåsan let his thoughts flow where they would. When he got hungry, he ate. When he got stiff, he stretched out with his head propped up on his pack so he could look up at the sky. He lay for a time and watched as high clouds moved past. At the end of the noon hour, Tåsan had a "pro" and a "con" list but no decision.

Only two things were certain. One, his schedule did not lack for one-off flights hauling nonsense goods from point A to point B. Mining machines, building supplies, things he didn't care about, and things he didn't want to know about. And two, he was starting to associate with several unsavory characters. The kind of denizens that live just outside the law and that operate in the darker side of life.

"Wouldn't father just love to know that!"

Further thought only threatened to bring on a stress headache so Tåsan donned his helmet and fired the rocket's thrusters.

"If I don't act to change my current course…I'll waste away."

• • •

Days of brooding and brooding for days did not get Tåsan closer to a solution.

"My business is failing. I don't think working for others is going to work for me. Corvus Space can only stay afloat for one more quad. I'm depleting my savings. I can't ask family." These were a few of the poisonous thoughts that Tåsan heard over and over until he would explode. *"Life is bleeding away."*

In his more lucid moments, Tåsan's thoughts were more imaginative. Maybe he should attract investors in Corvus Space? *"But then I wouldn't wholly own it."* Maybe he should take out loans against futures? *"If I default on payments then Corvus Space is gone."* Maybe he should rent or sublet space in the hangar to other pilots? *"Then I'm a landlord; it's too disruptive."*

Then one night a thought struck him and he wondered why it hadn't occurred to him before. *"Wouldn't it be so easy to just be a criminal?"* The absurdity of it made him laugh out loud. Still smiling, *"So what would my first step be?"*

Oh. Tåsan's mind ran with the notion of a life of crime. Humor aside, it presented an opportunity of creativity and problem solving that didn't weigh Tåsan down with portends of doom and gloom. Tåsan was surprised to find his mind exhilarated and completely clear of moral restrictions.

After all, it was just a fantasy. Right?

That night, Tåsan fell to sleep still entertained by the theory of doing illegal activities and waved it off as exactly that, entertainment.

But the next morn, as he opened his eyes to the hazy dawn, Tåsan's thoughts were already in progress, *"Start small to test the process..."*

The seriousness of it didn't surprise Tåsan at all. It was how his mind worked and yet it was a diversion that he could not let go of. He got a cup of strong tea and sat on a high stool at his worktable. After a moment, Tåsan pulled a clean leaf of paper into position in front of him, neatly on top of the schematics of his plans to modify *Tempest's* reverse thrusters. He picked up his stylus and bent to the task.

By the third cup of tea, Tåsan had outlined two fairly large and possibly difficult exploits. One, he knew that the Faradae Company on Sador routinely shipped large cargos of krennerite to various distribution points in the Hedorrion Galaxy and two, Tåsan knew that another ISA company shipped U308 from Thorium 4. Both crossed the Allodial Expanse, both without escort, both with minimal crew, and both very much alone.

By mid-evening, Tåsan had added a level of detail to his plans, rounding them out, so to speak. The krennerite and the U308 would fetch top tenges and should be off-loaded as soon as possible. Tåsan knew several characters that would gladly accept stolen goods without hesitation. He could arrange for the exchange to take place in a remote vector of the Rayten Galaxy. The whole exploit could be accomplished in less than one day.

"If Tempest was modified to increase speed and her fuel consumption maximized by 3.8 fifths, the time could be reduced exponentially..." Lists of needed supplies, contacts, and schedules readily appeared on the page, were modified, considered, and were revised to a detail.

Finally, Tåsan sat back and looked at what he had accomplished with a sense of pride that he hadn't felt for some time, and smiled, really smiled.

He ate a hearty meal, his appetite rediscovered. After his meal, he grabbed a Cirrus Ale and stepped out into the darkening night, taking a chair at the edge of the crushed rock courtyard where he could have an unobstructed view of the night sky.

As Tåsan unwound from the day, he chided himself for taking such a serious approach to committing a crime. *"However,"* he argued with himself, *"the details are flawless, the necessities have been considered and listed, and several solid contingencies named and answered."* He stretched his legs out and pondered his bootlaces. *"The only thing lacking is a crew…"*

• • •

As the end of the quad neared, Tåsan made arrangements to meet with his IGC buddies at a back alley dive in a more rowdy section of Brenton Kae. Why be seen, right? *Ari Arcturus* was scheduled to dock for maintenance in five days time and Tåsan felt excited about seeing his old friends and introducing them to his new ones…

Chris Phelan had flown as copilot on *Tempest* when Corvus Space was hosting a particularly stringent client or a large party that needed Tåsan's attention. Chris was from Thorium 4 and as such was tall and slender with skin the color of light copper. He was quick to grab new concepts and intelligent and Tåsan thought his piloting skill was of a high order.

Chris Phalen had kicked around Thorium 4 for a couple of solar years after university but found his talent for flying wasted amid the mining and shipping companies that dominated the economy. He worked at odd jobs, eventually finding himself in Merula and flying small shuttles for a local delivery company before seeing a notice for a pilot for Corvus Space. While the work schedule was inconsistent, Chris fell in love with *Tempest* and had developed a fondness for Tåsan.

Luan Oda was an exceptional mechanic with an extraordinary knowledge of inter-space vehicles, including propulsion and interconnectivity of ship-wide systems. She was small, barely reaching to Tåsan's chest. She had olive skin and wore her black hair short. Tåsan was struck with her piercing amber eyes that seemed to dance in the sunlight. She hailed from Helidor in the Hedorrion Galaxy and came to Corvus Space by way of Chris Phalen. Chris brought her along on one of his space runs, to introduce her to Tåsan, whom he encouraged to have a technical conversation with...about anything mechanical, anything at all.

Tåsan was impressed with her knowledge and when he asked her where she had acquired such a vast array of expertise, because she appeared so young, she answered in her soft, light voice that since she had lived four hundred sixty solar years, she had had ample time to learn and practice several subjects that interested her. Peripherally, she paid attention to Artificial Intelligence and its applications and had dabbled in armaments and explosives simply because it was thrilling.

Tåsan had listened to Luan cite her skill set with a drop of skepticism but he liked her right away and in the short time between then and now, had several enlightening conversations on the concept and adaptability of AI to a vast array of systems, biological not excluded, winning Tåsan over.

The third new friend that Tåsan was bringing to the party was Dhagáin. Dhagáin was a bit of a mystery but a master of mechanics. If it moved, he could fix it. He could read a schematic once and effect the changes with barely a question. He was from Zetta Ma in the Rayten Galaxy; he was tall, muscular from his years of working with heavy engine components and had dark wild-looking hair and pale green eyes.

It was some weeks into their association when one hot and humid day as Tåsan and Dhagáin struggled to seat an unyielding thruster cone to *Tempest* that Dhagáin pulled his shirt off in an effort to cool off when Tåsan found himself staring at Dhagáin's chest. It was covered in abstract figures and symbols done in colored ink and raised scars. It seemed to move as Dhagáin did and the intricacy of the design stopped Tåsan in his work. He had to ask about it and listened as Dhagáin explained that it was a depiction of an ancient Zetta Ma rune symbolizing a higher unity.

In the course of their employment with Corvus Space, Tåsan built a solid trust in Chris, Luan, and Dhagáin's skills and from that developed a friendship that went beyond the work environment. At times, Tåsan and Chris would share a lug of ale and talk about the ships they had flown, at other times he and Luan would linger over tea talking about AI possibilities and at still other times, Tåsan would listen as Dhagáin spoke of the Zetta

Ma outback or working in the iridium mines as a child. Dhagáin did not often speak, so when he did, Tåsan had the habit of listening.

At the appointed hour, Chris, Luan, Dhagáin, and Tåsan boarded *Tempest* and set course for the five hour flight to Brenton Kae, arriving several minutes earlier than scheduled and having to hold position while another ship pulled away from Slip 9E7, where *Tempest* would berth for two days.

Eventually, *Tempest* was docked and logged and the four made their way to the nameless dive, taking a table toward the back.

Tåsan had messaged Alyss, Castell, Darrian, Tao, Nikliss, and Annis of his arrival and had received acknowledgements that they were on their way. He ordered a series of small plates and asked that two lugs of ale be served, one at a time, and that he would pay the bill at the end of the night.

The first to arrive were Darrian and Tao quickly followed by Alyss and Castell. Five minutes later Nikliss arrived and Annis some small number of minutes after that.

The group was boisterous as introductions were made and everyone found seats. Shortly thereafter, the ale was poured and small plates arrived. Tåsan held his tankard aloft and toasted his dear friends and his new friends, thanking everyone for making the time to join him.

About thirty minutes in and as deftly as he could, Tåsan steered the table conversation by asking a question. "Is everyone truly happy in their current situation?"

There had been enough ale served to loosen a few tongues and Nikliss complained that patrolling the Allodial Expanse was boring on top of boring and nothing of what he thought it should be.

This kicked off a round of complaints...

Chris would welcome an increase in work thereby increasing his earned income.

Alyss said she was bored and lonely since Tåsan had left and that the current commander was a bit of a prig.

The IGC group all agreed that management was myopic and short sighted and longed for a change in command, someone younger and eager to expand responsibilities. None were

259

convinced that it would happen any time soon.

Tåsan told a story or two about sticky clients and falling revenues, apologizing to Chris, Luan, and Dhagáin that it was so. Then asked another question. "If you could change your situation, even if it meant quitting what you are doing and starting something new," nodding to Nikliss, "or more profitable," nodding at Chris, "and wholly more exciting," glancing around the table at everyone, "would you do it?"

Alyss answered first, "Yes, if it involved piloting a spacecraft."

"No," said Darrian, "I believe I've found my place. I like where I am right now."

"I would go," said Tao and turning to Darrian, "No offense my friend, and please don't get me wrong, I love working for you, it has been a wonderful opportunity, but I don't see where I would be anything but in your shadow." He lowered his eyes in humility, "I would change my situation."

Luan simply said, "Yes, I'm in." and Dhagáin nodded.

Tåsan looked at Castell who looked back at him with singularity. "No, I don't think excitement is reward enough," he said, "to quit my appointment and go off into the unknown."

Tåsan said, "Fair enough," adding, "Annis, your thoughts?"

Annis sat passively looking at Tåsan. "Give me a few more moments to consider all that is being said and weigh my thoughts and feelings against it."

Tåsan turned to Nikliss, smiled, and poked his jaw out and raised his brow as if to ask, "And you?"

Nikliss fairly leapt to his answer. "Yes, I would leave my situation as I fear if I stay I will lose my abilities. And, Tåsan, in my humble way of interviewing, my sub-specialty is ship's engineering." Then he folded his arms across his chest and smiled broadly.

Alyss said, "How about you, Tåsan? How would you answer your own question?"

Tåsan smiled and laughed in response. "Oh, yes. I would leave my situation for excitement and financial gain in a heartbeat. I have stressed too much and worked too hard and am still about to drown in a mire. For me it's an easy decision. Very easy." He found he was smiling for the opportunity of change. He looked around and his eyes met Annis'.

"I've considered my answer, Tåsan," she looked at him with ease. "While I am contented with my current situation, it is my future I am not that sure of. I have a large capacity for tolerance of the slow and sometimes ponderous management that typifies the IGC, but my capacity is not endless and I find myself often longing for change. I would welcome a more fast-paced situation where I can artfully use my skills to keep myself ready and sharp." She took a sip of her ale and gently set the tankard down. "Contentment is fast becoming inadequate. So, yes, I would change my situation."

The group fell silent, each to their private thoughts.

At length Tåsan spoke, "We deserve more. We deserve a better life, better treatment, respect, security." He looked at his friends. "It's not enough to just survive. It's degrading not to be able to pay the bills, not to have tenges to spend, to exist by routine, to march to one's end without looking from side to side, to live without enjoyment." The words flowed forward. "I for one would like to grab hold of life and live it more fully. Enjoy the little moments, not toil and descend into misery, or worse, poverty and regret." Tåsan talked on, "And I think I've come up with a plan to make that happen. It's a good plan, one that I like very much." Everyone was looking at him with a mixture of wonder and skepticism. "Rules will have to be bent," he added, "and laws broken, but the rewards will be worth the risk." Tåsan's eyes seemed to burn with anticipation. "Trust me, it's a good plan...are you in?"

• • •

On the return walk through Brenton Kae, Alyss and Annis shared their thoughts.

"This meeting and hearing how the others think about leaving the IGC," Alyss said, "has brought up why I joined the IGC in the first place. I really felt that it was my calling, my career, to be part of an organization that seemed to be on the cutting edge of technology and the forefront of space exploration. And don't get me wrong," she rushed on, "I value the training I received beyond measure. But there's something about the IGC that I can't put words to. Something dark. Something insidious." Her face reflected her thoughts.

261

Annis spoke, "There was always something just beyond any of Command's words. I'm not referring to the succinct way orders were given or the brusque communication of information. I'm referring to the unspoken ways in which Command acted. Unexplainable."

Alyss listened and nodded as she took in the words. "I watched with trepidation as Tåsan was forced out of the IGC without thorough consideration for his contributions *or* his potential." She unconsciously slowed her pace as she continued. "It made me wonder about their motivations *and* what my chances of real success are."

"I never had those thoughts," Annis added. "That is until these last few quads."

"Yes," Alyss agreed. "Everything crashed into the boredom of militaristic sameness."

Annis nodded in agreement.

"Now Tåsan is asking for a 'team' and I feel that I could leave with no hesitation," Alyss smiled.

"My feelings," Annis hesitated just a half-breath in reflection, "are that I am making the right decision to leave the IGC. To my surprise, after Tåsan left, I found that I longed for excitement and the opportunity to use my AI to its fullest potential. Maybe this is my time."

Three
Melted Into Air, Into Thin Air

Over the next small handful of weeks, a series of seemingly random actions occurred and although everything looked casual on the surface, they were not. The four IGC persons, Annis, Alyss, Tao, and Nikliss, decided it would be better to quit the IGC separately and not as a group. To that end, each surrendered their commissions citing a variety of reasons but keeping to the theme that the Commander of *Ari Arcturus* was a poor example of leadership that was probably reflective of IGC style, adding any number of other unspecified reasons meant to deflect coincidence.

Alyss and Annis took a small flat in Merula's west end, close to a trendy two-block area filled with cafés and night-life, basically taking a few days to transition into life outside the predictable routine of the IGC.

After Tåsan agreed that Nikliss could temporarily bunk at Corvus Space, Nikliss made a small and unobtrusive flop for himself in the machine shop area and kept busy in any way he could. He started by cleaning and sharpening all the hand tools and taking on small projects but soon became engrossed in Tåsan's schematics of things to come, making comments and studying output data.

Tåsan liked having Nikliss at Corvus Space and the two got along well. He found in Nikliss, a sounding board for changes he was developing and that Nikliss had an aptitude for ship's engineering beyond a casual interest. As it turned out, Nikliss was more than a pilot and an engineer; he was fast becoming a friend.

Tao went home to Jahved Tuk. He wanted to see his family, to tell them of his decision to leave the IGC and to assure them that he would be fine. He also wanted the opportunity to think about his new role as lead medical and how he would begin to organize a small but highly efficient med station aboard *Tempest*. He would return in two weeks time fully prepared and ready to go.

Alyss came out to Corvus Space daily and involved herself with modifying *Tempest's* action item list, and at first, helped to logically organize the list from beginning task to last, before carving out a large and very complicated job for herself, that of modifying pilot controls to account for the physio-monitors that were being first-stage tested.

Annis spent the first several days of IGC freedom on her own, appearing once or twice at Corvus Space but retreating again after only a short visit. Eventually, she revealed the reason for her non-communication. She appeared one sunny mid-morn bringing with her an exotic blend of tea buds and a variety of fruitlets. She invited everyone to join her in the galley for a short break and it was during this break, when everyone had gathered, that she spoke.

"I apologize for my absence and the veil of mystery that may have surrounded my activities, but I'm here now. I would like to offer in the way of an explanation, that I have been busy restoring myself. As my IGC partners know, several of my internal systems require a power source." Annis smiled, "For the sake of brevity, I'll not go into detail on that point at this time. I will, however, show what has occupied my time and attention this last week." And with that, Annis loosed a long, lustrous trail of material that had been gathered around her shoulders and slipped it off to reveal a stunning array of gems and stones and gold at her breastbone.

"Upon leaving the IGC, I was required to surrender the stones that aligned to *Ari Arcturus*. It is regulation and truth be told, the gems would have lost their potency with my separation from the ship." Continuing, "It took me awhile to find the right combination of stones that would align to *Tempest* but in the end I found them. Tåsan," she spoke looking directly at him, "*Tempest* will provide 'strength'," placing a finger on a stone, "'harmony and balance'," touching another, "'truth' and 'confidence'," pointing in turn to two other gem stones set around a large black hexagonal quartz that filled a center circle. "But above all," touching the quartz, "*Tempest* will provide 'protection'." And looking to the others,

264

added, "All the elements have come together at this time," naming them, "Fire, Soil, Wind, Water, and the force that unifies them, Storm." Nodding, Annis added, "All this bodes well for us," and stood smiling, "for our venture."

Almost at once the group started talking among themselves. Alyss jumped up and went to Annis desiring to look at the beautiful artisanship of the jewels and gem stones and gold wiring that enveloped them all and to declare, once again, the she would absolutely love to have Annis design a signature piece for her, adding, "In your spare time, of course," causing them both to laugh at the absurdity of "spare time".

However, Annis invited Alyss to join her on the courtyard, away from the others where she handed her a gift. Alyss looked at it carefully, recording its look and feel in her memory, and with a soft touch, opened the wooden box contained therein.

It was a brooch and as Alyss lifted it from the box, Annis told of it. "The large stone at the top is labradorite for power, next is citrine for creativity, followed by a fire agate," she hesitated long enough for Alyss to look up at her, "for the risk taker in you." Both laughed at the irony of the words. "The last stone is malachite, for confidence."

The stones were set in a gold backing and hung on a delicate chain of gold and titanium. Alyss slipped the chain around her neck and closed the clasp. "How could I ever repay you for this?" It was more of a sentiment than a question.

"No repayment required nor is it desired. It's a gift from my heart." Annis smiled. "There's just one other thing," she said as she picked a very small package from her pocket and handed it to Alyss. "It's not much but I knew you should have it."

Alyss opened the silken cloth to reveal a small, thin, pink ring that she immediately found to fit the middle finger of her right hand.

"Rose quartz. It represents the unity of us." Annis found other words, "The bond that ties us even through distance." She held up her right hand, showing the back to Alyss. There was a small, thin, pink ring on her middle finger.

• • •

The fair days of mid-solar were very busy for the recently

reconfigured crew of Corvus Space. Tåsan organized and assigned work items to crew according to their skills and at other times, according to their availability.

Tao had returned from Jahved Tuk as expected and made short work of setting up and organizing his med area and now made himself available for any task considered. Currently he was loading miscellaneous information and ship's manuals into onboard memory blocks, taking great care with its organization.

When Tåsan had first entertained the idea of heisting shipments and dealing with dark characters, he put together a cursory list of modifications to *Tempest* that would allow for increased speed and some level of defense. When his musings took on the more clear appearance of a plan, Tåsan got serious and added several levels of detail including not only mods to *Tempest* but considerations pertaining to the necessary "after crime" activities, if you will.

With everyone now working together, the task list seemed more manageable. Engine retrofits, console mods, and new docking ports for the modified Deployable Conversion Modules (DCMs) were seeing success and the addition of armaments and sensory arrays were being expertly handled by Annis. The list was tough but manageable.

Tempest was outfitted with state of the art equipment that would track and map the main shipping lanes. Many of the cargo ships traveling between galaxies had fewer crew on board with much of the work being done by drones, leaving only a pilot and one other crewmember managing the flight. A powerful scanner was installed and wired into the navigator console that would monitor ICG and local police activities throughout the hundreds of vectors that surrounded *Tempest*. A low rad beam would perform this surveillance operation without detection.

Before updated and much improved photon armaments and specialty arrays were fitted to the ship's exterior, several coats of chrysoberyl were added to the hull to help resist ultra-V blasts from local police and IGC ships that were sure to pursue them. Experience told Tåsan that the addition of two more coats of chrysoberyl would allow *Tempest* to absorb several more blasts before weakening. Tåsan also knew that by that time, *Tempest* would have out maneuvered and out run anything the IGC had.

The engines were expanded and converted to high-energy Rad-drives capable of jumping to hyperspace within seconds and reaching velocities above most hypersonic conditions. As Tåsan worked on this, he incorporated many aspects of his Spacial Propulsion theory, which now seemed to have moved from theory to development, soon to be a practice. *"Well,"* he sighed as he sat back on this heels admiring his work, *"fortune favors the brave."*

Once Tåsan embraced his new calling, he spent time considering other manageable, yet still unlawful, acts and compiled a fast list. From shuttling clients here and there Tåsan knew which resorts had the largest number of wealthy patrons on site and at what time of the seasons they spent their leisure time there. He also knew hotel safes would be brimming with jewels and tenges.

Along several of his planned routes, there were homes, government towers and mining outposts with little security and large amounts of accumulated valuables. This was going to be easy.

Another huge consideration was to procure and stow food, fuel and energy stores that could last for months. There was a possibility that *Tempest* could become "home" for a period of weeks or longer. Enough supplies had to be on hand and it looked like there needed to be more than *Tempest* could hold. Tåsan knew how to solve this. He secured several remote locations throughout the known galaxies, his favorite being a site on one of the Trimarian Planetoids; the most remote one. The one with no inhabitants.

He found a good landing site, a flat hard surface on a valley floor that was a short distance from a series of caves set into granite walls that were protected from casual view by outcropped spires and weathered overhanging cliffs above. Most importantly, the caves could be protected from electronic detection. Tåsan had explored the planetoid on a whim and was duly rewarded with ample space to set up storage and rough-living areas safe from the elements and undisturbed by all but the hardiest of Anuran lizards.

While Tåsan was assigned to the startup of Shadow Fast at

Supĕrus Tacere, he came across a restricted file, that he immediately broke into and copied after seeing that it was the protected technology of sensor distortion. Tåsan "borrowed" the jamming technology to render his remote area on the Trimarian Planetoid undetectable, under which, *Tempest* could land and any activity carried out would go unnoticed.

It took him four days to install and test the apparatus but in the end, it worked flawlessly and when the system sat idle, it was virtually undetectable. At one point as Tåsan was admiring his handiwork, he had to laugh at the irony of his "starting life outside the law" when apparently he was already living it, since he veritably stole the sensor distortion technology from Supĕrus Tacere.

The next step was to supply the Trimarian Planetoid "hideout", that Tåsan now referred to as Moonstone, with supplies and outfit it with temporary living quarters, allow for a power source, and house individual transport vehicles.

Along those lines, Tåsan, with the help of Dhagáin, transported most of the infrastructure and outfitted several sheltered areas into shop, storage, and living spaces. Nothing formal but separated enough so that "downtime" meant quietude, away from generators, lit screens, discussions, and hums. The one aspect of Moonstone that received Tåsan's full attention was the master console area where everything was monitored, adjusted, and tuned. There were screens and consoles and Rad-dev's that listened to space transmissions, IGC chatter, and shipping lanes. There were long-range sensors that picked up and mapped ship movements and reported speed, size, and compliment.

Alyss flew recon about the other two planetoids in the Trimarian cluster and found isolated areas where she and Luan deployed additional camouflaged sensors that widened Tåsan's surveillance capabilities by 34.18 percent.

Tåsan requested that his band of privateers, now collectively referred to as the *Tempest* Team, provide personal transport vehicles that would be hardy enough to fly them off of Moonstone to "anywhere else", in case there was a breach in their plans and there would be cause to disperse in a hurry. To that end, Moonstone was home to shuttles, Class-N's, and two DCMs that had been modified for long distance space.

All in all, Moonstone was a marvel.

• • •

Five weeks ago, Tåsan shut Corvus Space down, notifying his few remaining regulars that he was no longer in business, apologizing for any inconvenience to their schedules. At the time, Tåsan would have been hard pressed to say it wasn't painful to shut down his company, the thing that he poured so much of himself into, but as the days passed, he found himself more satisfied with the decision as he refocused his attention and energies into *Tempest's* retrofit and upgrades and searched out good plans for appropriations. In time, he again found his passion and vowed to put the past behind, to stand firmly looking forward, buoyed by his *Tempest* Team and energized by future prospects.

Today was one of his better days. Tåsan was at his loft workbench reviewing the detailed schema of his theory of Spacial Propulsion as integrated by way of nano-scale circuitry, when he heard the low hum of a Class-VII craft approaching from the south. He stepped to the window, curious to know who was drawing near.

Dhagáin and Nikliss had been working in the shop and upon hearing the vehicle, both had stepped to the hangar doors and stood watching and alert.

The Class-VII set down and momentarily the door depressurized and swung open and out stepped Castell Brann, his eyes wide in anticipation and a broad smile plastered across his face.

Tåsan stood long enough to recognize Castell, send up a verbal, "Oh look!" and hurry to the stairs, bounding down two at a time and rushing out to greet his friend.

"Oh! How good to see you!" Tåsan called out as he strode forward with arms spread wide.

"And you!" Castell called out. "Tell me it's okay that I came without notification, I did want to surprise you!"

"And you have done that, my friend!"

The two men gave each other a hardy embrace and stood smiling as Nikliss joined them. "Well, well. Come to join the *Tempest* Team?" he chided.

Castell shook hands with Nikliss, and answered the query, "As soon as I am tired of *Ari Arcturus* I will message you, but don't wait for me, that day is a long way off."

"Let's move out of the sun." Tåsan said, guiding the way to the hangar. "Can you stay long?" he asked.

"I'm on leave of duty but must report back in three days time."

"Perfect! You'll stay here of course, there's room and I will not take 'no' for an answer," Tåsan pronounced.

"Done," Castell finalized.

Dhagáin returned to his work after the formalities, satisfied that all was good.

The three men sat at a workbench sharing news. Tåsan was very curious how the IGC treated his leaving and asked if anything had changed.

"Your departure was handled in the only way the IGC knows how to do things," Castell explained. "They ignored it completely. The day you left, a new Commander reported for duty as if nothing had changed whatsoever." Castell frowned, "It was disturbing."

"Does *Ari Arcturus* enjoy expanded responsibilities?" Tåsan asked, hoping to hear that any of his parting suggestions had been enacted.

"No," was the simple truth. Castell said, "I spend most of my time in Engineering. The bridge is...too quiet since you two left," looking from Tåsan to Nikliss, "along with Alyss and Annis when they also left to become citizens," and hurrying on, "Speaking of which, where are they?"

"You came on the right day," Tåsan said, "They'll be here by dinner hour and what a surprise you will be!"

Nikliss gave Castell the grand tour of *Tempest* and the workspaces housed in the hangar after which he left Castell with Tåsan, saying that he needed to return to a pressing task and to assist Dhagáin with an e-net to console testing and would see him at dinner.

Tåsan chatted amiably about what had been going on since their last meeting, keeping most of the talk at a high level. Eventually, he and Castell ended up in the loft workspace and Tåsan left Castell on his own for a few minutes as he started a pot of tea.

Castell was drawn, like a magnet to nickel metal, to the papers and e-pads and in-laid screens that were scattered up and down the long worktable that dominated the loft space. He idly fingered the papers, scanned a schema of two then casually glanced through other sets of data until he caught sight of a particularly familiar set of drawings and notes. "Well I'll be..." he whispered to himself.

Tåsan stepped up to the table and stood opposite Castell, watching him. "What did you find?"

Castell looked up with a smile of delight and tapped his finger on a drawing, pointing to a complex set of drawn data. "You've finally named the thing," Castell said, "Spacial Propulsion With Integrated AI Assist, created and developed by T. Sulac and C. Brann," he read from the legend.

"I've made changes," Tåsan said excitedly. "Take a look at this..."

And just like that they were heads together and deep in discussion until dinner when the arrival of Alyss and Annis interrupted their concentration.

• • •

Castell stayed for two days immersed in engineering and development discussions with Tåsan and working with the *Tempest* Team wherever he could add a bit of value. Castell realized that he missed his friends more than he had been aware of and reluctantly took his leave to return to duty aboard *Ari Arcturus* after eliciting promises to keep in touch and swearing to do the same.

• • •

The autumn quad was nearing its end when Tåsan called for a team meeting. They were to gather at the end of the day in the hangar for a team update then continue to a trendy café in downtown Merula for dinner. His treat.

When everyone was present, Tåsan began, "I've been studying the task list and am very pleased. Through our diligence, we have completed all of the major retros and conversions to *Tempest's* systems and have managed to finish all but two of the Phase Two tasks, and this is to be applauded as the Phase Two list seemed to

271

grow with every effort we made."

Whispers of assent and nodding heads agreed with the note.

Tåsan continued, "You should be very proud of the work that has been accomplished here. Technical, physical, and abstract...its all come together, it has all tested true. Well done *Tempest* Team!" Tåsan stood, arms akimbo, smiling. "I've another topic of conversation for you, too. I've finalized a plan to appropriate a large shipment of osmiridium that is scheduled for slow transport through the Allodial Expanse mid-quad and it so happens that the Zorane Corporation is releasing a shipment of rare rhodium-3, valued for its use in space craft manufacturing that will ship at the same time but a few vectors away.

"I have arranged for the transfer of these metals and payment to occur just minutes after receiving them. The plan details are here in this doc," Tåsan held up an e-pad, "for your viewing pleasure." He leaned over and passed the information along. "I figure the take will be 42,000 tenges, minus 6,000 for expenses and fuel which will grant 4,500 tenges to each of us." Tåsan waited for that bit of information to be heard. "Not too bad for our first time out."

The team conversed among themselves for a minute or two before Alyss thought of a question. "Tåsan? After the shipments have been sold and transferred, do we return here to Corvus Space?"

"I'm thinking 'yes', unless something unplanned happens then we divert to Moonstone as a contingency."

Nikliss asked, "Are there other jobs lined up for us? Do we keep working?"

Tåsan answered, "I have several leads and have been in contact with two buyers. It'll take a few days to coordinate schedules, but yes, we keep working."

"I think it would be prudent," added Luan, "to monitor the waves and lines for any notice of this first job by the locals and by the IGC. It would also benefit us to closely monitor the Intersolar and Space Alliance comm waves. It's said that the top representatives sometimes think to handle their affairs themselves, without the involvement of the IGC."

"Really?" said Alyss more as a statement of surprise than an actual question.

Luan looked over at her and nodded, "Yes."

"Oh, good point, Luan," said Tåsan and turning to Dhagáin, "We had better modify our comm signal, realign two boosters, and add another six array switchers."

Dhagáin nodded, "I can have that done in two days, if Nikliss will wire the con-board, otherwise three days."

"I'm on it," said Nikliss.

"Anything else?" asked Tåsan, waiting, watching his team. "Let's go to dinner. And, if anyone thinks of anything else…" smiling, "you know where I am."

Four

Prevailing Steps

The atmosphere aboard *Tempest* hung heavy with anticipation. Conversation was minimal and clipped and it seemed, at a casual glance, that everyone was on the edge of their seats. In spite of appearances, Tåsan's team worked with the ease of experience and *Tempest* flew steadily toward her mission.

The time it would take to fly out to the predicted vectors, procure both cargos, meet with the buyers, transfer the goods and return to Corvus Space was marked as slightly less than three entire days. No extra time had been added to the schedule so it was important that everything go accordingly. And to this, the crew kept busy with the flight and with equipment checks.

Alyss and Chris Phelan, her co-pilot, took turns piloting the ship, finding that flying in six-hour shifts was an efficient use of the time. Early on, they devised a flight plan that would evade detection from passing ships that traversed the Allodial Expanse. Much of their six-hour duty stints consisted of monitoring the whereabouts of any Class-A and above sized ship, plot a course that would put *Tempest* outside their sensor radius and simply fly through. The constant attention to changing flight patterns began to wear on them at about hour five, hence the pilot changeovers. In their time off, they ate or slept or saw to systems checkouts.

Tåsan found the majority of his time was taken up with monitoring *Tempest*, acutely aware that the ship had been modified beyond a normal upgrade status. *Tempest* was well into the extraordinary upgrade phase and Tåsan was keen to take her into phenomenal.

He listened to her engines and frequently asked that she be sped up, slowed down, or held steady, making notations and conferring with Nikliss. He watched fuel consumption and how the AI segment of the Spacial Propulsion Assist reacted to changing flight demands. He evaluated and made changes as flight varied. Again, Tåsan took notes. After the first evaluation Tåsan mused to himself about how proud Castell was going to be upon hearing how well it operated during real flight.

For the rest of the team, time was spent on equipment checks and in Dhagáin's case, rechecks. He felt it necessary and a good expenditure of his time. Time was, in essence, a variety of activities for the team: study, rest, maintenance, and on task to one's discipline, all of which would be interrupted by the theft and off loading of osmiridium and rhodium-3.

• • •

"Commander," Alyss spoke into the ship's comm, "we will arrive at vector 207Bx4.4 in approximately twenty minutes."

"Acknowledged," responded Tåsan. "Everyone on station. Alyss," he continued, "I'll come to the bridge in five."

"Aye, sir,"

The mission of procuring the cargo of osmiridium would need five members to board the freighter. Tåsan, along with Luan and Chris, would immediately take command, securing the two pilots, leaving them unharmed but confined. Chris would re-program the heading, slowing the ship and engaging the auto-pilot. This would afford *Tempest* the "get away" time needed to leave the scene undetected. He would also monitor the console for approaching vessels or extraneous comm from the ship's limited company.

Luan would open the cargo bay doors, allowing Nikliss and Dhagáin to glide in on their modified DCMs, secure the space redi-containers of osmiridium and tow them over to *Tempest*.

All others would stay aboard *Tempest*, Alyss as pilot, Tao acting as flight engineer, and Annis on nav and tactical.

The heist went off without a hitch. The freighter's bridge was easily secured. It was rustic to say the least and probably hadn't seen an upgrade in twenty solar years. The two pilots were overcome by simply pointing a Hand-Laz at them. One had remarked that they were not paid enough to actually defend company property and both submitted to being bound to their chairs without a fight.

The osmiridium was secured and transferred without flaw and the five were back onboard *Tempest* in what seemed to be record time. In fact, it was excellent timing for a first heist.

Once *Tempest* was secure, Alyss took her, double quick time, out of vector 207Bx4.4 and marked the heading provided by Annis that would take them to vector 251Dx1 where the shipment of rhodium-3 was lazily making its way to its destination.

The flight time was measured at one hour thirty-two minutes.

Tåsan was on the bridge when Alyss announced their approach to vector 251Dx1 and he quickly detected the target space barge slowly making its way through Rayten's outer stars. It was a modified Class-K tanker and Tåsan knew that huge storage holds were usually located mid-ship, just behind the crew quarters' bulkhead.

Luan was positive that she would be able to open the massive pressure lock doors located adjacent to the storage hold. There was no need to pressurize the holds with atmosphere and in fact, that would hinder their efforts to move the rhodium-3 out quickly. The zero atmosphere and zero gravity would allow her, Dhagáin, and Nikliss to glide in on DCMs, locate the goods and guide their bounty out and away easily.

Tåsan and Chris would take the modified Class-N over, attach to the freighter's fuselage, covering a bulkhead door and laser cut the pressure bolts, effectively setting off alarms that signaled the loss of atmosphere, thereby sending barge crew scrambling about in a panic. Tåsan and Chris would quickly make their way to Bridge Control, commandeer flight command and modify the ship's path and comm.

Meanwhile, the DCMs would return to *Tempest* with the rhodium-3 where Tao would be waiting to help secure the haul and Tåsan and Chris would quickly return aboard their Class-N, leaving the barge locked on a slow course "away" with no comm.

That was the plan and as written it appeared to be a good one, but in actuality, was a bit different.

Everything seemed to go fine at first. Luan, Dhagáin, and Nikliss gained entry as planned but once inside the cavernous storage hold, quickly found themselves lost among the nonsensical mess of huge shipping crates, unlabelled containers, and random stacks of metal cases. There did not appear to be any order and, more to their dismay, there were no clear labels to indicate contents. Everything had symbols and logographics pasted haphazardly to their locking points but no written language.

After fruitlessly traversing three corridors through the hold and not locating the goods, Luan accessed her e-dev database and searched for anything related to rhodium-3. It took three tense minutes to locate the carbon symbol related to rhodium-3 and share this information with Dhagáin and Nikliss.

It took another five minutes to locate the transport crates and yet another five minutes to hook them to the DCMs and begin the trek back to the bay doors.

Tåsan and Chris found their way more difficult as well. They maneuvered the Class-N up against the fuselage door located just forward of mid-ship and began the process of laser cutting the pressurized bolts but found that it was taking longer that expected. The bolts were embedded in a type of metal that was resisting the intense heat of the laser, slowing progress. Tåsan was getting nervous about the time sink and the possibility that their presence would be detected and the barge crew alerted. He was about to call the mission off when the last bolt blew and ships alarms sounded throughout. It was then that Tåsan looked at Chris, shrugged and said, "In we go."

And in they went. The crew was indeed in a panic and in their haste, did not recognize Tåsan and Chris as intruders. In the chaos, Tåsan followed closely by Chris, jogged along the corridor to the bridge and burst through the door to find only the ship's Captain in attendance. He was standing at comm barking orders and demanding reports. He had just sworn in anger at his first mate in a language not clearly understood by Tåsan, leaving him to wonder at the epitaph, but that Chris had understood and found enough humor in it to laugh out loud, causing the Captain to round on them in anger. It took the Captain the briefest of moments to realize that Tåsan and Chris were not part of his crew. As his face showed signs of sudden comprehension, he immediately let go the stress of concern for his ship as his eyes focused on the Hand-Laz's pointed at him. He pulled himself up straight and faced Tåsan.

"I take it this is not a social call."

Chris motioned that the Captain was to move away from the comm and then stepped to the controls, studying the configuration as he said to Tåsan, "This is going to take me a minute or two."

Tåsan addressed the Captain. "Have a seat here, please." Indicating an extraneous data station. Once the Captain was seated, Tåsan quickly bound him and then walked the bridge until he located flight con and noting its displays, changed course and speed.

"You won't get away with this," intoned the Captain.

"Oh yes, we will," countered Tåsan.

"Do you know whose ship this is?" asked the Captain.

"Don't care," answered Tåsan. And turning to look at the Captain, added, "It won't change anything so save your words or I will restrain your speech for you."

The Captain nodded his understanding and sat back, resigned to his current situation.

Alyss' voice sounded in Tåsan's aural sen-dev, "What's taking so long?"

Tåsan touched his ear and answered, "Unavoidable delays. The others?"

"They report a slow progression. ETA is six."

"Aye. Noted."

Tåsan turned to Chris, "About done?"

Chris looked up from his screen tapping, thumbed one last icon and said, "Aye, all comm scrambled and misdirection has been broadcast on three waves."

"Good," said Tåsan as he turned for the door. Once he and Chris were on the other side, Tåsan fired his Hand-Laz at the door controls effectively melting then into a hot mess that shot sparks and oozed liquid down the wall panel.

They had made their way down the last wide corridor to their Class-N when a shot whizzed past them, just missing Chris as it grazed the wall to their left.

Tåsan and Chris dodged around the corner to the right and picked up speed. They reached the blown fuselage door and were scrambling into the Class-N when another shot was fired. Tåsan dove to the pilot's chair and fired the engines. Chris stood aside

278

the Class-N's hatch returning fire down the freighter's hallway until Tåsan started to pull forward and Chris closed and secured the hatch.

Tåsan banked around to port and spied the three DCMs with their cargo in tow just slipping past the threshold of *Tempest's* outer doors. He rammed the Class-N forward, speeding to the now half-closed door and slammed the thrusters into reverse on approach, sending the vehicle into a spin that carried it through the narrow hold door opening and into a skid on the deck plates before he cut the engines.

Alyss had *Tempest* in motion before the hold door was secure. Her voice, laced with concern, flowed across the bay, "Everyone alright?"

• • •

The osmiridium and rhodium-3 had been transferred to an unmarked space freighter and Tåsan had met with his client and received payment and had returned. *Tempest* was on a slow course back to Corvus Space and the team had assembled in the central area, eager to hear about mission results.

Tåsan retrieved a mug of tea from the galley and turned to address them. "I'll get to the main point," he sighed. "The profit from the sale of the goods was lower than originally thought due to the specialized market for such semi-rare and somewhat high profile materials. Instead of the expected pay out of 4,500 tenges apiece, I'm sorry to say," Tåsan plopped a woven sack onto a nearby table, "profits divided gives each of us 2,100 tenges."

The team registered murmurs of mild surprise at such a low figure.

"Do you think your contacts were being honest with you?" asked Nikliss, adding, "Considering their background, of course." causing a couple of others to nod at the irony of the situation.

Tåsan answered, "I do, for the most part but hasten to add that my limited experience in these types of matters probably weighs in a bit. Something I will strive to shore up in future."

There was a short minute of no conversation before Luan spoke, "We should use this mission as a sort of practice run. Examine the process and hone the steps so that the next time will be better." She looked at the faces turned her way. "If we consider

279

our actions for a moment, I'm sure we could come up with a list of lessons learned."

"The process was not bad," said Chris, "But we're going to need better tools and bigger fire power for defense. I could have used a hotter laser cutter, it would have saved a lot of time in the beginning."

Dhagáin added, "I'm going to increase the thruster power of our DCMs. What we have now was strained to pull some of the freighter boxes. I think an optional booster would improve capabilities."

Nikliss nodded, "I can help with that." Dhagáin nodded with assurance.

Tåsan spoke, "Alyss, I have questions about *Tempest's* performance, can we meet later?"

"Absolutely," she responded, "*Tempest* flew well, but we'll talk."

"And speaking of inadequacies," spoke Tåsan, addressing the group, "At one point, I thought to call the mission off, something we had not provided for. I think we all need to be ready to cut our losses at any given time, if something unforeseen warrants a hasty exit."

Alyss had been listening to the others when an observation occurred to her. "These two heists, while relatively simple, proved, at least to me, that we go in short numbered and very succinct, which is good," she acknowledged, "but for the least difficulty experienced, we are forced into another role, that of defense."

"That thought also occurred to me," said Chris, "at the exact moment Laz-fire skimmed past my head and I switched from engineer to security."

"Yes," said Tåsan. "I've considered hiring three or four mercenaries to act as mission guards so that we can put our full attention on our jobs."

Annis spoke, "Isn't that risky? Bringing mercenaries into the team?"

"Not necessarily into the team, Annis," Tåsan answered. "More on an 'As Needed' basis. And the only obligation would be to pay them for their services. There are an awful lot of these types of denizens around." Tåsan looked about. "It wouldn't be difficult to do."

"As long as you control the situation," Annis said, leveling a look at Tåsan.

"Agreed," said Tåsan before glancing back at the team, "We have one slow day of travel back to Corvus Space, let's talk about it again once we've landed." His statement was met with nods of approval and the group broke up, some to conversation and others to various ship's duties.

Tåsan took a seat close to a view port and gazed passively out at the distant stars slowly moving past the window. His thoughts drifted over the mission and how he was going to increase the value of future missions. *"Okay, now. Let me be honest, at least with myself,"* he thought. *"Missions are heists, simple as that."* If the tenges value of the heists was to increase, and he vowed it would, each heist plan should be evaluated very closely, every contingency accounted for, and every precaution taken. As the stakes rose, so would the risks.

~

The dark gray smoke was acrid and burnt his eyes to a teary blur as he stumbled through an endless maze of corridor trying to find the exit. The far off rumbling sounded closer and closer as the distance behind him closed and the brilliant flashes of light that foretold of an impending explosion momentarily blinded his progress. *"That was too close,"* the thought clearly pronounced.

Tåsan struggled to regain his balance and lifted his arm to wipe his sleeve across his burning eyes in an effort to clear his vision. He caught sight of the weapon he was clutching in his cramped fist and for the briefest of moments, wondered why he was carrying the murderous thing. Defense? Preparedness?

Another blinding flash of white hot light tore through Tåsan's awareness, this time the violent pressure of the explosion knocked him off his feet, bending him backward even as he flew forward, to land in a heap, dazed and disoriented. As he slowly turned in an effort to right himself, Tåsan howled with the sudden pain shooting up his right leg. He looked down and was

281

horrified at the sight. His leg was shattered and blood was soaking his pant leg and spreading out across the floor.

The heat of the destruction that was coming up the corridor was stifling the air and burning his lungs. "Get up," Tåsan shouted. "Get up and run or die here in a labyrinth of your own obscurity!" The condemnation of the words as they left his lips frightened him to the point of inaction. As his thoughts faded into the distance, the smoke swirled around him, cloaking his vision and confusing the scene and he slowly lost consciousness.

• • •

Tåsan opened his eyes. It was dark, his heart was pounding in his chest, his breathing ragged. He turned his head this way and that in an effort to understand where he was. The dream came flooding back to his fuzzy conscious as his loft at Corvus Space became more clear.

Tåsan breathed his heart into a slower rhythm and lay still trying to bring the details of his dream to the forefront where he could analyze it, as was his habit.

He swung his feet out and leaned forward in a shaky attempt to stand. It was then that the pain in his head, pounding with every heartbeat, dominated his awareness. Tåsan glanced at the time. *"Three hours till dawn."* Then standing on the icy floor, shocking him to reality, *"A cold shower, a hot tea, and a brisk walk should ease my pain and afford me the time to think."*

Tåsan found himself standing in the center of his loft looking at nothing in particular, troubled by his thoughts. *"Why do these dreams persist?"*

He reached for his e-dev and tapped out a message...((*Tempest* Team. Take two weeks off to relax and consider, then we'll meet again.))

Five

Sustained Measurements

Tåsan spent three days meeting with current and potential clients in his desire to become more familiar with the ebb and flow of the goods that moved without ISA controls, what goods were more in demand, and the dark mercari where it all happened.

The lessons came easy...handle all transactions fast. Set them up first, be sure of the details, be sure of your contacts, and be sure not to get caught. Stay fast, stay in the shadows. On the third day he learned that beryllitumn is in demand now but wouldn't be again for another two quads. And as it happened, a large quantity of the recently mined metal was scheduled to ship in ten days time. His client said that a middleman was lined up and ready. Tåsan agreed to the contract.

Back at Corvus Space, Tåsan mused about expanding his client base and thought to seek out additional contacts through casual conversation with a small handful of known clients. He also sought to shore up his knowledge of commodities and shipping schedules and remembered back to his IGC days of patrolling the shipping lanes, clearly recalling several corporate cargo ships and their manifests. He saw now that shipping was a seasonal thing. If you took a shipment then you must unload it or be stuck holding it for any number of quads before the mercari demand returned.

Sipping at his cold brew, a thought popped into his head. *"I'll bet that with little effort, I could find an IGC contact willing, for a handful of tenges, to pass along current shipping lane information. Yes. I'll pursue this in the morn."* Followed quickly by another thought, *"I think I'll reintroduce myself to the Vellosians. Wonder if they're still contented with their relationship with the ISA?"* He lifted his mug to his lips; *"Bet not,"* he smiled.

283

...

Two days later, Tåsan flew his Class-N to Merula for an afternoon in the seedier neighborhood hangouts that populated the south side. He intended to observe the locals and approach one or two of them with a job proposition.

Tåsan had never ventured into lower Merula before this day. He had no need and wasn't interested enough to be curious about the outlaw society that populated the streets.

He landed the Class-N on the roof space of a corner building. There he looked out over several blocks of run-down rises and unpainted stone and wood. Peering over the ledge, down onto the street below, Tåsan took in the sights and smells of old town. After a moment, he took the stairs down four flights to step out into the bustle of scoots and jetbikes and locals that clogged the intersection, he stood for a moment scanning the storefronts and watching the people flow up and down the avenue.

Tåsan spotted a likely bar front across the street and three or four doors down. It had a wide flyspecked and dirt crusted window facing the front but offered a filth-obscured view of the dimly lit interior. As he got a little closer, Tåsan could see three darkly dressed men sitting together about halfway down the bar. As he stepped through the door, he noted a raggedy old man sitting in a back booth, head resting against the seat back, mouth agape in a liquor induced stupor, breathing in a loud, raspy, irregular pattern.

The three men and the barkeep turned to regard Tåsan as he came forward and took a seat a couple of stools away from the group. He could feel their evaluating eyes drilling holes into his being as he adjusted himself and leaned his elbows on the bar. Once the barkeep had set an ale in front of Tåsan, the group of men returned to their conversation, keeping their words private in lowered tones.

Tåsan observed the men in short glances in the cracked and dirty mirror that ran the length of the bar and casual sideway looks, not intended to make them aware of his presence, just long enough to catch a word or two and take an educated guess about them in general.

The man sitting closest to Tåsan suddenly spoke aloud,

"What's your business here?"

Tåsan looked questionably down the bar at the group. *"Was he speaking to me?"* he thought.

The man sat looking straight ahead more or less at the filthy used bottles that lined the back bar. His companions, one smirking as he studied his half empty ale mug, the other leaning back on his stool, glaring at Tåsan, said nothing. The first man slowly turned his face to Tåsan and then swiveled on his stool until it was obvious that he expected an answer.

The seconds ticked silently by.

Tåsan set his mug down and slowly turned to face the group wondering if he should have brought a Hand-Laz with him. "I had heard that there were good, sturdy men round these parts, for hire."

The men had all positioned themselves as if expecting the conversation to erupt into a fray. The first man challenged, "Who told you that?"

Tåsan stood up and flipped two tenges onto the bar. "I guess they were mistaken. I obviously have the wrong place," and turned to leave. "My apologies."

The first man called out, "Wait." And stepped forward. "What kind of employment are you talking about?"

The barkeep moved to refill the four mugs and the men moved to a table, motioning for Tåsan to join them.

• • •

39536.64. *Tempest* team had returned from their furlough and now stood in uneasy groups, scattered about the Corvus Space hangar, nervously waiting for Tåsan to join them. He had sent a cryptic message to their e-dev's calling for a meeting where he would share news.

Tåsan was upstairs in his loft. He had finished his e-dev conversation, disconnected from the caller, and started down the loft staircase. He was greeted by and returned happy salutations to the team he had not spoken with for over a half month.

"I'll get right to the point," Tåsan announced. "I've lined up two important heists for us, the first to occur in two days time."

Murmurs rippled among the group.

Tåsan continued, "The second soon to follow." He took a step or two over to a workbench and leaned his weight against it, folding his arms across his chest.

"Let's not fool ourselves from this point forward. We have become outlaws, pure and simple." Tåsan looked about at the faces of his team. *"Good. They look un-phased by that."* Then continued, "This means increased security will be necessary; for us, the ship, and the heist."

Just then, the approaching sounds of roaring engines caused everyone to turn toward the hangar doors, with Dhagáin and Nikliss walking forward, alert and defensive. Dhagáin had grabbed a large bolt wrench from a bench as he passed.

"I've hired four mercenaries to provide for our safety. To ensure mission success. Sorry, heist success." Tåsan looked to the ever-closer thundering engines of several modified jetbikes as they neared and started to decrease in speed.

Striding out the doors, followed by the others, Tåsan raised a hand in greeting then waited as four leather and metal covered men landed and dismounted their jets amid a cloud of dust and noise.

The men stood in a loose group facing Tåsan and the others, each group suspiciously eyeing the other.

Tåsan broke the strained silence, "Good, you're here," and took a step to the side. *"Tempest* team, meet your new protection." Pointing to each in turn, "Fiann."

Fiann, a tall, muscular man standing squarely and closest, put two fingers to his temple and flipped them outward in a mock salute.

"Garrick."

A second man shifted his stance and thumped his chest with an open hand but said nothing.

"Kloet De."

A third man, less tall then the others, bearded, and carrying weight around his middle, raised a hand an uttered a guttural sound, "Ught."

"Aben."

The fourth man, smiling with pleasure, stepped to the front, made a slight bow and said, "Delighted to make your acquaintances."

Alyss felt a chill run down her spine and she looked to Tåsan wanting to give him an "Are you kidding" look but he was already moving on.

"These men are now working for me," Tåsan said, addressing the team. "They will provide security for our business and have agreed to work as needed. Introduce yourselves for a few minutes while I bring tea and a growler to mark the occasion."

Tåsan disappeared back through the hangar and up the loft stairs leaving the two groups facing each other in a deafening silence.

At long last, Fiann spoke, "As we now work for Sulac, these highly trained and skilled men," thumbing at his comrades, "and I, look forward to a long and rewarding association with you." Holding up his hands, palms forward, and tilting his head askance, added, "I know. I know what you're thinking. You're thinking, 'But are they any good?' and I can assure you," flashing a smile and leering slightly, "Yes. We. Are. We are that good," and laughed at what could only be an inside joke.

The other men joked and jostled each other and agreed with what Fiann had just pronounced then broke up as they mixed with the team and started to look over Corvus Space.

Aben hung back for a moment, passively watching as the two groups mixed and talked, then moved toward Annis. As he stood smiling in front of her, he introduced himself and asked her name.

"I am the nav and tactical officer, O'hAirt," she replied, looking at Aben in a mixture of calm and mild curiosity.

He leaned a half step closer. "Nav and tactical. Fascinating," he almost whispered.

"And you?" she asked, already knowing the answer.

"Oh me," Aben sputtered, affecting modesty, "I'm a security specialist. *Your* security specialist." He had walked a circle around Annis, looking her over. She stood this scrutiny with patience. "By the way, are you attached? Or are you free to follow your heart?" Aben winked suggestively, his gaze dropping to her breastbone as he moved a pointed finger toward her jewels.

In a flash Annis took hold of his wrist and effortlessly twisted it, threatening to break it, causing Aben to wince in pain. "Ah, there are always boundaries to be aware of. Wouldn't you agree?"

287

she smiled then loosed her grip on Aben's wrist. "And respect," she added.

He pulled free, rubbing and cradling his hurt wrist, the smile he was flashing earlier replaced by a guarded grimace, his voice measured, "Boundaries. Yes," Aben said holding up his wrist, "and restraint."

Annis said, "Restraint?" raising her brow to make her point and giving a slight nod in finality.

Tåsan had come through from the hangar workshop and froze at the sight of Annis holding Aben at bay by his wrist. He held steady waiting to see how it would play out, and relaxed when it appeared that they ended the confrontation in a civil manner.

Depositing the tea and ale on a nearby table, Tåsan invited everyone to help themselves and started a dialogue, "Beryllium. A metal alloy necessary in the manufacture of spacecraft. Truly a fascinating and rare commodity." He turned to the group, "A large amount of which will be in slow transit across the Allodial Expanse headed to the Niles Galaxy in two days time and it's ours." Adding, "And uridium-8. Another rare find, will be on a fast stop, four vectors away, coming from the Hedorrion Galaxy on route to Naiad Five." Tåsan helped himself to an ale and raised his mug to the group, "To success and reward in our new associations."

"Hear, hear!"

• • •

The plan was simple. Board the freighters, incapacitate the pilots, appropriate and off-load the two cargos. Done.

What wasn't in Tåsan's plan was the level of armaments the mercenaries chose to carry. Tåsan's team carried Hand-Laz's that in comparison looked like children's toys. The mercs carried serious firepower and appeared ready for war. It was a bit disconcerting; it was something Tåsan had not accounted for.

Tempest intercepted the Omega Lines freighter as it reached altitude of the outer stars and boarded her with little resistance. Tåsan, with one of the mercs, took control of the helm, tying the two pilots to their chairs and setting the freighter on a slow, safe heading to a far away space dock. Dhagáin and Nikliss procured the beryllium along with one merc, Kloet De.

With the first cargo secured in the hold, *Tempest* set course to intercept the transport from Thorium 4, which if calculations were correct, had entered the Allodial Expanse at vector 8F97.3 just minutes before.

Boarding went easily. Tåsan, Chris, and two mercs took command while Dhagáin, Luan, and two mercs made their way to the cargo hold. It was a large freighter and they stepped lively through the maze of corridors meeting one crewmember that Garrick immediately shot with a ten-degree stun blast to the chest, sending the surprised man to the floor in a heap.

Luan turned her gaze to Garrick, "Did you kill him?" she asked.

"No," answered Garrick in his gravelly voice. "Only stunned for an hour, maybe more." And kicking the downed man's foot, added, "Looks weak. Maybe more."

Dhagáin stepped around the scene, encouraging them to follow.

Alyss' voice sounded in Tåsan's aural sen-dev, "The clock is ticking."

Tåsan nodded to himself in agreement. He was still on the bridge, busy at nav. He glanced over at Chris. "Almost done?"

Chris was bent over the comm console, fingers flying, and jumped at Tåsan's sudden query. "This system is a nightmare," he answered. "It's a patch on top of a repair on top of an attempted correction." Then he jabbed at a few more icons and buttons. "But I think I've got it. Have sent a comm to the Chelic Corporation reporting a transport delay of five hours while a thruster is repaired."

"Good. We're almost done here," Tåsan said as he rounded to the vid-screen wall.

Chris watched as Tåsan pulled his Hand-Laz, took aim at an IGC ornamental award plaque hung with apparent pride amid several smaller accommodations and fired, turning the IGC logo to burnt mush.

"*Now* we're done," Tåsan declared.

~

Just as the last container was easing out the storage bay doors, in preparation for its space glide over to *Tempest*, an alarm sounded throughout the ship.

The team and the mercenaries froze for half a nano-second, eyes agog, before everyone leapt to action. Dhagáin, Luan, and Chris fixed the strapping on the cargo container and started to push it out the doors while Tåsan and the mercs turned to face the vast cavern of cargo bays, weapons drawn.

Soon enough, three Chelic Corp employees could be seen among the isles, stealthily making their way forward. Kloet De loosed a blast aimed at a container above one man's head causing the metal to burst into a rain of parts and debris. The man gasped in surprise as the debris knocked him to the floor. Garrick loosed another round along the metal floor plates to discourage the others from their forward travel.

With the uridium-8 out the doors and quickly gliding toward *Tempest*, the team mounted their DCMs and were leaving one by one. Just before Chris snapped his helm closed, he shouted to Tåsan, "Let's go! Move it!" The men scrambled to their DCMs, hastily laying down cover blasts and jettisoned out the bay doors in reckless speed.

Tåsan slammed his reverse thruster and jerked his DCM around and let go a round or two at the outer operation panel causing it to slam the doors shut. He turned his DCM and sped forward, calling out to Alyss to stand by for hyper jump.

As *Tempest* shot away from the freighter, she comm'ed Tåsan, "The alarms must have notified the local police. They are on course from Thorium 4. I've steered us away and will soon cut speed and change heading so as to look innocent."

"Perfect. Thank you," Tåsan replied. He was standing in the cargo hold with the others, feeling a bit numb as his mind retraced the last fifteen minutes. He spoke, directing his attention to the four mercenaries, "Well, I can plainly see the value of having you along. Worth your wage." Then speaking to all present, "Good job."

Tåsan glanced toward the two cargos. "Dhagáin, see that the shipments are relabeled and obscure the corporate brands." Tåsan turned to walk away, hesitated, and added, "We off load in two hours."

• • •

290

Dhagáin found Chris and Nikliss in the galley and joined their conversation already in progress.

"...makes my Hand-Laz look ineffectual. I may have to rethink my weaponry," commented Chris.

"Why would you need more firepower when your job is to secure command and alter comm?" asked Nikliss.

"Yes," interrupted Dhagáin. "What's your concern?"

Chris answered, "That as we move forward, opposition will increase, maybe to the point where I will need better self defense."

Fiann had stepped through the doorway in time to catch Chris' remark. "I overheard your comment," he said, startling the men with its suddenness, "and I will advise against it for your own sake." He sauntered to the galley and proceeded to pour himself a shot from a flask he carried.

The three men sat in silence watching him move. In a short moment, Fiann spoke again. "You are amateurs. Having an advanced weapon would make you reckless, a detriment to the..." and speaking as if searching for the correct word, inflected, "...mission." Smiling passively he continued, "Just do your jobs," Fiann said, pointing at Chris, "and leave weapons to those of us," pointing to himself, "who have far more experience than you."

Fiann tossed back his shot and quietly set his jigger on the galley counter and turned to face the men, almost daring them to challenge him.

None spoke.

• • •

Annis provided the nav and Alyss flew the ship on a forward sort of round-about course through the Allodial Expanse as three more robberies were carried out. They were small fairly insignificant jobs but important all the same. They were designed to take the focus off the main, more valuable heists, to confound the local police efforts, and as Tåsan explained, "To cause confusion, to make it appear that there are several independent thefts, not one."

So, in short order, a small shipment of Práxus wine, a miners union payroll, and four bags of raw gems were appropriated from their routes and *Tempest* fled into the outer stars of the Niles Galaxy.

Nikliss had been scanning all comm channels for the least

indication that *Tempest* had been indentified or that law enforcement, particularly the IGC, were close. To his relief there was not one word.

Alyss turned flight over to Chris and now sat alone in the galley with Tåsan. The others were scattered about the ship, busy with whatever.

"Today was quite the day." She looked at Tåsan who sat opposite her, apparently lost in thought.

He looked up, "And not over yet."

Alyss waited for him to continue.

"I will be more satisfied once we are back at Corvus Space and I've squared with the mercs. And only then when they are away." Tåsan took in a deep breath and huffed it out. He took out his e-dev and tapped out a message, looking it over before touching the send icon.

Immediately Alyss' e-dev chimed an incoming and she smiled as she saw it was from Tåsan but her smile faded as she read the content. ((Team – when we reach base operations, you are all granted one half quad off. Recompense will occur in the usual manner. Relax. Have fun. Wait for my next text. TS))

Alyss lowered her e-dev. Tåsan was watching her. "Is there a deeper meaning here?" she asked.

"I need time to plan our future activities," Tåsan replied. "It's one thing to hijack shipments of beryllium and uridium-8 but how many times can that happen without serious notice? Once," he pronounced. "I need time to be creative and more time to see the details." He sat looking at his fingers, choosing his next words. "After the others have left, would you like to take a ride over to the Lower East Grille in Merula with me? It's a favorite hangout of IGC trainees on a night out."

"Sure," Alyss said, then asked, "What's there?"

"Possibly information. I would like to hear what the rumor mill has to say about today's spike in robberies."

Nikliss' voice sounded in Tåsan's aural sen-dev, "We're five minutes out from our rendezvous coordinates."

Tåsan answered, "Thank you," and turned to Alyss. "And I could use some reliable company."

Six

Rumors Written on Air

The Lower East Grille occupied the entire first floor of a large corner building that rose three stories and was made of stone and brick and cobbles, and was adorned with hand hewn stone ribbons, leaves, and scrolls with lost lettering, all done by long-ago builders who once cared.

Tonight, the throngs of young IGC trainees, that packed the bar and jammed the booths along the windows, did not care that the old building had endured misuse to become worn and weathered. They cared for the lights and the music and for the laughter of friends. Lower East Grille sat center stage in an up and coming section of Merula collectively known as the Danelles that encompassed a half milia square area somewhat east of city center. The Danelles was an eclectic collection of old next-to-new next-to-refurbished next-to-abandoned. Most of it held promise, the rest, history.

The Grille, as the locals call it, is a working class tavern serving a long list of unusual intoxications. There is a huge oval bar in the center with tables and booths along two walls dimly lit by sconce and pendent, broken only by the swinging doors of the small, cramped kitchen that in spite of its size, served the best small bites around. The Grille is frequented by lots of IGC trainees and regulars from around Merula.

And it was thus when Tåsan and Alyss stepped inside, out of the crisp Merula night air into the overcrowded warmth of the east side hot spot.

After gazing around to familiarize themselves with the layout of the interior, Tåsan walked casually to his left.

Alyss made her way off to the right and after a handful of

293

seconds, slipped up to an opening along the bar, between two groups of friends. After another minute, one of the men she stood by became aware of her having a bit of trouble getting the barkeep's attention and turned to her, smiling. "It's always like this after quad finals." He raised a hand and leaning over the bar, called, "Whitley!" The tall slender Astorian, busy mixing a foamy concoction, turned her head and nodded her recognition.

The cadet leaned back in his seat. "Shouldn't be but a minute," and smiling, extended his hand to Alyss. "I'm Travers," quickly followed by, "Are you with the IGC?"

"Alyss," she answered. "Just a private citizen out for interesting conversation and a few good stories."

As the barkeep leaned over to hear Alyss ask for a Sadorian Frappe, Alyss glanced across the bar to see Tåsan chatting up two IGC trainees who were listening raptly then burst into laughter at something Tåsan had said, before she turned back to Travers and asked, "So. How did you do on your quad final exams?"

$$\bullet \bullet \bullet$$

Two hours later, Tåsan found himself seated next to Alyss ordering a pair of double shot Brandywines that arrived in small ornately carved quartz jiggers that glowed with interest. He held his up toward Alyss, who motioned her attention by raising her jigger up off the bar and looked for Tåsan to continue.

"Ahh," he said, "To efforts that pay." And tipped the liquid to his lips.

Alyss sipped the dark fermented sweetness and looked at Tåsan. "I've heard that the Omega Lines reported that one of their freighters had finally been located in sector 82E.5 where it had been adrift for seven hours." She suppressed her laughter into a wide smile. "Apparently, after many hours late to docking, Omega put in a frantic call to local authorities who, rumor has it, swarmed out of headquarters into a search but not knowing where to look, ended up wandering aimlessly until someone spotted the freighter."

Tåsan shook his head, "Unbelievable," was all he could add.

"And I've heard something else."

"Is it good?"

"Maybe better. The miner's payroll heist made the news. The

union is extremely angry, posturing with 'what kind of society do we live in that takes from others', and whatnot. They are threatening 'decisive action' and 'the highest retribution' and announcing that they are in discussions with the IGC about what can be done." Alyss turned in her seat to more face Tåsan. She looked him in the eye and levelly intoned, "They're blaming known privateers."

As a smile widened across his face, Tåsan nodded in satisfaction. "I talked with two trainees who are specializing in comm. One said that the IGC has told several ISA corporations that their problems were a matter for the local authorities. This has infuriated the corporations who have vowed that it is not settled. The IGC added insult to injury by requesting that the corporations 'keep them informed'."

Both Alyss and Tåsan laughed in humorous disbelief and tipped back the remains of their Brandywine.

Almost immediately, the barkeep was standing in front of them holding a bottle at the ready and on Tåsan's nod, refilled the jiggers and moved down the bar.

"Here's what I think," said Tåsan. "That the IGC wants the local police to look incompetent. In fact, they're probably counting on it. I think the IGC wants to use the situation to manipulate public perception. Then after some measure of time, to swoop in as heroes. To save the day."

Alyss took a moment to consider what Tåsan had just said. "That seems incredulous."

"Not if you knew my father."

• • •

Tåsan stayed with Alyss in Merula for another two days before returning to Corvus Space, and in that time, no additional news could be gained. The whole rush of chatter surrounding the day of heists slowed down and finally stopped. Everyone had moved on and nearly forgotten it had even happened.

Tåsan had decided to up the gain.

Seven
Along Came a Spider

It was settled. The next heist would be Aleia, an exclusive playground of the galaxy's most moneyed corporate leaders, located on a privately owned plot of land on Sador's moon, Eriop.

It was the peak of the solstice season and Aleia was festooned and polished and well stocked in an anticipation that had paid off. The hot springs resort was crowded with wildly moneyed merchants and corporate owners from throughout the galaxy.

The large and well appointed cloister of buildings and amenities are surrounded by stone walls half buried beneath tendrils of green and bronze Ozak vines. The walls are meant to add privacy for Aleia's exclusive clientele and to keep out intruders from the wild lands that surround the resort.

Inside the tall stone walls are hot springs and lush plantings with bright blooms and long swaying leafy tendrils, arranged to promote relaxation and enjoyment. However, the weeks of solstice brought a clientele looking for excitement, rousing times, and holiday cheer.

Tåsan had lit on the idea of robbing Aleia as a way to recoup the thousands of tenges lost on the last heist. He thought of it as an easy bonus, a reward for the hard work of his team.

The idea of Aleia came to him as he spent quiet time at Corvus Space. He had busied himself during the first two weeks of his coming home, monitoring the comm waves for any indication that local authorities or the IGC knew who was behind the much talked about day of heists. All he could gather was that it might have been the work of privateers from a neighboring galaxy. There were no real clues or reliable witnesses and without either, investigations went cold.

296

As Tåsan's concentration on the ever-fading comm news relaxed, he shifted his attention to *Tempest* and started to perform routine maintenance and subtle upgrades to her AI. It was during a particularly uneventful day that his e-dev chimed with an incoming message from Stellanova. Would he fly her to Cimtun 8? She has accepted employment with a company tasked with terra-building a new and modern city from the bottom up.

((Any time you say.)), he tapped out. ((*Tempest* is ready when you are.))

• • •

Three days later, Tåsan, with Stellanova as his co-pilot, lifted off from Corvus Space and flew a course to a set of coordinates along Cimtun 8's equatorial belt where Stellanova would start her terra-forming work.

Tåsan looked over at his co-pilot and said, "It's such a pleasure to see you, Stella, and you can't know how happy this makes me."

"Thanks!" she responded. "It's been much too long."

"It has. I think the last time we messaged was your graduation from university."

"I missed you at the ceremony. It was quite the celebration."

"I'm sorry, Stella," Tåsan leveled his voice. "I was busy and couldn't get away."

Stella looked at Tåsan and said, "I know it was because you didn't want to see father and I understand that but," she rushed on, "you might have met with mother and me."

Tåsan looked back at his view screen and fingered an icon. "That would have looked like a subversion to father and on top of all else, I didn't need that, nor do I need to give him an excuse to further chastise me or my life."

Stella was well aware that she had fuelled Tåsan's heated response so she gave him a bit of silence before venturing another subject. "What have you been working at lately?" she asked.

"Not much. Odd jobs. Quick flights," he replied.

"I notice," Stella said, "that you've made several rather major modifications to *Tempest*. She paused, watching Tåsan's face. "Is that a 70-ME laser cannon mounted to the fore panel?"

Tåsan turned to look at Stella, his brow furrowed in touchy concern, "Yes," he said shortly.

"What would you need a 70-ME for?" her voice a little challenging.

"For protection, Stella," Tåsan replied, his voice level and clear.

Stella did not take the hint and pushed again, "The thick coats of chrysoberyl and photon armaments along the fuselage tell a story more of battle than protection." Adding, "What are you into, Tåsan?"

He considered his words carefully. "Stella." He turned in his seat to face her. "I'm not 'in to' anything. I do what I must to survive in dangerous times." He could see her trying to form another question and sought to cut her off. "It's nothing for you to be concerned with. I'm fine."

They fell silent for minutes and more. Then Stellanova spoke. "I can see the dark modifications to *Tempest*, her name has been obscured with glyphs. I can only guess that you are up to no good." She held up her hand to stop Tåsan from protesting. "And while it makes me sad, I will not pry any further. You are my brother and I will always love and support you."

• • •

The rest of the trip to Cimtun 8 was over quick enough. Stella filled some of the time talking about her corporate project and her excitement in having such a prestigious appointment as her first employment out in real life. The subject of Tåsan's activities did not come up again until minutes before Stellanova was to disembark.

She stood at the gangway and faced Tåsan. "I don't know when we will meet again, but until then, please be careful. For me. Please be careful."

Tåsan smiled warmly and took Stella in a big hug. "Don't worry about me. I'll be fine. Promise."

She smiled back at him and then stepped through the hatch. She turned toward him when she reached the tarmac and raised her hand in farewell.

• • •

That night as Tåsan lay abed, floating in that place between wake and sleep, he saw a fog before his eyes and as he watched, it swirled and a face appeared, slowly coming from the undulating mist. It was the face of

298

Stellanova, and as Tåsan came to recognize her, the mist swallowed it up and it was then the face of his mother. He felt he must say something but the words caught in his throat as the mist changed and the face that was formed next was that of Alyss.

Tåsan's uncertainty at what was happening turned from confusion at the ever-changing face that appeared from the mist to that of complacency. He became aware that he felt no emotion at that moment. He was cold inside and only wondered at the realization of it, accepting that it was true, and at that instant, he was swallowed by the faceless mist and transported to a deep darkness that Tåsan guessed was a descent into the abyss of perdition.

~

Corvus Space had become a hub of excitement in the days following Tåsan's e-comm to the team inviting them to reassemble.

It had been weeks since the team was last together and as more and more members arrived, the air seemed charged with merriment. There were slaps on the back and warm hugs, smiles and laughter, and stories to tell as everyone caught up on what had been happening during the long break.

Over the evening meal that night, held upstairs in the loft, Tåsan talked about the changes he had made to *Tempest* and invited everyone to begin thorough checkouts of their stations starting the next day, "...because tonight is for celebration, friendship, and introducing the future," Tåsan announced with a raised mug of ale.

The meal went on amid laughter and tall tales and after the table was cleared and the glasses refilled, Tåsan took a few moments to review the *Tempest* maintenance logs and ask that supply lists be completed as soon as possible. "...and I'll tell you why," he paused and looked about the table, smiled and continued, "I've come up with a good plan, a very good plan that should make us an awful lot of tenges in the shortest amount of time."

Everyone looked to Tåsan with anticipation, eagerly waiting for him to continue.

"In seven days time, we will steal all the wealth from the rich and the richer who have converged for the solstice holidays at the Aleia resort on Eriop." Tåsan sat smiling at his reveal, very self-satisfied. But his words were greeted by concerned silence and questioning stares until Luan spoke, breaking the moment.

"Have you worked out the details?" she asked.

"The overall plan," Tåsan began, "is to gain entrance to the resort, blow the safe, and leave before the authorities arrive." He set his mug down and stood up, "Wait..." He went to the far end of this worktable and scooped up a pile of papers and his e-dev and soon returned to his seat, rustling through the short collection.

"I have several diagrams," he said as he started passing the pieces around. "I have obtained a partial guest list and it contains an impressive number of wealthy corporate owners who have booked in for the solstice. This is a big deal for these personages. They brag, they drink, they show off their wives, who, by the way, also brag and show off their jewels and all else their tenges can buy."

Now, conversation around the table had become animated and lively as the pages and the e-dev were looked over.

"The safe is too large to be carried away. It will have to be opened where it is and the contents emptied."

"The number of security personnel has to be determined."

"Timing will be a critical consideration."

"When would be the best time?"

Tåsan smiled to himself as he listened to fragments of everyone's discussion and evolving solutions to the task at hand. Eventually he spoke out, "I am pleased to hear all that is being said! Let's continue talking tonight about the main points, bring up questions and concerns and possible details but let's leave any final decisions for the day after the 'morrow. That way we all have individual time to think and consider and then, as a team, put the pieces together into a coherent timeline and a master plan." He took a breath and continued, "I've requested that our mercenaries meet with us in four days. We can inform them of their roles at that time."

The next two hours were filled with talk and questions and small disagreements. Eventually, everyone drifted away. Nikliss and Dhagáin to makeshifts in the hangar, Tao to a small lean-to he had set up just outside under the stars, and everyone else to small quarters aboard *Tempest*.

Tåsan, now alone in his loft space, poured another cirrus ale, turned off most of the lights, and sank into his overstuffed chair, his mind still running at high speed, in spite of the ale.

"...*field check the armaments, replenish fuel rods, test all op updates for accuracy, charge all weapons, verify provisions, check and double check plan specific list of supplies, ask for inputs...*" On Tåsan's mind ran until he started to relax and let his gaze wander out the window and into the dark night. As he sank further into the comfort of the chair, Tåsan's eyelids became heavy and as he blinked one last time, fell into a mercifully dark sleep uninterrupted by dreams or visions that took him, this night, far into the early morning hours.

• • •

The mercenaries had arrived hours after their expected time, offering vague and insinuating excuses as to why. The whole thing concerned Alyss who made a rather pointed comment to Annis about the mercs' untrustworthiness. Annis voiced her concern by simply looking at the four dark figures now assembling in the hangar and saying, "I agree. They bear watching."

Tåsan did not take an interest in the mercs late arrival other than to call everyone together and begin to review the Aleia plan.

One half an hour later, after the stage had been set and the player's parts discussed and spontaneous questions answered, Tåsan summed up.

"Just before dusk, we'll set down in an area roughly a milia from the south wall. Alyss, Annis, Tao, and Nikliss will stay aboard and wait for my signal. Luan, Chris, Dhagáin, along with Fiann, Garrick, Kloet De, and Aben, you're with me. We'll make our way to the reception office, secure everyone, and," addressing himself to Luan, "the safe will have to be blown with a small amount of boracite." Getting a nod of affirmation from Luan, Tåsan continued, "Chris, Dhagáin, Kloet De, and Aben, you will quickly secure our parameter, effectively keeping everyone else out of our way. When we have the goods, we retreat back across the gardens and out the south wall and across the flat. On my

301

signal, Alyss," looking over at her, "come in and pick us up." Alyss gave a slight nod in agreement.

Tåsan added, "Then we fly away." He looked around. Fiann was looking a bit noncommittal but had been paying attention. The other three looked bored and fidgety. His team looked confident. "Any questions?" Tåsan ventured.

"Just one," Fiann asked. "When do we start?"

• • •

Sador, along with its moon, Eriop, were several vectors from Naiad Five in its solar ellipse. *Tempest* was on course and had steadily closed the distance and was soon in a vacant piece of space on Eriop's uninhabited side and started her descent.

Alyss and Nikliss guided the craft through the maze of comm signals that made up Eriop's surveillance system and flew low and slow across the terrain, under all the known electromagnetic detection networks.

Anticipation ran high.

Tempest set down in a semi-remote area about one-point-five milia south of the Aleia resort. Annis had chosen a spot with the least treacherous track through the rough outback to Aleia's south wall.

The operations team assembled in the cargo bay and busied themselves with last checks before boarding their DCMs and signaling their readiness. When Tåsan was satisfied that everyone was on point, he drifted his DCM out the bay door and started in the direction of Aleia.

With the DCMs hidden behind a small rocky outcrop, the team made their way on foot reaching a slightly hidden access door in the wall within minutes.

Dhagáin produced a spy-fiber that he fed up to the top of the wall with which he surveyed the garden area for anything to be aware of. Seeing nothing and no one, he nodded to Tåsan that the way was clear.

Luan picked the door's locking mechanism and slowly pulled it open to reveal an overgrowth of vines. She smiled at the fortune of it and motioned for Tåsan to lead the way.

The band of eight moved stealthily through the manicured gardens, stepping quietly and stopping to check around blind spots before moving forward. They reached an unassuming side entrance to the reception office that Luan quickly opened for them.

Before going through, Tåsan looked at Luan, Fiann, and Garrick and using hand signals, told them that he and them would go straight ahead and to the left. Turning to the others, he signaled that they would go straight in then fan out to the right. Everyone nodded and readied their stance, anxious to move.

In they went.

Tåsan's group secured the rear of reception with very little effort, tying up four resort employees. Luan went to work on the safe, setting small amounts of boracite against the massive swing hinges before turning her attention to the complex locking medium.

The others had taken up defensive positions at portals and doorways. As Tåsan stood alert to the immediate area, he watched as two resort clients came through the doors and who were immediately met by Aben, who raised his blaster in a threatening manner, causing the couple to freeze in fear. Aben, with a leering smile, took a step toward the female, who shrank back from him. He smiled wider at her fear, reached out and plucked a gem studded piece from her neck, stuffing it in his pocket before wagging the blaster at her companion who immediately handed over two rings and a wallet. Aben then herded them to the counter where they were made to lay down on the floor.

Tåsan set his jaw and turned his focus back to Luan. She had drilled three little holes strategically about the lock and handle and had stuffed them with boracite. She looked up at Tåsan and with eyes wide, made shooing gestures, indicating that everyone must move back.

Tåsan made a soft whistling sound, gaining everyone's attention then signaled them to standby.

Unexpectedly there was the popping sound of weapons fire coming from the front of the compound. Someone had triggered a silent alarm alerting the local police. Immediately Garrick left Tåsan's side to join the others. Tåsan shouted to Fiann to stay with Luan and for Luan to, "Hurry up!"

Kloet De was holding his position at the doors but Chris, Dhagáin, and Aben had rushed outside and were exchanging fire with the local authorities.

Tåsan held position, protecting Luan and helping Fiann.

Suddenly there was a deafening explosion and a trembling underfoot as the boracite blew the massive safe door open even as it lifted the safe up into the air, slamming it back down.

Luan rushed back to the safe and frantically stuffed its contents into container packs.

The firing from the compound continued in measured spurts and one by one, Dhagáin, Chris, and Aben retreated back through the doors to reception, turning to provide cover fire as they did.

Tåsan shouted, "This way!" and the group ran back to where they had originally entered, some grabbing a container pack as they fled.

Alyss had tracked the police on the comm waves and had not waited for Tåsan's signal but instead had flown in and was taking fire from a police hovercraft. Annis was returning fire with equal force, crippling two cruisers and downing at least one hovercraft.

The ship was holding but the situation was getting too heated.

Tåsan and his team were making their way back to the south wall as fast as they could but the police had breached reception and were starting to swarm around the building, firing as they advanced.

One by one, Tåsan's team raced through the wall and ran the distance to their DCMs, firing them up and making haste toward *Tempest*. Tåsan had just gained his seat when he took a moment to check behind him. The police had taken up positions atop the wall and were firing at anything that moved. That was when he saw Garrick take a level ten weapons blast to the back. He was dead before he hit the ground. Tåsan leaned over and jammed the homing switch on Garrack's DCM and it lifted up and away.

As weapons discharged all around them, everyone made haste to close the distance between themselves and *Tempest*. As they hurried to get aboard, a police hovercraft zipped into view and as a cannon blast was loosed at *Tempest*, an officer leaned on his automatic weapon, striking Chris in the leg.

Alyss had the ship halfway into hyperdrive before Tåsan could secure the cargo doors. Everyone tumbled wildly to the floor as Alyss ignited the fuel and the ship lurched forward.

Eight
Whispers In The Dark

As *Tempest* reached the Zone of Demark, Alyss swung the craft sharply about and as *Tempest* turned on its arc, Annis loosed four rapid shots from the 70-ME laser cannon effectively blasting the starboard nacelle of a police cruiser into sparks and flame, and doing crippling damage to a second cruiser that had been following too close.

As *Tempest* completed its circular arc, Alyss resumed her course. She intended to fly at very high rates of speed out of Eriop's orbit around Sador and gain the Outer Stars of the Hedorrion Galaxy virtually undetected. Or at the very least, not followed.

There was a stunned silence as the ship accelerated into hyperdrive, reached a safe range and eventually leveled out at a steady velocity away from Aleia. Dhagáin reported to the bridge and went straight to engineering. Before settling down, he swept the ship for bugs or other electronic devices that would transmit their whereabouts. The bridge crew were at their stations verifying that they were out of sensor range of the police and any tracking gadgets that the resort may have been employing, but all were taking stock of what had just happened. After a moment, Alyss' voice crackled over the comm-unit, "Is everyone okay back there?"

Tåsan had come forward and took co-pilot command and was rapidly working icons and keys in an effort to take hold. He glanced over at Alyss. "Report," was all he said.

Alyss had been sitting forward in her seat, muscles taut and eyes alert. "Aye, Captain," she said without taking her eyes from her station. "We took several blasts to the hull from three local cruisers. The chrysoberyl remains intact. We have seventy percent armaments charge and fuel enough for two days of hyperdrive." She completed her status report with a question, "How are the crew?"

Tåsan sat back a bit and let his hands relax from his comm screen. It was good news to hear that *Tempest* made it through her first clash with authorities. He took the briefest of moments to feel proud of his craft before reality set back in.

"It's a good/bad situation," he said before he addressed Alyss, Annis, and Nikliss, who had stayed aboard *Tempest* as flight crew. "First the good," he continued. "The safe was absolutely loaded with wealth which we managed to appropriate." He looked down at his hands. "The bad is that it was not without cost."

Alyss and the others did not speak.

As Tåsan took a big breath in, his thoughts organized and he continued, "Chris took a blast to the leg, it didn't look good. Tao has the bleeding somewhat under control, however, Chris will need surgery very soon if his leg is to be saved. One of the mercenaries, Garrick, was killed during our escape." Tåsan fell silent but recovered quickly enough to answer any questions.

When everyone fell quiet, Alyss lowered her voice to ask, "What happened? How did the police get there so quickly?"

Tåsan only shrugged and shook his head slowly. "When you are sure that we remain undetected, set a course to within two milia of Corvus Space. We will drop the mercs off so they can be on their way."

"Aye, sir."

"Then set course to Moonstone.

• • •

To avoid detection, Alyss had flown a varied course pattern as *Tempest* made her escape from Aleia.

The mercenaries were dropped about two milia from Corvus Space. It was agreed that it would be safer if *Tempest* was not spotted in the vicinity. It was a short, smooth hike for the mercs needing very little effort. In minutes, they could be on their jetbikes and away.

Dhagáin and Nikliss had decided to disembark *Tempest*, too. Nikliss was going to stay at Corvus Space, as he always did, and Dhagáin, having nothing that required him to be elsewhere, decided to join him. They gathered camping supplies into rucksacks and asked to be dropped two days out from the hangar, preferring the rougher transition of a hike in the outback as a return to the relative safety of routine.

Tempest reached the Trimarian Planetoids within two days and slipped, undetected, down through the parameter sensor distortion beacons to land at Moonstone.

Immediately Tao prepped Chris for surgery. The weapons blast to his leg was traumatic. It had severed a major artery and shattered his femur, neither of which Tao could properly repair aboard *Tempest*.

Surgery took three hours and many minutes but in the end, Tao effected an almost perfect repair of Chris' leg. "He'll walk with a slight limp but will have full use of his leg," he reported to Tåsan.

"That's good news. Thank you, I was very worried."

"Tåsan. Jahved Tuk will be closest in nine days. I would like to leave at that time. I think I need to see my family. Luan has said that she will stay to monitor Chris' recovery." Tao glanced over at Chris, sleeping soundly, breathing evenly. "She has a moderate knowledge of varied medical skills and a great attention to detail. She's quite capable of taking care of him."

Tåsan answered, "If you think well of Luan's skills then I'm satisfied." Looking at Chris, "You've been invaluable, Tao," and turning back to face him, "I expect Chris will be fine. I trust your family is well and missing you." Tåsan held out his hand in friendship, which Tao took in his. Tåsan continued, "When I'm more clear on our future, I will contact you."

Tao smiled and nodded, "Good."

• • •

Nine days later, Tao boarded his Class-N and set course for home.

Under Luan's watchful eye, Chris was making a steady recovery. He wasn't quite able to stand without aid and wobbled when he tried to step forward but other than that, his appetite was good and he had started to decline pain management.

Luan had told as much to the others, easing their concerns, before asking Tåsan if he had a moment to spare.

"Of course. Over tea in the galley?" he responded.

When somewhat settled, Luan spoke. "I know a dealer whose

main interest, if you will, is in jewelry. He does not concern himself with its origins, only its potential value. My association with him goes back quite a way."

Tåsan's curiosity immediately kicked in. *"She's more complex than I ever imagined,"* he thought.

Luan continued, "I'm sure I can arrange to...*facilitate*...the sale of at least one half of the collection."

"What would you need from me?" Tåsan asked.

"Nothing more than your trust," she answered. "It will take as much time as it takes, but I will offer this in return," Luan looked down at her tea then back up at Tåsan. "I will visit Naiad Five and pay off the mercs." She held her gaze steady.

Tåsan responded, "Yes. Our mercenaries. As further incentive for their continued silence, maybe a bonus is in order."

"I'll assess that point and act accordingly," Luan replied. "I'll visit with Nikliss and Dhagáin while there and if there's anything comm worthy, I'll be sure to message."

Tåsan nodded his understanding.

• • •

Hours after arriving at Moonstone, Alyss and Annis began a thorough checkout of *Tempest* with a focus on the damage to the hull and sensors and completing maintenance on all of the ship's functions.

The busy work helped to keep them from obsessing over any consequences that resulted from the police battle at Aleia. They managed to hear any news of the situation from Tåsan, who was totally focused on monitoring several public comm feeds as well as two high-level comm lines, one belonging to the IGC that covered all of sector 972.1E5.

As of this morn, he had heard many accounts of the "Daring Aleia Heist" ranging anywhere from a few confident robbers to a hoard of crazed psychopathic beings no one was able to clearly describe.

While all of this comm was mildly entertaining, the information did nothing to alleviate Tåsan's concerns about what the authorities were doing about it. He needed to know current news and reached out to trusted friends within the IGC, framing his questions as friendly chatter. Nothing of import came from this.

Over the evening meal one night, Annis announced that all her systems aboard *Tempest* were one hundred percent and that there was no reason for her to stay longer at Moonstone.

"I have a task that I must complete that is compelling in and of itself," she said. "I must realign my power actuator."

"Your beautiful stones?" asked Alyss.

Unconsciously, Annis touched the jewels at her throat. "Yes. You see they are attuned to *Tempest* and recently this has given me over to some thought. I've reached the inevitable conclusion that I must separate my power source from *Tempest*. However," she continued her explanation, "a solution has presented itself. I just need time to effect it." She looked about her. "Captain Sulac," she intoned.

Tåsan responded, "Yes?"

"If you have nothing further for me right now, I think I might take my leave."

"Nothing comes to mind, Annis. When are you thinking of leaving?" Tåsan asked.

"I'm not in a rush, however Naiad Five will be within two days travel at the beginning of the next sidereal phase of the Enkaha constellation. To take advantage of that, I should depart in four days time."

Alyss asked, "Will you stay at our flat in the West End?"

"Yes. Indefinitely. Or until something else comes up." Annis smiled and glanced at Tåsan to see if he had picked up on her insinuation. She couldn't be sure as it seemed his thoughts were elsewhere.

Alyss spoke, "Good. I'm confident I'll see you there in a short time."

• • •

Luan saw to it that Chris steadily moved forward with his rehabilitation, pushing him to increase his strength and extend his "walk around" range. Under her care, Chris made remarkable gains and soon was ready to leave.

Luan offered to ride with him to his home planet Thorium 4 if they could stow one of the DCMs aboard Chris' 4-seat Hopper.

Tåsan lent a hand as they worked to remove the rear seats and secure the DCM in place. The extra weight made expanding the fuel cells necessary. It took one week to complete the modification but when it was done the 4-seat Hopper was good for two weeks of space travel before refueling would be required.

Luan finished the fuel-to-weight calculations with a satisfied smile. "We may have unwittingly invented a new vehicle," she announced. "Don't let the opportunity fade, Chris."

Chris laughed at the thought. "I'll be a mogul in no time!" he joked.

"This is a valuable modification," said Tåsan. "This extends your travel time by two hundred percent."

"More than enough time to cross the Allodial Expanse and gain ground on Thormium 4," said Chris. "Thank you all for your more than capable skills," adding, "I guess now there's no real reason for me to hang around."

Luan spoke, "There's a window of opportunity to launch the day after the morrow. Could you be ready then?"

"Yes, I think so."

"Good. We leave at 17084 hours."

• • •

At 17084 hours on the second day out, Alyss and Tåsan were the only ones left at Moonstone.

Late one evening, Alyss went in search of Tåsan and found him sitting outside in the darkness looking out across the landscape. The crunch of her boots as she stepped on dirt and stones, brought him back from his thoughts.

He turned his head to look at her and she smiled as she held up two shots and an unopened bottle of Tradorian Berrywine. "It's a good time to sit," she said, plopping down on a campstool and offering the bottle to Tåsan. "It has been a long day."

Alyss sat quietly as Tåsan worked the stopper loose and when the bottle was opened, offered the two shots while Tåsan slowly poured the amber liquid, careful not to spill. They took their first sips and seemed to relax.

"I haven't tasted this since I left the *Ari Arcturus*," Tåsan said.

"Seems so long ago," Alyss added.

Both fell silent.

Then Alyss said, "I'm sorry that Aleia turned into such a setback. I had no idea it would take so long to recover." She sipped

310

her wine and turned her gaze toward the outback. "Honestly, I don't think I gave much thought to encountering so much trouble. Something that I will avoid in the future." She looked at Tåsan.

Tåsan met her look. "We should have expected it."

Alyss furrowed her brow and asked, "Where do you see this going?"

He sized up the question as sincere but not having an exact answer for her, sought to lighten the mood. "I see it taking us all to riches beyond our dreams. To the good life and all that wealth can bring." He raised his shot in salute to the universe.

"If fortune stays with us," Alyss concluded.

Moments passed.

"What are your plans now, Tåsan?"

"Oh, I don't know. Probably stay here a while longer. You?"

Alyss nodded her head slowly as she studied her shot, her thoughts interrupted by Tåsan holding the bottle, ready to pour. She let him fill the small vessel to the rim.

She leveled a look at Tåsan. "I want you to know that I value our friendship almost beyond limit. Consider me steadfast in that. You can count on me. Always."

Tåsan smiled his appreciation.

"The last three quads have been," carefully picking her words, Alyss continued, "extraordinary. I almost can't catch my breath. And now that things have slowed down, I find that, to my surprise, I need time for myself."

Tåsan studied Alyss' face and could see she was in the throes of a conflict. She was wrestling with a dilemma. He held his words, waiting for her to continue. In a short moment, she did.

"I think I will leave Moonstone within the next day or two. I'm going home to my Merula flat. Maybe arrange a short visit with my father on Erontu." She fell silent but quickly recovered. "Will you go home for a visit?" she asked.

"No, definitely not," Tåsan said with a decisive note. "I've got a little work left here to do, then I want to think about what's next."

Alyss sat looking at Tåsan. When he looked back at her she nodded. "Okay then. I think I'll turn in." She stood up. "See you in the morn."

"Good night."

Tåsan sat back in his chair. The night air was chilling down but he didn't seem to notice. The lights from the comm area winked out, leaving him in the darkness of the night and alone in the quiet.

"It's amusing that I'm no longer concerned with my fate as it is now pretty much sealed," he thought. *"I do care for my team but they've made their choices and are largely on their own."* Tåsan poured the last drops of the Tradorian Berrywine into his shot, holding the empty bottle upside down, coaxing the very last drop to fall.

~

He couldn't quiet his mind. His thoughts were erratic and changed from one subject to another without pause. Tåsan could not catch them up and was starting to get irritated until he finally said quite clearly, "Stop."

The fast, confusing train of thoughts stopped.

Tåsan was determined to systematically work his way through the blur in an effort to make sense of it, to understand what was troubling him and to effect some sort of solution, if one existed.

Slowly his thoughts formed a long and unwieldy list but quickly his mind found resolution...

None of it mattered any longer. The desire to be accepted by Amans Sulac, IGC accolades and top honors, the humiliation of a career ending in rejection, the failed attempt to build a life of conformity, and now, more missteps. None of it led to satisfaction, none of it lasted. It was all of it, futile.

"Honestly, what's the point?" he asked himself. A sudden calmness came over him as he came to the inevitable conclusion: "It is all ruin, destruction, and annihilation that will certainly end in death. Embrace this and your mind will be free."

• • •

The sound of the e-dev as it came live jarred Tåsan from his sleep. He reached for it and through the fog of leftover dreams, focused his bleary eyes on the screen.

"Oh, Luan Oda," his recognition uttered, then awakening the device, "Yes, Luan."

Luan's soft and even tone flowed over the distance. "How are you, Tåsan? Is this a bad time?"

"I'm fine. The time is fine. Have you news?"

"Yes. The dealer acquaintance I have spoken about was extremely happy with my offerings, so happy in fact, he procured all and is interested in having first bid on anything further you may wish to liquidate."

"Perfect," Tåsan smiled slightly. "We should arrange the transfer of the remaining stock at a near point in time."

Luan continued, "Security personnel are well satisfied with their wages and have since been involved with other employment."

"Were there any difficulties that I should be aware of?"

"No. Everything is as it should be," Luan intoned. "I've been to see Nikliss and Dhagáin. They send their regards."

"As do I," Tåsan said.

"They are anxious to return to work. They joke about their skills rusting from non-use."

"Be assured. As soon as I have anything, I will be in comm. Until then, everyone should relax, look for opportunities."

Luan was silent as she considered Tåsan's words, then she spoke, "Until that time, Tåsan, fare well."

"I will and the same to you."

The e-dev went silent as the connection was severed.

Nine

Dreams of Purpose

It had been almost a full quad since Alyss had left Moonstone. She and Annis were away to their flat in Merula, Nikliss and Dhagáin were ensconced at Corvus Space, Tao had returned home to Javhed Tuk and Chris flew away to his home on Thorium 4. And Luan. Well, Luan was away. Where that was still remained a mystery.

In the days that followed the team's eventual departure, Tåsan managed to fill his time with busy work. At first, it all felt very important and most of the tasks he listed for himself set a sort of priority and gave purpose to his day. But as the primary issues gave way to lesser concerns which eventually wound down to menial tasks, Tåsan finally slowed down enough to realize that he was more than prepared and ready. It was time now to think about the "for what" part.

With satisfaction, Tåsan stood, arms akimbo, looking at *Tempest*, gleaming in the bright Rayten sun. *"Clean and bright. All systems in perfect working order, upgrades verified, and repairs effected. And with her chrysoberyl renewed and the glyphs repainted, she looks fierce, she looks ready."*

Tåsan became aware that he was smiling at the sight of *Tempest* and in embarrassment at his pride for his ship, lowered his eyes and kicked at a few pebbles just in front of his boot, but still, he felt his pride justified.

It was nearing dusk, his favorite part of the day when he would grab an ale and sit at the edge of the protected space beneath the sensor distortion units that ringed the compound. He would watch the light fade to blackness and stars appear

314

overhead.

Tonight, the small fiery planet, Kirmizi, appeared as a black dot on the face of the fading orange sun that was slowly receding into the northwest vista.

"It's a bit comforting to track the changes of season from this vantage point," Tåsan thought. But as soon as that restful thought finished, his mind raced on through the solar years to present him with a vision of himself, still sitting at the edge of Moonstone staring at the setting sun with nothing to show for it. Tåsan was taken back for a moment and with a huff of disapproval, he shuddered to shake the vision from his reasoning and clear the forlorn thought from his mind.

"That will never happen," he declared, then turned his thoughts to current interests.

At first, Tåsan sat quietly. He knew what he was about: gaining wealth with little effort and no adverse incidents. He closely monitored media comm for any mention of privateer activity thinking that such activities would hold the attention of local police, leaving other areas with little to no law enforcement presence. He monitored shipping lanes and cargo transports through the Allodial Expanse, mapping for consistencies and paying close attention to specific cargos and verifying their worth. He also kept an eye on IGC flights through the Expanse and throughout the three home galaxies.

Most of what Tåsan heard and scanned was routine and unchanging, punctuated by brief bursts of disorder, usually the local police were called in and while the incidents were numerous, they were of a lesser degree of crime, if you will, and the police intervention not very inspired.

On the other hand, when the IGC was obliged to intervene, the crime was of a higher level...more privateers, several ships, and almost always some sort of weapons violence. And to Tåsan's mind, the IGC did not always respond with confidence and a collective level-headedness. Through media reports and his own tracking, Tåsan noticed that the IGC success rate was below one half, with privateers escaping and costly damages to IGC *and* ISA property adding up.

"That," thought Tåsan, *"is a failing grade."*

315

Tåsan knew that the IGC's failed rate of resolving galactic criminality meant success and prosperity for himself.

Tåsan kept in touch with past contacts, gaining their trust as his own notoriety started to build. Over the weeks that Tåsan spent monitoring and observing the ebb and flow of crime and its consequences, he left Moonstone on several occasions, using his contacts and his new knowledge to engineer a half dozen strikes, anything from robbing a payroll shuttle to transporting illegal goods.

Tåsan monitored the comm waves, tracking his own crime spree only to see that he was always two steps ahead and long gone from the scene before any intervention showed up. This pleased him to no end.

One warm evening, as he sat sipping a cold ale, Tåsan came to realize two things. One, he was extremely good at planning heists. He had a real aptitude for it. The way he could analyze each plan, see it from different perspectives, and carry it to fruition was a thing of beauty. The other thing he came to know was that he didn't need the entire team for every heist. Some of the lawless actions he managed to complete involved only himself. But. Without a full team, crimes were on consignment and the gains limited. Nevertheless, all these activities, combined, proved to Tåsan that he could easily up the stakes and still stay anonymous.

Tåsan walked around with this newfound knowledge and a newly gained pride. Self-assurance seemed to show in his very mien. His step was sure, his thinking bold, and his confidence high.

It was time to leave Moonstone.

• • •

One week and three days later, Tåsan landed *Tempest* at Corvus Space. He had carefully prepared Moonstone for an unknown period of downtime by shutting down all technology and generating platforms and leaving the site virtually undetectable.

Tåsan contacted Nikliss and Dhagáin, giving them a two-day heads-up to his arrival, making a point of asking them to keep that to themselves.

Upon landing, both men came out to greet him.

As Tåsan disembarked *Tempest*, Nikliss, smiling broadly, called

316

out, "Hello! Hello! You look well!"

Dhagáin held out his hand in greeting as he approached and said, "Welcome home."

Almost the instant his foot touched terra firma of Corvus Space, Tåsan felt a flood of nostalgia wash over him. The satisfaction, the lessons of failure, the struggle, and the growth all meant something. And it made Tåsan happy to be back.

"It's been almost too long," Tåsan said as he took Dhagáin's hand and clapped him on the back before turning to Nikliss and doing the same.

"Let's see what you've done to the place," said Tåsan as he stepped toward the hangar's shop area.

Nikliss and Dhagáin followed Tåsan through the hangar doors. Both were smiling in anticipation and their excitement was heightened.

Tåsan took several steps through the doors and stopped. He stood silent and slowly ran his eyes from left to right, taking it all in. Nikliss and Dhagáin held their breath and watched.

"This is nice. This is very nice." Smiling, Tåsan went to one of the new workbenches and ran his fingers over the organized tools and polished surface then turned to his friends.

"You've taken great care of Corvus Space." And looking around added, "I dare say better care then I might have."

Nikliss stepped forward. "We were trusting that you would be pleased. We needed something to do in our downtime." He turned to glance at Dhagáin, who stood nodding in agreement.

Tåsan looked around again, this time noticing a piece of work in progress on another bench. "Oh, what's this?"

Dhagáin spoke as he moved toward the bench, "For the first two weeks we were here, Nikliss and I organized everything, filed things, and cleaned the dust away. When all that was done, we looked at each other and asked, 'now what'?" He glanced at Nikliss.

"We remembered seeing a partial design of an electro-charged twin boron fueled velocity enhancer on your design table upstairs," continued Nikliss, "...so we thought to develop it."

They stood waiting for Tåsan to take in what he had just heard and compare it with the apparatus that stood half-built among

317

parts and bits and wires strewn across the workbench.

Finally he spoke. "Watch the fuel sensor calibrations. I mused that the vibrations of the working cells would cause a miscalibration to report to the pilot's station." Tåsan was peering at a wired and tightly fit sensor pad as he spoke. He then straightened up and looked to the men. "Good job."

"We've tested a smaller version of it on one of the Class-N's," Nikliss said. "It really moves."

"It's a successful design, Tåsan," said Dhagáin. "We've taken it off the paper and into reality. I...we...felt that you would be pleased." He stood waiting.

"I am pleased." And after a brief moment of thought added, "I give the design over to you both," Tåsan declared. "May it bring you fortune!"

Nikliss became somewhat embarrassed, a flush rising to his cheeks as he shyly looked down at the floor in front of him.

Dhagáin nodded and smiled at Tåsan's generosity. "A Triton ale to celebrate!"

Pleased and animated, the partners stepped lively up the stairs to the loft.

$$\cdots$$

Two rounds of ale and forty-five minutes later, the three companions, sitting at the end of the long work table that dominated a large section of the loft, had caught up on most of what had occupied each of them during the weeks following Dhagáin's and Nikliss' departure from Moonstone.

"Dhagáin and I," continued Nikliss, "have more or less lived normal lives. We go into Merula for supplies and the occasional night out." He reached for his ale, "But otherwise we work and sleep here."

"So," said Tåsan, "you've started a small business repairing and modifying thrusters." The statement was a sort of question.

Dhagáin answered, "It was mostly accidental and the fates guided it from the start." He looked at Nikliss who nodded for Dhagáin to continue telling the story. "We were putting the modified Class-N through its paces out on the Cirrian Flats and were approached by three pulse rocket riders wanting to know how we had hyper-charged the 'N' and could we do the same for their racers."

Nikliss added, "We thought, why not? This was an opportunity to keep busy and make a few extra tenges for good measure."

"Turned out to be a lot of extra tenges. Seems that every university student who rides a pulse rocket wants to go faster." Dhagáin summed it up.

The group fell quietly into their thoughts for a moment until Nikliss asked Tåsan, "Have you been working on employment opportunities for the team?"

Tåsan chuckled at the euphemism. "Actually I do have one certain job and one maybe job in the works. There's an ISA shipment of krennerite coming out of Crosus to make its way slowly across the Allodial Expanse to a delivery point of 'Don't Really Care'. Not too difficult." He glanced at the two men who sat listening, then continued. "We could possibly complete that without the help of mercenaries. The transport is not fortified and not expecting trouble and the contact for the krennerite is flexible. The other job, not so much." Tåsan leaned forward to pick up his mug, noticing that it was only foam remnants and quickly glanced at the other mugs, both as empty as his. Scooping them up and looking expectantly at Nikliss and Dhagáin, said, "Another?"

Both replied yes.

Tåsan carried the mugs to the galley, intending to refill them from the growler that stood ready on the counter. "The other job is a bit more complicated. It's a larger job and will take more time to put together. We'll need the mercenaries and the whole team to pull it off."

Tåsan had just set the three full mugs down on the worktable when his e-dev chimed. He looked at the screen then up at Nikliss and Dhagáin. "I've got to take this," and snapped the dev on. "Yes. I'm here," he said as he turned his back on his friends and ambled away. "Absolutely." A brief second later. "Send me the coordinates." A breath or two. "I will contact you before the day is done." Listening. "To my agreement, yes." Tåsan had slowly crossed the floor and was standing by the window gazing out on his wild outback view. "I prefer QVs. More precise, less mess." Satisfied that the discourse had concluded, Tåsan disconnected and stashed his e-dev back in his pocket.

Turning back to his friends, Tåsan smiled. "No rest for the wicked," he proclaimed as an explanation for the interruption, as he regained his seat and his ale.

"So, about our next heist."

• • •

It took the team, minus Tao Vu, a short week to reassemble at Corvus Space. Tåsan's outgoing e-message asking that everyone make their way back prompted a call from Tao. He was sorry but he would have to quit the team. It was not a matter of funds as there seemed to be an adequate influx of tenges but a matter of what he could do in the time between one heist and the next. Spending time with his family only underscored his idleness. It made him restless. It made him miss his true calling. Medicine.

Tåsan had understood and told Tao as much. Being part of the team took a commitment. It was a lifestyle and to appreciate it, one had to embrace it fully. Tåsan broke the news to the others almost as soon as he could.

"It's not the end of everything. Tao did a good job setting up a medical bay and I'm certain we can manage most scrapes. In the event of something more serious, I have contacts. We shouldn't worry."

The heist of krennerite was quick and easy. The ISA owned corporation had loaded a small transport ship with the krennerite and put it on a painfully slow course through the Allodial Expanse to its destination on Erontu, some four vectors and five days away.

Tempest swooped in and procured the shipment. The crew, consisting of a pilot and a technician, were gassed unconscious and left adrift, waiting for discovery and rescue.

The krennerite was offloaded before the news of a crime had hit the e-media, and Tåsan distributed the profits as soon as he returned from the transaction.

"Not bad for a few hours of work," he had said.

Shortly thereafter, he and Luan entered into a discussion that led them up to the loft where they could talk without the distractions of shop noises or casual conversations among the others.

Tåsan said, "This is about the heist of IGC perks that will be in transit across the Allodial Expanse headed for Brenton Kae."

As Tåsan spoke, Luan made her way across the space to one of the overstuffed chairs positioned by the big windows. The sunlight streaming in made a patch of light on the floor. Luan lowered herself down into the comfort of the chair and extended her feet outward into the bright sun patch as if to warm them.

Tåsan continued, "I would like to know more about it before we set out. Tell me more about your relationship with the Vellosians, or as much as you care to tell, that is." He moved on, "I need to know about the ship that will carry the payload. Type, size, complement, armaments. That sort of thing." He paused and looked at Luan.

After a moment to organize her thoughts, she spoke. "I have known about the Vellosians since before they arrived in our space. They're secretive and guard themselves closely. I've worked with Vellosian merchants before." She gave a short laugh. "Small shipments of this or that are known to have gone 'missing' from time to time. However," Luan turned her gaze from out the window to Tåsan's face, and looking him square in the eyes said, "They are opportunists and they have a dislike for the Inter-Galaxy Command."

"I see," said Tåsan. "Possible comrades."

"Precisely," confirmed Luan. "They're very enthused about trading possibilities and agreements within the system but have come to resent the IGC for their arrogance and their attitude of entitlement. Seems the IGC has leveled a sort of tariff on Vellosian goods. A very greedy tariff."

Tåsan had never heard of such a thing. His face reflected his doubts when he asked, "Are you sure of that Luan? Are you sure the Vellosians aren't somehow mistaken about that?"

"Well, here's what I know," said Luan as she pulled her feet out of the sun patch and made to stand up. "The IGC stops the Vellosian trading ships, as it does *all* trading ships that cross the Allodial Expanse, and extracts what they call a 'safe passage fee' from them. This usually consists of a percentage of what the trade goods are perceived to be worth. The IGC takes a cut of the goods, a tithing of tenges, or both." She was headed to the galley and turned to Tåsan. "Tea?"

321

Tåsan was staring at the floor in front of him, his brow furrowed, his jaw set, deep in thought. Luan's voice almost startled him. "Oh, no thank you."

"Well this explains a lot," he thought. *"The storage bays full of Lingdon Práxus, father bringing home expensive liquors. He lied about those things being gifts of appreciation."* Anger made him stand up in reflex and under his breath he hurled a curse at his father.

Luan fixed her tea and returned to the big window chair and sat back down, indicating with a slight flourish of her hand that Tåsan should join her. When he was settled again and appeared to be listening, Luan began.

"I have contacts among the Vellosian diplomats and have been hearing of their mounting aversion to the IGC's policies and attitudes. One high-ranking diplomat went so far as to accuse the IGC of, and I'm quoting him here, 'A thinly disguised hatred and an obvious mistrust of the Vellosians.' A lesser ranking ship's officer who is in a privileged position among bridge crew and communication, has been heard to say that the IGC's higher ranking officers are acting more and more covetous toward what they are calling a technological imbalance between themselves and Vellosia."

Luan leveled her gaze at Tåsan.

He looked up at her.

"They, the Vellosians, are considering abandoning their trading enterprises here among us and returning to their home galaxy but before they decide on anything so final..." Luan took a quiet breath and looked at Tåsan as if to answer with the obvious, and shrugged as she said "they want a level of revenge." Luan had been sitting forward in her chair and now pushed back into the cushions and reached for her tea.

"Hah," Tåsan huffed in a not-that-surprised manner. "I'm a bit taken back but not wholly astonished at such a statement. It almost justifies all my doubts and suspicions of the IGC. I've always felt there were unexplained reasons for their behaviors. And now I know."

Luan had been intently watching Tåsan's face, noting the change of emotions that played out as he spoke until he came to a conclusion and his face seemed to calm and his jaw set. He had come to a decision. She waited.

At last he spoke. "I think now, the Vellosians and I have much more in common than either of us would have guessed...suspicion of the IGC's hidden motives and a growing resentment of them as a whole." Tåsan stood up and walked a few paces away and stood for a half moment in thought. Suddenly he spun around to face Luan and said, "I'm in. We hit the IGC."

Luan smiled and nodded.

For about an hour, Luan and Tåsan discussed the next heist. Tåsan and his team would steal, from the IGC, a cargo of expensive Vellosian liquor. It's a blend of fruit and flower buds from the rare Ashado tree that is only found on a Vellosian agri-planet. The blend is aged for twenty solar years and this entire batch is a mere five hundred bottles and, because of its rarity, commands top tenges. The greedy hands of the IGC extracted one hundred of these bottles as safe passage payment and the Vellosians are outraged.

Luan tipped the last of her tea to her tongue. "They want their liquor back."

Tåsan smiled, "Well, I think we can help. Would the Vellosians agree to a five bottle payment for the return of their property?"

"I'm sure that would be satisfactory."

"Then it's settled. We fly in four days time."

• • •

The Sub-class K transport ship was scheduled to enter the Allodial Expanse at vector 87A2.4 adjacent to the outer stars of the Hedorrion Galaxy. It was loaded with tariffs and goods and tenges extracted from several merchant ships doing business across the three galaxies.

It was a big ship with a crew of forty-five sub-workers and seven IGC officers. Its cargo hold ran from mid-ship along the fuselage to the rear with mechanics and crew quarters one floor above.

"Not all of the Sub-class K's booty would fit aboard *Tempest*," Tåsan said, "but as Luan has mentioned, there are higher profit goods to be found among the holdings."

The team was gathered in the loft space and sat or stood casually as the briefing continued.

"There is a section located about mid-bay that is reserved for richer rewards," Luan added. "The Vellosian liquor, cases of Valunde liquor and Lingdon Práxus, and aboard this particular transport, a shipment of neodymium metals."

Tåsan spoke, "I've set up the transfer of the goods. The neodymium is to be dropped off three vectors away. We'll facilitate the unloading and be on our way within minutes." He looked around at this team. "Any questions, so far?"

Chris Phelan spoke up, "I have reservations about hitting an IGC owned and operated transport ship. Wouldn't it make sense that they would be heavily armed?"

"It would make sense under normal circumstances," answered Tåsan, "but the IGC has grown complacent in their own good fortune of never having run into transport problems in the past."

Luan added, "They do not fear trouble because they are trouble. Their power is at the top of the ISA hierarchy. It's that simple."

"As a result, they don't pay much attention to their transports, so, no, we can do this. The seven of us can do this."

• • •

Tempest lifted off at 1587.3 and intercepted the IGC transport as planned, at vector 87A2.4 a few short hours later.

Alyss and Annis stayed aboard *Tempest* while the others rode modified DCMs over to the Sub-class K.

Nikliss and Chris headed for the air lock closest to the bridge while Tåsan, Dhagáin, and Luan aimed straight for the mid-ship cargo bay doors.

Alyss pulled back a few parsecs to follow the transport at an inconspicuous distance and Annis busied herself with monitoring and scrambling the transport's comm as well as monitoring several of the surrounding e-comm channels.

Nikliss blew the air lock bolts and both men gained access to the bridge without incident. As they entered, one crew member jumped up in shock and leapt at Chris, who backstepped and rammed his blaster stock into the aggressor's head, sending him down to the floor in a painful blackout before leveling his weapon at the remaining crew and announcing, "Any move, no matter how small, will be fatal."

Nikliss had moved to the comm station and disabled out-going signals before stepping over to the pilot station and slowing the ship's forward course. He touched the sen-dev at his ear and spoke in a hushed tone, "Bridge secure."

Tåsan had laser blasted the outer bolts on the cargo bay doors and he, Luan, and Dhagáin had floated in on their DCMs.

"Perfect," Tåsan responded to Nikliss' update, "Will signal when we're two minutes out."

Luan had found the desired cargo of Vellosian Ashado liquor and was busy harnessing it to her DCM.

Tåsan and Dhagáin were wrestling with very heavy crates of the neodymium metal and their progress was slow.

Luan had returned to the storage area and was now moving two large containers of the other targeted goods when she spied an oddly marked crate secured to the floor by a large heavy cable. Stopping for a closer inspection, she recognized the outer markings as a primitive language from Cimtum 8. It read, "IGC Deposit Only." Luan immediately laser cut the cables and lashed the crate to her DCM and started toward the bay doors. "I'm at capacity and will stand ready."

Tåsan responded, "Aye." He and Dhagáin had managed to tighten various straps and cables around their booty and were about to mount their DCMs. Tåsan's voice sounded in everyone's sen-dev, "Two minutes."

Tempest swooped in. Nikliss and Chris backed toward the exit, steadying their weapons on the crew. As they reached the alcove outside the bridge door and before it closed completely, Chris lobbed a smoke bomb that ignited with a flash of light. They hurried to the air lock and were away without further incident.

Meanwhile, some of the sub-crew personnel, alerted to the heist-in-progress, were trying to gain access to the cargo bay by laser cutting the door seals.

Tåsan confirmed that Dhagáin and Luan were ready and signaled them to take off. He waited until they were clear before he made his exit. After clearing the doors, Tåsan twisted around as to have a view of the open cargo bay doors and loosed a QV detonator through the gaping hole. It landed several meters into the hold and hesitated only a moment before exploding into a huge flash of white light followed by red sparks and a shock wave that decimated everything within view, leaving bits of IGC goods slowly floating out through the gaping hold into space.

Tåsan turned toward *Tempest*, now steadily positioned within easy flight, and sped forward, laughing with satisfaction.

When Alyss was sure all were aboard and the cargo doors pressurized, she turned *Tempest* and jammed the ship into hyperdrive, aimed at vector 93AE.

• • •

The neodymium fetched a good price and after it was discovered that the Cimtum 8 crate marked for IGC Deposit Only was loaded with thousands and thousands of vanadium tenges, Tåsan took an accounting and split the entire bounty among the team after giving Luan a hefty bonus, thanking her for her knowledge of primitive languages and her fast thinking.

"Oh friends," Tåsan happily called out, "what a profitable day this has been."

Smiling faces and satisfied murmurs agreed.

"Dinner is on me." Tåsan announced.

"And drinks are on me," Chris said before adding, "well, the first round anyway," he laughed.

Tåsan said, "Prep yourselves for leave. I'm asking for a two-week downtime before we go out again. Everyone should be ready before meeting for dinner at the Ryobe Bar and Café in downtown Merula around 21157 tonight."

Everyone busied themselves stashing their share of the day's heist into rucksacks or spare boxes and gathering personal items from around Corvus Space.

Tåsan had started to clear cups and mugs to the galley when he turned back to the team and said, "In the mean, I'll develop our next foray and monitor comm. Plan to return in two weeks." He finished with a warm smile.

~

Later that evening, as dusk turned dark, Tåsan closed his ledgers and stretched his back. He had been working numbers and calendars and notations for three straight hours and his head was swimming in its complexity.

It was very late and all had left or were retired but Tåsan. He was restless. He went downstairs to the hangar and walked aimlessly by the workbenches, touching surfaces and straightening tools. In short order he realized that his mind was crowded with thoughts to the point of overload. He stopped his rambling and decided to sit on the edge of the crushed rock courtyard and breathe. *"Maybe watching the last shreds of midnight fade and the stars move across the sky will give my mind focus and ease."*

Taking a seat facing the wild landscape, Tåsan's thoughts did calm but as the chaos quieted, one sensation started to turn over and over and become more clear.

"Oh fortunes, I am lonely. At another time, sitting quietly would be welcome but not tonight. Not right now."

Tåsan's thoughts followed a path he didn't really want to traverse. He remembered childhood friends and school buddies, he remembered university days filled with study and comrades. Several fond memories of his family flew by and of course, the pleasant times and friendships he made and retained while with the IGC. All of this made Tåsan smile and feel good. Up to a point.

"Yes but look at me now. Though I am surrounded, I am alone. Truly alone." Tåsan sighed into the dark night air and slowly traced the moonlit skyline of brush and scrub trees with his eyes and tried to brace up. *"No use indulging in self pity. It won't buy a mug of ale in any tavern."* The words did little to change his mood. Still Tåsan sat looking out to the stars, settling into a deepening melancholy that was slowly taking on the mask of desolation.

Tåsan sat for many hours. Thought of many things. But still he was alone.

Glancing at the lunar shine of Datos, now moving toward its zenith in the dark sky, brought Tåsan to the time and he shivered in the early morning chill. Realizing how bone-tired he was and how vacant his thoughts had been, Tåsan thought it time to turn in.

That night's dream was filled with endless nothing. Tåsan found himself traversing through endless corridors without doors, lit by an unseen glaring source that made his eyes hurt. He trudged on and called out for anyone to respond but silence remained. Once he thought he caught

327

sight of someone as they turned a corner ahead. It was just a glimpse and he called out as he started running in desperation to catch the figure. He skidded to the hallway corner and rounded it only to find an empty dead end.

Frozen for a moment in disappointment, Tåsan slowly started to realize that he was alone. Really alone. Still alone, and a small spark of anger flared in his mind. *"This is all father's fault,"* he heard himself saying. *"I have been forsaken by my family, outcast from my career, and abandoned by my friends."*

The dead end corridor swirled to gray and fell away leaving Tåsan standing on the edge of a precipice, his voice clear as the air across the ravine far below.

"This is all father's fault."

Ten

Infamy's Flip Side

Tåsan busied himself with monitoring multiple comm waves while he tinkered with an AI drone he imagined into a schematic, which he then developed into a viable plan, that he now had scattered about him on the long loft table. Pieces of luteium, bits of wire, and specialized tools littered the table for an arms-reach in all directions, gathered loosely around an already assembled circuit brain and transmitter.

Eventually the unit would be employed as a seeker. Launched from *Tempest* it would seek as programmed and compile and send data from its target, an IGC ship, perhaps, or a lone cargo transport.

With the local streaming comm wave running softly in the background, Tåsan's attention was wholly on adjusting the trans frequency of the seeker until he thought he heard the mono-voice report on a series of unsolved crimes. He snapped his attention to the comm and listened intently.

There had been an uptick in crime during previous quads, as reported by Special Focus Edition, FSN2Y, on this wave.

« Noteworthy as all pirate activity is, there seems to be an elevation, if you will permit me an opinion, » the mono-voice recited, « away from the endless pettiness of crimes against the ordinary Naiad Five citizenry where vehicles are stolen by ruffians for their temporary use or personal valuables are taken by force. Oh no, » the voice temporarily raised and then lowered, « what I'm referring to is the theft of larger quantities of valuable goods straight out of transport ships and right out from under the protection of local police. »

Tåsan had reached over to his comm relay and slowly twisted

the audio up a point or two. A smile almost one of pride, started to creep across his face.

The comm continued, « Owners of the affected commerce have logged complaints with their local police but as usual, the police have been largely after-the-fact and sadly, they continue to be ineffectual. Business leaders are demanding results. Interestingly enough, the police have raised the issue of escalating operating cost cuts; they cite the lack of staff and an aging infrastructure as two major blocks to their effectiveness. So for right now, there seems to be a stalemate. »

Tåsan returned the audio to its lowest point, gave another satisfied smile, and returned to work.

Later that evening, Tåsan took the Class-N into Merula for a light meal, telling Nikliss and Dhagáin that he would return late. In fact it was very late.

Tåsan walked the city center for a while looking through shop windows and soaking up the local atmosphere as he thought about what he might like to eat. In the end he settled for a bowl of hot serra grain topped with steaming hougla being vended from a cramped storefront café doing brisk business among the late night crowd.

As Tåsan leaned against the building front, munching his dinner, he overheard a conversation between two diners as they waited on their order.

"The police don't seem to be on the ball here," said one.

"When have they ever been?" chided the other.

"They seem to be okay with petty crimes, it's the serious crimes they can't get in front of."

"I don't hold out any confidence in them at all."

Just then their order was up and they faded away into the background of street noises.

After finishing his meal, Tåsan had only walked a block or two down the street before being enticed into a local bar by the bright light and music that spilled out of the open doors.

• • •

The team had reassembled at Corvus Space. They had flown in from various locations and were soon engrossed in friendly chatter with each other, telling tales and catching up.

Alyss found Tåsan aboard *Tempest*, elbows deep into a mod to the pilot's station. A front panel had been removed and Tåsan was busy splicing in new circuitry.

"What'cha doing?" she asked, her voice cheerful and relaxed.

"Oh," said Tåsan, "I'm setting a dedicated comm link for my AI bot. It needs to receive instructions and positioning information and return graphic data. All that has to be done on a low-rad wave to stay undetectable."

Alyss leaned closer to study the work but without knowing the more intricate functions of the AI bot, she couldn't tell if what Tåsan was doing was true or not. "I'll help with testing when you're finished," was all she could add. She sat idle, watching, then thought of something.

"I've been monitoring local news-comm lines and heard interesting bits of information coming from the Naiad Five sources but also from as far away as Thorium 4."

Tåsan had sat back on his heels and was studying his handiwork. He paused to look over at Alyss. "Do tell."

"As you know, police departments in both vectors have been vilified as of late, for their ineffectual handling of what is being termed, a crime wave." Alyss laughed at that and continued, "Most news-comm's are now full of opinions and solutions and while that is all so much filler, I heard a more serious report recently that claimed public opinion actually sympathized with the pirates. Not the lowly criminals, the daring 'Altruistic Outlaw' that has appeared as of late." Alyss held her point and watched Tåsan's reactions.

At first, Tåsan wasn't sure he had heard right and his face was that of serious consideration, brow slightly furrowed. And as the humor and irony of Alyss' statement became clear, his smile broadened and his eyes shown amusement. Alyss appeared to be ready to burst from stifled laughter.

"Are you serious?" Tåsan asked her.

"Yes! Every word of it."

"I've never thought of myself as altruistic, almost the opposite," he mused.

Alyss spoke, "Not only have the police bungled their way to ridicule, they appear to have lost public confidence and so much so that the scales have shifted in your favor."

"But why," Tåsan earnestly asked, "would I be labeled as selfless if I'm actually robbing someone?"

"Because you strive not to kill or maim in the commission of your crimes. And..." Alyss stressed this point, "...you are robbing the overly wealthy, not the average citizen."

Tåsan could only shake his head at the thought and smile in spite of it.

• • •

The team completed a series of profitable heists during the next few weeks making sure to allow enough time between each score to effect the look of randomness. And Tåsan's reputation grew still larger.

In spite of the near clumsy attempts by local police to effectively respond to the spike in criminal activities in their vicinities, many in the galaxies lawless community wagered that they could "get away with it, too," and stepped up their efforts. One result was that many clashes between criminals and law enforcement meant a significant increase in weapons fire. It seemed that the criminal world had exploded into a huge skirmish that covered two galaxies.

Tåsan was of two minds as he considered the current times. He was glad that the police were kept busy with the petty crime wave in progress. It allowed him to carry out his own heists almost undetected. Almost. On the other hand, everyone was more jumpy. The odds of an armed situation had increased because several of the ISA business representatives who ran regularly scheduled transports between the galaxies had increased security of their ships, some to include proto weapons and armed personnel.

As a result, Tåsan advised the team to increase the effectiveness of their own weapons and cautioned Annis that she may encounter resistance not only from police ships but also from the tankers and transports, themselves. Everyone was to stay sharp but not nervous.

Eleven

Slowly At First

"There's been too much criticism as of late and I mean it to stop."

The words spoken by Vice Admiral Caoin pierced the air with a stab of accusation, punctuated by his icy stare as he turned his eyes to each and every attendee at the meeting table as if daring them to contradict him.

Everyone there knew what Caoin was referring to. The news lines were having a field day reporting on, talking about, and interviewing anyone who would give a minute of their time. The topic? The spike in crime and the inability of the authorities to stop it and to restore civil tranquility.

Captain Amans Sulac spoke, "We certainly can't be held responsible for the complete incompetence of the local authorities."

Vice Admiral Caoin had moved to the window and now stood with his back to the officers gathered around the meeting table that occupied one end of his expansive office.

Amans waited for a reply from Caoin. None came. He then cut his eyes over to Captain Atrox who looked back at Amans, shrugged and feigned interest in a note page on the table in front of him.

Lieutenant Perda spoke, "Civilian police departments in all three galaxies have repeatedly bungled their jobs making it a matter for their electors. I don't see how that makes this our problem."

Caoin rounded from his position making a loud huff of an exhale. "Oh you don't, do you?" His voice barely under control, his eyes bright with anger. Turning his gaze down the table, he barked, "Legal."

Major Matorios jumped at the command. "Um, um, yes," he

stammered as he rustled through pages of a document. "I have it here," flicking a page and eying his way down to a point highlighted in yellow. "Here it is," he pushed his glasses up to the bridge of his nose and cleared his throat. "Inter-Galaxy Command," he read, "is not obligated to assist any agency involved with civil disturbances nor is the IGC," Matorios looked up and around the table, "and here it gets to the point," returning to the document page, "…to interfere unless said disturbances affect any…" he looked up to punctuate that last word, "any," he repeated, "asset or interest belonging to any member of the Intersolar and Space Alliance." Matorios dropped the document in front of him, slid his glasses off and sat back in satisfaction.

Caoin had been pacing back and forth as Matorios read the words. He now stopped and faced the table. "Well. ISA assets and interests have been affected."

Captain Atrox spoke, "Has the ISA asked for help?"

Caoin slowly turned his head to look at Atrox full on. "That is precisely the point. They have." He then spread his hands out to the table, indicating that the problem was now handed to the five officers present. "Discuss."

Amans, Atelli, Atrox, and Perda, with Matorios wildly thumbing pages of miscellaneous legal documents, burst into rapid conversation among themselves.

Caoin did not join in. Seemingly satisfied that he had presented the problem given him, he now turned from the table and walked the length of his office to take his chair at the huge ornate desk from which he administered his command.

Various statements and fragments floated across the distance. "…trying to appease the ISA.", "The IGC is too important to waste valuable resources on every little heist that occurs.", "…inept…", "The ISA are a collection of fat, self-centered whiners."

Caoin looked at the time and swiveled his chair around so that it faced the view out the expansive windows.

The voices of the group argued and agreed and raised and lowered as the minutes ticked by. Eventually a calm descended and the murmuring slowed to quiet.

"Sir?" Captain Sulac stood two paces from Vice Admiral Caoin's desk. The others, still seated at the table, all faced him, looking expectant.

Caoin slowly rotated his chair around and sat calmly, the fingertips of both hands forming a bridge in front of him, looking at Amans. "Yes," he said in a soft voice.

"Sir, I think we have a solution."

Caoin nodded once but said nothing.

Amans continued, "The IGC will flex its power with a show of strength," and stepped forward to place a carefully worded page in front of Caoin so he could read it.

~

Outraged by incidents of escalating crime against the assets of their members, an adhocracy of rich and powerful ISA organizational leaders met to form a plan of their own.

They would set a trap and bait it with a tempting combination of jewels, a beautiful Andorran Princess, crystals from the Nyoman mines on Sador, a safe full of tenges and one-half kilo of the rarest of all chemicals, boron, used for interplanetary star cruiser warp engines. Rumors would be circulated throughout three quadrants and an article placed in the e-edition of the Cirrus Times mentioning that security would be minimal due to a recent but faraway uprising that needed all available police.

But in reality, plenty of police and private security would be onsite and ready.

The ISA would accomplish what the IGC could not seem to do. That would show them. The ISA would demonstrate, once and for all, that it was their word, their superior intellect, and their skilled leadership that got things done. It would humble the IGC and they had better show some respect.

Twelve

Momentum

Tåsan had returned from a three-week absence from Corvus Space. While he was away and at Luan's urging, he met with a small contingent of unhappy Vellosians and listened with interest as they carefully told of their mistrust of the IGC. They felt that they were being taken advantage of in more ways than the outright tithing taken from every Vellosian ship entering IGC space. The price was outrageous and the Vellosians were tiring of it.

It was more then refreshing to hear that confidence in the IGC was eroding and mistrust growing from without the IGC organization. Tåsan was actually very pleased at this turn of events. When the Vellosians had completed their litany of grievances, Tåsan had but one question, "Want help getting some of it back?"

The look of relief and satisfaction on their faces was answer enough.

• • •

One day out from Corvus Space, Tåsan sent word for the team to reconvene. Almost immediately, affirmative replies came from Alyss and Annis, both anxious to get back to work. Luan messaged that she would be there the following day and of course Dhagáin and Nikliss were already on site.

Chris would arrive early as he was close and available and indeed, arrived within a handful of hours.

He was very excited to get back to work, but more excited to show off his newly acquired "safety precaution" as he termed it. Chris' safety precaution was a lithium powered ATW-50. An Advanced Tactical Weapon capable of blasting a sizeable hole through just about anything it was aimed at. Its true purpose was the ensured destruction of "the enemy," and at fifty pulses per 10÷9 that outcome was guaranteed.

Dhagáin sat passively listening as Chris chattered on about the weapon. Nikliss, on the other hand, listened with mounting apprehension. All he could think was that Chris was more dangerous than he had previously suspected. Chris would be the one getting them all killed.

"I've actually fired this baby several times," Chris was saying, "The recoil was a little unsteady at first but once I relaxed into it, it was a dream. Not too loud and very smooth." He was beaming from ear to ear as he stared almost lovingly at the ATW-50, now held gently in his arms.

Nikliss could feel the fear and mistrust rising in his chest. He felt trapped and he suddenly felt that he had to get away.

Chris made Nikliss jump when all of a sudden he thrust the weapon toward him asking loudly, "Want to try it?"

Nikliss felt his eyes go wide as he stammered, "What? No! No, I think I have to check on something. I have to see to something. My work." He jumped up and quickly moved away, confusion clouding his thoughts.

Chris looked at Dhagáin, "Interested?" as he proffered the weapon.

Dhagáin waved him off answering, "Not really." He shifted in his seat and lightly held his chin with his fingers looking at Chris with newfound curiosity. Finally he spoke, "So tell me Chris, why would you buy such a weapon?"

Chris patted the stock as he said, "Well, the way I figure it is like this. Eventually we're going to come up against a formidable opponent, one that is not going to hand over their tenges without a fight." Chris smiled with delight, his eyes dancing with excitement.

Dhagáin furrowed his brow slightly and made a small dismissive wave of his hand. "But an ATW-50?"

Chris laughed. "Simple. I want to win."

Later that evening Nikliss found Dhagáin alone at one of the workbenches. Assured that Chris and his "safety precaution" were not about, Nikliss asked what Dhagáin thought of the situation.

"Not much," was all Dhagáin offered at first. He glanced at Nikliss and could see the stress around his eyes and his face a play

337

of dark emotion. "This has upset you. What is it that you fear?"

Nikliss took in a deep breath and answered, "Having a hand blaster or a laz-stun is one thing. With those you can hold off anyone trying to stop your retreat. This I understand. Firing without much harm. But this!" his voice rose with the stress. "This is without care for the welfare of the team. Chris seems unstable." Nikliss looked at Dhagáin hoping to see agreement but Dhagáin stood steady, waiting for Nikliss to continue.

Nikliss, either emboldened by Dhagáin's silence or compelled by his own erratic emotions, tumbled forward. "I can't believe that he thinks he's safe with a weapon of that caliber. That weapon will draw attention, it will draw increased defenses, and it will draw death. I don't think I can work with that." Nikliss was worked up and breathing hard.

Dhagáin placed his hand on Nikliss' shoulder in reassurance. "Don't let your emotions play against your judgment. Try to relax. Nothing yet may come of it."

Nikliss seemed to calm with the advice. He thanked his friend for listening and retired to his makeshift to think and consider *"What would Tåsan have to say about it?"*

• • •

Tåsan arrived early the next morning as expected. After seeing to *Tempest* he made his way up to the loft thinking to find hot tea and maybe the remnants of a meal.

Dhagáin was there and so was Chris, who was sitting on the loft table swinging his legs nonchalantly.

After greetings and a fast update on team members whereabouts, Tåsan sat down at the galley table to spoon up a bowl of hot grains and pick at a piece of toasted bread.

They were joined shortly thereafter by Nikliss, who was roused by the excited chatter and noise drifting down from above.

Tåsan wiped his mouth and cleared his dishes to the sink before turning to the small band of friends and asking. "What's new here?"

Chris hopped down from his perch and with barely contained excitement, retrieved the ATW-50 from its resting place across two chairs, exclaiming, "Oh, this is something new!" holding the weapon in front of him and moving it slowly around so that Tåsan could admire it.

Tåsan stood stock still, his face held in check, looking from Chris to the very big weapon and back to Chris before saying, "That is an ATW-50. Its destructive forces are formidable. At a close enough range it can melt steel." Then he asked, "Why do you have it?"

A little of Chris' excitement left him. He looked at Tåsan and then, in brief confusion at Tåsan's lack of enthusiasm, looked at the weapon. In defense, he answered, "Law enforcement won't stay naïve for very much longer. This," he hefted the ATW-50, "will ensure the team's success."

"I see," said Tåsan. "You now see yourself as the main defender of our heists?"

"Yes, but moreover, the main defender of me," Chris replied.

Tåsan considered the comment, quickly bringing to mind that it was he, Tåsan, who recently asked the team to increase their mode of protection. He had not thought that anyone would have leapt to this level of weaponry. "Okay. But keep yourself in close check. Use that," pointing, "only in dire circumstances." He shifted his stance, "Understood?"

"Yes indeed and not to worry," Chris smiled, "It's all good."

• • •

"But it's *not* all good," Nikliss stressed the words. "It's dangerous to have that level of kill power with us." He looked pleadingly at Tåsan.

They were standing outside on the graveled edge of the wildlands having a private conversation.

"I've seen Chris handle several types of weapons, he's not unfamiliar with this one," explained Tåsan. "He'll exercise logic and weigh each situation toward the best outcome."

Nikliss was not reassured by those words. He had a mounting mistrust of Chris' mental fixation with bigger and bigger weapons. It was wrong. It meant trouble.

"I'm sorry I don't agree with you Tåsan."

"There's nothing to be overly concerned with," Tåsan added.

"I disagree. I am very concerned and I can't shake the feeling that the next heist will come to disaster." Nikliss hung his head in sorrow. "I don't think I can go on any heists with Chris *or* his

339

ATW-50." Nikliss then looked out over the wildlands for a minute and calmly continued, "I'm going to need time to think. Do me a kindness and keep our conversation private until I've thought it through."

"Of course," Tåsan responded. "Take all the time you need."

Nikliss appreciated the consideration. "We'll talk again tomorrow. Promise. And thank you."

Tåsan watched as Nikliss turned and slowly walked back to the hangar and wondered at what the morrow would bring.

And it came soon enough.

Nikliss had come to a critical junction in his life direction where he could clearly see two paths from which he had to choose. If he stayed as one of Tåsan's team members, while extremely lucrative, it held the likelihood of being shot, maimed, killed, or jailed.

"Any of those possibilities would absolutely outrank my enjoyment of any riches I would collect." Nikliss made a point of explaining that it was not wholly due to Chris' new weapon of choice. It was a culmination of several instances spanning several quads but most certainly it was his sense of unease.

Nikliss' final decision was to quit the team. He did not wish to continue in his life of crime. He had built a home business at Corvus Space. He was becoming a master mechanic and engineer to local spacecraft clients. He had been successfully completing repairs, retrofits, and upgrades and was familiar with most of the new technologies that were appearing on the market.

"I've weighed my options," Nikliss had said, holding out both hands. Looking at one, he said, "One path almost ensures my destruction. The other," holding up his right hand, "gives me joy and possibilities." He had shrugged to indicate the choice was obvious.

Tåsan accepted Nikliss' decision because he couldn't do otherwise. Furthermore, Tåsan would allow Nikliss to stay at Corvus Space if in addition to his home business, he would continue to provide mechanical and engineering support to *Tempest*.

Nikliss, in welcome relief, clasped Tåsan's hand and smiled through his response, "Agreed!"

...

The Intersolar and Space Alliance had begun a systematic campaign of applying pressure to local authorities to take control of the rising crime activities before all three galaxies became more dangerous than they currently were.

Various ISA members met with law agency commissioners, heads of political factions, judges, and other prominent business owners to further their agenda.

"Contact your subordinates, tell them to voice their concerns."

"Tell law authorities that they are not doing their jobs."

"Warn them that if this does not stop now, there will be consequences."

Eventually the news-comm got wind of the growing concerns of the ISA and made them a priority story and ISA members were more than happy to speak whenever a vid-dev was pointed at them.

"Police enforcement is ineffectual. What are they being paid for?"

"The law is very clear in regard to criminal activities...it does not tolerate them. Because law enforcement has so far been inept, do we assume that they do tolerate criminal activities?"

"Maybe it's time to appoint new commissioners."

Behind the vocal rhetoric, the ISA adhocracy continued to plan a trap. The idea had started some weeks ago at an initial meeting of several prominent leaders who fell into complaining of their transports being robbed and their most valuable goods taken with no regard. The meeting took on a change in direction when one member, in his frustration, blurted out, "We should do something!"

The others stared at him for a moment or two in silence as the meaning of his words took shape in their minds. Of course, they would have to handle this themselves. It is obvious that police and enforcement attempts were not satisfactory and, by the way, what right does Inter-Galaxy Command have to disregard ISA's official directives in this matter? The answer was, the IGC had no right and have proven that they cannot be trusted. The ISA would proceed without IGC support and if they were successful in stopping the criminal assaults on ISA member commodities, the

341

current IGC leadership would be out.

Once that was established, the adhocracy settled down and developed their trap.

Rich rewards should be the bait. Jewels from the famous House of Traderi, pure nyoman crystals from Sador, a rare collection of art on loan for a special showing, and of course a safe full of tenges.

The setting could be a party or a wedding, Yes, the wedding of an Andorran princess, resplendent in riches and accompanied by her royal entourage and her dowry. And if that weren't tempting enough, the cache would also include one-half kilo of boron, a very expensive chemical necessary for space flight.

There was but one more consideration…where should this plan take place? Various ISA members made suggestions but each were, in turn, noted to be inadequate until one possibility in particular was mentioned.

There is a small community of maybe thirty Helidorians who had established themselves on Iolite, Helidor's only moon. They sought to build a resort for themselves and erected a finite cluster of buildings to support that idea. To limit their isolation, they chose to host and cater events but only for the extremely affluent. No need to cheapen their purpose.

"I myself have held an event there. I might be able to persuade the committee to let us use their facilities."

Police and private security could masquerade as staff and management and others could hide themselves as the guests. The small community would be populated with heavily armed police and as soon as the "Altruistic Outlaw" and his band of rotten little thieves stepped into the well-organized scene, the trap would spring and the criminals would be apprehended.

This could work.

Small bits of information regarding the Andorran wedding would be "leaked" to news-comm's, but not played up too big. Don't want the event turned into a spectacle that would attract too much attention. Also, hints that security could be light due to increased criminal activities elsewhere in the galaxy were to be circulated to further tempt the outlaw and his gang.

Oh, the ISA adhocracy was so very proud of themselves. The

plan was foolproof. Not only would they be responsible for ending the biggest crime spree to date, they would succeed in thoroughly humiliating the IGC.

This was going to work.

~

Tåsan had met with a small Vellosian delegation to hear details regarding the movement of a large and costly cache of goods by the IGC. Tåsan had earned their trust upon the return of the rare and expensive Vellosian Ashado liquor the IGC had procured from the Vellosians earlier that solar year.

Their gratefulness and newfound trust in Tåsan led them to partner with him in the execution of another big heist. Maybe others, too, if this proved to be profitable. The Vellosians would not take part, oh no. They were merchants and business opportunists only. They would, however, take a percent of the booty as payment for the reliable and very accurate information they provided.

With manifest in hand, Tåsan spent several days perusing the list of goods, contacting his sources to secure offloading, and monitoring the IGC transport schedule to ensure its precise location, speed, crew compliment, and defense capabilities, as well as suspected armaments that may be employed.

The most spectacular goods proved to be the easiest to transfer. There was a shipment of gems, including acanthite gems and calaverit, rubies worth hundreds of thousands of tenges, and a cask of almost priceless azure diamonds. Tåsan's fences were beside themselves with desire to possess gems of that quality that could be cut smaller to disguise their original form and sold for untold sums. That concerned Tåsan less than his asking price, which was met with almost no hesitation.

Among the other goods on the manifest, the items that Tåsan was most interested in were an assortment of macroscopic detection units and particle analytical systems bound for the IGC base, Supĕrus Tacere, on Eros. He might have to help himself to a unit or two before offloading the remaining gear.

• • •

A short week later the team had assembled, *Tempest* was checked, rechecked, and ready, fence contacts were scheduled and standing by, and the IGC transport was exactly on course.

The team was onboard preparing for liftoff.

Alyss would pilot *Tempest* and Annis would sit as navigator and comm officer, take out all comm and vid sensors on the IGC transport, and handle all on-board weaponry if needed. Chris, Dhagáin, and Luan were secure for flight and waiting for action. Tåsan stood behind Alyss, looking over her shoulder at the display console, noting with satisfaction that, one by one, all of *Tempest's* systems came alive and reported ready.

"On my mark," Tåsan spoke, glancing at Alyss and Annis who nodded in response. "Lift and burn."

Tempest shuddered ever so slightly as she rose from the tarmac of Corvus Space. As the craft slowly ascended, Tåsan could see Nikliss far below, standing at the hangar doors, hand over his eyes to shade against the sun, watching. When *Tempest* reached the Zone of Demark, Alyss set course and speed to intercept the IGC transport. It would take nine hours to reach the transport's coordinates.

Tåsan made his way to the galley where Chris, Dhagáin, and Luan were making themselves comfortable as they waited out the travel time. When they were within an hour of their target, they would perform system checks on their transports and review strategy.

Tåsan thought to sit with them for a few moments before returning to the bridge.

"Everyone ready?" he asked as he dropped into a seat by a view port.

"Aye," replied Chris.

"Yes," replied Dhagáin.

Luan smiled and nodded.

"We're flying trim for this heist," said Tåsan. "I saw no reason to employ mercenaries believing that we can handle any given situation that may arise."

Luan came toward Tåsan, offering him a mug of tea that he readily accepted.

"Thank you." He sipped the slightly bitter liquid. "You all have reviewed the transport's schematics and are familiar with bridge and cargo bay locations?"

Everyone nodded.

"This particular IGC transport is considered to be under-staffed," Tåsan continued, "and under-guarded. But I find that a bit hard to believe in light of the type of cargo they carry." He sipped at his mug. "Our number one rule for this heist," Tåsan said, leveling a look at his team, "is to stay sharp. Be aware of your surroundings, and do your job efficiently and with as little disruption as possible." Tåsan glanced and nodded at the others, silently asking for confirmation that readily came. "Good." He rose and left the others to talk among themselves and ready themselves for the heist.

• • •

"One hour," Alyss' voice sounded in Tåsan's sen-dev. He had been in the cargo bay performing system checks on the modified Class-N that he and Luan would take out to the transport ship.

Tåsan tapped his sen-dev, "Aye. Send the heads-up to the others, Alyss."

Dhagáin was the first to arrive to the cargo bay. He nodded acknowledgement to Tåsan and started checkout of his modified DCM, ensuring fuel capacity was high before continuing on.

Luan came through with Chris, both fairly silent and looking intent. Chris was carrying his ATW-50. It was holstered in a sort of sling type affair that slid from front to back to allow a quick retrieval. For something so unwieldy, it slid forward with ease, straight into Chris' grip, ready to fire within an instant.

Luan joined Tåsan in the Class-N, taking her co-pilot seat and beginning her checkouts. "How does she look?"

"Good," replied Tåsan. "Fit and trim."

Luan nodded with satisfaction, "Exactly as required."

• • •

The hour blew by faster than expected.

Alyss held *Tempest* two vectors away waiting for Tåsan's signal. Annis scanned the area and it stayed clear, reporting that it was void of any other ship, the nearest one being an hour out.

Tåsan gave the signal and Alyss swooped in within two hundred meters of the transport. She slid up close to the ship's underbelly where *Tempest* could stay undetectable for a period of time and then called out.

"Go."

The cargo bay doors opened and Dhagáin and Chris on their DCMs flew out closely followed by Tåsan and Luan in the Class-N.

The transport's cargo doors were disabled and opened within seconds allowing the vacuum of space to rush in. Dhagáin and Chris darted inside and separated as they scanned the storage isles for their targets.

Alyss' voice sounded in everyone's dev's, "Two minutes."

Tåsan flew the Class-N forward to a bulkhead door and positioned the 'N' close enough to loose laser pulses that soon obliterated the securing bolts and watched as the door slid off from the ship and float leisurely away. He and Luan gained entrance adjacent to the bridge and worked fast to laser their way through.

Alarms were sounding throughout the ship, triggered by the sudden loss of air pressure as fuselage doors blew off.

Tåsan and Luan found the bridge crew scrambling to get into their pressure helmets for a source of air. They were not expecting trespassers and looked to their captain for an explanation but he stood still, looking very confused.

Tåsan waved a Hand-Laz at them. "Have a seat. We won't be long."

Luan shut the alarm off and nudged the transport's course off by some twenty vectors and its speed up some five or six nautical meters before blasting the console to a molten mess.

"Five minutes," Alyss' voice sounded.

Tåsan and Luan backed out of the bridge and made for the Class-N. Just as they moved away from their position, Tåsan jettisoned a QV into the cavity and watched as a white flash pulsed out of the gaping hole. "That will keep 'em on the bridge."

Luan guided the 'N' around to the transport's cargo bay, intending to take on a payload.

Dhagáin and Chris made good use of their time.

Dhagáin secured three large crates to his DCM and now stood next to it waving the Class-N to come forward. He positioned five more travel crates in the doorway and intended to help load them up.

Chris was astride his DCM and talking into his dev, "Have located the containers of technology that are now fastened tight, ready for transport."

"Seven minutes."

Tåsan waved him off and Chris started toward *Tempest* now positioned a stretch of meters out.

With the last crate aboard the 'N', Tåsan signaled Dhagáin to leave.

"Ships approaching!" Alyss' voice sharp with stress.

"Luan, away!" commanded Tåsan as he secured the access door. The Class-N lurched forward.

Suddenly *Tempest* turned about and fired her photon cannons. *PHING...PHING...PHING.* The splash of light across her chrysoberyl as she absorbed incoming UV blasts was intense. Annis was anticipating the attack blasts with great accuracy and returning fire with well-placed shots to the oncoming swarm of ships.

Dhagáin pushed his DCM forward and amid oncoming UV blasts, recklessly zigged and zagged his way toward *Tempest*.

The Class-N lunged forward, firing its small intensity lasers and launching all available QVs into the fray.

PHING...PHING.

The attacking ships were closing in range and had started to scatter outward, firing wildly.

Dhagáin had just maneuvered his DCM through *Tempest's* bay doors when a 4-seat hopper dove past the hull, releasing a powerful blast that struck the rear jet panel of his DCM causing him to lose control and crash in the far end of the bay.

"Now! Now! Now!" Alyss screamed into the sen-dev comm. "We have to leave NOW!"

The Class-N dodged its way through the melee, closing the distance between them and *Tempest*. Tåsan, his eyes steady on the fight, threaded through the space.

Luan had taken control of weapons and was inflicting damage on several of the smaller attacking craft.

PHING

Tåsan caught sight of Chris several meters to port. He had cut the cables that had secured his goods and was speeding his DCM straight at the on-comers. Tåsan could hear Chris' voice crackling through the dev.

"You filthy teropt bugs!" Chris yelled through his rage. "You'll not finish what you've started!" He was guiding his DCM with one hand and firing the ATW-50 with the other, each recoil threatening to unseat him.

Tåsan shot for the bay doors, slamming to reverse engines just as the 'N' dragged its belly across the metal floor plates sending a blinding array of sparks in all directions.

Shaken but not down, Tåsan and Luan unstrapped and leapt to the door.

"Where's Chris?" Tåsan demanded.

Luan answered, "He took a cannon blast to the chest. I saw him partially disintegrate before floating free from his DCM. He didn't make it."

Tåsan touched his sen-dev, "Alyss! Get us out of here!" The words barely spoken before *Tempest* jerked to portside and accelerated away from the fight.

Several of the largest ships attempted to follow but *Tempest* out-sped them all and eventually even the most worthy of the adversarial ships was left far behind.

Annis reported that they were out of range and free to change course, which Alyss immediately did.

Tåsan stood looking around at the damage done to the Class-N, the cargo bay, and to Dhagáin's DCM. His first assessment was, *"Messy but not too bad."* Then he asked the bridge for a report.

Luan had gone to Dhagáin and found him slumped against the twisted wreckage of his DCM, a gash in his leg slowly soaking his quilted space suit red with blood. He smiled a weak smile and shook his head in partial disbelief.

Luan placed her hand lightly upon his shoulder and spoke, "Isn't it just your fortune that Tao taught me a bit of surgery before he left."

Dhagáin huffed a short laugh, holding his middle as he groaned with the pain. "Just don't amputate anything."

"Come on, I'll help you up," Luan said and pulled on Dhagáin's arm and he stood himself up and let himself be guided as he limped along with Luan to the med station.

Tåsan had gone to the bridge and now conferred with Alyss and Annis. "You say those were IGC ships?" he directed his question to Annis.

"Yes, several of the identifications returned as registered to the IGC and I recognized one of the Class-C interceptors. *Celestial Hook.*"

"Humph." Tåsan's brow furrowed and his mind raced. "Maybe they just happened along, out on a practice course, all by chance." He trailed off into thought, not really convinced by his own words.

Alyss spoke, "*Tempest* took several UV blasts but sustained little damage. Our laser cannons need several hours to recharge and I used a great deal of fuel for our hasty withdrawal."

"Do you think we were identified?" Tåsan asked.

Annis answered, "No. I scrambled their sensor arrays. Well, the ones I didn't destroy at any rate."

"Good. Thank you. Set course for Corvus Space."

Thirteen
What Were The Odds?

The atmosphere at Corvus Space was a sobering mixture of explanations and silence. Everyone wanted to know what had happened and the more the story was told the more details started to emerge.

Two hours after touchdown, Tåsan had called for a team meeting, inviting everyone to the loft. He thought to give everyone time to settle down and to contemplate the scrimmage, and mark their actions down to the smallest of details. He needed to know everything.

As a way to clear his mind and to organize his thoughts, Tåsan hopped on his pulse rocket and rode out into the wildlands. The sun had passed its zenith and shone softly through a haze of clouds that hung in the sky to the northeast. The pulse rocket hummed steadily and the cool air washed over Tåsan, making him shudder with the sensation. His thoughts a jumble of story and clarifications.

"There was always a risk. We knew that. It was an accepted fact. Was there something else we could have done? Something else we could have planed for?" Tåsan stopped his ride but did not dismount. Looking out at nothing in particular, he continued, *"Things went well up until the approaching ships got near. Then the situation changed."*

Tåsan blew through his memories then filed several questions that he intended to ask the team. He ended his internal monologue with a thought to losing Chris Phelan. *"I had thought he had more self-restraint. I should have known better and I'm sorry for his end."*

Tåsan started up the pulse rocket and rode slowly back to Corvus Space.

The meeting was a somber affair. Tåsan started the narrative by

350

offering a remembrance of Chris.

"...He was a good co-pilot who liked his career and loved his friends. I know he will be missed."

There was a quiet among the team so before continuing Tåsan hesitated a handful of seconds while he took in a deep breath. Then he turned the conversation to the main point.

"I would like to walk through the entire episode from start to end with everyone's observations and actions, in detail, overlapping throughout. I need to see a dimensional picture of the heist. Forgive me but I will be frequently interrupting to ask for clarification or for your own thoughts."

And thus it went for two hours. Halfway along, Luan had made tea and brought a small platter of fruitlets that seemed to put some life back into the conversation.

Annis was saying, "Unless someone held a hand recorder, none of the ships sensors or vis-recorders were operational. I had disabled them when they first appeared. As that goes, they had no means of identifying *Tempest*."

"I immediately swung to," Alyss added, "and evaluated distance and aggressor's compliment, and determined weapons range. I fired within a split second of their crossing that mark."

Dhagáin spoke, "That was a clear indication for me to race back to *Tempest*."

Tåsan looked thoughtful. "At that point, Alyss, how many ships were closing in on us?"

"Seven. One Class-A cruiser, two Class-C interceptors, and a handful of hoppers and Class-N's. Nothing smaller," she added.

"I don't think this group was out on any kind of practice run, as I first did." Tåsan mused. "I'm of the opinion that they were on course straight for the transport. Or for us," he said.

"That never occurred to me," said Alyss. "It seemed straight up a coincidence. If it had been planned, then why the Class-N's?" She shook her head in dismissal.

"She has a point, Tåsan," said Luan. "Why bring p-shooters to a significant battle?"

"Okay, I see your points," said Tåsan, "Well taken, but our lesson should be, don't be caught unguarded next time."

• • •

351

Tåsan divided the take from the heist equally among his team and it had come to a tidy sum for each of them.

Soon thereafter, Alyss, claiming fatigue from the day's activities, announced that she was leaving to go home. Annis was also ready to go so would ride with her.

Luan said that she would stay one night to look after Dhagáin's wound but thought it would be fine the next day and would depart soon after changing the derma-med one last time.

Nikliss was keeping Dhagáin company as he rested in his makeshift.

Luan had busied herself with cooking a pot of stew that when finished, she left it on the heat telling the others to help themselves. She spooned a portion into a bowl, fixed a mug of tea and retired to *Tempest's* galley for some alone time.

Later that evening, Tåsan visited Dhagáin to check up on him. "Is there anything I can get you?" he had asked.

"No, thank you. Nikliss has done a good job of being my runner tonight. A bit of a worrier, I suspect," Dhagáin said. "But I wonder if we may talk for a short while?"

"Sure," Tåsan answered as he moved to take a seat.

"I think the blast to my leg," Dhagáin said as his hand moved to the bandage, "actually woke up my brain." He organized his next thought. "I think this was my last heist." There. He said it. But before Tåsan could comment or question, Dhagáin spoke again, "I have observed a steady increase in weapons violence since we began our systematic approach to crime."

The statement made Tåsan laugh a bit. "It was to be expected. The more we heisted, the better we became."

Dhagáin, relieved that Tåsan had not reacted to his reservation in a negative way, offered a small explanation. "When I first joined your team, it was for the excitement of change. I was fairly unencumbered and available. And the prospect of riches was very convincing." He looked at Tåsan, his brow raised, his head cocked, "*Very* convincing."

The two friends laughed a bit.

"But seeing Chris blasted from his DCM only made me wonder what is in my future? I've been happy working with you and for you, Tåsan, but I believe I have had enough excitement and I certainly have enough riches. It's time I started again." Dhagáin fell silent having said what he needed to say.

Tåsan nodded. "Would you consider staying at Corvus Space and continue as mech-engineer to *Tempest*?"

"I would consider it an honor," Dhagáin's smile widened.

Tåsan stood up and reached to shake hands. "Maybe Nikliss would offer you a position with his new company."

"I would take nothing less than partner," Dhagáin exclaimed

~

He lay slumped in a heap on the cold, hard ground. The scent of burnt flesh swirled around him, moved by a fetid breeze.

Tåsan could not move his head, it felt pinned by a heavy weight. His limbs lay motionless, unresponsive. He opened his eyes trying to peer through the darkening mist but saw only vague movements in the blurry periphery.

Sounds came to his ears. At first he could not make them out but as they became louder, they became frighteningly clear: the flapping of wings. Tåsan could only think it was the harbinger of more bad news and his heart felt heavy and he sought to close his eyes to escape.

Large black birds flying high above had started a descent. One by one they came closer to Tåsan's prone body, squawking and cawing as they dove.

Each black bird had one word it repeated, and with every repetition, Tåsan sank further into unhappiness.

Abandonment

Betrayal

Denial

Lies

Death

Then silence.

Tåsan opened his eyes and before him stood a huge black bird, head tilted, looking steadily at him.

"Your life is ebbing," the bird spoke. "I can see sadness in the void." It stepped closer, leaning down even closer. "It's too late, it's too late," it screeched. "It's too late!"

353

Fourteen

Step by Step

The Intersolar and Space Alliance plan to capture or kill the Altruistic Outlaw and his gang could not have gone any worse.

The Helidorians consented to the use of their enclave as the setting for the trap, convinced by the top ISA representatives that their plan was absolutely foolproof and any damages would be sufficiently covered and the Helidorians well compensated.

The scene was prepared as if for real. Lavish decorations lined the main street that led to an expansive hall where the imitation wedding celebration would be held. Inside the hall were tables enough to accommodate two hundred and fifty "guests", each table was set with expensive dinnerware and each place setting a gift, presumably of some value.

Flowers and streamers and sparkling lights hovered above, while soft silken material added warmth and comfort.

The gift tables were stacked high with boxes of all sizes to fire the imagination about what they might contain, and cases labeled with exclusive vintage logotypes littered the surrounding floor space.

It was a setting worthy of a royal wedding, the wedding of an Andorran princess.

The ISA had recruited a large number of private security persons and filled out the remaining positions with local police, who were more than happy with the prospect of regaining their reputation that had, of late, been taking a beating at the hands of the news-comm reporters.

Everything was ready.

The news of the lavish wedding had been carefully leaked, the small community and the celebration hall extravagantly decorated,

354

and the security and police had been richly dressed and heavily armed. Everything was in place.

What could go wrong?

As the time ticked down, and the advertised celebration start-time neared, several approaching ships were spotted. Then several more, then dozens more and still more ships, large chasers and ten-crew runners, descended upon Iolite. Closely following and jamming the sensor screens were a half-a-hundred solo flyers swarming like a plague of insects.

The shooting began shortly after the first mercenaries landed and the ensuing mayhem only escalated as more and more pirates, privateers, and mercenaries circled the enclave, firing cannons before landing their crafts and disgorging their foot soldiers.

Security and police had expected one ship, one Altruistic Outlaw, and maybe five privateers. They were shocked by the sheer number of overrunning pirates and hastily set up a line of defense. Leadership was nil and it showed in the panic of finding a safe barrier and shooting whatever moved.

The pirates were not unused to violence and weapons play so returned fire with zeal. After all, there were untold riches, gems, expensive goods, and a princess to be taken. Right?

An hour passed before the last shot was fired and the end result of the ISA's grand plan was horrific. Eighty-two security and police lay dead and seventy-nine others were badly injured. Less than one-third remained standing, and those were busy tending to the wounded and rounding up any of the privateers that had not managed to escape.

The small Iolite community was in total ruin. Not one building remained whole. All were shot and blasted almost to dust.

Reports of the disaster flew out on e-dev's and comm lines with the speed of lightning. One such report, filled with visuals and expletives, hit the desk of one Vice Admiral Caoin.

~

"This is inconceivable. Ludicrous. Beyond belief." Caoin banged the riff of papers down on his desk and looked at Captain Amans Sulac seated before him. "And yet, here it is."

"If I may, sir," Amans said. "The ISA may have just handed us a gift. Two, if you will."

Caoin sat back in his chair, curiosity reflected on his face, and waved a hand at Amans, signaling that he should continue.

"This horrific disaster, orchestrated solely by the ISA, is solid proof of their collective incompetence and that of the local authorities as well. Their massive bungling of their so called trap has completely eclipsed our pale attempt at capturing the altruistic," Amans' inflection of distaste underscored his contempt for the privateers' moniker, "...gang as they pilfered our transport. The ISA now stands in judgment by us." Amans leaned forward, his face almost twisted in malicious joy as he spoke, "We own them, now."

Vice Admiral Caoin took it in, sitting still, eyes steadily on Amans while he spoke. He now moved to clasp his hands on the desk before him, nodding, "Yes. We. Do."

"I have a request, sir. I would like to be appointed special counsel leader of a task force in charge of the apprehension and imprisonment of the Altruistic Outlaw." Amans sat back with a shrug, "Or his death. However it works out."

"Done," said Caoin. "Reassign who you will and keep me informed."

Amans, clearly very pleased, snapped to his feet, "You will not regret your decision, sir. I will start right away." He walked to the door, opened it to leave and turned to Caoin, "Thank you."

• • •

The first thing Captain Sulac did was to give his project a nice title, that of "Inter-Galaxy Command Office of Special Counsel." Next, a title for his position as head of the new group, "Commander in Charge." Third, a budget. Fourth, appointees. Lastly, a written directive that would clearly state Special Counsel's jurisdiction and their objective.

"...to capture or to eliminate the unidentified, but significantly dangerous criminal dubbed the 'Altruistic Outlaw'," Amans spoke into his v-translator. He pressed a couple of directive tabs and stabbed his finger down on the send/distribute icon that launched his missive out to his newly formed team. Amans wanted them informed before meeting with them, he glanced at his e-dev, in fifteen minutes time...

Standing at the head of the table looking impressive in his new uniform, Amans addressed the group. "We are here to investigate crimes against the IGC and the ISA. I have full authority over the actions of this office and the full support of the Admiral's office with oversight provided by Vice Admiral Caoin. As you can see, our pedigree is impressive," Amans said as he looked around the table. "Now, let's get to work."

Within hours of his first special counsel staff meeting, Captain Sulac ordered several prominent Intersolar and Space Alliance personages to appear before him in two days time. The meeting went very well.

The corporate leaders had started a diatribe focused on the shifty circumstances that undermined their success, and Amans sat quietly waiting for them to run out of steam. When they had talked and argued their way to near silence, he spoke.

"The point is not what external forces caused your great plan to fail. The point is that your limited thinking, ineffectual planning, and total incompetence caused the death and maiming of one hundred and sixty one individuals, possibly the worst slaughter in mid-history."

The group sat gaped-mouthed at the words.

Amans stood up. He wanted to appear bigger than the corporate shills seated about the room. "Your plan failed because of *you*," he emphasized as he paced slowly back and forth. "And because of your failure, the IGC must now step in to clean up your mess. Which we will do...*without*...your further assistance." Amans spun around and glared at the group. "You will be required to provide restitution to all affected parties and underwrite the work and investigations performed by this office."

One of the group started to say something but Amans held up a hand to cut him off, "There will be no objections or questions."

Amans positioned himself center and looked at each and every corporate leader with severity.

"This meeting is over. Get out."

• • •

The IGC's Office of Special Counsel, under the direction of Amans Sulac, sent a network of spies and investigators out into the public with one objective: track down the Altruistic Outlaw. Find out where he is based, the individuals working with him, and those

357

who know him.

Amans sat at his desk, arms folded across his chest, feet crossed at the ankle. He seemed to be staring at the messy piles of paper and oddly placed e-dev's that littered the desktop, but his eyes were not so much focused on the clutter as they were searching his memories for all the documented instances of lawlessness attributed to his prime objective.

"A good strategy is developed from a strong foundation of facts and figures," Amans thought. "Yes, facts," he said aloud as he touched his e-pad and asked that his aide immediately come to his office.

"You are to search all records for every single instance of crimes against the IGC or ISA assets and I would like this set of data delivered to me by end of day."

"Yes, sir," the aide snapped a salute and left quietly.

Amans was starting to feel good about his new command. *"If all goes well, this would spell a promotion and a significant bonus."* Smiling, he sat back in his chair, and let the dream of grandeur play on. *"I'll establish a timeline of the crimes. Knowing where the outlaw has been will surely point to where he might go next."* Amans absently picked at the papers on his desk, then as an idea came to him, plucked up his e-dev and started a search for a list of persons who had had any contact with the outlaw. Amans searched for the names of pilots, transport captains, comm persons, anyone who could help build a profile. *"A composite of his face, his appearance, and his character will advance my success."*

After several moments of typing and clicking, Amans had a short list of possible collaborators that he immediately transmitted to his field operatives with an order to extract details and to leave no fact behind.

"That fool Caoin should have thought of this weeks ago. His sitting at Vice Admiralty is a mockery of Inter-Galaxy Command beliefs." Amans said aloud to no one but himself. "Maybe I'll just take that ranking from him," he mused and then with a small huff of mirth, returned to his e-dev.

• • •

Captain Sulac, Special Counsel Commander, met with his aide and two of his most trusted and prodigious intelligence agents to discuss all intel collected to date and to analyze patterns and consistencies related to the current crime threat. Amans refused to use the term Altruistic Outlaw, preferring, instead, the more apt descriptor, Menace.

His small team, seated about the meeting table, was intently studying the graphs, papers, crime scene photos, interviews, and various other bits of data that were spread out in a messy array along the table's length.

Amans spoke, "We have an impressive collection of information and statistics but they are full of inconsistencies and contradictions. For instance, this point," he held up a piece of paper and pointed to a specific dot floating somewhere in the middle of a crowded field of dots, "represents three or four crimes being committed almost simultaneously." He put the paper down. "Which crime belongs to the menace?" asked Amans, quickly adding, "If any of them do."

His query went unanswered.

Amans continued, "And what the tophet is this?" as he tossed a sheaf of papers down the table so that they fanned out as they skidded along.

The others reached out to examine what the pages contained, curiosity creasing their brows.

Amans did not expect an answer. "I'll tell you what they are. They are two dozen entirely different composite drawings of the face of one," he punctuated the word and repeated it for further emphasis, "*one* criminal's face." Amans stood up, leaning forward on his hands now placed firmly on the table in front of him. "How is this explained?"

One investigator started to speak, "It's just that..."

"Never mind," Amans cut him off. "We need to hone in on this. We need further clarification of collected data," he said as he waved the page of dots in the air. Amans pulled in a soothing breath of air and sat back down. "Go back to the witnesses and fix these descriptions. There has to be someone out there with a better memory than this." Amans waved a hand over the table in front of him and there was no doubt among the aide or the two investigators present that Amans was registering disgust.

Just then Amans' e-dev chimed an incoming call, the screen reported that it was Vice Admiral Caoin. Amans looked to his team and held up a finger indicating that he would take the call.

"Captain Sulac here." Listening to the voice on the line. "Yes. I'm reviewing current status with my team."

Amans' aide's e-pad chimed and he lifted the lid to see an incoming message advising him to launch NKKZ-app to see the latest news-comm. And this he did.

Amans tilted his head, "No sir, I haven't seen it."

The aide turned his e-pad to the others and clicked up the audio.

Amans squinted and leaned in toward the e-pad to gain a better look then, intently focused on the news-comm, said into the e-dev, "I'll call you back," snapping the device off.

« There seems to be a confusing number of reports coming from several points in the Rayten Galaxy, particularly from Jahved Tuk, concerning a very upsetting event that has just occurred close to their outer stars. » The comm-reporter, whose image was telecast on the screen, touched their ear, nodded and continued, « Yes, a crime-in-progress turned shoot-out was reported moments ago. We do not have the details but will keep you informed… »

"Snap that off," barked Amans. "Get out there now. Find out what's happening."

The investigators were on their feet and moving toward the door.

Amans commanded, "I want timely reports." And turning his head, "Got that?" he shouted at their backs as they left.

"Yes, sir," they called back as they retreated away.

~

Upon hearing from a reliable source that a freighter loaded with valuables was scheduled to dock in two days time on Jahved Tuk, Tåsan made a quick decision to hit it.

"My source," Tåsan was saying, "is confident that this freighter is transporting a large shipment of uridium-8 from the Chelic Corporation mines on Thorium 4. "Hah," he exclaimed, "Fun fact," eyebrows raised and nodding, "father owns interest in the Chelic Corp."

"Just how reliable is this source?" asked Alyss.

"Very," replied Tåsan before moving on, "There's also three kilos of boracite that my source is very interested in and a small amount of boron supposedly just laying about waiting to be pilfered."

"Doesn't it seem a little convenient?" Alyss looked skeptical. "Could there be something else going on here, something you haven't been told?"

Tåsan was thoughtful for a very brief moment before answering. "I admit that on the surface the heist looks sketchy, but I've been told that with the recent spike in crime, most merchants are taking precautions. This one in particular has hired a freighter from a small company with the intent to fly unnoticed."

Luan had been quietly listening and now offered her opinion, "I can make queries among my friends, Alyss, to confirm Tåsan's source information, if that would help to put your mind at ease."

Alyss, visibly uncomfortable, said "Thank you, Luan." And turning to Tåsan, "It's not that I doubt what you're saying," slowly shaking her head, "It's that I'm not confident that your source has enough information to make a move on."

"Okay," said Tåsan. "Let's say that the heist comes to nothing. The worst that could happen is that we took a joy ride and burnt some fuel. The best to happen is we win again."

"I know you're right," admitted Alyss with resignation, "Okay, we're good. I'm good."

The remainder of the day was spent readying *Tempest* and fueling the DCMs in preparation.

The plan was to shadow the freighter for a parsec then, if all was clear, disable comm and vid and quickly move in to boarding range. It was determined that since it was an older more worn freighter, Alyss would pilot and sit weapons and Annis would take control of the freighter's bridge while Tåsan and Luan secured the payload.

The entire episode should take no longer than fifteen minutes. Everyone was to arm up, choosing large capacity hand stuns and high frequency lasers. Tåsan was not expecting too much trouble from the freighter crew so did not think large overbearing weapons would be necessary.

The hour came.

The freighter was indeed old and worn, and sported scuff marks and dents along her fuselage indicating sloppy docking practices. But most importantly, she was slow and alone in this sector of space.

Alyss few *Tempest* in close and Annis, the first out of the bay doors, flew forward ahead of Luan and Tåsan, reaching the freighter's outer hull access door and began laser cutting the securing bolts. Luan was next to reach the door and assisted in the effort.

Annis was first through the open access and quickly moved through the cramped passageway to where the pilot and co-pilot sat strapped into their command seats. From behind them, Annis loosed a short blast from her Hand-Laz targeting the comm unit panel, blowing it up. The pilots had not noticed her approach and jumped with the suddenness of the sparks that spewed from the comm panel and began to struggle against their seat straps in a panic to start their safety recovery.

Annis said, "Not to worry. All is fine," and zapped both of them with a mild stun shock, effectively putting them to sleep. As they slumped into their seats, Annis smiled with satisfaction, then busied herself with redirecting the freighter's path and locking the controls.

Tåsan and Luan were searching the second of three storage bays when they heard what could have been the report of a hand-blaster.

Tåsan touched his sen-dev, "Report," he voiced.

Silence.

"Report," he repeated.

Two seconds clicked by. "Two security in passage," Annis' voice rang in everyone's sen-dev's. "I'm pinned down between the bridge and bay one."

Alyss spoke, "Standing by."

"Hold position," Tåsan ordered then indicated to Luan that she was to move her now loaded DCM to the hull breach and return to move Tåsan's as well. He was going to enter the passageway and make his way to Annis to assist.

Alyss, her voice reflecting her focused concern came over the sen-dev's, "I can help." She pulled *Tempest* out of stationary hold and swooped up and over the freighter, hitting it with UV blasts that rocked the ship enough to put it into a slow turn to port side.

Meanwhile, Tåsan had gone some yards up the passageway and managed to surprise three security characters as they were making their way to the holds. He stunned one before they noticed him and as the other two dove for cover, Tåsan stunned another with a medium level blast to the back, sending the individual tumbling down into a heap.

Annis' voice on the sen-dev, "Passageway secure, I'm making my way aft."

"Step carefully, there's security on deck one," Tåsan said.

Alyss cut in, "Three ships closing fast, moving to defense mode."

Tåsan charged down the passageway blasting his laz and his stun to create a cover for himself and hit the third guard with a laz to his upper arm that made blood soak out, just before a stun hit his chest, forcing the guard backwards and down to the floor.

A noise made Tåsan suddenly turn and raise both his weapons, his muscles tight, his fingers pressing on the blasters' release mechanisms.

It was Annis.

The sight of Tåsan ready to blast her pulled her up short. She stood stock still as Tåsan realized the situation and let his muscles relax. They briefly smiled at each other then quickly turned and ran toward the cargo bays.

UV blasts rocked the freighter making their progress unsteady but not impossible. When they reached bay two, Luan had successfully loaded all three DCMs with the goods they had come for and was standing ready at the hull breach.

Tåsan took a moment to notice two prone bodies on the floor then touched his sen-dev, "Alyss."

"Hang tight. Two down. Chasing the third." Alyss had outmaneuvered the IGC ship and blasted their guidance and comm system arrays and had pushed it, with one last UV blast, into a rapid twirling motion away from the freighter. *Tempest* was no equal match for the two local police ships that accompanied the IGC into the sortie. Alyss blasted the tail off of one ship just as she gave chase to the other that turned and ran. She planted four well-placed blasts right up its thrusters, killing all engines and sending it adrift before bringing *Tempest* back to the freighter's location where she found Annis, Tåsan, and Luan aboard their DCMs holding position, waiting for her.

As soon as the DCMs were aboard and the bay doors secured, Alyss pointed *Tempest* away from the outer stars of Jahved Tuk, choosing a long and meandering course back to the Niles Galaxy, home to Corvus Space.

"Ah, Luan," Tåsan said as he helped her unload the crates of goods from her DCM, "you never cease to amaze." Tåsan dropped a fairly heavy case to the floor and pried its latches open, lifting the lid and revealing the contents.

"I thought something special for you," Luan replied as Tåsan lifted a Particle Analysis System up for closer inspection. "I know how you love technological toys."

"A gesture that won't be forgotten. Thank you." Then turning to include Annis, Tåsan said, "When we're finished here I would like to meet on the bridge."

Twenty minutes later, Tåsan was addressing his team. "We did very well for a small team and for being surprised by guards. I think it all went *very* well."

"I didn't like having an IGC ship arrive," said Alyss, "Although it was a little exciting to make split-second combat decisions, again."

"I felt very confident that no harm would come to us," said Luan. "We've trained and prepared and were ready."

Tåsan added, "We'll split the booty at Corvus Space. Alyss, take us home."

~

Amans Sulac listened again to the IGC bridge recording, following the words as closely as possible.

« Stand by, we're approaching vector 8721.e9 approximately one point 10÷2 sectors out. » (a lapse of ten seconds) « Incoming! » (called out the navigator) « We've been hit, sir. Port side destabilizes down to thirty percent. » (nothing) « Another direct hit, this time to the nav array. » (garbled static) « Target that ship! » (the captain shouted) « Nav is down, sir. Can not comply. » (responded the co-pilot) « We're in free float. »

The recording ended with a long sequence of static until it went silent.

The IGC law enforcement fighter ship sent to deal with the situation in progress was only slightly larger then the two police cruisers deployed as assistants. The pilot and co-pilot had been debriefed immediately upon their retrieval...eight hours later. They were located five sectors from the disabled freighter, adrift with no nav, no comm, and no sensors. They had been grilled for two straight hours and made to tell absolutely everything they could remember about their encounter with the privateers, their ship, and any observance made no matter how small.

This report and the bridge recording were submitted to Captain Sulac as fast as it could be compiled. Amans now sat alone in his office, reading and re-reading the report and playing the audio over and over, his thoughts focused.

"This does not feel like a band of random mercenaries. It looks to be too specific. That freighter was a target." Amans thrummed his fingers on the table. *"Who knew about that freighter?"* He knit his brow and leaned closer to his e-pad, staring at the words on the screen. Then an idea struck him and his face relaxed as he sat back in his chair turning his thoughts around in his mind. *"Yes, that freighter was targeted."*

Amans sat up and jabbed a finger at his e-pad, summoning his aide to answer. "Compile a list of all IGC goods that have been stolen from IGC possession during the past five quads," he stated then disconnected the comm before the aide could answer.

"Yes, yes, yes," Amans said aloud. "A picture is starting to form," he added, self-satisfaction evident in every word.

• • •

Two days later. Vice Admiral Caoin was standing in Amans' office demanding an explanation. "The ISA owner of that freighter is on my e-pad and e-text about every hour demanding to know if we have caught the perpetrators and recovered his stolen shipment." Caoin tossed a few message tags onto Amans' desk.

"I've been busy with my own investigations, as you have directed this commission to do. You will have to take this matter," Amans pointed to the little mess of tags in front of him, "up with the acting commander of the Tactical Deployment Department." Amans stood up looking passively at Caoin, who faced him across the desk, fuming.

"Someone will have to answer for this," Caoin shouted.

"Then let it be the acting commander."

Caoin stormed out the door.

Amans smiled and almost laughed out loud as he gathered up the comm tags and dropped them in the wastebasket.

• • •

That night, Corvus Space was quiet. The booty had been split, ship maintenance completed, the supper meal eaten, and the galley stowed.

Everyone had faded away. Alyss and Annis to Merula, Dhagáin and Nikliss to themselves and Luan retired to *Tempest* to "...do a bit of recon," as she put it.

Tåsan had poured a generous glass of the well-aged Vellosian liquor he now owned and had made himself comfortable in his loft space intending to familiarize himself with the operations of the particle analyzer Luan had gifted him.

He decided to sit in one of the overstuffed chairs by the windows and as he sunk down into the cushions, he realized how bone tired his body really was. He sat for an untold number of minutes, sipping his liquor and looking out at the wildlands beyond, now silhouetted in the late evening light.

As dusk slowly turned to night, the stars appeared overhead, brightening one by one until countless bright dots of light suddenly shone across the dark sky canvas.

Tåsan sank further into the chair, whose cushions seemed to welcome and support him with warmth. He felt good. He felt safe. He felt happy.

> The stars shone above and a warm gentle breeze brushed past Tåsan's face, soothing his thoughts. He was riding his pulse rocket, watching the wildlands roll by, marveling at its beauty hidden half-seen through the veil of darkness. Alyss was with him and she raised her hand to signal that they should turn their course just ahead.
>
> Tåsan's excitement grew even as his anticipation unfolded. The turn in the path was toward a brightly lit room framed in a dark fog. As he and Alyss approached, their pulse rockets faded from reality and Tåsan found

that he was now walking toward a familial scene dotted with smiling faces of family and friends, who were all surprised and very happy to see him.

With fondness, Tåsan greeted everyone and accepted their joyful declarations and desire for his good fortune, in stride. He was moving among the well-wishers, happy and contented when he casually turned to his right and saw, standing just a few steps ahead, Stellanova.

Tåsan hesitated for only a fraction of a moment then rushed forward in his joy.

The dark gray fog closed in and Tåsan opened his eyes to the stark darkness of the loft, realizing that he had awakened from a dream.

He pulled his e-dev from a pocket and pressed a series of iconographs and letters and touched the send icon. ((Are you awake?)) Less than a minute had passed when the dev chimed a reply to his query. ((Yes!))

Tåsan chose a setting and put the device to his ear, "Hello my sweet little sister. It's so good to hear your voice! Tell me what you've been up to."

Fifteen

Turn Up The Fire

Captain Sulac, wielding his influence with the Vice Admiralty, ordered a significant increase in IGC patrols and surveillance all along known trading routes with special importance given to tracking IGC freighters and sub-freighters.

Since that time, reports had been crowding in from several sectors of space. The reports show an uptick in petty crimes closest to popular trade and docking zones such as Brenton Kae and Cimtum 8, usually committed by privateers who target small transports and easily taken goods.

The local police have been working additional time and have literally stuffed their holding facilities with petty criminals and privateers.

The IGC, in their stepped up role of law enforcer, have been busy engaging privateers as well. Those caught were turned over to local authorities. Those who chose to run were chased down and subjected to IGC's rule of combat…strike hard and win.

Amans sat with his aide, reviewing reports from the past ninety-two hours.

"The segment total of crimes is numbered at three hundred forty one, of which, the IGC was involved in exactly twenty seven," Amans read the statistics aloud. "Where will I find the descriptions of the incidents related to that number?" Amans glanced at the aide stirring in front of him.

"There on page four, sir," the aide replied. "It follows the statistical data and graphing of the crimes. You may sort by date or by level of severity," he added, "whichever is more convenient."

Amans thumbed down the e-dev screen and found what he was looking for. Only two of the twenty-seven IGC interventions involved anything significant. Amans dismissed the other twenty-five incidents as useless information and was inclined to toss out one of the remaining two crimes of interest as well.

"Tell me," Amans said as he turned his e-dev toward the aide and pointing at a report entry, "who were the individuals involved in these two crimes?"

"Those records were not included in this report for the sake of brevity. But I can get them for you within the hour."

Amans nodded his head and turned his e-dev back, then a thought started to form. *"None of these petty skirmishes come up to the caliber of expertise displayed by our Altruistic Outlaw along with the gang of thieves."* He shifted in his seat. *"We have to look deeper. We have to find connections and similarities."* Amans considered his train of thought then ordered the aide to action.

"I want the names of the criminals involved with these two specific altercations." Amans repeatedly tapped a finger on his e-dev screen. "I want them brought here and questioned until we know 'who they know' and 'what they know' and I want it now."

~

Leaving his technology behind, Tåsan spent the following week riding his pulse rocket out into the Naiad Five wildlands. Some nights he would return to Corvus Space. And some nights he would not. On those nights, he camped out under the stars and let his thoughts run as they would. He enjoyed his sojourns into the wild where no others intruded, where he answered to no one, and seemingly where he was responsible only for himself.

After several days of riding, observing the natural world, and living without a schedule, Tåsan felt relaxed and restored. He returned to Corvus Space and after completing the maintenance to his pulse rocket and stowing his gear, he took a long hot shower that seemed a fitting end to his recreation and a return to the well known.

Tåsan had fixed a meal for himself and sat in the loft galley spooning the deliciously warm concoction of heated grains, powee nuts and fruitlets, while sending a message out to Alyss and Annis. Would they be up for a visit? He would like to come into Merula the following afternoon. He could be at their flat before late afternoon, or whenever was convenient for them, they could visit

369

for a while and he would take them to dinner. Yes?

Yes.

• • •

"Right on time," Annis said as she opened the door then stepped aside so Tåsan could enter.

"Hello! You look well," said Tåsan as he leaned in for a hug.

"You made it!" exclaimed Alyss as she appeared from up the hallway, spreading her arms for a hug.

"I've brought a chilled bottle of Lingdon Práxus," Tåsan said, holding the bottle for inspection. "I know you have three glasses."

The friends made their way to the kitchen, chatting small talk and laughing as Annis opened the bottle and Alyss set the glasses on the counter. When the wine had been poured, the friends stood in a loose group. Tåsan held his glass up and said, "To today."

"Hear, hear."

Annis said, "Let's get comfortable and catch up," and motioned that they should move to the living space.

When they were seated and settled and most of the light conversation observed, Alyss said, "This is such a nice surprise," and addressing Tåsan asked, "Is there something in particular on your mind? A special occasion?"

"Yes and no," Tåsan answered. And they waited for him to continue.

"I have been missing our social get-togethers where we leave our business for awhile and just be friends," Tåsan said, looking a small bit embarrassed. "A twinge of nostalgia, I guess."

Alyss said, "Back to the days of IGC training where we had no worries, eh?" laughing.

Grinning, Tåsan added, "Yes. What about all those spiny little Muroidea beasts? They're nothing!" he laughed.

Encouraged, Annis said, "Not to mention the high pressure and compressed deadlines of the Shadow Fast Fighter. A walk in the park."

"Hear, hear!"

As Tåsan refilled their glasses, the conversation followed the natural path of remembrance as each friend talked about a special time or a notable memory shared with the others. They laughed, they joked, and they added details to the stories, until eventually, the conversation wound down to chatting about what each of them had been up to lately.

After that, the three friends wound down a bit more.

Annis took note of the thoughtful nature of Tåsan's face and said, "You seem to have something on your mind. Is it something you could share with us?"

Tåsan seemed to steel himself just a bit. He took a deep breath and said, "I've had occasion to think about and consider several things relating to myself. To be more specific, where I've been and where I'm going."

"That sounds very serious," commented Alyss.

"It is in a sense," replied Tåsan, "but not so serious as to cause undue concern," he explained, hoping to put her and Annis at ease.

In the way of an introduction to his reasoning, Tåsan told of his weeklong trek into the wildlands and a little bit of the inevitable life review that accompanied most lone journeys.

"...and two things became more obvious," he continued. "Sooner or later, my current vocation will come to an end. If I'm fortunate enough to call that end myself, well then, I'll be an awfully rich and extremely happy individual." Tåsan reached for his glass of Práxus, taking a small sip to punctuate the happy story.

"And..." prompted Annis.

"And..." agreed Tåsan, "If I'm unfortunate and my end comes to me courtesy of the IGC or by way of a proton blast, well," he said, "I can see that I would be leaving a few loose ends."

Alyss spoke, "I think we've all had those considerations since we've chosen this path. Those thoughts aren't extraordinary and they certainly aren't yours alone."

"Yes, I know that, Alyss, I'm merely saying that I've moved on my thoughts of an untimely end to my life of crime."

Tåsan saw the looks of uncertainty on the faces of his two best friends. "Let me explain, please, no protests," he said to calm their fears as he retrieved his e-dev.

Alyss looked over at Annis but could not read her emotions by her face. Annis looked back at Alyss and smiled a pale smile. Neither was comforted by the exchange.

At last Tåsan found the electronics he was looking for and

371

spoke, "I've amassed a fortune in goods, property, tenges, and technology. It would be a shame if it was all lost." He consulted his e-dev. "I've thoroughly thought about this and have documented my decisions," handing his e-dev to Alyss because she sat closest to him. As Tåsan continued, Annis moved to Alyss' side to share the e-dev screen.

"I'm giving Corvus Space, the business, the land, the shop, and all the tools to Dhagáin and Nikliss." Tåsan sat back, looking relieved that he had finally breached the subject. "Annis, I'm giving Moonstone to you."

Annis had a look of surprise flow across her face.

"Alyss, *Tempest* is yours." Tåsan held up his hand, "No protests." He chided.

Alyss caught herself and remained quiet, nodding at Tåsan.

"Luan will appreciate that I'm giving her my encoded book of fences, contacts, clients, and ne'er-do-wells. It should amuse her for a short time. Supplemented by ownership of the modified DCM that she prefers."

Tåsan sat smiling, very pleased that the conversation had gone so well. Alyss and Annis were surprised by the revelations and sat quietly, trying to process the information.

"Dinner?"

"No," said Alyss, "not just yet," quickly following up with a question. "Where is all this coming from, Tåsan? What has brought this particular subject to the forefront, enough so for you, that you've gone to this level of planning?"

Tåsan looked at Alyss. She was clearly struggling and trying to understand the emotional drivers of his decisions. He spoke with consideration, "It's really the end result of my self-analysis. I had occasion to ask myself 'where am I going?' and since I have no sight into the future, I came up with basically two logical paths. And it was abundantly clear that I lacked a good plan." Noticing that Alyss had let go of some of her initial reluctance, Tåsan continued. "It seemed natural for me to do this and I'm pleased that I did. It's done."

Alyss looked at Tåsan and he looked at her, "You know how I like a good plan," tilting his head and smiling.

That seemed to take the seriousness out of the conversation

and helped return it to the lightness it deserved.

"I've reserved a table for us at the Lower East Grille," Tåsan said. "I hear they serve the finest Tradorian Berrywine tenges can buy." He raised his brow and looked expectantly. "Ready?"

~

A week had passed when Tåsan received a message from Alyss. Could she come for a visit? He replied yes, a visit would be great. He was taking *Tempest* out for a test of her latest AI, would Alyss like to ride along?

The two were on the bridge monitoring the operations of three separate drones that had been launched earlier. Tele-screens were reporting that the drones were performing as designed.

Alyss took the opportunity. "Last week, when you spoke about transferring your property and goods gave me pause."

Tåsan took his eyes off the flight console and turned slightly to look at Alyss more fully.

"As I puzzled out your motivations, and I fully understand your decisions," she added, "I came to a crossroad in my own path." Alyss earnestly looked at Tåsan. "And it gave rise to a question that I thought was one that I would like to talk with you about."

Tåsan moved to put *Tempest* on auto, programming her to pace the drones for two more parsecs then bring them home, before turning his full attention to Alyss. "Anything you want. I'm yours."

Alyss smiled and nodded appreciatively. "My crossroad presented me with a dichotomy...when is enough, enough?" Eyes lowered, she twiddled a switch on the co-pilot's console as she organized her thoughts, then continued. "We've all become very rich. I, myself have more than enough tenges to support myself well into the future. Well into any dreams I may have about that future. However," she hesitated a scant moment, "will any future I have be as exciting and treacherous as flying against the IGC has been?"

Tåsan knew he couldn't answer that question but offered a response, "In the beginning, the goal for me *was* tenges. I was on the edge of losing everything and becoming desperate. When I found that tenges were so easily gained, my goal subtly changed to finding and honing my skills of planning and managing. Of course," Tåsan shrugged and smiled slyly as he continued, "I've enjoyed my life of crime. It generally feels good to stick it to the IGC."

Alyss laughed in agreement.

Tåsan said, "Since my alone time in the wildlands, I find myself restless again. I can't exactly put my finger on it but I'm restless."

"I know what you're saying," Alyss offered. "And," she added, "the IGC really isn't the bumbling organization they lately appear to be. They're just slow to move, slow to get moving."

"Yes, they won't remain obtuse for much longer. They have already stepped up their presence. Two quads ago they were absent, preferring to leave petty crime up to the poorly trained local police. Now they seem to be everywhere," Tåsan said.

"They still send their smaller, unimportant ships out, but," Alyss stated, "it won't take them long to correct that."

"I've noticed a marked increase in IGC interventions that involve weapons use. I don't think," said Tåsan, "that the IGC is interested in convicting criminals as much as they are interested in putting on a show of strength."

Alyss added, "That fits right in with their egos and we know from experience how important that is to them."

"These kinds of thoughts have led me," Tåsan said, "to conclude that the IGC is getting serious and probably to the point of weapons warfare."

Alyss nodded. "Which brings us back to 'when is enough, enough?'"

"In a way," Tåsan said, "I may already be answering that question." Noticing the enquiring look Alyss gave him, he added, "Give me some time to work the details. Then we'll talk again. At the next team meeting."

The remainder of the flight went very well. The drones performed their reconnaissance and gathered their data with exceptional clarity. Tåsan was very pleased and said as much as he turned *Tempest* toward home.

~

"Well, well." Captain Sulac stood, arms folded across his chest, glaring at the Vellosian seated at the table in room a1C, a small, stark room reserved for interrogation.

"Imagine my surprise," Amans continued, "at seeing you here."

The Vellosian, a low-ranking ships technician, sat uncomfortably in a stiff backed chair, under the glare of the overhead lights. He looked up at Amans. "Am I supposed to know you?"

Amans ignored the question. "You were brought here because you were overheard telling an acquaintance," Amans looked up at the ceiling as he recalled a fact or two, then leveled a look at the Vellosian, "I believe you had met at the Karona Bar on Brenton Kae, that you have information pertaining to Vellosian participation in certain illegal activities."

The Vellosian shrugged his indifference.

Amans smiled. "You will tell me this information. I assure you." He stepped to the door, opened it and addressed the two guards standing outside, "Take him to Department S, and remand him to Major Sarti. No comm, no food, no water."

Then turning to the Vellosian, "We will see how strong your will is very shortly. Also," Amans' voice was dripping with sucrose, "your Vellosian counterparts will not be informed that you are here with us. You are very much alone."

The guards stepped in and roughly grappled the Vellosian to his feet, half dragging him out the door and down the hallway.

Amans stood for a long moment watching the figures retreat down the hall then turned to go about his day.

"An interesting turn of events. A Vellosian among the throngs of privateers brought in." Amans was very pleased. *"This has opened up another avenue of possibilities. Yes. An interesting turn of events."*

~

The team had assembled as Tåsan requested and now were scattered about the loft space attentive and ready.

Tåsan had been small talking about this maintenance list and that upgrade idea when he turned the subject team-wide.

"Is everyone generally happy with the rewards we've garnered? I'm talking about the rewards we've received as a team. Have they been adequate?" Tåsan paused, expecting an answer

375

that came in the form of several positive comments along with satisfied looks and big smiles.

"Good. I'm glad because what I'm about to say should not come as too much of a surprise." Tåsan pulled in a breath and quickly organized his next sentence. "I've been put on the trail of a fairly lucrative heist. It should play out as the largest take we have ever seized. We will need mercenary reinforcement, a pretty good strategy, and a fool-proof getaway plan."

The team looked expectant.

"And this brings me to my main point," Tåsan hesitated just long enough for his team, Luan, Annis, and Alyss, to turn their full attention to him. "I've decided that this will be the last heist."

Annis nodded her head as she considered the news.

Luan had a look that said she had been expecting Tåsan to find another occupation sooner that later.

Alyss just smiled her encouragement and agreement.

"We've been highly successful in our pursuit of riches," Tåsan said. "So much so that I almost don't know what to do with it all." He then gave a short laugh and added, *"Almost."* To which there were agreeable comments.

"Be very clear about this heist," Tåsan said, "it's big, it's important, and it will not be without risk." He looked around before continuing. "The IGC has increased its law enforcement presence and their fire power. They're very serious about making a reputation for themselves and have become unpredictable except that they are dangerous. *That's* predictable."

Tåsan stood up and noticed that his legs were a bit stiff. He stretched them out as he spoke, "Ready your stations and your weapons. We fly in one quad. I'll have more for you then."

Part Three

The Descent
Into
Redemption

The fog was thick and acrid and burnt Tåsan's eyes as he strained to find his way forward, one thought turning over and over again in his mind, *"I've been here before."* His advance was slow as he picked his way over and around...were those rocks? stumbling and bracing for a fall. Tåsan managed to keep his feet but his progress was impeded to the point of frustration. But on he went.

Just as his abilities started to ebb and his muscles fail, a faint voice sounded in his ear, "There you are."

Tåsan froze, straining to hear more. He stood for what could have been an eternity before the voice, barely audible now, sounded again, "Where have you been?"

Tåsan dared not utter a sound for fear of breaking his concentration. His breathing shallow, his heartbeat slowing, Tåsan gradually turned his head from right to left as he tried to peer past the now disappearing fog.

Suddenly a hand thrust forward, startling him with its closeness. He was sure he hadn't seen anyone so near him. Where could that have come from?

"Take my hand," the voice said, sounding clear and unmistakable.

Confusion began to cloud his mind, but Tåsan blinked his eyes shut and opening them again, strained to focus. This was help. He reached out and felt the firm, strong grasp take hold of him and begin to pull him forward. His fingers were held tight as if in a vice. Concern turned to awareness and then Tåsan heard the voice again.

"You will have to pay for what you have achieved."

One

Insidious Footfalls

Emboldened by the small gains forward, Captain Amans Sulac decided that a marked increase in the IGC crackdown on crime was long overdue. He ordered more IGC presence throughout the three galaxies and assigned six additional long distance Battle Class-W's to patrol the Allodial Expanse.

Amans felt that the increased level of offence, an active approach to finding and punishing the Altruistic Outlaw, was justified.

It all seemed to be moving along according to Amans' grand plan, which pleased him to no end, until late one day a very disturbing report came in.

The details were sketchy at first. There had been an altercation some vectors out, close to the Niles Galaxy outer stars. An IGC ship had encountered what appeared to be a robbery in progress. They immediately called for support that was rendered to them by a Class-W within minutes. Upon entering the given vector, the Class-W found the IGC ship engaged in weapons exchange with two unidentified ships and they wasted no time as they immediately joined the fray.

Amans sent out a communiqué demanding more information and in short time it came.

A shuttle full of patrons leaving the Niesus Resort had begun a rendezvous with a larger ship, a Class-VII, that was to take them to a main terminal on Sador and from there they would arrange for individual transportation needs.

The shuttle had just arrived when a privateer ship swooped in and fired haphazardly, disabling its guidance array before it turned and fired at the Class-VII, that by this time was firing back.

The IGC ship engaged in battle immediately and when the Class-W arrived, the scene had taken on the appearance of a full out war. The Class-W wasted no time. It blasted the privateer ship to fragments and mistaking the shuttle for a second aggressor, sent a well-placed UV blast that blew it in half.

The result was gruesome. An estimated eight privateers were dead and the maimed bodies of twenty resort patrons floated slowly through space mixed with pieces of three ships and bits of luggage.

Amans was furious. It was as if all his work, all his strategizing, and all his plans had been for nothing. All wiped out in the length of a breath. He immediately ordered a lockdown on the scene. A cleanup was to be completed now and all situational data transferred to him before being deleted from the source devices, cleaning up yet another incompetent mess.

He had to think.

• • •

"There has to be guarantees," Delegate Mekela Kress said with finality. He was sitting on a rather comfortable sofa situated at the far end of Captain Sulac's office. He sat with his arms folded across his chest, jaw set, looking rather defiant.

Seated opposite and looking slightly perturbed at Kress' persistent obstinate nature, Amans choked back the urge to have Kress thrown into solitary confinement and be done with it.

Kress spoke again, "There is nothing I can help you with if my requests are not met." He stared blankly at Amans. "Now," he continued, his voice softening, "we've been talking so much but gaining very little, how about a drop or two of brandy to set us both right?"

Amans stared for a short length of time at the delegate before picking up his e-pad and entering a sentence or two. He thought to himself, *"I can see he is unmovable,"* then aloud, "Yes, I agree, Delegate Kress, my aide will be here shortly…"

Just then the aide slipped through the door steadying a tray holding an ornate jasper decanter and two carved quartz tumblers that he set on a low table in front of Amans and left as silently as he came.

"The finest brandy known to the three galaxies, from the

380

exclusive House of Rytos of Metamere. You may have heard of them, Delegate?"

"I'm aware of them, certainly. They are rumored to be an excellent distillery. Possibly good enough to rival the oldest houses of distinction of Vellosia." Kress leaned forward in anticipation.

Amans slowly poured a short measure of the dark, thick liquid into the tumblers, over the thin strips of citrus peel at the bottom. He could see the anticipation on Kress' face. *"Good,"* Amans thought, as he handed the drink to Kress.

• • •

"So. We have an agreement," Amans pronounced, his voice barely covering the exasperation he felt.

The last two hours were spent in discussion with the Vellosian delegate, Mekela Kress, but to Amans it was an exhausting two hours spent arguing.

Amans ordered another bottle of Rytos brandy be brought in because Delegate Kress displayed a serious tolerance to its intoxicating properties. Something Amans had not counted on. Then he furtively told his aide to, "Sit over there, be quiet and record everything."

Kress said, "I would like to go over each point," he smiled, "So there can be no mistakes, ah, for clarity. Don't you agree?" Kress smiled again much like a reed feline might do before devouring its prey.

Amans smiled back, nodding as he answered, "Of course, Delegate Kress. Anything to satisfy." Then thinking, *"You'll be smiling out the other side of your face before we're through."* And turning to his aide, wagged his hand indicating that he wanted the aide's e-pad given to him.

"Point one," read Amans. "Delegate Mekela Kress will not be prosecuted, according to ISA corporate rule of law for," Amans paused to look up at Kress who was tipping his tumbler of brandy to his lips, "treason," he said in a tone of finality.

Kress nodded at Amans and saluted with a wave of his hand.

Amans could feel anger just behind his tongue but held himself in check. Continuing, "This would include any Vellosian currently in detention. Moving on," Amans paged the e-pad forward. "Point two contains this verbiage…To avoid criminal charges for aiding,

381

abetting, collusion, or rendering any level of assistance or cooperation to the criminal dubbed the Altruistic Outlaw, you will name that outlaw and all known associates of said outlaw upon the immediate signing of this binding document."

Kress was pouring yet another glass of brandy. "Yes, yes." He pushed back into the cushions with an audible sigh of pleasure.

Amans continued, "Point three. Vellosian membership in the ISA is revoked for one solar year. At the end of said time, you may reapply and be reviewed and considered for new membership." Looking at Kress he thought, *"How nice to be bored with the legal implications of impropriety looming over you,"* Amans' anger was slipping out of control. "Point four," he almost spat. "All future activities involving any Vellosian in any sector of the three galaxies will be strictly monitored. And," Amans set the e-pad down and straightened his back. "And any action that you take, not specifically covered by this legal and binding document will be considered outside the scope of this document and subject to scrutiny and/or legal proceedings that could include, Delegate Kress," his tone sharp, his eyes steady, "prosecution to the fullest extent."

Kress glanced over at Amans. "Sounds so serious."

Amans shrugged. "Could include a prison sentence."

"Ahh," Kress said, "such are the legalities of the ISA." He then set his empty tumbler down on the tray that held the second empty bottle of Rytos brandy and struggled to move his weight to the edge of the sofa and gain his feet. Once standing, he brushed his clothes smooth and faced Amans.

"I insist upon one other detail. A very important one." Kress was steady and his voice level. "I, and by extension any Vellosian, will not be held responsible, in any way, for any damage resulting from our little collaboration. Furthermore," Kress tilted his head and looked for any sign of agreement from Amans, "if successful, and it will be I assure you, my fee stands at forty percent."

Mekela Kress stood waiting for Amans to react one way or the other. Getting nothing, he continued, "When you have that finalized," he waved a hand at Amans' e-pad, "and approved and stamped and validated," Kress said, "or whatever it is you need to do, contact me. I'll be aboard my ship, *Salvificus*." Kress moved toward the door and the aide jumped to open it.

"Thank you for the brandy, Captain Sulac. It was a delight."

Amans waved the aide out and sat quietly, deep in thought. He could not help but to think there was something Kress was not telling. He seemed too uninterested in the legal repercussion of his actions, as if it all had meant nothing. *"There's something more,"* ran through Amans' mind. *"There's something more."*

For the better part of an hour, Amans sat and thought about all the data and the whisperings concerning the outlaw, his prime objective. And as he sat, several more puzzle pieces fit together. It seemed odd, didn't it, that the Vellosians directly profited from multiple robberies of IGC property? How could that have occurred if not from direct involvement? They had to have directed the outlaw menace to the IGC property. Provided intelligence. Maybe even participated.

"So. Delegate Mekela Kress. I will win this game of secrets you think yourself so clever at playing. You will not leave the three galaxies unmarked," Amans declared as he sent out another directive to his field agents.

• • •

It took close to four painfully slow weeks for Amans to compile the information he desired. His operatives and agents had squeezed every last bit of information possible out of suspects and informants and had shadowed Vellosian ships throughout their travels and in doing so, uncovered a wealth of evidence that implicated them in several punishable crimes.

Today, Delegate Mekela Kress was back in Amans office, under what Kress thought was an invitation to sign their previous agreement.

Amans was seated at his massive desk and did not stand when Kress was escorted in by the aide, who had beckoned Kress to sit in the visitor chair opposite Amans.

Kress, visibly uncomfortable in the barely cushioned straight-backed chair said, "Ahh, Amans, couldn't we move to the more comfortable sofa?"

"No." Amans looked up from his e-pad and stared intensely across the desk at Kress before he rose from his seat to then stand, leaning against the front of his desk, arms folded, staring at the

Vellosian seated before him.

"You've been informed as to why you are here?" Amans asked.

Mekela Kress smiled a friendly smile and replied, "Yes, I'm afraid so." But offered no other comment.

"There have been further developments in your case," Amans paused, then said, "Mekela," his voice dripping with an offensive tone, "that we need to discuss. It seems that you have been implicated in a series of crimes, many of which are considered to be subversive in nature." Amans statement lacked a friendly manner. "Subversive to the Intersolar and Space Alliance, to which you belong, and," unfolding his arms and standing up straight, "to the Inter-Galaxy Command."

Mekela Kress laughed nervously and spread his hands outward as he said, "I'm not exactly sure what it is you are referring to."

"How about this for example," Amans said, "Let's refer to the robbery of an IGC transport ship where one hundred bottles of Ashado flower and fruit liquor were taken and that mysteriously showed up on the market less than a half-quad later."

"That could have been done by anyone," the delegate protested.

"But it wasn't," Amans glared at Mekela Kress. "It was done by a specific outlaw. One you have had clandestine meetings with."

"I protest!"

"Save it, Delegate Kress," Amans spat the words out in disgust. "Save it for your hearing."

Mekela Kress was visibly shaken and darted his eyes back and forth as if searching for an argument or at least a plausible explanation.

Amans regained his captain's chair at the head of his desk before continuing. "You see," Amans spoke calmly, "I was not quite satisfied by our last meeting. I was bothered by something, something I could not put a finger to." Amans almost laughed at the curious look on Kress' face. "Naturally I did what any officer would do when faced with a situation such as I found myself in…I ordered my troops, if you will, into battle." Amans smiled at his little play on words and leaning back, said, "As a result, several very valuable, new and interesting facts have come to light."

Amans smiled deliciously as he explained...

It seemed that in addition to IGC surveillance of Vellosian trade routes, the ISA had made note of their direct contacts with various Vellosian traders and had shared this information and their impressions of the Vellosians among themselves. After a short amount of time, the ISA had built a sizable database of information. Enough so that a map of their trade routes had been built. "The ISA is nothing if not thorough in their business dealings," Amans had said.

The ISA trade route map was overlaid onto the IGC's observations of Vellosian meanderings, "And guess what this provided?" Amans had asked as Kress fidgeted in his seat.

The trade route meanderings map was overlaid once more with a record of IGC freight lines and, "Behold," Amans smiled, "it revealed two positive points where Vellosian ship movements intersected with crimes against IGC and ISA transports."

The ISA also turned over copies of their long list of complaints against the Vellosian merchants, alleging that the Vellosians employed underhanded methods in their agreements, frequently substituting inferior goods where valuable goods had been promised. "That, my dear Mekela, is fraud," Amans had added.

Mekela Kress was dumbfounded by the accusations. He sat motionless except for his eyes that nervously moved back and forth as he searched his mind for words, any words that would defend him from the charges Amans had put forth. None came.

Amans, truly enjoying the moment, let Kress squirm for two more moments, and then continued. "And if that isn't enough to have you detained for many...many...quads, I have here in my hands," lifting his e-pad and nodding at Kress, "proof that you have worked with this wanted outlaw in the past. Most recently during the robbery of a shipment of uridium-8 from a Chelic Corporation freighter."

Kress tried to protest but Amans held up his hand to stop him. "Tut-tut, Delegate. Don't waste your words. Your ship was seen at vector 971E-3A on three occasions transferring goods from an unidentified Class-C interceptor to your holds. The ISA observer thought it odd that you were loading goods out in space and not at a qualified facility such as Brenton Kae. However, at the time, they let it pass, owing it to your rather unconventional ways."

Amans was thoroughly enjoying his superior position.

Kress was defeated. His face showed none of the bravado he usually displayed. He was looking at Amans, silently imploring him to have a small bit of compassion. He held up his hands in front of him and meekly asked, "Now what am I to expect?"

Amans smiled with his thought, *"I've got him."* Then he sat back, rested his elbows on his chair arms and locked his fingers together in a show of satisfaction. "Here's how this will now play out, Delegate Kress," his words sharp and clear. "First you will tell me everything you know concerning the outlaw menace, your every dealing with him, and every rumor you've heard. Leave nothing out."

Amans touched an iconograph on his e-pad, summoning his aide, who immediately rushed through the door and took a seat behind and off to Amans' right. He sat easy, staring noncommittally at Kress.

"Second, you will approach this criminal and enlist his and his associates expertise in the commission of a very rewarding robbery." Amans looked at Kress and watched as resignation settled his features. "For this, you may freely leave the three galaxies and IGC space for one solar year."

Amans watched Kress closely. "Do you agree?"

The delegate looked optimistic, as if a lifeline had just been delivered.

Amans could not have been more pleased.

Mekela Kress sat quietly for only a brief moment before speaking, "I humbly apologize for having misjudged you in the past. I do agree to your proposal," and bowing his head slightly, added, "When do we begin?"

Two

Iniquity Flares

As Delegate Kress talked, the overall picture of the crime events that Amans was focused on, became much more clear. Amans had pushed the interrogation along with questions and requests for dates, locations, and other clarifications. And his analytic mind had raced along sorting, comparing, and filing.

Five hours in, Amans noticed that Kress had lost some of his energy and the color had drained from his face. He had called for a break and invited Kress to sit on the sofa to which he quickly agreed. In the meantime, Amans had reviewed the session notes, culling pertinent data and building a profile of the Altruistic Outlaw that was leaving little doubt as to his identity.

After another three hours, Amans had called for the session to end and for Kress to be detained.

"You will be our visitant until our business has concluded," Amans had informed Kress. "Refresh yourself. We will meet sometime later to develop our strategy."

That was hours ago.

In the intervening time, Amans reviewed and considered all that had transpired that day and on previous days and the more he thought, the more convinced he became. And the more convinced he became, the more anger built until finally, snapping out of his obsessive deliberations, Amans snatched up his coat and left his office.

• • •

Amans arrived home late. He had called for a family meeting, asking Rebetta, Arron, and Stellanova to be present.

"I thought you should hear what I have to say before it becomes common place news."

The small group, seated in the living space, waited quietly for Amans to continue.

"Some weeks ago I began an investigation into a notorious crime wave and since then have uncovered many facts. Facts that have served to build an almost undeniable profile of the main criminal involved." Amans jumped to his feet and took two quick paces across the room before turning back to his family.

Stellanova, clearly aware of her father's barely controlled anger, gently asked, "What is it, Father? What has upset you so?"

Amans pulled in a strong breath of air and measurably let it back out in order to control his voice as he spoke the next words. "It's Tåsan. Tåsan is the Altruistic Outlaw the IGC seeks."

Confusion and questions erupted.

"Are you sure of this, Amans?" asked Rebetta, clearly distressed.

"I am not the least surprised," said Arron, slowly shaking his head in condemnation.

"It's not true," Stella demanded.

"There is irrefutable proof. Sightings, witnesses, testimony," Amans said with finality. "I do not like to be argued with, Stellanova. You would do better to hold your tongue."

Rebetta started to cry in her shock and anguish and Stella moved to her side to comfort her, murmuring, "It's not true, Mother. It's not true."

Amans waited as his family quieted down from their initial shock. "When I began to put it all together, I did not want to believe it either. But as evidence piled up, I could not deny it any longer." Amans could not control the anger that had been roiling under the surface for some hours but steadied himself and said, his voice sharp with renewed anger, "He has betrayed me. He has betrayed this family."

"That's a very strong accusation, Father," Stella said.

Amans rounded on her, "You have been warned to hold your tongue, Stellanova. You do not know what I know. You are in no position."

Stella shrank back from the scolding and sat quietly as Amans ranted for minutes and minutes about all he had done for Tåsan, how he had enabled Tåsan's career, given him solid advice, had made himself available, and on and on.

Eventually Rebetta calmed herself enough to ask, "How are you going to handle this, Amans?"

"Yes," Amans huffed. "This revelation has put me in grave concern for my career. This scandal would jeopardize everything I've worked for. I have thought on this long and hard." He looked at his family's upturned faces. Rebetta and Stellanova showed signs of expectation. Arron showed resignation. Amans continued, "I will treat this situation no differently than if the criminal was any other low-life being. I will be as harsh as need be to prove there will be no nepotism. Prove beyond any slight doubt that I will not adversely influence IGC law in any manner. I will not tolerate any interference to my career."

Questions, comments, murmurings, and choked voices babbled on for a number of moments. Amans ignored it all.

"I advise you all to hold this information to yourselves." Amans gave a severe look to each of the three. "I will not be moved on this. Do not question me further."

And with the last word spoken, Amans left the group and shut himself into his study, remaining there until the early hours.

Three
Modus Operandi

The predawn began its slow progress toward a brighter sky, obscuring the night, and covering the cold stars with the promise of the day to come. The distant call of an Avabird, flying high above, announced its presence and a small breeze stirred the underbrush.

Tåsan shifted in his sleep and then slowly opened his eyes to the brightening haze of his loft space. He had been away from Corvus Space for a number of weeks and had almost forgotten what it felt like to sleep in a real bed under familiar and warm covers. He lay for scant minutes reveling in its warmth until he was moved to rise for the day.

Today would be busy. Tåsan had arrived home late the night before and had left *Tempest* where she was berthed without doing his post-flight maintenance. He would need to see to that today.

And so he did. With Nikliss and Dhagáin's expertise to assist, all flight and engineering systems were checked, refueling done, and armaments restored. As all system reports were logged as successfully concluded, Tåsan completed the final inspection of *Tempest's* outer hull, her arrays, and her intakes, occasionally running his hand over her smooth, cool surface.

It was late afternoon when all the checklist items had been completed and in reflection on the work, Tåsan was very pleased. The number of systems needing recalibration or tweaking was minimal and the range of differences miniscule. *Tempest* was true.

Tåsan thanked Nikliss and Dhagáin for a good days work and coaxed them to take the evening off, to relax. He, himself, was going to retire up to the loft to work. He would see them on the morrow.

From the remnants of root vegetables and vine berries he found in the galley stores, Tåsan put together a large bowl of warm grains and seeded fruitlets and made a place for himself at the loft table among his various notepapers and e-pad schematics. As he sat munching his meal, his thoughts ran over the work he had affected during the past weeks while away as he decided on what was to be his final heist.

In his typical approach to any given heist, Tåsan first considered the logistics...where would be the first and best location to engage, how valuable are the goods, what resistance to taking said goods would they encounter, and most importantly, what is the pay-out.

Tåsan smiled to himself, *"Tenges in, tenges out."*

This particular heist was vastly important to Tåsan. It was to be his last one, and to his way of thinking, it should be big and as a way to thank his team and his various colleagues, it should be rewarding.

After several hours of reading and rereading his notes, reviewing flight paths, considering which fence or dealer would be best for offloading and would they be available or not, Tåsan got down to logistics. His intel had advised him to be prepared to encounter mid-level security, so Tåsan wanted to line up several mercenaries to round out the team and act as guards. Tåsan was also given ships schematics so had worked out where and what it would take to breach the hull, and how to quickly locate and remove the goods, that to Tåsan's annoyance, seemed to be spread throughout three different cargo bays.

"Well okay," he had thought, *"Inconvenient but not that tricky."*

The consideration that took a great deal of Tåsan's attention was the escape route. It had to be fast and it had to be precise. It also had to be peppered with rendezvous with his contacts, each prepared to receive and pay for the agreed upon goods in a timely fashion. Minutes counted.

After all the goods were sold and tenges collected, Tåsan would fly *Tempest* to a pre-designated coordinate, pay off his team and the mercenaries, and have them disembark *Tempest* to their private transports and then to go their own way.

At this point, Tåsan would fly *Tempest*, with Alyss as co-pilot,

391

either back to Corvus Space or to somewhere else. He hadn't quite made his mind up about this but felt that even an impromptu decision at the last minute on the matter would be fine. Maybe he and Alyss would take a jaunt together. Maybe she would like to go to Erontu, visit her father, and camp in the outback for a week while thinking about the next phase of their lives. *"She dreams of a big house on a large piece of land. Maybe we can figure out what that might look like,"* Tåsan mused.

Tåsan leaned back and looked at the papers and e-pads in front of him. They were no longer a scattered bunch of data and maps strewn about the table. They were organized and coherent. They were solid plans and schedules and Tåsan was very satisfied.

"This is going to work," he thought.

After taking a break from the plans and stepping outside for a breath of the chilly night's air, Tåsan decided that a neat tumbler of Tradorian Berrywine would be nice. He also decided to use the next hour to contact his receivers to set up times and coordinates affixing the schedule into a smooth, fast transition. Afterward he would rest. It had been a good night's work.

Tomorrow, Tåsan would go into Lower Merula to meet with Fiann to talk about his interest in joining the team for one last profitable event, and could he recruit eight other trustworthy individuals to join them.

Things were coming together nicely.

• • •

"Well, this is it," said Tåsan. He had welcomed his team back to Corvus Space about an hour earlier that morning. He had provided a large pot of tea and invited everyone to get as comfortable as they could as they waited for a small band of mercenaries to arrive, which they did about twenty minutes later, roaring in on modified jet-bikes, 4-seat hoppers, and charged out Class-N's.

Tåsan let everyone settle down before addressing the group. "I know we've all talked to one another during the past dozen weeks, so we all know, without surprise, that this heist is the last heist we will work on together. Before getting down to details, let me say up front that this journey has been exhilarating…and profitable," he said, cocking his head and smiling. "And I've loved every minute of it."

Small chatter and huffs of laughter softly rippled through the group. Tåsan continued.

"Let's start with the prize. There is a Class-K transport, the *Steady-1* that will be loaded with pricy goods whose last scheduled stop before proceeding to an auction house on Titus, is Halide on Metamere. When *Steady-1* leaves Metamere space it will be hauling treasure such as we have never seen." Tåsan picked up his e-pad and read, "Art and artifacts, rare and highly sought after paintings and statues, objects from an ancient civilization dig site on Eros. Technology," Tåsan emphasized, "*cutting* edge technology bordering on revolutionary…Spacial reality augmenters, a 4-D converting device, robotics and drones, and my personal favorite," Tåsan put the e-pad down, "neural interfacing devices." He looked around. Many of the mercs looked confused. Tåsan said, "Trust me, these items will fetch top tenges." At which the mercs then smiled and nodded. Tenges they understood.

"The payout will be substantial and once we understand the logistics and security of the *Steady-1*, the risks should be manageable," Tåsan said. "Are we ready to go to work?" he asked. Tåsan had been standing as he addressed the group but now moved to take a high stool at the long table and he bid the others to join him.

The next hour was spent reviewing the technical layout and readiness of *Steady-1*, storage bay locations and the easiest way to gain entry, location of the most valuable goods and a list and description of them, bridge location, and course and speed.

There were discussions about crew compliment, how many would join security to defend, where would the most resistance likely play out, and did Tåsan know what weapons might be used.

"On-board weapons use would be limited to something that would not pierce the inner and outer hulls so I would expect that a D7R-Laz would be at the top end," Tåsan replied. "Although my advice is to be prepared but not to the point where you are the cause of a hull failure."

The discussions continued for a bit longer until it seemed to Tåsan that just about every aspect of the heist had been covered. He then asked if there were any questions.

Alyss asked if *Steady-1* would have escort ships since it was carrying such a valuable cargo.

"No," Tåsan had answered, "There has been no news-comm at all about this. It's believed they're relying on secrecy to shore up their security."

Fiann wanted a little more guidance on personal weaponry and wanted to know who was responsible for the explosives.

"Side arms are your personal choice, however, bring an adequate number of rounds and charges. Also, I recommend lightweight body armor, but make sure it does not slow you down. I need you to be able to do your jobs as described. Timing is important. Explosives are mine."

Tåsan nodded at Annis, acknowledging her question.

"How reliable is the source of this intelligence?" she asked.

"Very," Tåsan started, "I have met with three independent sources and all of them have outlined almost the same things about schematics, systems, weapons, schedules, and crew," he said. "I've found that these sources have, in the past, been extremely reliable. They're Vellosian." Tåsan smiled, "They like profit." He looked around, waiting for anything further.

"Okay." Tåsan concluded. "Make your preparations. I will see you again at the pick/drop point, fully charged and ready to fly in exactly two days and," glancing at his e-pad, "nine hours."

Luan rose to go to the galley. The mercs ambled out to their rides, jostling each other and laughing at jokes. Alyss descended the stairs and disappeared among the workbenches and Annis lingered behind wanting to speak with Tåsan privately.

"If fortune favors us, Tåsan," Annis smiled, "this heist will not be the last time we meet," and from her pocket she drew a small silk packet and offered it to Tåsan.

He looked slightly surprised as he reached out to accept the gift.

Annis continued, "During my last journey into the wilds, I was moved to find these stones. At first I wasn't sure why this was so important as they did not really belong to me. But as I held the stones and gazed at their every feature, it became clear. The stones belong to you."

Tåsan was holding an amulet that was hung from a braided titanium cord, up to the light so he could see it more clearly.

"The largest stone," Annis said, "is black phantom quartz. It inspires courage and resolve."

"Something I will need a lot of in the days to come," Tåsan quipped.

Annis nodded, a faint smile shown over her thoughts. "The green stone is an obsius stone that represents love and compassion and the last stone, the dark one with green hues and red splotches is a bloodstone." She took a brief moment to watch as Tåsan held the amulet close so he could look at its details. "Bloodstone is strength, it is courage, and it is vitality."

Annis paused and when Tåsan looked up at her, she said, "It is you, Tåsan. What you are and what you will be."

"This is priceless," Tåsan said as he slipped the cord around his neck and adjusted the stones to hang straight. "Thank you."

"Yes." Annis was glad. "Good." Then added, "We meet again in two days and...eight and one half hours." And smiling, she turned to go.

Four

Nothing to Chance

As *Tempest* neared parsec 107e5-A, Tåsan verified that the last of his buyers were standing by and ready to receive the goods they had bid for. He had plotted a fast escape course through the Allodial Expanse, lining up the drop-offs in order to make their get-away as succinct as possible. Now he was on the bridge, peering out into the darkness ahead and checking the lighted display screens along *Tempest's* console.

"Slow to inertial frame 5.8, Alyss."

"Aye."

Tempest slowed to her position some number of vectors out from where *Steady-1* would escape Metamere's atmosphere and gain course and speed as they headed for Titus.

The plan was to intercept *Steady-1* approximately seventy two hundred nolans away from Metamere just as it reached the outer stars of Rayten Galaxy. *Tempest* would shadow *Steady-1* to the designated coordinates then immediately disable her comm and nav arrays, then move into position and execute the heist as discussed.

Alyss would hold *Tempest* steady. Annis would stay on weapons and defense, plying offense where needed. Tåsan and Fiann would seal the bridge, trapping a number of crew within then make their way to the cargo bays. Luan and Aben would lead some of the mercenaries to the holds and manage the appropriation of the exact goods they were after, while the remaining mercs would provide security. As each transport was loaded and ready, it would deploy back to *Tempest*.

If there were no glitches, the heist would move forward smoothly and methodically. It could all be over in less than thirty-five minutes, and that timed out to be so much faster than a rescue ship could effect an arrival. Tåsan was confident that that wouldn't happen because all possible contingencies had been accounted for.

"Sensors have picked up *Steady-1* two thousand nolans from Rayten's outer stars," Alyss announced.

Tåsan touched his sen-dev. "Ten minute countdown. Ready yourselves," he announced to his extended team.

Steady-1 emerged through the outer stars and repositioned her course. *Tempest* held her position and moved along keeping pace with *Steady-1* but staying outside sensor range.

"Two minutes," Tåsan announced, then looked to Alyss, "Ready?" he asked.

"Yes, all systems are ready," she replied.

"On my mark," Tåsan held his gaze on the console steady. "Initiate," he directed.

Alyss lit the engines and *Tempest*, with assured power, leapt forward to her command and overtook *Steady-1* in less than one minute.

By the time *Tempest* was alongside *Steady-1*, Annis had plied three surgical laz-cannon shots that cut the comm and nav arrays and severed one of the propulsion engines, sending it floating away in a cloud of sparks.

The mercenaries, led by Tåsan's team, disgorged from *Tempest's* loading bay doors quickly followed by Tåsan and Fiann, who shot forward to the outer hatch that would lead them to the bridge. They quickly gained entrance and made for the bridge, but were stopped by a small band of armed security. Tåsan tossed a percussion cap down the hall that stunned the guards, sending them down to the floor. He and Fiann made the distance to the bridge entrance and wasted no time melting it shut with handheld laz blasters.

Once inside the cargo holds, Luan posted guards at the door and led Aben and the remaining mercs to the goods. They were quickly loading whatever Luan pointed to onto the transports when weapons fire turned their attention to one of the doors that led out to a corridor. Luan shouted to the mercs to pay attention to the grab and to step it up. When the first transport was loaded, she waved it off. She then turned and yelled out, "Kloet De! Help at

397

the bay doors!" Kloet De left what he was doing and rushed toward the doors, pulling his weapon to the ready as he disappeared among the stacked cargo containers.

Tåsan and Fiann did not make their way aft through the ship's corridors but before they left, Tåsan blasted the trans-lift controls and lobbed a QV down the connecting corridor. They went out the way they had come, mounting their transports and speeding along the outer hull to the blown cargo doors. On his approach, Tåsan saw one transport fly recklessly out through the breach and head for *Tempest*. As he and Fiann rounded through the jagged gap in the hull, they were assaulted by weapons fire and quickly dismounted and ran for cover.

A second transport, awkwardly loaded with goods, rumbled past them out into space.

Alyss' voice sounded in Tåsan's sen-dev, "Ships approaching at a high rate of speed." An instant later, *Tempest* loosed a series of cannon bursts. Tåsan turned his attention momentarily to *Tempest*, now framed through the ragged hull opening. Alyss was wrestling *Tempest* to starboard then to steady then to port, skillfully avoiding incoming UV cannon blasts. He turned to glance at Luan and Aben who had just completed loading a third transport. Firing for cover, Tåsan moved up through the containers, focused on the doors from the corridor where Kloet De and three mercs were fighting to hold their line. In the next instant, as Tåsan watched, a blinding flash of light exploded near the door and two of the mercs were lifted up and tossed backward, maimed and clearly dead. Two of the mercs protecting the transports immediately ran forward to cover the now open positions. One took a blast to the chest and fell lifeless to the floor.

Tåsan touched his sen-dev and commanded, "Away! Everyone away!"

Chaos erupted as mercs and team scrambled to escape while still firing on the oncoming security, who by then had broken through the corridor doors and were spilling into the cargo hold and advancing.

Tåsan threw two QVs. One rolled out the doorway and ignited in a hot flash of destruction, causing security to retreat. The other blew a stack of containers into shards of molten metal and sparks, taking out much of the weapons fire that had been concentrated there.

Kloet De with only one merc still with him turned and ran toward their transports with Tåsan and Fiann providing cover fire. Luan, Aben, and two mercs had already cleared the hull and were fighting their way back to *Tempest*.

"Tåsan! Now!" commanded Alyss.

Fiann stood up and, walking backward, fired wildly in the direction of oncoming security, taking many of them out. He yelled to Tåsan, "Come!"

Tåsan bolted from his cover and ran to his transport just as Fiann mounted his and shot out the hull breach. Seconds later Tåsan followed after hesitating long enough to lob a fistful of QVs that blocked security from following.

As soon as the loading bay doors were pressurized, *Tempest* jerked to port and banked hard as she gained speed. Alyss and Annis quickly surmised that a clean get-away into the Allodial Expanse was impossible. The way was blocked by two IGC Battle Class ships, four cruisers, a large number of Class-C interceptors, and, on a high-speed course to their current coordinates, the crown jewel of the IGC, the *Ari Arcturus*.

Alyss called out to Annis, "The way is clear through Metamere space," and she ignited the thrusters.

Annis, her fingers flying and her eyes searching, said, "Course plotted and engaged."

"Aye," responded Alyss as she banked *Tempest* through a wild serpentine path toward Metamere.

Tåsan's voice sounded in Alyss' ear, "Report!"

"Escape through the Expanse is wholly blocked. I'm taking *Tempest* into Metamere space and out into the galaxy where I'm sure I can lose the Class-W's and *Ari Arcturus*." Alyss paused the briefest of moments waiting for Tåsan to comment on that little revelation. None came so she continued, "We may experience interference from the cruisers and interceptors but I am confident we can shake them."

Tåsan spoke, "I'm on my way." And in less than a minute he was on the bridge where he noted Alyss intent on piloting *Tempest* and Annis working weapons. "How are we doing?" he asked.

399

Alyss answered first, "Not as well as desired. The course through Rayten Galaxy was complicated enough but I'm afraid it's going to be more difficult. There's incoming ships, Class-C's from the surface."

Tåsan had strapped into the co-pilot's seat and busied himself with the logistics.

"Annis," he called out, "your success rate, please."

"With current weapons charges, maybe sixty percent kill rate." She answered. "The shields will fail if they take a small number of additional direct hits. I estimate as few as five." Annis looked up from her controls and screens.

"Orders, Tåsan?" Alyss queried, glancing at Tåsan whose brow was furrowed with concentration, his mind working to assess possibilities.

Those mere moments of silence passed as slowly as hours until Tåsan finally spoke. "Take her down to Metamere, land her as close to Halide as you can. We'll take our chances among the population of the city rather than try to scatter through the wildlands." Then flipping a ship-wide comm icon to address everyone, Tåsan said, "Our way through space is blocked. Our only choice is to land and attempt to escape as individuals." He hesitated. "Small fortune is with us today and if it holds we will meet again on the morrow. Until then, ready yourselves for an abrupt landing and hasty disappearance." Tåsan switched the comm off and speaking to Alyss, "Auto pilot as much as you can and ready your exit. I'll stay with *Tempest* and follow when I can." And turning to Annis told her, "Switch your console to mine and join Luan and the others in the loading bay."

Annis nodded and readied her consoles and stood up to leave the bridge. She exchanged a brief look with Alyss as she did so. Alyss smiled and held up her right hand so Annis could see the thin pink line of the rose quartz ring she wore. Annis held up her hand in return and smiled with sincere friendship then turned and left.

Tempest bumped and shivered as she dropped through Metamere's atmosphere. Tåsan said, "It's time, Alyss," and stood up, ready to take the pilot's station.

Alyss stood too, but in a moment of emotion, threw herself into

Tåsan arms and held him tight. "You will follow as soon as *Tempest* is down. Right," she said in more of a statement of fact than a question.

She was shivering slightly and Tåsan held her close. He pulled back just enough to look at her face, almost getting lost in her beautiful steady dark, cobalt blue eyes. "I will follow. Trust that we will see each other soon."

Alyss straightened up, declaring, "Good," and made her way to exit the bridge without looking back.

Tåsan quickly took over the controls just moments before *Tempest* broke through the upper atmosphere only slightly easing her descent speed. His plan was to plummet toward Halide, skimming the outskirts of the city until he spotted a likely landing site where he would set her down.

Luan's voice was in Tåsan's sen-dev, "Your DCM is ready."

"Aye, Luan," Tåsan said, "Thank you."

"Fortune to you. Fare well." And the sen-dev went silent.

Tempest rocked with an incoming UV blast but held as Tåsan returned fire and lowered her altitude five more clicks and steadily guided her down, down, down.

"There," he thought, *"There's the perfect zone."*

Tåsan struggled with the controls as two more UV blasts struck *Tempest* jerking her down and to starboard. When he got her fairly level again, he activated ship-wide comm and called out, "Away! Away at will!" trusting that the opportunity was clear to all.

Moments later, *Tempest* violently shuddered as she skimmed the planet's surface, the noise of which was deafening with sounds of metal screeching and the fuselage ripping apart until *Tempest* jarred and twisted to a sudden stop.

In an instant, Tåsan was on his feet and bolting toward the hold as sparks and smoke bellowed out from the bridge threatening to choke his lungs and blind his way. Entering the hold, Tåsan saw that all the DCMs, except his, were gone. The thought, *"Good. They made it,"* flew through his mind before he reached his DCM and fought to get it upright and ready to fly.

As he threaded his way out through the crushed hold doors, he was greeted by the sight of Kloet De lying on the ground with a huge blistery hole through his left side, his eyes staring wide but blank. Seven meters beyond, the bloody, twisted body of one of the mercs lay pinned under a smoking DCM.

At first sight, Tåsan feared he would find others but thankfully he was spared. The sounds of weapons fire whizzing past his head snapped Tåsan alert and he blasted the DCM forward in a direction that he thought was away from the shooters and toward the city's outskirts where he planned to lose himself on the city streets. Too late he realized he was in the middle of another firefight.

The sky was full of IGC interceptors holding their positions and firing cover for the many, many peacekeepers and local police that swarmed over the terrain shooting wildly.

Tåsan jammed his DCM to a halt and dove for cover. From the corner of his eye he spotted Fiann and Aben trying to pull one of their fallen companions out of the fray into a bit of safety along a back alley just behind them. As Tåsan turned to look more fully, Aben took a blast to the shoulder that violently twisted him around in silent pain as he fell backward, dead.

Fiann, seeing that helping his friends was of no use, fell back into the alley, taking aim and downing four IGC peacekeepers as he did.

Tåsan rushed forward, lobbing a QV that momentarily halted the throng of advancing peacekeepers and giving him the scant time he needed to make it to Fiann's side. Fiann nodded his surprise and managed a smile as he quickly reloaded his auto weapon and took aim. Tåsan nudged Fiann's arm in camaraderie and then also took aim and fired. He had stood up to make a clear shot when he saw a flash of weapons fire, aimed into the approaching peacekeepers, coming from roughly forty meters across from his position on the other side of the street.

It was Alyss. She was astride her DCM, now in pulse rocket mode, steering with one hand and blasting her sidearm with the other as she made her way toward Fiann and Tåsan.

Tåsan's thoughts were shocked into silence. He managed a faint croak before touching his sen-dev, "Whaaat?" he sputtered.

"Couldn't just leave," Alyss shouted, then turning her attention back to the battle, let out a war cry as she plowed forward.

The legion of peacekeepers and police seemed to grow in

402

number and soon were spilling into the alley and over the entire area such as a plague of hungry insects would do within sight of a grain field.

In the next moment, Tåsan felt slammed backward with the heavy force of a pressure such as he had never felt before. It blew his weapon from his grip and weakened his legs. He felt himself falling in slow motion and turned his eyes to Fiann.

Several peacekeepers had burst into the alley and were piling onto Fiann who struggled wildly in a futile effort to escape.

Tåsan then looked to Alyss. A number of peacekeepers mounted on jet bikes had pulled close to her and were forcing her to slow when one kicked her in her side, causing her to tumble off her rocket and into a mob of police that had surrounded her.

As Tåsan slowly fell backward, noise from the battle, yelling voices trying to be heard, and the fire and smoke that was all around him, started to fade and he knew then, as his eyes dimmed and his hearing receded, that he was losing consciousness. His last clear thoughts, before being overtaken by oblivion were for his team and for Alyss. He saw her face just before the darkness.

Five

A Pale Victory

Slowly, slowly, ever so slowly did awareness return to Tåsan. His head hurt and his eyes watered in the harsh artificial light and as he fought to wake fully, nausea swept over his aching and battered body. Soon, he realized that he was alone in a small, cold holding cell. As he tried to shift his body he found that he was held fast by chains around his wrists that led to a thick metal ring in the wall. As the fog in his head cleared, Tåsan heard a soft hum that emanated from far below that told him that he was aboard a ship and in transit...but to where?

The cell door opened with a scrape and a thud and in stepped Captain Cullen from the Inter-Galaxy Command. Tåsan had studied under Captain Cullen while still at the IGC academy, and liked him for his fairness and the genuine concern he always displayed for the trainees. However, the Captain's face was not filled with concern or sympathy now. It was cold and hard as he looked at Tåsan for what seemed a long quiet eternity before he spoke.

"Commander Sulac, you have led a group of hostiles and with them, have committed several heinous crimes which caused the direct death of many and the peripheral death of innocents. You are guilty. How guilty will be determined in a tribunal of law and judged by those appointed to hear your case and render a decision. Until that time when you will be brought before this tribunal, you will remain in the custody of the IGC under heavy guard."

"Sir," responded Tåsan, "How many of my crew members survived, who is here under confinement?"

"There were only three members of your nefarious group to be captured. A career criminal with a long list of serious infractions who goes by the name Fiann. A criminal of little consequence with

404

no proper identification papers that is simply being referred to as Case 41872. The third person of interest is someone you know. Her name is Alyss Brannick. All four of you will be tried and all four of you will be sentenced."

Tåsan's mind raced with the news that only three of his team were captured and wondered if any of the others had made it safely away. "Am I allowed to communicate with them?" he asked.

"No," was the only word Captain Cullen said before turning and leaving.

Less than five minutes had passed when the sound of the cell door lock disengaging brought Tåsan from his sullen thoughts.

Amans Sulac stepped through the opening followed by his aide who carried a chair into the cell and placed it a short measure from where Tåsan sat shackled.

"Father," said Tåsan in somber recognition.

Amans stood silently as the aide placed the chair and quietly left, closing the cell door behind him. Amans sat down never taking his eyes from Tåsan's face.

Tåsan waited.

Finally Amans spoke. "You have been the cause of so much pain and destruction." He fell silent. Tåsan could see the cords in Amans' jaw clamping down.

"Father, I..."

"Silence," Amans commanded, his voice low but firm. At last he spoke again, "The Altruistic Outlaw." Amans made a huffing sound as he forced air from his chest. "Such a nice distinction for such a ruthless black heart. Your crimes, the ones we know of, have spanned the three galaxies, caused a great loss of life, is to blame for the destruction of valuable property, and is directly responsible for a growth in crime never before witnessed. It may take generations to undo what you have done."

Tåsan had been looking at Amans as he spoke and had the feeling that deep down, Amans was enjoying himself although his outward appearance was coldly civil and to the point.

"And you had nothing to do with this," Tåsan said with a touch of accusation in his voice.

Amans ignored the comment. "You have betrayed me, Tåsan. You have betrayed your family, you have betrayed the IGC, and as bad as all those things are, they do not equal your betrayal of yourself." Amans suddenly stood up. "It seems your crimes have a greater value than your principles."

The door pushed open and the aide rushed in to retrieve the chair. Amans stopped at the open doorway and looked back at Tåsan. "There is a touch of irony here," he said with a wry smile. "Your ruination will be my success. For my facilitation of your capture, I've been promised a promotion." Amans shook his head, briefly looked at Tåsan, and left.

Six

Deep Into The Rabbit Hole

Tåsan was not certain of the next period of time. It could have been days, it could have been weeks.

The cell that held him was barren except for a metal frame for a bed, one blanket for warmth, and a glaring light fixed to a very high ceiling. It was a harsh light that was never turned off. It burned constantly. The only other object in the white box of a cell was a monitor array, its ever blinking lens always watching. In more lucid moments, Tåsan found this humorous as he was kept shackled to the wall, his movements were very limited. What was there to see?

Tåsan did not try to communicate with any of the guards that rarely entered his cell. They were wholly disgusted with him and let it be known by their angry glares or the under-their-breath snipes. They were IGC. Tåsan's biggest crime was that he used to be IGC but he was not IGC now.

The slow arduous journey from Metamere to the Inter-Galaxy Command station on Naiad Five took so long that Tåsan had begun to wonder if his cell, the angry guards, and the endless light weren't actually his punishment. Which always brought up the question of how long would it go on for.

Eventually the answer came. The transport ship docked at Brenton Kae and Tåsan was transferred to a shuttle. This he knew was happening because two guards came into his cell. One held a formidable sidearm aimed steadily at Tåsan's chest as the other unlocked his wrist shackles from the wall. Tåsan's legs were stiff and cramped with pain from inactivity and he stumbled as the guard pulled him upright and pushed him out the door.

Tåsan tried to hold himself with dignity. He had not lost his self-respect even if his appearance begged to differ. The sight of him, battered with old bruises and taped up gashes, and shuffling along in filthy clothing, could only bring up revulsion, *"Tinged with disgust,"* Tåsan thought with a silent smirk crossing his face.

It was nice to breathe fresh air and Tåsan greedily pulled in lungful after lungful as he limped from the shuttle to the facility where he would now be held.

They passed no one in the long, softly lit hallway Tåsan was marched down. As they moved along, he noticed e-screens at every doorway and knew they were monitors of the rooms beyond. None of the doors were labeled and all looked the same. No sounds emanated from behind any of the doors.

Tåsan became aware of the sound of his own footfalls as they echoed through the corridor and the isolation of it chilled his thoughts.

Tåsan was taken into a large room where he was handed a set of clean clothes and allowed to bathe. He took his time in the hot water and soaped himself twice, putting extra care into cleaning the cuts that dotted his arms and right leg and looking after the feverish gash on his forehead.

When he was dressed and feeling quite whole again, a guard pointed to a chair and told Tåsan to sit and wait for, "the doctor." The view from the chair was of a medical set-up. There were shiny tables and a glass-fronted sideboard that held miscellaneous items like bandages and ointments.

Presently, the hallway door pushed open and the doctor came through. It took Tåsan a scant breath of a moment to recognize his friend.

"Tao!" Tåsan said in his joy. Tao Vu was a comrade from the IGC training academy who had been assigned to *Ari Arcturus*, and was part of Tåsan's *Tempest* team.

Tao furrowed his brow and gave a faint but sharp shake of his head and said, "You will address me as Doctor Tao Vu or as Doctor. Nothing else. Understood?" he asked.

Tåsan was a bit taken back but answered, "Yes, Doctor."

Tao busied himself gathering supplies to the shiny topped table and rolled it over to where Tåsan sat. He hesitated a moment as he considered the items on the table.

"Ensign," Tao addressed the guard who stepped forward. "I don't seem to have the appropriate 20-M non-woven bandages. Go to the central supply and get them, please."

"But sir," the ensign waved his arm in Tåsan's direction and started to object but Tao spoke again.

"It's fine," he said, adding, "Where's he to go? Just hurry back."

"Yes, sir," said the ensign and was gone.

Tao turned to Tåsan, "Friend," he smiled.

"Oh, Tao," Tåsan managed before Tao cut him short.

"We must be quick," as he looked to the door and lowered his voice. "I have news. Luan got away. She outfitted her DCM with a prototype distortion unit that apparently works. She sent word shortly after. Annis made it away. She is fine. Alyss did not get away. They're holding her on another floor in this facility."

"Is she okay?" Tåsan asked.

"Yes. I've seen her. She's fine." Tao said to Tåsan, "Give me your arm," which Tåsan did allowing Tao to treat some of the major cuts on it. He continued, "No news of your capture has been made public. No one knows you are here."

Tåsan shook his head slowly as he took it all in.

Tao said as an afterthought, "The IGC also managed to capture a couple of career criminals."

"Fiann," said Tåsan.

"Yes, but I do not have access to him or the other fellow."

Just then the ensign returned with the bandages. Tao accepted them and silently resumed cleaning and stitching Tåsan's wounds. The ensign resumed his position as guard and all conversation ceased.

A scant half an hour later Tao was gone and Tåsan was being taken back down the hall and introduced to his new cell. It was exactly like the other but with a small table and two hard-backed chairs.

"Well at least that's something," was Tåsan's only thought.

~

Exhaustion took its toll and the payment was sleep. Uneasy sleep.

"Where...," Tåsan uttered vaguely as he struggled

409

back to consciousness, willing the dark swirling fog to leave his mind and clear his vision. He closed his eyes tightly in an effort to block the brightness that flooded in but could not stop his thoughts from racing forward and jumbling into an almost incoherent babble.

"Where am I? And what is this place?" Tåsan rocked his head to the side and strained to hear anything that would help to answer his questions. By now his eyes were partly open although what he could see was blurry and misshapen. He tried to move but found his arms pinned as if by heavy weights and they remained non-responsive to his repeated actions to free them. He lay back, motionless.

As he lay quietly, Tåsan's mind calmed its frantic pace and he slowly became aware of the last few moments that played out across his mind, before...this. "But what is 'this'?" he had to ask. No answer came.

Tåsan relaxed his memory. *"We flew in, boarded and secured the crew, procured our goods, and then...and then all of a sudden we were under fire,"* he reviewed. *"That was no accident."*

Awareness blurred into a dark fog and once again Tåsan could feel his anger rise as he strained against it. Fighting the futility of his actions, he gave one last furious jerk that sharpened a pain in his hands. He dared to look at them and found they were broken and chipped and falling away and he could feel his chest tighten and his jaw set with hard, cold anger until suddenly, Tåsan could see clearly through the fog even though nothing was there. Anger and rage filled his head until he thought he would explode.

Tåsan knew who the betrayer was and he screamed out the name now burnt in his mind, "Amans Sulac...*Father!*"

410

Seven

Stubborn Facts

Three weeks after landing at the IGC flight field on his home world, word came that Tåsan's hearing would begin the following week. In the days that made up that week, Tåsan had several visits from various IGC officers whose main reason for coming was to inform Tåsan on court protocol and how he was to conduct himself during the official proceedings.

At one point, Tåsan had asked, "Will I be given an opportunity to speak on my behalf?"

And the answer was, "No. The judges do not need any level of discourse from you. However, they may ask you to clarify a piece of data or fill in a small detail but don't count on that. They have everything they need."

To which Tåsan asked, "So what's the point?"

The court officer had popped his head up from his e-notes as if shocked before the expression on his face faded to steel and his tone became insulted. "Tradition," was all he said.

When court officers decided that Tåsan's preparations were complete, the visits stopped and Tåsan was left to wait out the remaining time alone.

When the day arrived for Tåsan to be transported, armed IGC guards escorted him to a waiting chamber outside the main court gallery. It took two hours to fill the gallery with the landowners and other wealthy citizens from the ISA who were more than interested in a satisfactory resolution to the Altruistic Outlaw problem. Interestingly enough, a small group of Vellosians filed in and took seats close to the front. The remaining seats were filled up with IGC officers, relatives and friends of those who lost their lives, and a fair number of nosy and curious citizens and, of

411

course, those who never tire of observing their licit system in operation.

Tåsan sat facing a long narrow window in the stark, dimly lit holding room in which he was to wait until summoned into court. The window afforded a view of the court proceedings and Tåsan had watched with curiosity as the gallery slowly filled to capacity.

The armed guard that was assigned to Tåsan had warned him that he could not be observed or heard by any of the seven judges or by anyone in the gallery. "No words or actions from you will be tolerated," he had been informed. "It's best if you keep silent."

After all observers had registered and filed into the gallery, the Acting Tribunal Attendant called for silent attention and having deemed it so, beckoned the three attending judges and the four sub-judges to come forth. The judges filed in, taking their seats on the two-tiered dais at the far end of the court. The gallery was then duly admonished to keep silent throughout the orations. Any outburst would mean expulsion and a penalty. After the judges had whispered and conferred among themselves, the lights began to dim. As the lights were lowered, one could begin to make out a lone spotlight aimed at a small, round platform that stood in the center of the gallery in front of the highly polished judiciary bench.

Tåsan watched as a shackled prisoner was brought through the shadows and made to climb the two steps up to the lighted platform. Tåsan recognized that it was Fiann and studied him more closely. There were bandages on his left shoulder and the purple remnants of a facial injury lingering under his eyes. Otherwise he was upright and didn't look too worse for wear.

Fiann stood tall as the Acting Tribunal Attendant read the list of criminal charges. All the judges except one busied themselves rustling papers or looking at e-dev's giving Tåsan the impression that they were trying to keep up.

Tåsan peered through the distance in an attempt to look closer at the lone staring judge that sat leaning an elbow a little lazily on the right armrest of his high-backed chair with his cheek resting on his cupped hand. When the attendant finished reading the charges, this lone judge lowered his resting arm and leaned forward in his chair.

Tåsan pulled in a short breath as he recalled that face. It was

Magistrate Adrobach. The one and only Magistrate Adrobach of the *Starlight* Episode that Tåsan remembered as the single most certain point where the IGC began their systematic approach to undermining his IGC career.

Adrobach was speaking to Fiann. His tone was matter of fact and barely audible. "Case 80919, also know as Fiann, there is a long history of your erroneous behavior, however, you now find yourself standing here guilty of multiple homicides and the serious crime of larceny against Intersolar and Space Alliance members."

Fiann turned to the gallery and raised his arms up to encompass the spectators and loudly addressed his audience, "Justice! You call this IGC justice? I call it..."

At Fiann's interruption, Adrobach had waived a guard forward ordering him to silence Fiann.

The guard rushed forward and hit Fiann in the side with a hand weapon that discharged an electrical jolt that doubled him up and dropped him to the floor. He lay rolling and twitching, his face twisted into a grimace.

Tåsan's reaction was to bolt upright but he was acutely aware that his guard had moved forward and stood ready to intervene. He held his tongue and watched.

Adrobach picked up where he had left off. "You are guilty on all reports."

Fiann began to groan in pain and was attempting to stand up.

"All factors of your crimes have been recorded and considered."

The heavy chains that bound Fiann banged against the balusters that surrounded him as he gained his feet and turned toward Adrobach.

"This panel sentences you to 185 solar years of confinement to be immediately followed by 102.5 solar years of servitude to repay the amount of nine hundred twenty four thousand vanadium tenges as claimed against you."

In a last attempt of defiance, Fiann wiped the stress and spit from his mouth on the sleeve of his prisoner jacket and faced Adrobach with a wide toothy grin.

Adrobach glared at Fiann and pronounced, "Judgment rendered," and slammed his gavel once, producing a sharp sound

413

that reverberated off the walls.

Fiann, still smiling at the judges, was pulled down from the platform and pushed and prodded from the courtroom.

Tåsan sat a little bewildered and wondered if he would ever see Fiann again.

Several minutes passed in silence until the judges appeared ready to continue and Magistrate Adrobach wagged a hand at the guard standing at the far end of the room.

Immediately a slice of light shone through an opening door, filled with fuzzy gray shadows, cut across the floor and then, just as abruptly, was gone. A prisoner, accompanied by a guard, shuffled through the dim courtroom and mounted the steps to stand on the platform.

"Oh, Alyss," sounded in Tåsan's mind and he sat a little forward in his seat as his attention sharpened. His thoughts ran smoothly along. *"She appears to be well. There's no bruising on her face. No evidence of bulky bandaging."* Tåsan realized he was holding his breath and slowly let out what was left and in relief that Alyss appeared well and whole, slowly pulled air into his lungs and relaxed his straining muscles.

All the judges were turned around and leaning toward Adrobach who seemed to be conferring with them on certain points or details. This little skirmish continued until all the attending judges eventually agreed with whatever they were being consulted about, nodded their heads and returned to their seats.

At length Adrobach spoke, "Case 98704, Alyss Brannick. Due wholly to your status as pilot, we have found you guilty of aiding in the commission of a multitude of crimes against corporations belonging to the Intersolar and Space Alliance and aiding in the violent and damaging destruction sustained by the Inter-Galaxy Command." Adrobach paused to look up at Alyss who stood straight and tall, passively listening to the proceeding. He stared at her for an uncomfortable minute before lowering his eyes to his e-dev and continuing.

"In light of your admission of your participation in key crimes and your acknowledgement of receiving stolen vanadium tenges as payment for your unlawful services, this court has agreed to a reduced punishment. You will be sentenced to a period of time to a penal colony. The length of time to be communicated to you at a later date. You will also, prisoner Brannick, be made to pay restitution for damages directly attributed to your actions, no less than four million five hundred seventy five thousand vanadium tenges."

Tåsan couldn't believe he was hearing correctly. Alyss was never anything but pilot. She never used weapons of any sort and when she did it was for her defense only. Why was she being sent to a penal colony? Why was her financial burden so high?

Magistrate Adrobach, satisfied that the disposal of this prisoner's sentencing was complete, called for the guard to remove Alyss from the courtroom. She looked neither left nor right as she was being led out.

Tåsan, in his agitation and anxiety, leapt to his feet and rushed forward to the window yelling, "Alyss!" as he thumped the glass with his shoulder and shackled wrists. Instantly he felt an electric jolt to his ribs and barely heard the guard say, "What did I tell you," before crumpling down to the floor in pain.

When the courtroom returned to quiet and the judges stopped clicking their e-dev's, and all was ready, Tåsan was pushed and prodded through a side doorway and directed to the center of the room. It was a very long walk across the floor through the dim gallery to the lighted platform and after mounting the steps and steadying himself, Tåsan found he was somewhat blinded by the spotlight and had difficulty making out the faces around him. As his eyes adjusted to the light, Tåsan could just make out some of the faces in the stands and to his great surprise, there sat Luan. She nodded her greeting and just as Tåsan was going to say something to her, he stumbled at being pushed by the guard. When he looked again, she was gone. He slowly scanned the remaining crowd looking for a friendly or familiar face. When he had twisted around to his right, Tåsan saw among the strangers, Stellanova. Her eyes were red from tears but held steady as she gazed at Tåsan. He smiled and raised his hand only slightly in recognition and all too soon, Magistrate Adrobach broke the silence.

"Tåsan Sulac you are here to face punishment for the crimes of Larceny, Sedition, Conspiracy, including the inducement of others, Assault and Manslaughter." Tåsan turned his attention to

415

Adrobach, his thoughts fully silenced. Adrobach continued, "The seven Judges have read the reports, viewed technical renderings of everything involved with your crimes, consulted tribunal law scripts, and conferred among themselves." Adrobach skimmed his e-dev forward several pages, found what he was looking for and continued. "Some of the most damning evidence of your mental qualities was obtained through confidential witness interviews. There were accounts of your unrestrained anger, one involving an altercation outside an establishment where you brutally inflicted physical harm on an outstanding ISA member. Another witness recounted you leveled an unwarranted death threat against a cooperating victim during one of your heinous crimes."

Tåsan recalled the incident outside of The Game of Twenty bar where he throttled Tezzo Maluki for molesting his sister, Stellanova. He smiled at the recollection. The death threat he couldn't recall and set it aside as a nervous recollection on the part of the witness.

Adrobach had seen the smile cross Tåsan's face and it inflamed him to no end. "During the various stages of deliberations, Prisoner Sulac," he spat, "we tried to keep in mind that you were once a celebrated Commander in the Inter-Galaxy Command and a very accomplished starship pilot. However, it is our belief, and it is evidenced by your crime spree, that you are beyond a simple redemption of electorate service and must pay the price of a full penalty. Law among the three galaxies is very specific on this matter and you may well give thanks that we, as a civilization, have evolved past court ordered death sentences and hard labor prison camps to a humane rehabilitation system involving penance and reconciliation accompanied by strict supervision."

Ardobach had completed his lecture and sat for a split second as he glared at Tåsan before returning to his e-dev. "It is decreed and demanded that your condemnation is for a period of 237 solar years, but will be increased to 300 solar years if you do not fully comply. Particulars will be conveyed to you by the Judicial Director's Office and you are to be held, in solitude with no outside contact, until which time you will commence the penalty." And with that, the gavel struck home ending the proceedings, giving Tåsan a start and sending chills down his spine.

Immediately the court gallery erupted into shouting and confusion as the observers leapt to their feet in an effort to spread the news to those outside. The Senior Judge had to shout to be heard above the dim, "Tribunal Attendant. Remove the prisoner!"

Above the uproar Tåsan could hear Stellanova calling his name and he turned to find her. She was straining to lean over the gallery railing, her arm outstretched in a futile effort to touch him, her eyes sad, her voice cracking with emotion. It broke his heart. "Be well, Stella!" he called out. "Fortune be with you! Be well!"

The guard gave a guiding shove and Tåsan was led out of the gallery and transported back to his now too familiar holding cell. One day later a representative from the Judicial Director's Office arrived. There were three fast hours of paperwork and signing this and signing that before the representative produced a lengthy paper outlining the explanation of the details of Tåsan's pending term of reconciliation.

Eight
Tradition As Guide

The Judicial representative had provided Tåsan with a copy of his sentencing terms conveniently titled Document of Reconciliation.

Tåsan sat on his cot with his legs pulled up reading through this document and wondering what had just happened. He was trying to organize his thoughts while also trying to understand the terms of his punishment.

As Tåsan read through the document, he started to realize just how severe his penalty was. The details were almost frightening.

The first section of the document pertained to the sentencing, the basics of which Adrobach had announced at court. Tåsan was to be exiled to PSCN1298, an infrequently used penal colony, for a period of 237 solar years. If it was found that Tåsan was non-compliant, this could be increased either incrementally or fully to 300 solar years. Compliance rules were outlined later in the document, in Section II. Tåsan's sentence also contained a stipulation that, as part of his rehabilitation, he "Must carry out philanthropic deeds, specifically those that will provide technological advancement for the intelligent growth of the inhabitants of PSCN1298."

Tåsan lowered the document and cast his eyes across the cell to a stark white wall. *"What exactly does that mean?"* he mused.

Section I contained three more entries. Tåsan will not be allowed any familiarizing contact with the inhabitants nor will he be allowed contact with off-worlders. Any attachment to indigenous beings is prohibited and will automatically sever ties to the three galaxies, dooming Tåsan to a life on the penal colony. He must stay within the boundaries set by the terms of his sentence and a required number of philanthropic deeds must be carried out

418

with all details of said deeds transmitted using 1024 code.

Tåsan would be allowed to take tribunal ordered accoutrements to the surface with him. The transport capsule that will deliver Tåsan to the penal colony surface will carry basic environmental survival items: a therm/vent tent, warm clothes and a sleeping quilt. A kit containing small hand tools and forty thousand vanadium tenges will also be included.

Tåsan's eyes felt strained. He had read and reread Section I in a futile effort to escape the facts. Instead, he had almost memorized the pages and now sat thinking about it all. He was about to continue reading when the cell light dimmed and brightened again.

Tåsan looked up at the bare light, *"Ah, the warning. Light out in ten."*

• • •

Tåsan slept fitfully that night, waking frequently and tossing in a dreamless agitation. He woke tired and struggled to shake the fog from his head throughout the morning meal. When he felt better, he picked up his Document of Reconciliation and began to read.

Supervision will consist of constant monitoring by means of five physical implants equipped with Universal Meta-Luristic Tracking Devices that are coupled with vaporizer mechanisms in case of deviation from the program. The tracking devices contain sensors that detect altitudes above 95,286.22 nolans and will trigger a fifteen-point warning allowing Tåsan to return to nominal altitude before activating the imbedded vaporizers. IGC wardens will conduct periodic unannounced visits in order to observe that sentence stipulations are being met.

Notes will be taken during the observations and added to Tåsan's file and reviewed on a periodic basis. Judges comments will also be recorded. Communication of these results will only occur if they negatively affect the length of the sentence term.

"In other words," Tåsan thought, *"my sentence stands firmly at 237 solar years but could be increased if I am found in noncompliance."*

Tåsan put the document down and sat for a second before getting up and stretching his arms up over his head to flex his spine then he launched himself into a half hour of strength and endurance exercises. When he had finished, he sat back down and went at the document again.

The Compliance section was pages shorter than the other two sections that described sentencing particulars and monitoring. Tåsan read the legalese and abbreviated it down to its basics...Good behavior counts and the sentence is deemed completed when 237 solar years are served *and* the requisite number of philanthropic deeds, stated as six total, have been accomplished. At that point Tåsan would be allowed to return to Naiad Five. Free.

"Well, there is that."

Tåsan fidgeted with all the information and instruction that his Document of Reconciliation had communicated up to that point. He put it down and thought about it logically, trying to apply it. The results of that mental exercise were futile. Without knowing more about PSCN1298, Tåsan couldn't put a plan together. It was all becoming too much for Tåsan who could feel himself going into information overload. He could actually feel his eyes starting to glaze over.

When his evening meal was brought in, Tåsan took the opportunity to ask that the guard deliver a message to IGC Legal requesting supplemental information on PSCN1298.

The guard smirked but said that he would make Tåsan's request known.

~

That night, after the light was out, Tåsan lay on his bunk looking out into the deep pitch of blackness that surrounded him and thought about his future.

His immediate future was assured. It had been clearly outlined by the IGC judicial system. He was to spend a predetermined amount of time on a penal colony in servitude. That part was clear. What wasn't clear was the path he must choose to effect the true completion of his sentence.

There were too many uncertainties, too many unknowns. It was all starting to be very confusing and Tåsan was not used to feeling perplexed and lost. It was the same as being in freefall with no guidance system.

He didn't like it.

Stress grabbed his chest and slowly the icy fingers of fear

reached out.

Grrrrr...

"What was that?" shot through Tåsan's mind as he bolted upright and strained to see through the darkness. He sat very still and focused his hearing.

Grrrrr... sounded again.

Terror gripped at Tåsan and he tried to call out but his voice would not come.

Then panic hit. Tåsan's mind flew through words... *"No weapon, nowhere to hide,"* then *"RUN!"* all but shocked Tåsan until he spun sideways to gain his feet and race away into the dark.

Nine

The Tyranny of Fate

The days rolled into one big cycle of light on, light off, punctuated by periodic interruptions from guards and IGC legal representatives.

Tåsan's request for information on PSCN1298 had been denied. Somewhat. He did not receive anything tangible that he could study, instead, what he got was a curt reply from one of the legal representatives when in an offhanded manner, the rep said, "It's a planet many, many quantum shifts from here. Several legal systems use it as a penal colony, and, oh yes, it's populated with barbarians and brute savages."

This did not help to alleviate any of Tåsan's concerns so in the long run he tried to be optimistic telling himself it would be all right and to let it go.

The guard that brought this mornings meal had informed Tåsan that today was the day that Tåsan would begin sentencing preparations.

That was some number of hours ago and all Tåsan could do was wait for the time to click down. Eventually the cell locking mechanism sounded and the door slid open. In came two guards and what Tåsan guessed was a medical aide, who stepped in and motioned for Tåsan to come with him, actually saying the word, "Please." Tåsan had heard no words of warmth from anyone since being captured in that dingy back alley of Halide, and smiled in his appreciation.

Tåsan was walked down the hall and into a brightly lit medical bay and told to sit in a chair adjacent to several glass-fronted locked cabinets and many odd-looking apparatuses.

Within minutes, the Chief Medical Officer arrived. It was Tao

Vu, who nodded in greeting to Tåsan and waved the guards out of the way.

"By orders of Vice Admiral Amans Sulac," emphasizing his words, "I am to be the attending physician today," he spoke to Tåsan holding his attention for a moment to indicate that he was not happy about the circumstance of their meeting again.

Tao readied a metal tray with small bottles of antiseptic, gauze patches and a small tray of computer modules retrieved from one of the cabinets. From a drawer, he pulled a metal contraption that his assistant hooked up to a valve protruding from the wall closest to the chair where Tåsan was seated.

Tao said. "You are aware of the decree that you are to have Meta-Luristic Tracking Devices implanted as part of the monitoring process, right?"

Tåsan answered, "Yes, Doctor," and steadied himself.

"This will pain you less if you don't move. I apologize if it causes you too much distress." Tao wiped liquid pharma antiseptic on the surgery spots and with the guards holding Tåsan still, used the high-pressure air delivery mechanism to shoot five implants into Tåsan's wrists, his ankles and the base of his skull. The pain was intense but passed quickly and all too soon, Tao Vu was gone.

On the return walk to his holding cell, Tåsan was informed that the Inter-Galaxy Command starship, *Ari Arcturus*, would transport him to PSCN1298 where he would be deported to the surface to begin his sentence.

Ten

Is This Par?

The *Ari Arcturus* was berthed at Brenton Kae and when Naiad Five's orbit was at its closest, Tåsan was transported by way of a shuttlecraft that docked directly into one of her cargo bays. He was promptly marched down empty hallways and vacant trans-lifts as he was delivered to his holding cell.

To Tåsan's surprise, his security restraints were then removed. He could only think that another form of discipline would take its place but before he could ask, one of his guards told Tåsan that he could expect a visit from the *Ari Arcturus* Commander and to just relax. Both guards then left and Tåsan was alone in his new quarters, free to move about.

The cell where Tåsan was to be held during the voyage resembled a small but fairly comfortable room. It was not what Tåsan expected. Like his previous cells it had a bed and a table with two chairs but this cell also had a sitting area, a private wash, and a galley cabinet that held mugs, glasses, and a flask of water. There were no windows, to Tåsan's dismay, and the ever-present security monitor was there but overall it was actually nice. Compared.

Tåsan had been sitting for some time on one of the more comfortable chairs when the door mechanism sounded. In reaction, Tåsan stood up and turned to face it. The door slid soundlessly open and in stepped the Commander. He was tall and slender with golden eyes and skin the color of copper. The Commander was from Thorium 4.

"My name is Bremman. I am the Commander of *Ari Arcturus*," and extended his hand in greeting. "And you, of course, are Tåsan Sulac."

424

Recovering from his initial shock at the politeness offered, Tåsan stepped forward to take his hand. "Yes, sir, that is correct, and if I may say, this is a little awkward."

"Shall we sit down?" Commander Bremman motioned toward the sitting area and took a seat.

When they seemed more settled, Commander Bremman spoke. "I've read your IGC file and what stuck with me was not the unfortunate circumstances you now find yourself in, it was your near brilliant career with the IGC." Bremman stood up, "Mind?" taking short steps to the galley cabinet and bringing two glasses and the water flask back with him, setting the items down on the low table.

Tåsan immediately poured two glasses, offering one to the Commander first.

"Thank you," said Bremman taking a small sip. "You excelled during IGC training, garnering several commendations through the quads. Several of your instructors submitted glowing reviews and comments to your file. Oh, I can see by your reaction that this is news to you," Bremman said.

Tåsan was indeed surprised. "Still, it's nice to know."

Bremman continued, "Trainees are never made privy to instructor's thoughts. No need to complicate things further." Continuing, "Your hard work paid off. You were assigned to *Ari Arcturus* as her first commander. Quite a feat."

"Thank you Commander Bremman. I was very proud of this ship."

"And that brings me to the reason for my visit." Bremman cleared his throat and took on a look of seriousness. "In respect for your noteworthy accomplishments and your tenure as an IGC Starship Commander, I have afforded you certain freedoms. This quarter for instance," Bremman moved his arm to indicate the surroundings, "is much better than the usual prisoner holding area. And," Bremman added, "you will not be restrained while in residence."

Tåsan looked around and said, "Yes and I appreciate it," as he subconsciously rubbed at his wrists.

"The guards will be outside the door, if you are in need of anything, within reason, you understand," Bremman looked at

425

Tåsan for acknowledgement before continuing, "Just ask."

"I do not take this kindness lightly," Tåsan said. "I will not betray it."

"Good," Bremman said as he stood up to leave. "I'll send some reading material and a small stock for the galley." Bremman continued to speak as both he and Tåsan slowly moved to the door. "The voyage to PSCN1298 will take roughly four weeks at an extremely high rate of velocity. We will have opportunity to meet again but for now I must return to duty."

Bremman turned when he reached the door and Tåsan took the moment to say, "Thank you for your trust. Until we meet again," and put out his hand to the Commander who took it and smiled before he stepped out and away.

A short time later, a small supply of galley stores were delivered. There were herbs for tea, dried biscuits, additional water, and a small basket of fruitlets.

A scant minute after, an e-pad arrived loaded with three books: Life in the Distance, The Roots of Technology, and Primitive Mythologies.

After reading the three titles and registering a pulse of shock, Tåsan thought to himself, *"Well, I've been warned that PSCN1298 was populated by barbarians."*

He opened book one and began to read...

'PSCN1298 is a fairly young planet, among many other planets and stars and gasses belonging to a solar nebula roughly 2.537 million light-nolans from the three galaxies. It was born from violent volcanism that formed the primordial beginnings of organism evolutions.'

Tåsan stopped reading. Knowing about events that had occurred in the distant past did not help him. He put the e-pad down and went to the galley cabinet to make tea. He would return to the story at another time and thought to ask if it would be possible to keep the e-pad during his exile. As he waited for the tea to brew, a thought jumped into his mind, *"If PSCN1298 is two point something million light-nolans away and it will take four weeks to arrive, just how fast is Ari Arcturus traveling?"*

• • •

Tåsan arranged his sleep cycles to be as regular as he could in light of the fact that he was not certain of the time. His wake cycle consisted of meals, two sets of exercise movements, reading, and moments of reflection and contemplation of the future. To make his time a little more stimulating, he frequently mixed up the order of his activities but Tåsan's interest was wearing thin. Confinement didn't suit him.

Unexpectedly one day, he had a surprise.

"Oh! Today fortune smiles on me!" Tåsan exclaimed as he jumped to his feet and hastily moved toward his visitor, Castell Brann, giving him a hearty embrace before taking his hand and saying, "It's so good to see you!"

Castell returned the greeting in kind, "This is a good day! You look well, Tåsan!"

Tåsan stepped back and spread his arms wide, "As well as can be expected. Come in, let's sit, how long can you stay?"

Castell motioned to one of the hallway guards who came in carrying an armload of things that he set on the table and after receiving a thank you from Castell, quietly left the quarters.

The friends sat as comfortably as they could all the while catching up.

"I'm Chief Engineer now," Castell said, "Back aboard *Ari Arcturus* after several quads aboard the newest Stratos Class ship, *Sudden Storm*, as her primary test engineer."

"So you've moved up ranks, good for you," Tåsan added, then asked, "Are you happy?"

"Yes. I spend my free time aboard ship in research. It's very rewarding," Castel smiled. "Oh, I want to tell you that I stay in touch with your sister, Stellanova, and she told me very strictly to tell you that she is fine and not to worry about her. She's been very disapproving of the way the IGC has handled your situation."

"Stella," Tåsan lowered his eyes for a moment then asked what she had been up to.

"She's rising in the Biomechanical world. It would not surprise me if she becomes the premier terra-forming expert of her time," Castell explained.

This made Tåsan very happy to hear but he jumped subjects, "How long can you stay? Should I make tea?" he looked expectantly at Castell.

427

"As long as two hours then I must report to the bridge, but I'm here not only as your friend but on request of Commander Bremman. He has asked that I explain several technical points of your deployment to PSCN1298. And yes, you should make tea," Castell added.

As Tåsan made tea, Castell sorted through the items that he had brought with him, laying several of them out along the low sitting area table.

"You will be allowed to take warm clothes, a survival shelter, and a small kit of hand tools," Castell said, "And I have included documentation on how to navigate hostile environments."

"Anything like the marshy fen on Erontu?" chided Tåsan.

"I think worse," said Castell before adding, "in some circumstances."

"Then thank you for the docs," said Tåsan, his voice tinged with uncertainty.

"You must absolutely understand this, Tåsan. The capsule that you are to be deployed in will land at predetermined coordinates, you are to vacate it and retrieve your belongings quickly because the capsule is programmed to self-destruct. It will collapse and burn itself into an unidentifiable molten ash." Castell was looking very seriously at Tåsan.

Tåsan was taken back but managed to ask, "How long do I have?"

"Roughly twelve minutes," was the answer. "You need to pack your things and leave the area as soon as you are able. It would not do to attract attention to yourself so soon."

"Okay. Understood," Tåsan nodded.

Castell then launched into a technical explanation of the survival shelter and how it could be configured in a number of different ways depending on need. It could provide for over-night or accommodate longer periods. "Say, up to a quad and a half."

Castell handed over tech guides and miscellaneous informational documents for Tåsan to look at, adding that they would be on board the capsule as well.

When Castell had wound down his overviews, satisfied that Tåsan understood all the technical aspects of his deployment gear, he sat back in the chair and stretched his legs out before him.

"There's one last thing you need to have," he said.

Tåsan looked up from a specification sheet and said, "Yes?"

Castell produced a smallish box and handed it over.

Tåsan took it and opened it exclaiming, "Parudi Rule!" in his excitement, "I haven't played this in ages!" Then, tilting his head and smiling at Castell said, "Do you have time?"

One fast game later and it was time for Castell to leave. The friends had to say goodbye.

Tåsan said, "It has been great to catch up, I've missed us," adding, "Would you look after Stellanova while I'm gone?"

Castell did not hesitate, "Of course. Please don't worry about her at all, she's in good hands, or maybe I should say, I'll be in good hands. She's very capable, you know?"

"Yes. And determined," agreed Tåsan.

Castell held his hand out, "I'll be here when you get home."

Tåsan took his hand, "I'll send word as soon as I touch down on Naiad Five," and smiled.

The friends embraced and clapped each other on the back while mumbling parting salutations and wishing good fortunes.

All too soon, Castell was gone.

• • •

Tåsan read and studied and reread every scrap of information he could get regarding PSCN1298. Its season cycles, weather patterns, geography, biomass, horticulture, and biology. He managed to stumble upon an obscure lecture concerning PSCN1298, included as a footnote of a larger text that was titled Linguistic Anthropology of Primitive Cultures. If Tåsan hadn't been so concerned with surviving his legal punishment, the subject might have fascinated him. As it was, this short lecture, padded with empirical data and waning into philosophic musings, presented a picture of a culture in chaos. It was more frightening than assuring.

The short number of days passed all too quickly. Interestingly enough, as the time for Tåsan's deployment neared, the more calm and assured he became about being launched into two hundred thirty seven solar years among primitives.

With two days remaining aboard *Ari Arcturus*, Commander Bremman came to sit with Tåsan one last time.

"I trust you feel better prepared to serve out your sentence, now?" Bremman asked.

"Yes," answered Tåsan. "Much better than being stranded with absolutely no suggestion of 'where' or 'what' I'm surrounded by." He smiled at his joke, "We already know the 'why' part."

"Well, for my part," Bremman said, "I'm happy to have helped you at least for your beginnings. And," he quickly added, "I intend to be here for your return home. I intend to be the Commander of the ship that retrieves you and delivers you back to the three galaxies."

"In good part to your generosity," Tåsan said, "thank you again."

Commander Bremman stood up and Tåsan did the same. "Until that time then," Bremman said putting his hand forward, "may fortune be with you."

Tåsan took the commander's hand and said, "Fortune to us both," and smiled a warm goodbye.

• • •

The view from the forward windows of the bridge was strikingly beautiful. A slowly rotating planet of subtle blues, clouded with white and gray, shone brightly against the dark, star-dotted expanse of space.

The bridge lightly buzzed with checks and rechecks as all hands stayed intent on their mission.

Commander Bremman addressed his Chief Engineer, "Lieutenant Brann, what is the status of the deployment capsule?"

Castell answered, "Capsule secured and ready to deploy on your command."

"Very good, Lieutenant. Stand by."

The bridge hummed quietly while display screens flickered as they tracked data. The reverie was interrupted by the navigator's voice as she said, "Sir, we are within range."

"Stand by," Bremman said as he watched the scene out the bridge windows. "Lieutenant Brann. On my mark." Bremman hesitated as he looked over at Castell, who raised his eyes in response. "Deploy."

Castell said, "Capsule away," just as the jetted capsule shot out of the cargo bay and streaked along its path to PSCN1298.

Moments later another jetted capsule, on the same path, lighted the darkness of space as it followed.

"*Sudden Storm* reports their payload was successfully deployed," the Communication Officer said.

Commander Bremman had stepped forward, closer to the windows and now stood watching as the two jet trails neared PSCN1298 and punched through the misty cloud cover. "Fortune to us all," he said before the two jet trails disappeared.

Eleven

PSCN1298

Tåsan's capsule shook violently as it dropped through PSCN1298's atmosphere on its flight path. The capsule was coming in low and at a high rate of speed and from PSCN's surface, resembled a fiery meteor streaking across the sky.

Eventually Tåsan felt the assist jets fire and the craft respond as it dropped its rads per second down to almost nothing. He held his breath and tensed his muscles in anticipation of what was to come next. Touchdown.

The capsule skidded and bounced along for four hundred rough meters before jerking to a stop.

Tåsan waited a fraction of a moment, stunned by the landing, before gathering his wits and working the air lock that momentarily loosed its magnetic grip on the hatch seal and relaxed with an inrush of air. He pushed the hatch open and away and sat up to look about.

The first thing he saw was snow and ice and shivered as the cold air seeped through his flight suit.

Tåsan snapped his attention back to the capsule, *"Twelve minutes...maybe now only eleven minutes to self destruction."* He hurried to stand up, and ignoring the stiffness of his legs, started hauling his supplies out of the capsule, tossing them as far from it as he could.

Tåsan stopped long enough to retrieve his thermal outerwear and as he hastened to put it on, a fiery streak appeared on the horizon, catching his attention. He stood curiously watching the small fireball and clearly saw three assist jets fire and the object drop in velocity and altitude as it plummeted downward. Concern for his safety and welfare turned his attention back to retrieving his goods. The clock was ticking.

With all speed, Tåsan removed his cache from the capsule and moved it to a safe distance. He had barely dropped the last item into his collected pile when the capsule made a series of popping sounds that ignited an electrical fire. Tåsan watched as electrical pulses rippled across the capsule's sides, sparks popped here and there, and black smoke billowed out to drift away on a light wind coming from the north. Tåsan then remembered the sighting of the other streaking object and turned to look in the general direction of its landing. He stood in the desolate quiet for a moment until his eyes began to wander across the landscape, eventually returning to the crash site of the other capsule.

Tåsan pulled in his breath with a sharp huff. There in the distance was a figure, featureless and black against the snowy backdrop. It was pulling a sled and headed straight for him. Tåsan quickly remembered Castell's warning to clear the area before being detected and in a half panic turned to his belongings and tried to reason out how to collect them and leave in a hurry, but almost instantly he realized he could not make that happen.

He decided to confront the stranger and turned to face them, who by this time had closed the distance and now had their arm raised in salutation.

Tåsan raised his hand to return the greeting and started walking forward. He managed about half the distance that separated them before recognizing the smiling face that approached.

"Alyss!" he cried out as he started to run.

Alyss could not contain her excitement any longer. She dropped the lead rope of her sled and ran to Tåsan who caught her up in his arms as they came together in a rush of emotional excitement, frantic greetings, and muffled cries. They slowly sank to the ground still holding each other in a hug trying to catch their breath and hurriedly asking, "Are you okay?" and answering, "Yes, all the better now."

As Tåsan held Alyss, he could see black smoke billowing up and away in the distance. It reminded him again that they should vacate the area. "How are you feeling?" he asked.

Alyss moved to take her weight off of her knees and took a

good look at Tåsan. "You've lost a little weight," she said.

"I'm fine really, actually very well."

"Good," Alyss said. "I think I'm a bit lighter but better for it."

"I think we should pack everything and move a few kilometers away from here," Tåsan said, adding, "I've been warned about the indigenous ones."

"Agreed," Alyss said, "I'll go get my sled then help you with yours."

・・・

After Tåsan and Alyss had added a nice warm layer of thermal outerwear to their clothing and packed their sleds, they trekked ten kilometers along the snowy northwest mountains until Tåsan spotted a sheltered area tucked into a rocky crevasse that he thought would conceal their presence.

They hauled their gear up and set to work making camp. It was then that Tåsan noticed that the gear Alyss had with her was nothing like his. Curiosity got the better of him and he took a closer look, noticing that she did not have a survival tent but did have a brazier, an item missing from his gear.

He stopped working to ask how that came to be.

Alyss paused in her work to say, "There is a very long story attached to that answer that I will gladly tell you but would rather start once we're inside, settled, and warm." She looked at Tåsan. "Next to a nice fire," she prompted.

"Okay," was all he said before turning back to setting the tent up.

・・・

The very long story Alyss related to Tåsan, over hot tea and nutri-cubes, started with her capture in Halide on Metamere.

When the peacekeepers swarmed over her, she felt a heavy blow to her abdomen and must have passed out. When she woke next, she had suffered a broken rib and all cuts and scrapes aside, sported a huge purple bruise on her midsection that took weeks to disappear.

As with Tåsan, Alyss, too, was kept in solitary confinement for an extended period of time but as she related, "I didn't mind. I was clear on why I was in IGC custody so I used the quiet to think about how my situation was going to play out. And somewhere in the quiet I came to the conclusion that I was going to affect the outcome."

Alyss began to use her knowledge of their heists as bargaining chips. She would offer a bit of data in exchange for bending her sentence ever so closer to Tåsan's. "Keep in mind," she had said to Tåsan, "I had no idea what they were planning for you, but to my way of thinking, the IGC would most likely make an example of you."

Eventually she was transferred to *Sudden Storm* and had access to IGC Legal who pressed her for more heist details. "The names I gave up were of those who had already died. Everyone else," she shrugged, "I didn't care to know. And here's why my gear is different than yours," Alyss offered. "Apparently Castell has some influence with *Sudden Storm's* First Engineer, who was tasked with designing my survival items list."

"That makes sense, Alyss," said Tåsan. "My transport was aboard *Ari Arcturus* where *Lieutenant*," Tåsan emphasized, "Castell Brann is Chief Engineer!"

"Oh!" exclaimed Alyss, "Did you get to see him?"

"Yes, and he's well and he's happy. Not about this," Tåsan said looking around, "But he loves his work and is doing well within the structure of the IGC."

Alyss smiled at the news and fell silent as she gazed into the fire.

Tåsan fell silent too, until he thought to say, "This campsite seems to offer what we need for now. We should think about staying here a week or so while we get our bearings."

• • •

That night, the first he could remember in a long while, Tåsan fell to sleep easily, with his arms around Alyss.

A snippet played out in the bright haze of a dream…

Before him a vast landscape filled his view, pristine and untrodden and a feeling that it was so incredible threatened to overwhelm him. As he stood quietly, Tåsan felt the stress leave his chest and he relaxed into the moment and silently watched as the bright day of his dream slowly faded into night.

435

Tåsan was lost in his amazement when suddenly he was jolted by the touch of someone next to him. He turned his head and Alyss was by his side, smiling and pointing upward. Tåsan looked up and before his eyes was a vast and unbroken view of a clear night sky dotted with stars that twinkled and shimmered in the darkness.

As Tåsan stood in astonishment at the beauty of it all, he heard a voice say, "I will never leave you."

And the dark haze that surrounded his vision slowly closed in to provide rest.

• • •

The next day, Tåsan and Alyss woke feeling refreshed and stayed under the warm therm-blankets, feeling no need to rise to the day so soon. They spent the next hour sharing ideas about how that day and a few others should unfold.

"It seems," said Alyss, "that there's no hurry about anything right now, short of running out of supplies, that is."

"I think we should take today," offered Tåsan, "to get a feel for where we are on this planet. Are we in an untamed outback? Are we close to any kind of civilization? That sort of thing."

Alyss added, "I have maps we could study."

"And," Tåsan said, "I'd like to look around outside for a short time." Then he yawned and stretched out his arms. "Ready to get up?"

• • •

After the morning meal, Tåsan and Alyss sorted through their gear and took inventory of their rations.

"Our food stores will last us three weeks, maybe four if we're careful, and that's without finding berries or grain or tubers as supplemental," Alyss observed.

"We can make a passive search for things like that while we're outside," Tåsan said.

"Are you finding anything noteworthy?" Alyss asked, nodding at the miscellaneous items of gear spread about the tent.

"Yes," answered Tåsan, "I'm finding that we have an extremely noteworthy friend in Castell. Our two sets of gear make one almost perfect set." He reached for an e-pad and tilted it so

436

Alyss could see the attached handwritten note. "It reads, 'The charge is limited to five hundred eighty PSCN1298 hours and the e-pad is loaded with historical information only. Use judiciously. All current PSCN1298 data and relevant observational information is tangible. Fortune be with you, CB'."

"Oh, Castell," said Alyss, "is such a true friend."

"The other things here will make our camping life easier and we have a small variety of hand tools that will come in very handy."

Alyss organized the food stores back into the transport cases while Tåsan did the same with the gear, separating it from the books and papers he intended to spend time reviewing.

Before the late day meal, Tåsan and Alyss agreed to venture outside, "After which we will want to get warm and stay warm," Alyss had said.

Tåsan peeled back the tent flap and they stepped out into the most beautiful snow scene either had ever experienced.

Spread out before them was a vast wilderness blanketed in winter. The land formed a wide valley of rolling hills lined on the Northwest and the Southeast exposures by snow covered mountain peaks. Tall trees hugged the lower mountain elevations displaced by shorter trees that still held their needles and outcrops of black rock that spread across the width of the valley.

"Hear how quiet it is," said Tåsan as they stood still to observe the view.

"Father would love this," said Alyss.

As if on queue, the call of a soaring bird cut through the distance, the sound sharp and lonely. Both Tåsan and Alyss scanned the sky looking for the source.

"It seems we're not alone," observed Alyss.

"Let's explore," said Tåsan as he picked his way down the rocky ravine that led to the valley below.

They spent over two hours trekking northward stopping frequently to look at bare-limbed plants and black boulders. They saw animal tracks and bird prints in the snow cover prompting Tåsan to observe that the animal tracks revealed a small group, maybe five "whatever they are" had passed through the area a number of days earlier.

On the trek back to camp, before darkness fell, Alyss spotted tiny little green leaves poking through the icy snow and stopped to dig them out, prying from the frozen soil, a fat tuber that promised the possibility of edibles.

By the time they were back inside their tent with the brazier glowing and the tea brewing, both Tåsan and Alyss were still flush with the excitement of their discoveries.

"Maybe food sources are plentiful and we won't need to worry about rationing so much," noted Alyss. "I'll deal with the tuber later, but I am encouraged to look further."

"I'm encouraged by only seeing animal prints in the snow and not boot prints," said Tåsan. "There are no outward signs of civilization. No smoke from fires, no lights from windows. I think we're sufficiently isolated and generally safe in this campsite."

That night, Tåsan and Alyss slept well. Not from stress and exhaustion, but from a new feeling of passion and confidence.

• • •

For the next quad, Tåsan and Alyss spent their time in the study of their new planet. As Tåsan had mentioned, "It wouldn't do to wander out of our valley without some sort of preparation for the inevitable encounter with any of its inhabitants."

First they studied the planet's place in its galaxy and from that, its seasons and weather. Alyss took an excited interest in any horticultural information she could find among the texts and papers Castell had provided. From that she learned what edible plants looked like and when they were plentiful. Her studies were rewarded by her finding winterberries and a variety of tubers on her and Tåsan's outings. Their foraging supplemented their food stores by weeks.

Tåsan found interest in the anthropology, both social and biological, of PSCN's inhabitants. After the study of one of his books, Life in the Distance, he was relieved to find that, "Their physical development resembles ours in a lot of ways, even if their intellectual development lags far behind." To that, Alyss had observed, "Then it makes sense that this planet is used as a penal colony. Anyone serving time would blend in."

As they studied the geology of PSCN1298, they soon found where, on its surface, their capsules had landed. It was in the

438

northern hemisphere where the weather was severe in the winter and not so severe in the summer. "Which keeps the population small," Tåsan had remarked, "To our advantage."

Their closest neighbors were eight hundred kilometers further north. After some discussion and further thought, Tåsan and Alyss agreed that when they broke camp the direction they would travel would be north. The logic they were following dictated that their first encounters with PSCN1298 inhabitants should be limited. "We would be able to better contain the situation," Alyss had summarized. So in preparation, they studied the language and social proprieties of the "Sámi."

In passive discussions about their future, Tåsan and Alyss agreed to stay nomadic until they gained a deeper knowledge of, "Just about everything." They wanted to understand the desirable locations as well as the undesirable. "It wouldn't do to stumble into a Sand Sea without guidance," Tåsan had said.

They would also need to ramp up on social, artistic, and technological gains of PSCN's inhabitants if Tåsan and Alyss were to accomplish their six philanthropic deeds. They had a very small kit of hand tools but strongly doubted that that, combined with their mechanical creativity, would be enough. And until they knew what they had to work with, most planning was futile.

And so Tåsan and Alyss spent their first weeks on PSCN1298 in study, in exploration, and in each other's company.

• • •

When winter began its slow transition into spring, Tåsan and Alyss knew the time was nearing when they would break camp and begin the trek northward.

Realization came in the form of melting snow that formed rivulets that swelled into streams. Flocks of water birds and tree dwellers appeared, calling to mates and singing the season.

Almost overnight, trees and shrubs started to push out buds and early blooming flowers nudged through the last remaining patches of snow.

• • •

Today is the day.

Tåsan and Alyss rose early, eager for the day. They ate a good morning meal and spent two hours stowing their gear and

439

breaking camp.

Alyss took an extra moment to clear any trace that they had been there, in homage to her father's words, "The outback does not belong to us. We have no right to leave boot prints in disrespect for the natural inhabitants of such a wondrous place."

After moving everything down the rocky crevasse to the valley floor and reconfiguring the sled rails to wheels, Tåsan and Alyss stopped to take one last look at what they had done and to ask if they had everything, did they forget anything.

Satisfied that all was as it should be, Tåsan looked at Alyss, she returned his light gaze, and then he put his arms around her. He stood embracing her for a few seconds of time before letting go and stepping back.

"This is it, Alyss," Tåsan smiled, "Today we begin the adventure." He turned to look once more at "their" valley then looked back at Alyss. "Are you ready?"

"I am," she replied.

Other Works By N. K. Hart

The Innocence Of Power – A modern day suspense thriller

Up The Crime Ladder – One humorous week in the lives of
Henchmen

The Future of Crime – Further adventures of the Henchmen

Swimming Through Air – a collection of short stories and musings

Available through Tangible Press.
http://tangiblepress.net

www.ingramcontent.com/pod-product-compliance
Lightning Source LLC
Chambersburg PA
CBHW020503020726
47493CB00001B/162